WATCHFUL WISTERIA

Wisteria Witches Mysteries

BOOK #4

ANGELA PEPPER

CHAPTER 1

THIS IS THE STORY of how a little red fox saved my life.

Wednesday morning, I was walking to the library, enjoying the dappled sunshine in Pacific Spirit Park. I'd taken my headphones out of my ears so I could listen to the chirping birds in the canopy above. One particularly squawky bird began making a ruckus, silencing the others.

About five feet ahead of me, there was movement at the side of the trail. The bushes rustled, and a red-furred animal emerged, staggering toward me before dropping at my feet. It was the size of a Shiba Inu breed of dog, but its tail was nearly as long as its body, and distinctively bushy with a white tip.

A fox.

In the middle of a woodsy city park. Early on a Wednesday morning.

I looked around, my fingers crackling with potential. I noted, with cool detachment, my witch powers surging through me. I was almost good at this! After only a few months of practicing my novice witch powers, the sensation of blue plasma pooling in my hands had become regular. Not *normal*, because normal's just a setting on the dishwasher between Lite Wash and Heavy Pot Scrub, but *regular*. Common. Typical.

This fox, however, was new.

And new meant dangerous.

I took a few cautious steps back, my boots crunching through dried leaves. I smelled the coppery tang of blood coming from the fox. There was a dark streak of blood along its side, where the red-orange fur turned to white underbelly.

The fox lifted its glistening black nose and whimpered. Gold-green eyes dotted with oval-shaped pupils stared up beseechingly. The animal's long white whiskers shivered as it took panting breaths. Even as pity squeezed my heart, I noted that its white fangs looked very sharp. I was glad I'd worn leather ankle boots that day.

We locked gazes, and I felt something unexpected. Familiarity. I had healed a wounded wolf in this same forest, which accounted for some of the déjà vu sensation, but there was more.

Was this fox the shifter version of someone I knew? The supernatural residents of Wisteria were all so secretive about their powers. Those familiar gold-green eyes could belong to anyone. Then again, the fox could simply be someone's pet. I scanned the woods again for signs of trouble. It was still early on a Wednesday morning. The weather was cool and sunny, the air thick with the promise of summer heat by afternoon. I hadn't seen another soul since I'd stepped on the trail that ran through Pacific Spirit Park. All was quiet. Too quiet. The songbirds were silenced. The tall redwoods didn't even whisper in the breeze.

The fox whimpered and reached out one black-socked paw to touch the toe of my boot. With the movement, the fox's thick fur on its side parted, revealing a deep wound that cut through muscles. I winced as I felt a sympathetic pain in my own ribs. I heard heavy, pained breathing. My own.

I got down on my knees on the dirt. The fox needed healing. And wasn't this exactly what I'd been training for? My aunt had been stabbing, burning, and slicing herself repeatedly—all in the name of my education. And now here was a wounded animal. Here was my final exam.

I rubbed my hands together, turning the blue plasma from destructive energy to healing energy. I chanted the focusing spell in the Witch Tongue. I reached toward the fox, whose trembling was making the dry leaves of the trail rustle like a chorus of pleas for help. The tangy scent of blood made my eyes water.

I hesitated, hands tingling.

My awareness stretched out, so that I saw myself frozen in that moment, as though drawn in a storybook. How could this be a final exam? I was in the woods, not my aunt's floral-decorated sitting room. This wasn't a controlled environment. Since when does a fox emerge from the bushes of a city park and throw itself at a person's feet?

The animal licked its dark lips and fixed me with a too-calm expression. The eyes shifted between green and gold and back again. What was this magic? Who was this beast? A chill slipped in between my muscles and my bones, snaking up and twirling around my heart. This constriction in my chest was something I hadn't felt much until recently.

Fear.

A shrill voice pierced my thoughts. "Careful! Careful!"

I turned, expecting to find bushes parting to reveal my aunt. But there was only the greenery of trees and ferns. No glamour disguise and no Zinnia.

Up in the branches overhead, blue feathers flashed against the greenery. A blue jay fluttered down on silent wings, landing on the ground near me. He wore the colors of the male of the species, and he looked like the king of the forest with his downy white belly, black feather accents, and coat of many shades of blue. The bird cocked his head, fluffed up his perky, pointed crown, took three hops forward, and pecked the fox on the mid-point of its bushy red tail.

"Hey," I said. "Don't be mean."

"Careful," came the shrill voice again, in time with the bird's beak opening.

The fox glanced over at the blue jay then back at me. Was the fox thinking what I was thinking?

A blue jay who talks? Ziggity! I knew this bird. It hadn't been around lately, but I'd heard it talk before, in my own back yard.

I nodded at the fox's wound and asked the bird, "Did you do this?"

The bird squawked, "No!"

No? Maybe it was the limitations of the corvid's speech, but its *no* had sounded a wee bit guilty.

"A likely story," I said.

"Zara, be careful," the blue jay squawked.

My mentor's voice rang in my head. *We ought to use our minds and senses before we resort to magic.*

I clasped my hands together, keeping the blue plasma compressed.

The fox didn't move except to breathe, which sounded laborious.

The bird hopped around the fox and gave it a sharp peck on the haunches. The fox turned its long muzzle with surprising speed and snapped at the bird. The blue jay evaded the sharp canine teeth with an undignified retreat.

"Go ahead," the bird squawked, looking at me with cold, black eyes. "Do your trick."

Do my trick.

"Okay," I said evenly. I would do my trick, but first I had questions. "Blue jay, if you didn't attack this fox, who did?"

The bird gave me the tiniest of shrugs. The feathered crest on its head smoothed down.

"Do you know who this is?" I pointed to the fox with one plasma-clad finger.

The bird opened its beak and let out a CAW CAW.

"I know you can talk," I said. "Want to try that again? Who is this fox?"

The bird gave me another shrug and a CAW CAW. It flapped its wings and took to the air with an indignant squawk. The bird winked out of sight above the forest canopy.

The fox, meanwhile, said nothing. Not even a whimper. Its pink tongue lolled out limply. Those eerily familiar gold-green eyes were losing their shine. Good or bad, trap or test, the animal was going to perish if I didn't do something quickly.

I rubbed my hands together once more, refocusing my healing powers. I wasn't supposed to use my magic in public unless I had a really good reason. I'd already been grounded once for my carelessness. Was saving a fox worth the risk?

My hands were trembling, and it wasn't from the pulsing plasma.

When had I become such a scaredy-cat?

* * *

THIRTY MINUTES EARLIER

I'd woken up that Wednesday morning with every intention to stop by my next-door neighbor's house before work. Chet Moore had a book I'd negotiated for and won, fair and square. Not only had I located his fiancée's spirit and gotten her back into her body, but I'd also helped rid the Department of Water and Magic of a traitor.

Now, a book of great knowledge was mine for the reading. And yet, for the past two weeks, I'd been coming up with excuses to not pick it up. When a librarian procrastinates the acquisition of a powerful book, you know there must be more to the story.

As excited as I was to get my hands on what my daughter and I jokingly referred to as the *Monster Manual*, my eagerness was dampened by my fear of Chet's fiancée, Chessa. She and I had shared many things recently, including my body. And this sharing had come with a cost.

While I hosted her spirit, Chessa's memories had embedded deeply and become my own. Her emotions became mine. Her love for Chet Moore had become my love. Her lust for his body had become my... Well, you get the picture. I felt what she felt, and still did. And the crazy thing was, my crush on Chet had been doing just fine on its own before I got a dump of her feelings. He was a handsome and responsible single father who lived right next door, conveniently enough.

If Chessa ever found out how I felt, it might conjure up that ol' green monster, jealousy. And not just your standard garden-variety jealousy. Chessa was the descendant of powerful creatures. Her ancestors had ruled the depths of the deep blue sea, and other places across time and space.

You would think that knowing my handsome neighbor had sleepovers with a mythical sea monster goddess straight out of an H. P. Lovecraft story would be enough to keep me away from his house. And you would be absolutely right. I hadn't set foot in the yard since she'd returned to the land of the living. Chessa scared me to the brink of incontinence.

I'd only caught a glimpse of the ethereal blonde's "true form" for a few seconds, and my mind had blown a gasket. Ever since that day at her sister Chloe's baby shower, I had kept my distance. Heaven forbid I slipped and said something flirty to Chet. All my witch powers wouldn't do me a lick of good once a vengeful goddess decided to use the inside of my skull as a candy bowl.

And so I stood on the sidewalk in front of the Moore family's blue house that morning, frozen with fear. Yet I craved the book I'd won. Would the tome be bound in leather or wood? Would the pages have that wonderfully funky, decaying, delicious old-book smell? And what magical treasures awaited inside?

Something chattered. My teeth. I was shivering under my leather jacket despite the warm summer weather. *Well, Zara? Are you going to stand on the sidewalk like a ding-dong all day?*

No, I answered myself. *I'll have to go to work eventually.*

I clenched my fists, stabbing the tips of my fingernails into my palms as punishment for my cowardice. I wanted the Monster Manual so badly, but my feet wouldn't move.

Where had the real Zara Riddle gone? I was once the girl who had the courage at sixteen to bring a child into the world on my own. I'd had the guts to pack up my life and move across the country for my career. And recently, I'd taken the whole surprise-you're-a-witch bombshell with grace and enthusiasm. I was the woman who, upon encountering a chasm, retreated just enough to gain speed for my leap. And now I couldn't even walk up a few steps and knock on a door.

Out of the corner of my eye, I saw my neighbor, Arden, approaching on the sidewalk.

He stopped beside me, thrust something in front of my face, and asked, "Have you ever seen the likes of this?"

In his palm was a chunk of stone, in the shape of a rat. Someone with an active imagination might say he was holding a petrified rat. If that same person were to see the collection of stone hornets, mice, and single stone turtle displayed inside my daughter's room, that person might wonder if there were a gorgon or two frequenting the neighborhood. And that person would be right. Chessa's triplet sisters, Chloe and Charlize, weren't as powerful as Chessa, but both had magical snakes in their hair and could turn living creatures to stone with a touch.

"Wow," I said to my neighbor, who was a friendly gentleman enjoying his retirement years. "The detail on this rat sculpture is exquisite. Who's the artist who did the carving?"

Arden dangled the petrified rat by its stone tail. He glanced left and right before answering in a hushed tone.

"It's not carved," he said. "A monster did this." He spat as he repeated, "A *monster*."

"Art is so subjective," I replied with a light laugh. After years of working with the public, I was a master at avoiding certain requests. When it came to discussing politics or having a look at weird moles, I stonewalled by cheerfully misunderstanding unwanted invitations.

I leaned over and gave Arden's dog, a brown Labradoodle named Doodles, a pat on the head. "Is it true these Labradoodles are hypoallergenic? We've been looking for a pet. Just a low-maintenance one."

"Low maintenance? You have to walk a dog multiple times a day. You should get a cat."

"People keep telling me that," I said, which wasn't entirely true. Most people, upon discovering I'm a librarian, ask me how many cats I already have and don't believe me when I say zero.

"Doodles likes kitties," Arden said. We chatted about cats and dogs, and the joys of pet ownership.

Then something interrupted our conversation.

A blue jay. Tweeting at us from overhead, as though it wanted to join in the conversation. Was it the same one I'd seen the day I moved in?

I gave Doodles one more pet and then said goodbye. I walked down the street, the task of getting the book pushed off to tomorrow again.

I'd taken the long route to work, through Pacific Spirit Park.

I hadn't remembered the blue jay until now—now that I was about to put my hands on the wounded fox and use magic to heal its injury.

Zara, be careful. That was what the blue jay had said.

"You're testing me," I said to the fox.

The animal blinked slowly. The light was fading from its eyes.

CHAPTER 2

I ran.

With the bleeding fox cradled in a sling I'd made from my leather jacket, I ran all the way to the nearest veterinary clinic.

My aunt and witch mentor was always lecturing me about not using magic to solve problems that could be fixed with regular means. She would be proud of my choice this morning. Why risk using magic when modern medicine would do the trick?

The fox didn't even wriggle in the sling.

As I burst through the door into the vet clinic, the fox was so still, and I feared I'd made the wrong choice. I clenched my jaw and fought back raw emotions as I hurriedly explained to the young man in the white coat that I had a small animal that needed emergency treatment.

The veterinarian simply nodded and handed me a tissue. He knew the drill.

When he saw that the animal wasn't a dog or a cat, he barely raised an eyebrow. He took the fox into the back room and began shuffling things with an urgency that gave me hope. If the fox had been too far gone to save, surely the vet wouldn't be muttering under his breath and banging around for supplies.

"I should have been faster," I muttered to myself. I stared down at the dark-red dirt on my hands. The light around me shifted, as though my mind was lifting a veil, and I saw that it wasn't dirt on my hands. It was blood. My blouse was clean, but the inside lining of my leather jacket was soaked in fox blood, as were my hands.

There was so much blood for an animal that barely weighed twenty pounds.

"You can wash up in that sink," the vet said in a soothing tone.

I walked over to a sink and methodically washed the blood from my hands. When I'd healed Chet in the forest, there hadn't been this much blood. The magic might have sopped it up, or maybe I'd been too distracted to notice. There'd been the bird attack, the new powers, and the nude man. Shifters are able to keep their clothes on when they turn into their animal forms, but Chet had disrobed. I later learned that Chet had a reputation for getting naked, especially when he prepared to do battle.

"You can handle this," the veterinarian said, his tone still soothing and relaxed.

It was exactly what I needed to hear. I dried my hands with paper towel and then used the wadded paper to soak the worst of the blood from the inside of my jacket.

I asked the vet, "Anything I can do to help? Is it just you here today?"

"My assistant, Fatima, will be in later," he said. "You can go up front and write down your contact information so I can call you with an update."

I didn't want to leave the fox, but I did as the veterinarian requested. I wrote my name and cell phone number on a notepad. I hovered in the reception area, catching glimpses through the doorway. The vet spoke to the fox in a hushed tone.

I called out, "How bad is the blood loss? Can you do a xenotransfusion with canine blood?"

Without turning to face me, the vet said, "I don't want to risk a hemolytic reaction." He reached up and adjusted the transparent tube snaking down from a bag of clear fluids. He glanced over his shoulder at me. "Are you a nurse?"

"Librarian," I called back. "I pick up all sorts of things." I straightened up the pamphlets on the clinic's front counter. "I should be at the library right now."

"Then go to the library," the vet said firmly. "I'll call you as soon as there's news."

I stayed at the counter, watching. The only part of the fox I could see was the white tip of its bushy tail. The tail drooped over the edge of the stainless steel table, as limp and lifeless as a fake-fur Halloween costume.

I checked the time again. I wasn't quite late for work, yet I wasn't much use here. I folded my leather jacket with the fox blood on the inside and draped it over my forearm.

I should have healed the fox right there in the woods. This is the lesson I was supposed to learn today.

The vet continued speaking softly, saying something about a needle to numb the area for stitches. He followed it with, "Promise not to bite me, and I won't bite you."

The tail twitched, which I took as a positive sign.

I quietly slipped away with my fingers crossed for a good outcome.

* * *

"Zara, slow down." On the other end of the phone call, Zinnia let out a huffy sigh. "I can't understand a word you're saying when you talk like you've had five cappuccinos."

I pulled my phone away from my ear and made a face at it to calm myself. I was inside the washroom at the library, which was where I made all my secret phone calls, since a hushed library isn't the ideal place for talking about secret supernatural stuff. One of my coworkers, Frank Wonder, was a flamingo shifter, so he would understand, but the others were non-supernatural until proven otherwise.

Slower, I repeated my description of the morning's events to my aunt. As my mentor in all things witchcraft, she was my best and only resource, at least until I got my hands on that Monster Manual.

She interrupted me before I could finish telling her about the kindly veterinarian.

"Whatever devious thing it is you believe I'm involved in, you are mistaken," she said crisply. "I would *never* harm a defenseless creature simply to test you, Zara. Or trap you. Or whatever it is you think I did."

I wanted to believe her. She'd hidden things from me before, but our relationship was stronger now. Ever since she accidentally killed me that one time, she'd been working hard to regain my trust.

She was quiet on the other end of the line. I visualized her mouth forming a tight pucker. I had plenty of memories to draw upon, since it was easy to offend my aunt. She had all sorts of boundary lines, and if you crossed one, it was like setting off a laser alarm in a museum; you were in trouble. Often, I would cross one of her laser lines deliberately to provoke a reaction and get it out of the way. My favorite tactic was teasing her about her clothing or decorating style. This phone call, however, had poked her on a deeper level. A not-so-fun level. She sounded genuinely hurt. Or at least her silence did.

I checked the display on my phone to make sure the call hadn't ended.

"Sorry," I said. "I'm sorry if it sounded like I was accusing you."

There was some background noise on the call—the clinking sounds of a busy cafe.

"And I apologize for snapping at you," Zinnia said.

"Now what do we do? About the fox?"

"Zara, just because we're related doesn't mean all of your problems become my problems. Maybe you should consult Chet Moore, since it concerns one of his... animal buddies." She said *animal buddies* with a note of disgust.

"I was afraid you'd say that."

"Fear is a gift," she said with an ominous tone. "Talk to Chet, and be careful. Try not to throw yourself at him. What's that word Zoey calls you?"

"Turbo-flirter."

"Right. Don't do that."

"Sure." I made a face at the phone again. And then, with a conversational tone, I asked, "Whatcha doing?"

"Waiting." She breathed out noisily, making a windy sound over the phone connection. "My associate is late for our meeting. Tansy is never late."

"Any chance your friend Tansy is a fox shifter? Or a talking blue jay? That bird knew my name."

"Zara, I prefer not to discuss such matters over an unsecured line, but let me assuage your curiosity. No. My associate is neither of those things."

"Tansy," I mused. "Isn't she the lady who supplies your special seeds and herbs?"

"Yes..." She trailed off, and I imagined her wishing she hadn't told me anything about her plant supplier.

"So, she could have made a potion and transformed herself into another form, right? Like a fox?"

There were only the background clinking sounds of the cafe. I pictured Zinnia's mouth scrunching in on itself until her whole face disappeared.

I asked, "Do you want the address of the vet clinic? To see if the fox is someone you know?"

"I'm sure my associate will be along any minute now. Thank you for your concern. Good luck with whatever it is that you've gotten yourself into."

"Come on. You know you're curious. Who is the fox? What's the deal with the talking blue jay?"

"Curiosity killed the cat," she replied.

And then she ended the call.

* * *

I got on with my day, helping library patrons with their requests and then helping myself to the previous day's leftover birthday cake in the staff lounge.

Kathy Carmichael, the head librarian, came into the break room with a tiny cough to announce her presence. She lifted her chin and sniffed the air like a woodlands creature. From her bright orange-brown eyes to her round glasses and pointed nose, Kathy always reminded me of an owl. She stalked toward the leftover cake like a hunter. From the look of the twigs and dried leaves in her hair, Kathy's morning had been as woodsy and adventurous as my own.

I asked her, "Did you bring enough twigs to share?"

She twisted her head to the side quickly, brown curls whipping. "Pardon me?"

"You have twigs in your hair, boss."

Her cheeks reddened. "Oh, fluffernuts." She patted through her brown curls and pulled several twigs from the tangled depths. She frowned at the sticks in her hand. "They say no good deed goes unpunished."

"And what kind of good deed were you doing this morning before work?" I reached up and checked my own hair for twigs. I'd cut some corners while running through the woods with the fox and wouldn't be surprised to find souvenirs in my own hair. I did have one small burr that came out with a strand of hair. I tossed both into the trash surreptitiously.

Kathy repeated my question, "What kind of good deed?" She pulled out another twig as she scrunched her face, making her beak-like nose even pointier. "The kind of good deed that kicks you in the butt when you turn around." She finished with her hair and brushed at her hip and butt as though dusting off dirt from a boot.

"Sounds colorful." I slid off my stool and put away my dishes. "Before I go back out to the circulation desk, let me serve you up some birthday cake. It's only a day old. Would you like one piece or two?"

She blinked twice, slowly, like an owl. Huskily, she answered, "Leave the lid off the box, walk toward the door, and don't look back." She repeated in a dramatic whisper, "Don't look back."

There were four and a half pieces of cake remaining in the box. I tiptoed toward the door as requested and did not look back.

Before I reached the desk, my phone rang. The call was from Dr. Katz. That was the name of the calm, young veterinarian. Dr. Katz! Ha-ha! Had his name drawn him to the field, or was it just a pun-tastic coincidence?

I silenced the ringing, waved to the young library page who was covering the desk, indicating I'd be right back, and kept walking all the way out the front door. I answered the call once I got outside.

"This is Zara Riddle."

"Ms. Riddle?" It was Dr. Katz himself, with his calm, soothing tone. He sounded older over the phone. "Your fox is stable now. I've closed up the wound, and he's recovering nicely. He's a champ."

I breathed a sigh of relief. "Thank you so much. You're a lifesaver. Literally."

He chuckled. It wasn't the first time he'd heard that compliment.

"Ms. Riddle, you can pick him up this afternoon. I would offer to keep him overnight, but I'm sure he'd be happier at home with you."

Home with me? "What are my other options?"

"Ma'am, if you're worried about the cost, don't be. My assistant tells me it's all been taken care of."

I'd been pacing back and forth in front of the library entrance. I stopped in my tracks. The fox's medical bills had been taken care of? What exactly had I stumbled into? None of this made sense.

Just then, a Department of Water (and Magic) van drove by slowly. The driver was my neighbor, Chet Moore, and he lifted his chin when we made eye contact. I waved. He waved back and then pulled over to the side of the street.

On my phone, the veterinarian kept talking, letting me know the clinic's hours. I thanked him, promised to pick up the fox before closing time, and ended the call.

I crossed the street, circled around the front of the DWM van, and pulled on the handle for the passenger-side door. It was locked.

Inside, Chet gestured for me to wait. He turned toward the back cargo area before pressing some buttons. Heavy mechanical parts shifted around inside the van. It sounded like a gate closing. Once the metallic grinding stopped, he unlocked the passenger door for me.

Don't be weird, I told myself. But I knew the command was futile.

I jumped into the passenger seat and immediately asked, "What's the deal with the fox and the blue jay?"

He gave me a startled look. I was onto something, I was sure of it. A half-baked conspiracy theory unfurled in my mind.

"Corvin is a blue jay shifter," I said, my tone accusing. "Don't try to sidestep my question and pretend he isn't. Blue jays are corvids, so your son's unusual name all but gives it away." I shook my head. "I can't believe I didn't figure it out before. I've been seeing that blue jay around the neighborhood, ever since I moved in. Watching me. I should have known it was your son."

Chet narrowed his eyes at me. He picked up a paper coffee takeout cup from the van's drink holder and took a sip, all the while watching me with curiosity.

"Unless Corvin's *not* a blue jay shifter," I said. "Is he a fox?" I widened my eyes and covered my mouth. "Chet, I would have used my powers to heal him right there in the forest if I'd known the fox was Corvin." I lowered my hand to cover my heart. "I'd never dump your son at a veterinary clinic. Not knowingly."

Chet made a sour face as he glanced down at the takeout cup. He swished his mouth from side to side then shrugged and took another sip anyway.

"You're not reacting," I said. "Corvin's not a fox, or a blue jay."

He raised his eyebrows.

"You don't even know what I'm talking about," I said.

He made a clicking sound with his mouth and pointed at me, as if to say *you finally guessed one thing right*.

I nodded as the picture came together. "You just happened to be driving along by the library because this is a main street, and you saw me pacing up and down the sidewalk, then waving you down like a madwoman, so you pulled over."

He made the mouth-click sound again and winked.

"Because you're one of the good guys," I said.

His right eye twitched.

"You deserve an explanation for all of this." I rubbed my neck self-consciously. "Long story short, I might be the proud owner of a pet fox."

He quirked one dark eyebrow.

Chet could be talkative when he got going, but judging by the dark circles under his eyes, he didn't have the energy for it at the moment.

I cleared my throat and carried on our one-sided conversation. "Since we're on the topic of foxes, would you mind stopping by my house after work?"

He tilted his head to the side. We hadn't been alone and face-to-face with each other in a few weeks, not since I'd bumped into him at a grocery store and helped him select a cantaloupe. I'd been avoiding him, but my success made me think he'd been helping by also avoiding me. Wisteria wasn't that big of a town.

"You could bring that book over," I said. "But mainly you'd be coming by to take a look at the fox."

His brow furrowed.

Something in the back of the van, hidden from my view by a metal barrier, made a gurgling sound—like the hunger pangs of a very large stomach. What size of creature had a stomach that big? The van rocked from the movement of something colossal shifting around in the back. I took that as my cue to exit the van. I yanked the handle and pushed the door open.

Chet's hand landed on my left forearm. I froze into stone. He was touching me. Multiple circuits fired up in my brain confusingly. I was wary of the gurgling monster, but now I was more concerned about the presence of a certain man's hand on my arm.

"Zara," he said, his voice hoarse.

Not to be overly dramatic like a hormonal teenager, but my name had never sounded so sexy.

Was I breathing? I answered by baring my teeth in what I hoped was a normal smile.

He said, "I can look in on you tonight." He turned his head away and coughed lightly. "And the book is all yours for the taking," he croaked. "Sorry I haven't been around. I haven't been myself. I must have caught a flu bug or something, because I've been about half my usual self."

Half his usual self was still a lot of man and wolf. I nodded at the metallic barrier separating us from the mysterious cargo. "Don't worry about coming over tonight. Not if you're sick. You look like you could use a night off from weird things."

"I'll come have a look at your fox," he said. The corner of his mouth turned up in a hint of a smile. "I have a way with strays."

I have a way with strays. His hand was still on my arm. I got a flash of one of Chessa's memories: Chet, play-fighting and tumbling with a black dog, a Labrador retriever. The two of them wrestling. Chet laughing while the dog licked his face.

"I bet you do," I said with an eyebrow waggle. "You certainly have a way with me."

"I do?" He yanked his hand away from my arm. The ghost of his touch turned cool on my skin.

Whoops. "Never mind. See you later." I kept smiling and jumped out of the van quickly, before I said something else I'd regret.

Along with Chessa's memories, her flirtatious feelings had infected me. I tried to be cool and detached around Chet Moore, but instead I was the exact opposite. It's like when you're walking over a grate and you think, "Don't drop your keys down there," and you reach for your keys to make sure they're secure, but you fumble and drop them right down the grate. I'd jumped into Chet's van thinking, *Don't be weird,* and then immediately started gushing information and making inappropriate overtures.

After tonight, I wouldn't talk to him ever again. Not even in an emergency. It wasn't worth risking Chessa's wrath. After all, I liked my skull right where it was, on top of my body.

CHAPTER 3

"YOU MUST BE the fox lady," said the young woman at the veterinary clinic's front counter.

"Is it that obvious?" I looked down at my purple blouse and blue jeans. "But I don't *look* like some circus person who keeps exotic animals. Not today, anyway." I grinned, thinking of my closet full of costumes and fun clothes. "For a change."

The young woman pressed her full lips together in an adorable smile. She had a perfectly round face, olive skin, and wide-set, sparkling brown eyes. She wore an oversized pair of white cat-eye glasses that were so wrong they were right.

She tilted her round head to the side and squinted up at me. "You know how some pet owners look like their pets? That's you, to a T, with your beautiful red fox hair. Even your eyes are the same green."

"They're hazel."

"Same thing."

Not really.

She pursed her lips and squinted again. "I'd love to get a picture of you posing with your fox. After he's recovered completely, of course."

I fluffed my red "fox" hair self-consciously and smiled down at the young woman. "I've never been asked to model before. Not with my clothes on, that is."

She pushed her white cat-eye glasses up her short nose and laughed. "I find that hard to believe!" She pointed to a calendar hanging on the wall. The picture for the current month was a glamorous portrait of a well-fed black cat with a snow-kissed white chin and white whiskers. She explained, "That's our calendar we send out at Christmas. All the pictures are taken right here in Wisteria. The models are all amateurs. Some months we have pictures of pets with owners, but some are just the fur-kids." She said *fur-kids* like it was a regular, everyday word.

"It looks very professional."

"Thanks! If you let us put your photo on next year's calendar, I'll be sure it goes with one of the longer months so people can spend a full thirty-one days admiring you and your fox. Definitely not February."

"You're very sweet." I leaned over the counter and checked her name tag. "Fatima." I glanced around. The vet clinic's waiting room was empty. The corkboard on the wall contained no posters from people who were missing foxes.

"We'll be shooting in the fall," she said.

"Let me think about the photo shoot. I'm not sure how long I'll have the fox. The custody situation right now is temporary."

"Of course!" Fatima moved to the left with a quickness that surprised me. I'd assumed she was sitting on a chair, but she was on her feet and had been the whole time. She was quite short, under four feet. She stepped up onto a platform to use the computer, tapping away speedily with small hands.

Fatima said, "You're all paid up, so you can take your little man home now."

"About that," I said. "Why is my bill paid? Is there a charitable fund for wild animals?"

Fatima blinked at me, her brown eyes becoming unfocused behind the white cat-eye frames.

"It was a man," she said in a flat tone. "A large, muscular, African-American man. He came in, and he paid for the bill. He talked to the fox for a few minutes, and then he left." Her tone stayed flat and vague. "I don't know who he was. He didn't leave his name."

"Did you see his name on his credit card?"

"He paid cash."

"Are you sure?"

She nodded slowly, her eyes still unfocused. Her head tilted to the side, as though she'd suddenly grown weary of our conversation and was dozing off.

A large, muscular black man? She could have easily been describing Knox, one of Chet's coworkers at the DWM. Knox was a shifter who could transform into an enormous bird. I'd always thought of Knox as a gentle giant, but it occurred to me that he might practice his aerial combat skills by hunting. Had the fox been his prey? If so, why would he pay the veterinary bill and then leave the animal behind with no explanation? The whole thing was getting weirder by the minute, and I'd seen a lot of weird things since moving to Wisteria, so that was saying a lot.

Fatima blinked and snapped back into focus, her head upright once more. "Come with me." She waved for me to walk around the counter. "I'm sure your *fur-kid* will be happy to see his mommy."

I snorted to myself. I'd been called a few things, but being referred to as a fur-kid's mommy was a first.

We walked past an examination table and into an alcove with stacks of roomy cages. The fox's cage had been labeled Mr. Fox, as though the big bushy tail wasn't enough of an identifier.

True to Fatima's promise, the little guy did seem happy to see me. He lifted his pointed muzzle and rotated both big dark ears to face me. He was all ears and fur. What a cutie! His gold-green eyes blinked with recognition as he unfurled the bushy tail he'd had wrapped around his small body. And was that a smile on his black lips?

Fatima called over the veterinarian.

Dr. Katz joined us in the alcove. In his soothing tone, he described the emergency treatments he'd given the fox. He used the technical terms to describe the extent of the damage, and he didn't pull any punches. The injuries had been deep. I swallowed hard, regretting the valuable seconds I'd wasted in the forest, being indecisive and chatting with that nosy blue jay.

I thanked the veterinarian, and he excused himself to check on the cage directly across the alcove.

He opened the grated door and poked at what I'd assumed was a fluffy white sheepskin blanket. The lump rose up and took the shape of a long-haired white cat.

"That's a good Boa," the veterinarian cooed. "Good girl. Wave goodbye to the charming Mr. Fox. This nice redhead lady is going to take him home now, and you'll have the place all to yourself tonight."

The cat showed her intense concern by yawning lazily.

Fatima saw me watching Dr. Katz with the cat. She asked me, "Would you like to adopt Boa? She's currently looking for a *furever* home."

"Did you say *furever home*?"

Fatima grinned, her teeth as white and pearly as her glasses frames. "That's what we call adoption."

Of course. Fur-kids went to furever homes. I'd know that if I'd ever owned a pet before.

The vet chimed in. "Boa's a lovely girl, and she'd make a lovely addition to any household. She's up to date on all her shots and ready to curl up on someone's lap. Wouldn't you like that?" He gave me a hopeful smile. "Some people think a white cat with long fur might need a lot of maintenance, but I assure you Boa is quite capable of grooming herself. A little dab of fur-ball medicine once a week is all she needs."

"Let me think about it," I said. "Why is she called Boa? She's not part snake, is she?"

Fatima and Dr. Katz exchanged a knowing look and snickered. The vet explained, "She showed up here with no identification, and she reminded us of a feather boa." And then, speaking very slowly, as though I was quite foolish, he said, "Cats are no more related to snakes than humans are related to, say, birds."

"Right," I said, though I happened to know otherwise.

The veterinarian scooped fluffy white Boa from her cage and murmured sweetly to her, "Let's go get some sunshine in the courtyard." As he walked away, the cat peered over his shoulder at me and raised one pink-toed paw, as if to say, *Don't forget about me.*

Behind me, there was a metallic clinking sound as Fatima operated the latch on the fox's cage.

"We had to use our high-security latch," she said. "Foxes are notoriously clever about foxing their way in and out of places they shouldn't be."

"Great," I said flatly. Did I really want to take this clever animal home with me?

"Good boy," Fatima said as she looked him over. "You haven't touched the stitches, so you may not need the Cone of Shame." She scratched under his chin as she explained the after-care treatment for his wound. He would need oral antibiotics plus a topical cream.

She asked brightly, "Any other questions?"

"Yes. Sorry to be a bother, but could you describe to me again the person who paid my bill?"

Once again, her eyes unfocused, and she stared blankly past me, this time in the direction of a cat poster on the wall.

"It was a petite Asian woman with short hair," she said. "She was elegant and regal, with the most dazzling bright-blue eyes."

I felt my eyebrows rise. "Did you say a petite Asian woman paid the bill? Not a large black man?"

"She was short-haired," Fatima said with a slow nod.

I turned my head and looked at the poster in her field of view. It was an artistic photograph of a Siamese cat walking daintily along a tree branch, staring at the camera with bright-blue eyes.

Magic!

The veterinarian's assistant was under a spell. Whoever had paid for the fox's treatment had done so under a glamour, a magical disguise. I'd been disguised by magic once, as a bush. And I'd seen my aunt transform herself into an old man. This spell affecting Fatima was a bit different, it seemed. The memory itself was changing.

I turned to the fox, who still appeared to be smiling.

Mr. Fox, you've got some questions to answer when I get you home.

But first, how was I supposed to get him home? I'd brought him there wrapped in my leather jacket. I'd zipped out on my lunch break to take the blood-soaked jacket to a dry cleaner, so I didn't have it with me. What I needed was a portable cage, or even a car. I could call for a taxi, assuming they wouldn't see the fox and refuse service.

The fox got to his feet and waved one front paw. He seemed to be beckoning me to lean forward. Did he want to tell me something? Whisper it in my ear?

I leaned in, and he jumped onto my shoulders with seemingly effortless grace.

He settled in for a shoulder ride, comfortably balanced on my shoulders with his paws draped forward over my shoulders.

Fatima smiled at us with adoration. "What a beautiful family. I love how your hair blends with his fur."

"Thanks," I said, feeling weirdly vain. Did she think I'd chosen to own an exotic animal because we matched? I wasn't shallow like that. Or was I? His fur did complement my hair.

The fox nuzzled my cheek with its wet black nose.

Fatima looked down at my feet. "The lady who paid the bill was wearing those same boots," she said. "Exactly the same."

"I'm sure," I said. *I'm sure you believe she was, thanks to that spell.*

I patted my fox companion on his sable paws, thanked the assistant and the vet, and began walking home with my furry, rust-colored scarf.

CHAPTER 4

THEY SAY YOU can get used to anything if given enough time.

It took me two blocks to stop worrying about the fox falling off my shoulders, and a third block to find the pleasure in parading around with a genuine fox scarf.

"This is actually fun," I said to the fox.

He responded by tickling the tip of my nose with his bushy tail. I smoothed down the tail, ruffling my fingers through the thick, luxurious coat. The bright-red fur was both softer and denser than it appeared.

"I hope you don't mind me petting you. For the first time in my life, I finally understand why people wear fur coats."

The fox puffed out an indignant snort, right next to my ear.

"So, you do understand what I'm saying, Mr. Fox. You comprehend human speech."

He gave me an ear twitch and nothing more.

"You're not going to make this easy on me, are you?"

The fox rested his chin on my shoulder and stretched out his dark sable paws, letting them hang down languidly along the neckline of my purple blouse.

I reached the end of the street and asked the fox, "Left or right? I'd be happy to take you right back to where you belong, if you'd just give me a hint."

The fox closed his green-gold eyes and let his head go limp. He was playing dead.

"Cute," I said.

There was a clip-clop sound behind me. By the sound of it, a woman in heels was hurrying toward the corner where I stood waiting to cross the street.

"Excuse me," the woman said. Her tone was anything but polite. "Ex-cuuuuuuuse me," she repeated, more aggressively. "Hey! You with the fox!"

I turned around to find a short fifty-something woman with gray curls around a rectangular face approaching me. She wore a dark-gray suit and hard-soled shoes that clip-clopped like hooves. One of her curls stuck out from the center of her forehead. She had rounded shoulders, and her upper body was tilted forward as she came toward me, giving her the appearance of a charging rhinoceros.

I replied politely, "Can I help you?"

She stopped charging and pawed the sidewalk with one hoof-like foot.

"Fur is murder," she spat. "It's wrong. You should be ashamed of yourself."

I might have agreed with her message, but I sure didn't like her tone.

Mr. Fox was still limp around my shoulders, playing dead. I gave his tail a tug as I smiled sweetly at the Rhinoceros Woman.

"Ma'am, you should take a closer look at my scarf before you start hurling accusations."

She clip-clopped right up to me and leaned in close, frowning. She reached out and tentatively poked the fox on its dark, wet nose. The fox gave no signs of being alive. The woman recoiled and crossed her arms.

"You sick person," she spat. "You're wearing a corpse!"

"He's alive." I tugged the bushy tail again, harder. "I swear, he was alive a minute ago."

The woman gawked at me with bugged-out eyes. Her whole rectangular-shaped face was twitching, as though her muscles couldn't decide what expression to make. The horn-like curl on the center of her forehead trembled with outrage.

"Wake up," I said to the fox. "You've had your fun, now open your eyes."

"You're a psychopath," declared the woman. "Or a sociopath. Or both. Your parents should have drowned you at birth!"

The fox made a growling sound but didn't open his eyes.

I raised my hand. "All right. You've made your point about wearing fur, ma'am. Now if you'll just let me be on my way—"

The woman lunged forward, hands raised, and grabbed the fox's front paws. His eyes flashed open immediately, and suddenly his jaws were snapping, his sharp white teeth just inches from the woman's face.

She released the paws, shrieked, and stumbled backward. She tripped, and her arms windmilled helplessly as she teetered backward off the sidewalk.

At the same moment, a city bus was rapidly approaching the same space occupied by the top half of Rhinoceros Woman's body.

I jumped forward, reaching for her arm. Her eyes bulged with terror. She was more afraid of me than falling. She yanked her arm out of my grasp, propelling herself even more rapidly toward the front of the bus.

There was no time to think or debate. I used my telekinetic magic to catch her on the back and bounce her back up onto the sidewalk. It was ridiculously easy, much simpler than trying to grab her with my hand. Once she was upright, I latched onto her hand and dragged her to the middle of the sidewalk. The bus roared by without so much as a honk.

"Phew," I exclaimed theatrically. "I thought you were going to slip through my fingers, but then luckily I snagged the hem of your jacket."

She made a gurgling sound as her rectangle face contorted. Her rhinoceros-horn curl was now damp with sweat. She twisted her head to look at her back and kept twisting, twirling around like a dog with something on its tail.

"My back," she muttered. "Something touched me on my back." She stopped twirling and stared after the bus as it trundled down the street, its aura of raw destructive power decreasing by the second. "Something invisible," she said.

"Invisible? You mean like wind?"

"No! An invisible force!"

She was onto me. I needed to change the topic. Fast.

I pointed across the street, at a familiar-looking man in a suit the same shade of gray as the woman's.

"Hey," I said to the woman. "Who's that suspicious guy over there? What do you suppose he's up to?"

The man across the street noticed me pointing and stopped walking. He broadened his shoulders and pushed back his jacket to put his hands on his hips in a Superman pose. It was good ol' Detective Bentley. I'd missed teasing him at the bakery this morning. He looked stronger and more rugged than he appeared when he was eating donuts.

Rhinoceros Woman swiveled her head to stare at Bentley. While she was distracted, I made my escape. I walked swiftly down the street, turned down a side street, and didn't look back. I listened for the clip-clop of her shoes, but to my relief, she wasn't chasing me.

The fox on my shoulders made a sound not unlike a human guffaw.

"You're a monster," I said. "You nearly got that woman killed, and you made me... do something I didn't want to do."

The fox pressed his wet nose against my cheek and gave me an apologetic lick.

"You're still a monster," I said.

The fox sighed, rested his muzzle on the front of my shoulder, and gazed up at me. Those green-gold eyes were still so familiar. I felt a confusing mix of emotions I hadn't experienced in a long time. I was annoyed, but having fun in spite of my reservations.

We left the downtown core, and my walking slowed as I neared my neighborhood. The hills felt steeper with the additional weight of the fox on my shoulders. He was mostly fur, but he had a few solid pounds underneath the fluff.

I received a few curious stares from my fellow Wisterians, but nobody dared to talk to the sweaty redhead with the live fox on her shoulders.

As I turned onto Beacon Street, I noticed a cacophonous clanging followed by an ominous groaning. It was the sound of a large structure being strained. Was someone doing a home renovation? There were more clangs and groans. It didn't sound like the typical hammers and saws of construction. The groaning reminded me of a school field trip to an auto wrecker yard, where all of us children had cheered as the auto crusher squashed a rusty old car into a cube.

The fox's ears straightened up, and he raised his head. His shiny black nose pointed straight at the corner of the street, where my house sat.

As I drew closer to home, it became clear the horrible noises were coming from my house. My daughter had been planning to come straight home after school, so she was presumably inside the house. What was she doing? There was more clanging. My pulse raced. What was happening?

I ran up the porch steps two at a time and yanked on the door. The handle was unlocked; it turned, but the door didn't open. The door didn't even budge. I yanked again, but it was like pulling on a brick wall.

I banged on the door and pressed the doorbell button. I couldn't hear the cheery ding-dong of the doorbell over the clatter. If I didn't know better, I'd guess a six-man wrecking crew was inside, tearing up the hardwood floors and ripping out plumbing.

"Zoey!" I banged on the door. I tried using my magic to shove the door from the other side. It still wouldn't budge.

My shoulders felt lighter. The fox had jumped down and was now pacing the porch, stepping gingerly on the rear paw that was next to his injury. His pointy sable ears kept swiveling left and right.

"Mr. Fox, do you know what's going on?"

He let out a single YIP.

"Did you say 'yip,' as in yes?"

He tilted his head to the side. I might have found the head tilt adorable under different circumstances.

I rubbed my hands together, feeling my powers growing while my mind raced for answers. My lips got ahead of me and curved into a smile. *Zoey's powers?* Despite my fear over the noise, I had a glimmer of hope. Perhaps my daughter's latent witch powers had finally kicked in and she was doing something amazing with her magic.

I ran down the steps and around the side of the house. There wasn't much space between our house and the Moores' house, and today the breezeway seemed even narrower.

I cupped my hands around my mouth and called up, facing her bedroom window. "Zoey!" And then, for maximum effect, her full name. "Zolanda Daizy Cazzaundra Riddle! Open your window right this instant!"

The air shimmered before me, twinkling with the visual signs of my magic that only I could see. The window flew open with a bang. The cacophony of noises continued, louder.

Zoey's face appeared in the window, her red hair swinging out over the ledge as she leaned down. Her skin was as white as snow, her cheeks flushed with patches of pink.

"Mom? What are you doing to the house?" Her gaze darted over to my animal companion. The fox sat by my feet, his bushy tail wrapped around his front paws, as calm as could be.

"Me? What are *you* doing to the house?"

"It's not me," she said, and then, softer, in a tone that felt like ice in my heart, "Mom, I'm scared."

"I'm coming up. Throw me down your ninja rope."

"Can't you just..." She looked at the fox and frowned. "Is that a red fox?"

I turned to look at the fox. His elongated mouth was open, and the corners of his black lips were curled up. He was smiling, all right. No doubt about it.

"You're doing this," I said to the fox.

He clamped his muzzle shut and gave me the cute head tilt.

"Stop it right now," I growled. "You can mess with other people, and you can mess with me, but don't you *dare* mess with my daughter. She's up there by herself, and she's terrified, and it's all your fault."

The fox licked his nose.

My powers rose up inside me, the pressure like rushing water straining against a concrete dam with cracks forming.

In the controlled, barely audible voice I'd been trained to use for the Witch Tongue, I commanded the fox to stop whatever it was he was doing.

Cease your mischief now. I command you.

My ears rushed with power, drowning out the sounds of wood and metal groaning. I cupped my palms and directed my command at the creature's head.

The fox lowered his muzzle to the ground and covered his eyes with one sable paw. He shook. He trembled. His fur rippled.

And then he changed form, into a man.

The man was fully clothed, shorter than average, with rust-colored hair. The side of his brown jacket was dark with blood.

"I knew it," I said.

He removed his hand from over his eyes and blinked up at me with gold-green eyes. *Those eyes.* Now I knew why he'd looked so familiar.

"Zara," he said hoarsely. "Did you really know it was me?"

"All along," I lied. "Who else would it be?"

CHAPTER 5

I CLAPPED MY HANDS together to keep from zapping the man with more of my spell.

I'd already hit him with a dangerous amount. Shifters aren't supposed to change form while injured. Chet had told me it wasn't so much a rule as a physical impossibility. But when I'd commanded the fox shifter to *stop its mischief*, my spell must have forced the shift back into a man. I'd broken the rules of nature. Surely there would be a price to pay for my brute force.

The man, whose name I knew was Rhys Quarry, gave me a sheepish grin.

"Hello again," he said. "Can I offer you a hug?"

"Go hug yourself," I spat out.

Zoey, who was still leaning out of her bedroom window, cried out happily, "Pawpaw!"

Rhys Quarry, my fair-weather father, turned away from me and beamed sunshine up at my daughter. "Zozo! You remember me!"

"She's got a great memory," I said under my breath. "And so do I. An excellent memory."

Zoey called down, "Pawpaw, are you really a..." She cupped her hands above her head, imitating fox ears.

He stammered and kicked at some loose pebbles on the ground.

I cocked my head and grabbed my father's arm. "Rhys, do you hear that?"

He blinked and gave me the hurt look he always made when I called him by his first name instead of Dad. I'd been calling him Rhys since the first time he'd let me down —age five.

"What? I don't hear anything, Zara."

"Exactly," I said. "The noise inside the house has stopped."

"Ah." He waggled his rust-colored eyebrows. "Let's try the front door again."

I led the way back to the front of the house. This time, the door opened easily. I stepped in cautiously, looking around for signs of danger. The air was filled with dust, and the hall mirror was crooked, but other than that, everything looked about the same as I'd left it.

I ran up the stairs to check on Zoey. My foot caught the top step, and I nearly went sprawling.

What the...? I turned and frowned at the stairs. Rhys was coming up slowly, gripping the railing.

Something was different. My body had a muscle memory of the staircase and hadn't been expecting that last step at the top. Was it possible all that groaning and banging was my house growing an extra step on the staircase? For what purpose?

"Pawpaw," Zoey cried out. She launched herself into her grandfather's arms.

They hugged in the upstairs hallway. He stumbled backward, chuckling. "Easy, Zozo. You're not so little anymore. I think you might be nearly as tall as me."

She pulled back and straightened up. "I'm sixteen now. And I'm at least an inch taller than you, Pawpaw."

I raised my hand to interrupt. "Can I just point out the irony that the man you call Pawpaw happens to have four paws?"

Rhys gave us an embarrassed shrug and a crooked smile. His rubbery features were almost comical in their exaggerated movements. He swept his hand through his rust-colored hair and then stuffed both hands into the pockets of his brown blazer. I stared at the bloodstain on the side of the jacket. Had the blood transferred from his fur to the fabric, or had he been injured first in human form? I had so many questions, I didn't know where to start.

"Surprise," he said, casting his gaze up at me, his gold-green eyes squinting under his rust-colored bushy eyebrows.

"And what a surprise," I replied. "You're a supernatural."

"Yep." Another shrug. "Your dad's a real catch. You might say he's a genuine fox."

I rolled my eyes.

Rhys gave Zoey a rubbery grin. "And judging by your utter lack of surprise, little Miss Riddle, I'm guessing you two both know all about shifters and goblins and things that go bump in the night."

Zoey's mouth made an O shape. "Goblins are real?"

"Sort of." He bobbed his head from side to side. "Mostly, it's just an expression." He cast his gaze down and shuffled his feet, scuffing his shoe over the dusty wood floor. "So, how are you finding your new powers, Zoey? Did your witch magic kick in on your sixteenth birthday?"

I quickly clamped my hand over Zoey's mouth. "Don't answer that. Our family secrets are not for him to know. You know what Aunt Zinnia says."

Zoey blinked once. I released my hand, and she said, "Secrets revealed are trouble unsealed."

Rhys asked, "How is Zinnia these days? I haven't seen her since your mother's funeral."

"Never mind Zinnia," I said. "What were you doing running around the forest? It's amazing you just happened to cross my path right when you had a life-threatening injury. Some might say unbelievable."

His eyebrows rose high. "There's nothing amazing about a life-threatening injury. Sometimes a coincidence is just that. Plus you know what they say. Magic has a mind of its own."

"I've heard that a lot," I said coolly. "But recent events have opened my eyes. Sometimes what seems to be a fun coincidence is just the tip of an iceberg of lies." Like when your new neighbor tricks you into bonding with him over a shared history you never had.

My father scuffed his shoe over the floor again. "Well, I don't know what to say, Zarabella. The injury was genuine. I'm still in real pain."

Zoey made a sad noise. "You're hurt, Pawpaw?"

"Don't you worry, little one." He patted his brown blazer right above the bloodstain. "The old man's on the mend already, thanks to your mother's quick thinking." He moved his hand over to his stomach. "Is anyone else famished?"

"Don't change the subject," I said. "How did you get hurt?"

He reached out and grasped the newel post to steady himself. "I was enjoying some morning exercise in one of your quaint little town's lovely parks, and a giant bird came at me from out of nowhere." He let go of the newel post and used both hands to dramatize his story like a master. "I was alone one second, and then the great winged beast was upon me, snarling as it grasped me with its razor-sharp talons." He shaped his hands into claws and snapped at Zoey playfully while growling.

"Birds don't snarl," I said. "They caw or screech."

"Are you sure about that?" His rubbery features twitched between amusement and innocence.

"Yes," I said. "Vultures aren't capable of cawing, so they make throaty hisses."

"How romantic," he said. "I'm sure their throaty hisses are very appealing to the other vultures."

"Was the bird really snarling, or would you care to change your story?"

He made a fist with his free hand and swung it. "I'm sticking to my story, girls. It was a giant winged creature, dark and scary as a plumber's crack. Maybe it wasn't a bird, but it was certainly an unprovoked attack."

Zoey asked, "Why are you here? Did you come to see us?"

"I had been hoping to see you." He fixed his green-gold eyes on me. "I phoned your mother a couple of weeks ago, and she said you were still too busy getting settled to entertain visitors. She said she was busy with cantaloupes, whatever that meant, but maybe there'd be time later this summer."

"I told you not to come to Wisteria," I said. "Not ever."

His eyes twinkled. "Semantics." He snapped his fingers. "Now, which of these rooms is your guest room?"

"We don't have a guest room," I said. "This house has only two bedrooms upstairs."

He walked over to a door and put his hand on the doorknob. "Oh? Then what's this?"

Zoey and I exchanged a confused look. The last time I'd observed that section of wall, it had been wall. Not a door.

He winked at me before pushing open the door. What lay beyond was an entirely new room, one I'd never seen before.

The guest bedroom was fully furnished, with a bed and a small desk. The linens were neutral and timeless, not unlike those of a chain hotel room.

Zoey's jaw dropped open.

Laid out on the bed was a change of clothes, in my father's signature style—trousers with a plaid shirt and an old-fashioned tweed jacket that would look right at home on a traveling salesman from a 1960s movie.

He picked up the clothes and came back without a word, walking past us toward the bathroom. He whistled a catchy tune. Then he closed the bathroom door, and the shower water began running.

He called through the closed door, "I hope you don't mind if I freshen up before dinner!"

"Freshen away," I said.

Zoey was still incapable of speech as she stared into the new guest bedroom and then back at me.

"You sure have a lot of different kinds of shampoo," he called out. "Any recommendations?"

"Whatever you want," I said. "Don't get your stitches wet. Dr. Katz's assistant said if you chew on them, I'll have to put the Cone of Shame around your neck."

Zoey raised her eyebrows. "Cone of Shame?" She grinned.

"I'll be careful," he promised.

Zoey walked down the hall and opened the door to my bedroom. "Uh-oh," she said.

I followed and looked over her shoulder. My spacious bedroom had shrunk to make room and was now simply adequate. My closet had narrowed to match. My clothes were so tightly packed they were practically complaining about getting wrinkled.

Zoey led the way to her bedroom next. Like mine, it was also smaller than it had been the day before, though not by as much.

She looked at me, her hazel eyes wide.

"You need to be more careful," she said.

"Me?"

"I think you should have given me notice, at the very least. I was sitting on my bed, reading, when the house started making all these snap-crackle-pop noises. I thought we were having an earthquake, so I tried to get outside to safety, or at the very least into a doorway, but my door slammed shut on its own, and I couldn't get it open. I couldn't even get the window open, then a few minutes later, it just opened on its own."

"I guess the window opening was my magic, but the extra guest room wasn't me. Not unless I'm casting spells without being aware of it."

She gave me an exasperated look. "A little warning would have been nice." She shook her head. "Show-off."

"Zoey, I did open your window, and I did force my father to shift into human form, but I swear I didn't cast any sort of make-a-new-room spell on the house." I looked up at the corners of the ceiling and whispered, "The house must have done this on its own."

"Really? That is so..." She trailed off, glancing around the room.

"Creepy? Disturbing? Downright rude?"

"Wonderful," she finished. "What a great house!" She patted the wall next to her light switch. "Good house. Good girl."

I snorted. "You wouldn't be lavishing praise on the ol' gal if she'd stolen more square footage from your bedroom. I'll have to sleep standing up tonight. Assuming I can even sleep at all, knowing that my own house might decide to squeeze the walls in on me like a trash compactor inside a big spaceship. How happy would you be if your mother was a small cube?"

"That depends. Would you be small enough to cart around in my backpack? I think I could work with that."

"You're twisted and strange, just like this house."

She grinned.

The sound of my father whistling in the shower floated into the room.

"Listen," I said, invoking my Serious and Wise Mom Voice. "I know your grandfather can be charming and fun, but you can't trust him. If he asks you about magic, say nothing. Change the topic to school or politics or religion or anything but magic."

"But he's one of us. He's a shifter."

"Apparently." I widened my eyes and took a deep breath. My father was a shifter. A fox shifter. The knowledge kept hitting me in waves. *Folks, meet my father, Rhys Quarry, the red fox shifter.*

Zoey poked me on the shoulder. "That means you're half shifter, and I'm a quarter shifter. Unless my father was a shifter, in which case I'm three-quarters shifter." Her normally smooth forehead wrinkled. "And if I'm three-quarters shifter, that would explain why my witch powers haven't kicked in."

She took three steps back and sat limply on the edge of her bed. She held up her hands and examined the palms as though seeing them in a new light.

Softly, she said, "Mom? What am I?"

The dust in the air tickled my nose, but I resisted sneezing. My vision blurred.

Zoey looked up at me, her eyes as wide and trusting of me as they'd always been, even when she was a baby. She was still my baby, my little girl. Everything was happening so fast. I wanted us to both turn into foxes right then and there, so I could curl my body around hers and cover us both with my big fluffy tail.

The wrinkle on her forehead turned into a furrow. "You don't even know what I am," she said.

"You're my daughter," I said. "You're Zoey. Nothing else matters."

Her eyes narrowed, and the frown deepened. "You're just saying that because you don't know anything. And you won't even let me talk to the other people who might have answers for me. Pawpaw wanted to visit before now. He phoned you, and you told him not to come. Now he's only here by accident. He probably had to hurt himself just so you could give him the time of day."

I wagged my finger at her. "There. You just said it yourself. He *did* stage that accident. He hurt himself on purpose to get access to our family. You need to keep—"

She interrupted me. "Our family? You mean *his* family. We belong to him, too. I know he wasn't the world's greatest father to you, but he's the only grandpa I've got. It's not fair of you to keep us apart. It's not fair." Her gaze flicked around the room. "This house knows better than you. She made space for him in our life. Literally. This house is a better mother than you."

I took a step back, reeling as through slapped. *She doesn't mean it,* I told myself. *She's a teenager dealing with hormones, a new town, and magic, all at once.*

"Okay," I said softly. "If both you and the house want to give him a chance, then it's two against one. I know when I've been beaten." I bowed my head. "I'll give your grandfather the benefit of the doubt." Except I wouldn't. I would let him stay in the guest room, but I'd be watching him.

Zoey said nothing. She'd probably been gearing up for a big battle and had nothing prepared in response to me being agreeable. I nearly smirked with pride over having surprised her. *Good mothering, Zara. Always one step ahead.*

"Fine," she said.

"Fine," I agreed. "But please, Zoey, please don't trust that man any further than you could toss his little fox body. Rhys Quarry is an opportunistic man. If he asks you about magic powers, it's because he's already got a buyer lined up and waiting."

Her face twitched. She didn't want to believe me. She heard my warning, but it went in one ear and out the other.

"A buyer?"

"He's always called himself a business matchmaker," I said. "I assumed he was just a traveling salesman who didn't want to admit he was a salesman." I came over to sit on the bed beside her. As soon as I sat, she shifted away, just far enough so I couldn't put my arm around her shoulders. The rejection stung, but I had to keep talking. It was important that she knew the truth.

"Zoey, I only saw the man once a year. I didn't have a clue what he did the other three hundred and sixty-four days a year. But now, in light of the whole thing with the whiskers, black nose, and bushy tail, I'm guessing there's a lot more to Rhys Quarry than I ever imagined. He was never brokering manufacturing space or negotiating corporate partnerships. It must have always been magic stuff."

Without looking at me, she asked coolly, "How does a person making a living doing that?"

"That would be a good question for you to ask your grandfather. Now's your opportunity to find out. You're a smart girl. Make the best out of this situation." *And get me some information I can use against him.*

She crossed her arms. "I don't like it when you do that thing with your voice. Stop trying to trick me by pretending that I've won."

"I'm not trying to trick you."

"Don't patronize me." She leaned even farther away and growled, "Stop talking already and leave me alone. Can't a person have five minutes of peace and quiet to think her thoughts?"

As much as I didn't want the last words of our conversation to be her giving me a bag of heck that I didn't deserve, I knew better than to pick a battle nobody could win. I got up and left my teen daughter to her thinking.

I went to my smaller bedroom and pried a jacket out of my closet. I walked back out to the hallway and announced loudly, for the benefit of any family members who might be listening, that I was going out to pick up some food for dinner and would be back in an hour.

Then I left the house. As I walked down the front steps, I used my phone to send Zinnia a plea to meet me at the Thai restaurant halfway between my house and hers. *It's urgent,* I messaged.

She wrote back: *I'll be there in ten minutes.*

I glanced over my shoulder at my house, a gorgeous three-story Victorian Gothic, painted red. The wisteria vines twisting along the front porch accented the bright gingerbread detail around the windows and eaves. Kids in the neighborhood had been calling it the Red Witch House since long before I'd moved in.

If they only knew the full story. The house had a mind of its own, and had conjured up a guest room without my permission.

Two blocks later, I stopped abruptly and stared at my hands. The news about my father was still hitting me in waves. I was half shifter. Could my hands turn into paws? If Rhys Quarry was a fox shifter, did that make me less of a witch?

No wonder Zoey was confused. I was the adult in our relationship, the one who was supposed to have all the answers, and I didn't even know what we were.

CHAPTER 6

PERHAPS I WAS projecting my own jumbled-up emotions, but the owner of the Thai restaurant looked like she'd also had a taxing day.

May Meesang stood slumped over the restaurant's counter, with her cheek propped up on one hand and her elbow on the counter. She didn't notice me walk in and offer her usual cheery greeting. I couldn't see her eyes. Either she was staring down at the piles of paperwork on the counter, or she had fallen asleep standing up.

I cleared my throat and shuffled my feet on the bristles of the restaurant's welcome mat so as not to startle her. She didn't move.

"May, is everything okay?"

The petite woman startled, her chin falling from her palm and nearly hitting the counter before she caught herself. She looked up with wide eyes and flashed me a welcoming smile.

"Zara! Everything is okay now that you're here."

I looked down to see what she'd been snoozing over. It was a pile of half-opened mail.

"Lots of bills in there," I said. "A stack that big would put me to sleep, too."

May groaned and pushed the pile aside. She got a mischievous look and kept patting the edge of the stack, like a cat in a funny internet video, until the papers fell off the edge of the counter and into a drawer she'd opened with her other hand.

As I watched this, I remembered the description I'd gotten from the veterinarian's assistant. Fatima said that a petite Asian woman with short hair had paid for the bill. She'd been staring at the poster for a Siamese cat, but she could have been describing May.

May had a triangular face with a pointed chin, and small, wide-set eyes that were probably naturally brown underneath her blue contact lenses. She'd shaved her head a few weeks back in support of a family member going through an illness. Her dark locks had grown back quickly in an adorable pixie cut with a spiky tuft on the crown from her swirling cowlick. She was a few years older than me, but the cut made her look as young and energetic as a teenaged skateboarder.

As I wondered about this, she leaned sideways to look behind me. "Where is your daughter?"

"At home."

May straightened up and looked right at me. "You two must have had a fight."

"How did you know? May, are you a psychic?" I gave her a playful, sidelong look.

"Your child is sixteen, and she's full of fire, like her mother and her great-aunt. It doesn't take psychic powers to make a lucky guess." She closed the drawer containing her mail with a solid shove.

"That's a good trick," I said, nodding at the now-clean counter. "I leave my mail on a hall table so it can give me dirty looks when I accidentally make eye contact."

May ran her small finger across the fringe of dark hair along her brow.

"The mail isn't so bad these days," she said.

"How's your cousin?"

"Very good, thank you." She clasped her hands together girlishly. "In fact, my cousin is doing so well that I want to celebrate by going dancing, but my husband is such a mean grump." She frowned dramatically. "He won't take me. He doesn't like my hair this way. He says I look like a little boy." She flicked at the spiky tuft at her crown. "I wish someone would talk some sense into him."

I laughed. Was she just making conversation, or did May believe I could convince her husband to take her dancing? Her small blue eyes twinkled at me knowingly.

I kept thinking about the vet assistant's description, and how well it matched both the Siamese cat and May. The woman's family was from Thailand, which had been known as Siam prior to 1939.

May tapped a blue ballpoint pen on a pad of paper. "Ordering takeout tonight? If you bring that fiery daughter of yours some *Kai Pad Med Mamuang Himmapan*, that sour teen attitude of hers will turn so sweet."

"Can't hurt," I said with a smile. "How's your day been? Did you get up to anything interesting?"

"That depends on if you would call shopping for spices and preparing marinades interesting. How about you?"

"Just librarian stuff, plus a few trips to a vet clinic." I watched her for a reaction.

She handed me a takeout menu. "Sounds expensive. I didn't know you had a pet."

"Me, neither."

Someone in the kitchen attracted May's attention with a question. I looked over the menu, and when she returned, I ordered way more food than three people could eat, as usual. I didn't know what my father liked, but I figured chicken was a safe bet. Foxes love to snatch farmers' chickens—at least if children's picture books are to be believed.

"No rush in the kitchen," I said. "Zinnia's meeting me here for a visit so I can fill her in on the latest family drama."

May winked in her friendly way. "I'll get two tall glasses of Thai iced tea ready. Take a seat anywhere you'd like."

I walked into the Thai restaurant's small dining area and chose a table for two in a quiet corner. I would be able to cast a privacy bubble spell while my aunt and I talked, but I still retained my normal human instinct to seek privacy the regular way. And for good reason. There was no need to attract the attention of people who might wonder why they could see our lips moving yet not hear our words. Smart witches keep a low profile and try not to attract attention. Parading around town with a live fox on one's shoulders is a good example of what *not* to do.

Zinnia arrived at the same time as the milky, sweet Thai iced tea.

I jumped up from my chair and gave her a hug. She didn't so much hug back as receive the hug neutrally, as was typical for my aunt. As I took my seat again, I recalled telling my father to *go hug himself.* I could have been nicer, but in my defense, it had all been such a shock.

Zinnia cast the sound bubble spell and gestured for me to go ahead. I filled her in on everything that had happened with my father, starting with his surprise phone call a few weeks earlier.

When he'd called, I'd reacted poorly to hearing his voice. The first thing I'd done was demand to know how he'd gotten my new phone number. My human defenses must have been on high power due to my grocery store interaction with Chet Moore, and I'd taken it out on my father.

Did he deserve such poor treatment? I'd been much nicer a few months earlier, when I'd needed something from him. That probably painted me in a bad light.

Why did I feel how I did? Why did hearing his voice or seeing his face make me tense with anger? My heart told me I couldn't trust Rhys Quarry, yet my head wasn't so great at putting it into words.

"It's a complicated situation," Zinnia said sagely. "Sometimes the past is a ghost who takes up residence in the dark closets of your mind."

I tapped my forehead. "This place gets a bit crowded sometimes."

She raised one eyebrow. "At least you've solved the mystery of the fox."

I gave her a suspicious look. "You knew," I said. "You already knew who it was, because you've always known my father was a fox."

She gazed into my eyes and tapped her fingers on the table. She was a mirror of me, reflecting my suspicious expression right back. Zinnia was only sixteen years older than me, the same gap as between me and my daughter. Most people mistook us for sisters. Some even took us for twins, which she pretended not to take delight in. She and I had the same thick, red, wavy hair, the same hazel eyes, and the same pale, slightly temperamental skin. But she had an air of old-fashionedness that made me think of her as being a full generation older than me. She didn't swear, not unless you considered *floopy doop* as a curse.

"You knew," I repeated, my voice tinged with accusation. "You knew about Rhys, and you never told me. This explains what's happening with Zoey. Or, should I say, what's *not* happening with Zoey."

Zinnia's mirror-like reflection of me softened as she sighed. She spoke softly. "How long?"

I held up my hands. "How long? Uh, since forever and always?"

"No," she said crisply. "I mean how long will it take you to forgive me for my sins of the past and stop accusing me of keeping secrets every time something new presents itself in your life?"

I frowned. The sweet taste of the milky tea in my mouth turned cloying.

"Floopy doop," I said. "Now you're angry, too."

"I am?"

"Now everyone's ticked off at me. First Zoey, now you. I can't win. I knew it, right away this morning, that I was being tested. I just didn't think it would be like this."

"Stop talking nonsense," she said. "I can see you're upset, Zara. You haven't even said a single word about my new vest, so I know it's serious."

"Your vest!" The mention of her clothing was as good as a slap on the face. I did a cartoonish double take and took in her outfit. "Does the Rose Petal Tea Room know you've stolen their curtains?"

She swirled her milky tea with a long-handled spoon before taking a delicate sip.

"No, wait." I snapped my fingers. "That's the chintz fabric from their seat cushions. From the one by the window seat for two."

"For someone who claims not to love florals, you certainly have a knack for spotting pattern similarities."

She took another sip and set the glass down an inch closer to me than it had been before. "Now that we've gotten your tantrum out of the way, let me assure you, whether you believe it or not, I had *no idea* your father was a supernatural being."

"Fair enough. I know you and my mother weren't very close, and she and my father could barely tolerate being in the same room together. She would grit her teeth nonstop on the mornings she handed me off to him for the annual daddy-daughter day." I made the gagging face I always did whenever I heard or said the phrase *daddy-daughter day*.

"I'm sorry to hear that," Zinnia said. "That must have been very hard for you."

I rolled my eyes, the way I do when someone uses those therapist-approved empathy-handbook phrases on me. *That must have been very hard for you.* Ugh. I wanted to be heard, not managed.

"Don't roll your eyes at me."

"I was looking at the ceiling. A person can still look at the ceiling, right?"

In a patronizing tone, Zinnia said, "You're smart enough to make the best out of whatever life throws at you, Zara."

I opened my mouth to say something cranky but stopped myself. She was sounding an awful lot like how I'd sounded back in Zoey's bedroom. And I was sounding a lot like a petulant teenager.

"Sorry for acting like such a ding-dong," I said, bowing my head. "Rhys brings out the worst in me, but you bring out the best in me, which is why I both need you and appreciate you."

"Apology accepted. What do you need?" She reached for her purse.

I eyed her purse, which I knew regularly contained enough narcotics to knock out a full-grown man.

"That depends. What are you offering?" I licked my lips. "Do you have anything that will knock me out until the family reunion is over?"

She made a tsk-tsk sound and pulled out her phone. She didn't usually check messages in front of me, which meant she was excited or worried about something. I remembered her mentioning the associate who was late for their meeting that morning.

"How's your friend?" I asked. "You were worried about the lady who grows the eleven secret herbs and spices. Any news?"

Zinnia frowned at the phone and then returned it to her purse.

"Well, she's not dead," she said.

"Is that what you tell people when they ask about me?"

She fought a smile, but the smile won. "Sometimes." She waved her hand between us. "Don't worry about Tansy. She's always getting herself into trouble. I have a feeling she's up to something dangerous yet again."

"Sounds like someone I'd like to meet."

"Soon," she said. "Back to the issue of Rhys Quarry. While he's at your house, see if you can't do a little digging for information."

"About shifters?"

She made a face like she'd eaten something bitter. "No. I mean figure out where your mother's money went after she passed. I'm not interested for myself, of course, but I did find it unfair that you and Zoey didn't get anything substantial."

"Mom died broke. She spent her last penny on those experimental treatments that didn't pan out."

Zinnia raised one eyebrow. "You would do well to treat everyone with the same suspicion with which you treat me."

A smiling man with a shaved head approached our small table. "And what are you two whispering about over here?"

Zinnia and I both popped the bubble spell at the same time.

"We're talking about you, August," I said. "Why won't you take your lovely wife dancing? Are you too embarrassed to be seen with May and her little-boy haircut?"

August, who was far too nice to deserve such harassment from me, wrung his hands together nervously.

"No, no," he said. "It's the opposite. With her hair cut that way, May looks ten years younger. Me, I have two left feet and no rhythm. If I take her out dancing, someone's going to steal her away from me."

I looked across the table at Zinnia and raised my eyebrows. "Should I do my best to convince this man to take his wife out dancing?" *Using magic,* I implied with a knowing look.

She pressed her fingers to her chin then nodded, giving me the go-ahead to use magic.

I silently cast one of the "bread and butter" witch spells I'd learned—the one for bluffing. I'd learned a number of new spells in the last few weeks, but Zinnia's prediction about the Pareto Principle held true. Eighty percent of the time, you only had use for the same basic spells.

Once the spell sparkled to show it was active, it only took me a minute to convince August he should take his wife dancing.

After he walked away, Zinnia complimented me on my speed and accuracy.

"Not bad for a novice," I said with a shrug.

"You're no longer a novice," she said. "I'm happy to see you gaining more control over all of that raw power."

A moment later, we heard May shrieking. We both turned to see her throwing her arms around her husband's shoulders.

"August was an easy one," I said. "Deep down, he wanted to go."

I watched the happy couple together. When I returned my attention to Zinnia, she was staring blankly past me. I turned to follow her gaze. There was only a wall and some simple posters of Thailand.

"Hello?" I waved my hand in front of Zinnia's face.

Nothing.

The color drained out of her lips, making them as white as her face. The effect was startling.

I reached across the table and grasped both of her shoulders, shaking her gently. "Aunt Zinnia?"

Her white lips parted, and she said with a croak, "The bones. Spit out the bones." The voice was not her own.

I shook her harder. "What?"

Her lips gradually turned pink again, and she tilted her head as she looked at me curiously. I released her shoulders and leaned back in my chair. I glanced around the half-full restaurant. Nobody was staring—not openly, anyway.

I recast the sound bubble spell and described to her what had just happened.

"It's probably nothing," she said. "I get these snippets sometimes. When you cast a spell, it opens a crack, and other things leak through."

"Things from *the other side*?"

She waved her hand. "More like the crackle you get on your car radio when there's another signal nearby."

"Do you think it came from May?" I relayed my suspicion that the restaurant owner might have been the one who paid the veterinary bill.

Zinnia explained that she'd known May and August for a few years, and she doubted they had anything to do with magic.

"It was merely a blip," she said. "They increase in strength as you get older, and during certain phases of the moon."

"Like PMS," I said.

She shook her head. "Oh, Zara. You have *such* a way of putting things."

"What does 'spit out the bones' mean?"

"Zara, if I knew, I would tell you." She blinked her hazel eyes twice. "Honestly."

CHAPTER 7

"Is this all the food you got?"

My father raised one rusty red eyebrow and gave me a rubbery smirk. I was reminded of the German compound word *backpfeifengesicht*, translated as *a face in need of a fist*.

I shook my head and continued setting the table with our best dishes; the plates were different sizes, but all were the same shade of white.

"We can always order more," I said in a high, stretched-thin voice. "Let's see how we do with all of this first."

"My eyes may be a touch bigger than my stomach," he joked.

"I'm starving," Zoey said. "I could eat all of this myself. I wonder what you'll eat, Pawpaw?"

He held his hands up in a paw-like gesture. "Juicy field mice." He licked his lips with an irritating smacking sound. "Have you ever eaten juicy field mice? They're delicious." He lowered his voice to nearly a whisper. "But there's just one problem with juicy field mice. And do you know what that is, Zozo?"

Zoey leaned toward him on her chair, hanging on his every word. "No. What?"

In a high-pitched voice he declared, "They wriggle around in your tummy!" He lunged forward with his paw-like hands and tickled my sixteen-year-old's sides playfully.

Zoey squealed as though she was five.

I rolled my eyes for the benefit of no one. They were both too busy with the tickling and laughing to notice if I'd suddenly caught on fire.

I opened the foil takeout containers and began piling food onto my plate, banging the serving spoon loudly.

Rhys and Zoey eventually got control over themselves and started piling up food as well.

I noted that neither of them thanked me for getting the food. And then I noted that I didn't want to be the sort of person who notes all the times they aren't thanked, much less comments on it. Nobody signs up for parenthood expecting to get thanked. I sighed inwardly, like a good martyr, and started eating.

Zoey kept gazing over at her grandfather with childlike wonder.

"Pawpaw, will you turn into a fox for us after dinner?"

Rhys paused with his food-laden fork midair and looked at me as though requesting permission.

"Suit yourself," I said with a casual air. "You can turn into a rutabaga for all I care."

He sniffed. "Isn't that a vegetable?"

"It's a Swedish turnip," Zoey said.

He gave me a hurt look. "I won't be turning into a fox or a rutabaga or anything else for a while," he said. "Not until this nasty cut on my side has healed."

I wagged my finger at him. "No licking, or you get the Cone of Shame around your neck."

"Will you put it on me using witchcraft?"

I stabbed my fork into my food. "Witchcraft? Honestly, Rhys. You have quite the imagination."

He turned to Zoey. "Your mother's witch powers are very strong. She forced me to shift my form. I couldn't have done it on my own. Not while grievously injured." He glanced over at me, something akin to respect in his gold-green eyes. "Your mother is very powerful, indeed. She's grown into quite the witch."

I only twitched my mouth from side to side while I chewed my fried noodles. I wasn't going to give him the satisfaction of admitting to being a witch.

He wasn't letting up easily, though. He asked me, "Are you enjoying your powers?" He watched me intently, his gold-green eyes still foxlike in my mind. "Don't be shy. Do a spell for your old man. Make him proud."

"I don't know what you're talking about," I said in what sounded like my aunt's snippy tone.

"My darling daughter, I have excellent hearing, especially in fox form. I heard you utter the Witch Tongue."

I narrowed my eyes at him. Humans weren't supposed to hear our spells, but I didn't know the rules for shifters. He might have heard my spell, but it seemed more likely he was bluffing.

Zoey asked him, "Was Grandma Zirconia also a witch?"

I levitated her fork out of sight of my father and poked her on the side of the forearm. She swatted the fork away and continued ignoring me.

Rhys looked directly at me, his bushy rust-colored eyebrows raised comically high. "Should I answer? I don't want to share anything you wouldn't want your impressionable young daughter to know." His eyes twinkled.

He was enjoying this, enjoying my discomfort. And he knew I was dying to know more about my mother's abilities. He *had* to know.

"Go ahead," I said casually. "Was my mother a witch? Aunt Zinnia says she wasn't."

His mouth made an O shape, and he let out a Santa-like ho-ho-ho chuckle. "That sounds like Zinnia, all right." He raised his chin and sniffed the air. "How was your meeting with your aunt tonight?" He sniffed again, deeper. "I'm surprised she hugged you. I never pegged her as the hugging type."

"Wow," Zoey said, her hazel eyes wide with amazement. "You know about them meeting and hugging just from smelling her?"

He tapped the side of his nose. "A fox *knows* all with his fox *nose*." He winked. "A little play on words."

I didn't want to take the bait, but I had to know. "So, my mother was a witch?"

"For a while," Rhys said. "But she didn't practice." He looked down at the table, and his expression softened. "She didn't want to be a witch, and when she had the opportunity to get rid of her powers, she took it."

I turned away and let this revelation settle. What he was saying felt true enough. My mother had been such a restrained person. She sought the approval of her clique of friends by trying to out-perfect them. If her best friend, Sandra, got new wallpaper in her powder room, my mother would get new fixtures plus new lighting and wallpaper in hers.

Witchcraft wouldn't have appealed to my mother at all. Magic is messy and wild and secret. Of course my mother would have rejected magic, just like she rejected me and all of my mess.

"There's the look," Rhys said softly, staring at me intensely. "Zara, I see it all over your face."

I frowned and leaned back in my chair.

He was smiling, but it was a genuine smile born of happiness, not his rubbery salesman grin.

"You're such a bluffer," I said sullenly. "You don't see anything."

"I saw it shift across your face, Zara. Now you understand your mother much better than you ever did when she was..."

"Alive," I finished. "But it's a bit late now for understanding, don't you think?"

"Oh, it's never too late to—"

"Don't," I said, interrupting him. "Don't waste your breath. I'm a full-grown woman, and I know who I am. I know what matters." I pushed my chair back and stood. "I guess I'm not that hungry after all."

I left the dining room, left them to their reunion.

Zoey called out after me. Her voice was drowned out by the sound of the doorbell ringing.

"Doorbell," I yelled as a reflex.

My daughter's chair scraped as she got up to answer the door. Answering the doorbell was one of her official house duties, and we usually had fun with it, but not tonight.

"I got this one," I called back. "You stay back there with Pawpaw and finish at least half of that food."

I ran to the door and swung it open, happy for a distraction.

Chet Moore stood in the doorway with a brown-paper-wrapped package the size of a fiction hardcover in his hands.

"Hi there," I chirped, happy to see someone I wasn't related to. "Rough day?" I looked over the dark shadow on his chin. "I swear your stubble has become a full beard since I saw you this afternoon."

"Could be better," he said, his voice as croaky as it had been earlier. "I'm here to see about your stray animal. Just me. Corvin's out with Grampa Don, and Chessa's busy tonight." He peered around me. "You have company?"

"That's the fox," I said. "He's my father, as it turns out. Mystery solved."

Chet rubbed the dark stubble on his chin and twitched with discomfort.

"Your father is a shifter," he said.

"A red fox. Yes."

Chet's shoulders rose up with tension. He could pour on the charm when he wanted, but his default state was to look like he didn't understand how he'd gotten to wherever he currently was. His eyes often flicked around as though his top concern in any situation was identifying the exits. And I loved him for it. Or at least Chessa did, and so the part of me caked with her spiritual residue loved him for it, even though I was trying very hard not to love him.

"Then I'll leave you to your reunion." He turned to walk away, the package still in his hands.

I had the urge to reach out and grab onto his arm like a drowning person to a life raft, but I steadied myself. Flirting with Chessa's fiancé was bad. Grabbing him was worse.

"Unless..." He stopped walking. With his free hand, he rubbed his throat as he turned to look back at me. "Would you be interested in going for a drive to get some ice cream?"

Ice cream? It wasn't as bad as flirting or grabbing, but it wasn't great.

I tried to say no, but my tongue slipped, and it came out as, "Sure!"

CHAPTER 8

WISTERIA HAS MORE than its fair share of places to get ice cream, but Chet wanted to go for a drive up the coast to the next town.

I climbed into the passenger seat of his civilian vehicle and quipped, "Chet Moore, going out for food the next town over is something married men do with their mistresses."

He looked even more uncomfortable. "How would you know?" His voice cracked twice.

"I read a lot of books."

He coughed into his fist. "Westwyrd is barely a different town from Wisteria," he said. "I swear it's worth the drive. There's this little seaside place, and it looks like a tourist trap, but they have the best ice cream you've ever tasted." He looked out his side window at our houses. "But we could go somewhere closer if your family will miss you if you're gone too long."

"Odds are they won't notice." I fastened my seat belt. I was thankful to be in Chet's civilian vehicle, with no rumbling monster behind us. I still peeked over my shoulder to check, just in case. "Let's hit the road and keep going," I said.

Chet started driving.

I kept looking at the brown-paper-wrapped book on his lap.

He saw me looking and handed me the package.

"Go ahead and rip your way in," he said. "Don't pretend to be polite and restrained on my account." He shot me a knowing look. "I know better."

I snorted and immediately ripped off the paper.

It was, as I'd expected, the DWM book of magical creatures that I'd been promised. Or was it? The codex was titled *Second Year Intermediate Economics*. But that was just the cover wrapper, surely. How clever to disguise a magical tome as a second-year college textbook. I opened it. There was no crack of the spine. This wasn't a new copy. I could live with that, but the contents were disappointing. The inside matched the cover. Chet had given me an economics textbook. Or had he?

"There must be some trick to this," I said. "A special light bulb? A decoder ring? Don't tell me I need a bookwyrm. My last one died a hero before I could even give him a name."

Chet glanced over. His green eyes were growing livelier by the minute.

"Try holding it the other way around," he said with just a trace of gravel to his voice.

I rotated the open book and turned it away from myself. "Like this?"

He guffawed. "With the pages facing you but upside down."

"That's not what you said," I teased.

We shared a laugh, and the tension caused by my fear of his fiancée lifted. My upper body softened. I wasn't holding in my breath anymore. Why, oh why, couldn't I enjoy Chet's company like this every day? I would love having him all to myself. Why had I worked so hard to pull his fiancée back from the brink of death? Just because I was a good person? Bah.

I looked at the book again, following his instructions. The text shifted, blurring, and then revealed something new. The real text. Excitement fluttered in my chest. *Secrets revealed are trouble unsealed.* Sure, but how bad can it be when it's the book of secrets you've been waiting for?

For the rest of the drive to Westwyrd, I did the simple yet magical thing that had always come naturally to me; I lost myself in the book.

Chet had to poke me on the arm to get my attention. "We're here." He gestured to the seaside patio next to where we'd parked. "You can bring the book in with you, but people might notice something strange about the beautiful woman reading an economics textbook upside down."

I replied, "Good point. I'll leave the book behind." My cheeks felt hot. He'd referred to me as a beautiful woman. *Smarten up, Zara. This is the same man who did nothing but lie and manipulate your entire family until you turned the tables with a spell. Don't fall for his charms or his green eyes or his lips. Those lips sure can lie.*

We stepped out of the vehicle and stopped to take in the view. A long, sandy, gently scalloped beach lay before us. The wooden boardwalk was dotted with just the right amount of people, walking and riding bikes. The ocean beyond was flat and smooth, like a blue satin sheet. Above us, the sky was turning purple, with the promise of a spectacular crimson sunset.

Chet was suddenly beside me, his elbow touching mine.

"I already knew about your father," he said.

I whipped my head around just as an ocean breeze caught my hair and tossed it around like dark-red fire.

"You did?" *Of course you did, you liar!* I growled, "Mr. Moore, is there anything in my life you aren't meddling with?"

He took a step back, hands up in surrender. "Easy now. I only found out today. Corvin was in his bedroom, and he heard the loud construction noises next door. He was worried about Zoey. He was watching when he saw you and the fox show up. He saw the fox turn into Zoey's grandfather. He told me everything." Chet still had his hands up in surrender as he added, "Don't bite my head off."

I said nothing.

Chet relaxed his hands and rubbed his neck. "I nearly had my head bitten off once already today, and that's more than enough."

"You can't blame me for jumping to conclusions," I said. "Given our history."

He nodded toward the brown wood-sided building connected to a patio five times its size. "Let's put a bookmark in our history file for now. Come on. I'll buy you some ice cream."

I nodded, dialed down my paranoia, and walked into the building.

The Northern Stargazer Cafe offered the usual food you'd expect to find at a beachside hut—corn dogs, french fries, chicken strips, and a variety of national-brand frozen dairy treats. But the real spectacle was a cooler full of extravagant-looking ice cream in two dozen flavors, all made fresh on site. I ordered a double scoop of cherries jubilee. Chet ordered the most expensive thing on the menu, a legendary sundae called the Kraken, because it was big enough to sink a ship.

We found a seat on the open-air patio. Waves lapped on the nearby rocks. The sun felt warm, and the ocean breeze felt cool. It was, I noted, perfect. Or it would be, if I weren't there with a man who belonged to a scary sea goddess.

I picked up a cocktails menu from our table and perused it to distract myself. The back of the menu had an unsettling photo of the Northern Stargazer, which was an actual creature that the cafe was named after. The fish, with the unappetizing name of *Astroscopus guttatus*, had bulging eyes and a toothy smile that resembled a broken zipper. According to the write-up, the Northern Stargazer buries itself in the ocean floor, waits for something tasty to float by, and then uses jolts of electricity to jolt the prey before unzipping its hideous maw and gobbling the small fish or crustacean whole.

As disgusted as I was by the creature's unphotogenic face, I felt some bit of connection. I could also zap creatures with my electricity. I rarely gobbled crustaceans whole, though.

Chet leaned forward. "Whatcha looking at?"

I snorted, and a childhood taunt came out of my mouth. "Your girlfriend." I turned the menu card so he could see the bug-eyed creature.

As he looked at the sea monster, I studied his face, seeing it clearly in a way I never could when his green eyes were fixed on mine. His face looked extra wolfish tonight with the dark stubble along his jaw. His hint of a beard glinted red in the evening's sun. If he grew a beard, it would certainly be redder than his dark mahogany hair. His long face, prominent cheekbones, and hollowed-out cheeks could make him appear fierce at times, but he was as close to relaxed now as I'd ever seen him. The two and a half wrinkles on his forehead were barely visible.

"Yes," he said of the Northern Stargazer. "I do see the resemblance."

"It was just a dumb joke. I didn't mean Chessa."

He raised one dark eyebrow. "You didn't?"

I looked around for a change of subject and clapped my hands. "Ice cream time!"

The waitress set the Kraken Sundae between us with two spoons and then handed me the double-scoop cone I'd ordered. Did she really think I was going to eat my ice cream and then Chet's? I definitely would, if given the opportunity. But how could she have known? Had word of the Riddle Girls' amazing powers of ingestion traveled this far up the coast already?

Chet pulled his dish close and began eating.

I watched with fascination as he dug into the Kraken Sundae, which was a mass of ice cream on a bed of brownies, angel food cake, and sliced bananas, topped with salty peanuts and chocolate-covered pretzels.

With his permission, I cast the sound bubble spell so we could talk freely. He politely prompted me for more information about my father. I filled in the blanks as best I could.

"What does this make me?" I asked when I'd finished telling him about my day. "Am I a witch or a shifter?" I licked the sweet ice cream from my lips and added, "A shifter like you?"

He cast his green eyes up and down me while he rubbed his scruffy chin. "Have you ever turned into a furry creature with four paws and a big, bushy tail?"

"No."

"Then you're a witch. It's usually the dominant gene, so to speak." He rotated the Kraken Sundae to attack it from a fresh angle. The monstrosity was speckled with shelled pistachios and gummy bears on the side I hadn't seen yet.

"Someone should have informed me," I said bitterly.

"Zara, go easy on the guy. It's hard being a shifter. And it's hard being a dad."

I nodded and said icily, "Good to know whose side you're on."

Chet abruptly jumped up and went to help a woman with a walker get her chattering teacup and saucer over to her table. She thanked him, and he chatted with her amiably. She was a tourist who wanted to know if it was true that the area was full of strange creatures.

"No, ma'am," he answered. "I understand that Agents Mulder and Scully from *The X-Files* did a thorough sweep of this region, and you'll be quite safe."

She laughed, got him to take a picture of her in front of the sunset, and then finally sent him back over to our table. She gave me a sly smile and a wink, as if to say I was a lucky lady.

I winked right back. It felt good to have my situation envied, even if the admirer had it all wrong.

Chet returned to his seat, dug into his melting sundae with renewed vigor, and asked, "How long is your father sticking around for?"

"I don't know." I'd been licking my ice cream slowly to make it last. Why must unpleasant things always take so long while good ice cream is practically over before it starts?

With a casually upbeat tone, I asked, "What's new over at the Moore house?"

"Not much. My house hasn't shuffled out any new rooms, unlike your place."

"I meant, how are things with Chessa? Is she recovering from... *the incident*?"

A darkness overcast his eyes, turning them black. "You mean *the incident* in which she was held captive and unconscious for a year, having her eggs harvested against her will, as though she was no more than a factory chicken?"

Yeah, that incident.

"We don't have to talk about it," I said. "I wouldn't have asked, except I feel a connection with her. Does she ever talk about her connection to me? I've always wondered if it goes both ways."

"She hasn't said."

He kept his eyes on the sundae and ate in silence.

I started biting into my cherries jubilee cone. I'd changed my mind about wanting this moment to last.

He said, "You should have your house talk to my house about this room-shifter stuff. I'd like to get my attic turned into an at-home office. And free sounds like the right price."

I smiled. "I'll see what I can do."

"Any new ghosts?"

"Sadly, no," I said, frowning as I pondered my true feelings as evidenced by my unfiltered response. *Sadly, no?* I'd sounded disappointed.

"I'm sure another one will be along soon enough."

"Chet, is it weird that I feel like I'm missing out? I've only had one genuine ghost so far. The others were people who weren't quite dead. I was hoping to get a brand-new one and really do things right, from the start."

"Like having a second kid."

I laughed. "Let's not get crazy."

"How would you do things differently with a new ghost?"

"I'd try to get more help. I'm told that in their spirit form, they're just a recording of themselves, basically running their highlight reels, but I don't believe it. There's an intelligence present. Perry Pressman helped me renegotiate my mortgage and get thousands of dollars back."

"You want to monetize your abilities?" He scratched his scruffy chin and furrowed his brow.

"Nothing like that."

"Why else would you want help from ghosts?"

"I meant help doing whatever it is they're sticking around for. Help getting them closure."

"Zara, if you're lonely, there are plenty of living people around. Don't try too hard to get close to ghosts. They'll drag you out of life with them."

I raised my eyebrows. Was he thinking about my situation or something that was bothering him?

"If there's a murder that needs solving, getting the victim to communicate directly could be helpful."

He shrugged. "Some things take time. Don't rush a process that needs time."

"Never mind," I said. "You wouldn't understand anyway, wolf boy."

"Fair enough. You're probably right." He stared out in the direction of the water.

You're probably right. What a craptacular way to kill a conversation. It was the most passive aggressive way to say, *You're wrong,* while still appearing to be reasonable. It was totally a Chet thing to say, too. I could feel it in Chessa's residual memories, feel her irritation at him blending with my own.

A moment passed. My annoyance at Chet also passed. It had been a long day, and this moment by the sea was too beautiful to waste on grudges.

He shifted in his seat and said, "In answer to your question about missing out, my answer is no. It's not weird how you feel. Once you come into contact with such power, it's hard to care about the things you used to. Everything changes in the blink of an eye once you discover your life's purpose."

"My *life's purpose*," I repeated. "For the last sixteen years, I've been so focused on surviving from day to day that I haven't given my life's purpose a lot of thought."

"Well, here we are." He lifted his stubbly chin to point to the sunset hues painting the ocean-side scenery like a watercolor landscape. "A sunset for your deep thoughts."

He got a wistful look as he stared out over the ocean. The bright light gave his skin an orange hue.

This is new, I thought, watching Chet instead of the pink clouds in the sky. *Entirely new.*

I searched my memory—including Chessa's emotional residue—for a memory of this place, and of Chet at this place. I found nothing.

"You never brought Chessa here," I said.

"It's out of the way." He finished his last spoonful of sundae and looked up, locking his eyes on mine. "How did you know that?"

"Lucky guess," I said, turning to watch the sun's rays paint the water red.

CHAPTER 9

AFTER CHET AND I finished eating our ice cream and enjoying the sunset, we ordered takeout in insulated pints to bring back to our respective families.

We returned home to Beacon Street in the dark.

Inside my house, I found Rhys and Zoey in the living room, playing a card game. He was teaching her poker. *Naturally.* I dropped the ice cream off with them and then sequestered myself upstairs to my bedroom—which seemed to have shrunk by a few more inches—to read my book.

I started with a topic I'd experienced firsthand: bookwyrms.

The book confirmed what I'd already learned the hard way about bookwyrms. They love causing mischief. The book had several anecdotes about bookwyrms convincing people to kiss them, which usually resulted in face blackening, paralysis, bladder dysfunction, and memory loss. I'd been fortunate, thanks to my witch strength, to only have my mouth turned black. My coworker Frank had been less fortunate.

Bookwyrms, the editor of the book suggested, might be responsible for some fairy tales, such as the ones in which princesses are convinced to kiss toads and other icky things in search of their prince.

Bookwyrms are creatures who fall somewhere between plant and animal, in a bizarre zone only made possible by magic. You can dry and powder the bookwyrms into dust then add other powders and liquids to form a non-sentient dough that can be used for a variety of purposes. One compound is excellent for removing dried candle wax from textiles and carpets. Another compound restores warts. (Why anyone would want to *restore* a missing wart is a mystery to me.) However, if a supernatural creature or "dirty witch" lavishes too much praise or affection on a bookwyrm, it can "spoil" and become sentient, which then leads to mischief.

The description of dirty witch made me pause. I wondered if it was a typo. My bookwyrm had become sentient, so did that mean I was dirty in some way?

Zinnia had warned me to be careful with the bookwyrm dough, but she hadn't given me specifics. The ball of pale-green dough had seemed so innocuous. Had she not known the dangers, or had she intentionally skipped over them? She might have assumed hearing about possible sentience would have made me even more curious. And she would not have been wrong. I mean, really. Who doesn't love a mischievous pet? Well-behaved creatures aren't nearly as interesting as naughty ones. The same could be said of humans.

After reading more than I'd ever wanted to know about bookwyrms, it was already two o'clock in the morning. I was getting sleepy, but I'd flipped forward to the section on mammal shifters.

To my surprise, the book contained several sections on shifter etiquette. I thumbed through pages listing all the many taboo subjects you must never broach with your Friendly Neighborhood Shifter. For example, if a shifter is a rideable animal, such as a horse, you must never presume that you can ride him or her. And you must not request a shift for entertainment value. The list of What Not To Do was exhaustive. And by my rough count, I'd already broken at least ten of the rules, five of them within hours of discovering Chet was a wolf shifter. I had a chuckle to myself over my blunders. According to the book, the only safe question to ever ask a shifter is, "Would you like some food or drink now?"

On the other hand, the rules for conversing with shifters weren't vastly different from proper manners. You'd never ask a person to perform a trick, give you a shoulder ride, or explain their mating rituals. Not unless you were very good friends.

One paragraph specific to red fox shifters was particularly interesting:

Red fox shifters, unlike most sensible mammal shifters, do not find witchcraft repugnant. They are morbidly fascinated by redheaded witches in particular. Some academics theorize that the bushier-haired ones remind them of their red-furred mothers and fond memories of the family huddled together inside fox dens. When the distasteful subject of witch-shifter liaisons arise, one must keep one's pity and curiosity under control. Resist the urge to discuss or even condemn the idea of carnal witch-shifter relations, no matter how revolting.

In spite of my gratitude for the treasure trove of information before me, I found myself despising the person or people who'd put together the book. Who did these people think they were? I checked the front matter. The page glamour kicked in as it did when I turned more than one page, and I was staring at the upside-down listing of the editors of *Second Year Intermediate Economics*. I relaxed my vision, and the page went blank. No information.

And then I realized, through my sleepy haze, that the back was the front in my upside-down version. I flipped to the other end of the book and relaxed my vision at the appendix.

My view blurred and refocused, and then a single line appeared: Edited by Jorg Ebola.

Jorg. There was no dieresis (double dots) over the letter O. I tried sounding the name in my head. Some people named Jorg pronounced it the same as George, but I had a feeling this particular Jorg had a specific German pronunciation in mind and would correct you if you got it wrong. Jorg was probably pronounced *yerg* or *yerk*. Yerk seemed right for someone whose prejudice against witches kept coming up in the text.

I wondered, was Jorg Ebola prejudiced against all witches, or just the particular ones he deemed dirty and revolting? Whoever this editor was, I hoped he was still alive. I wanted to meet up with him some day, wearing my pointiest, witchiest boots, so I could kick him in the shins.

I tried to cross-reference the fox shifter information with witches, but the book had no dedicated section on witchcraft. Were we not considered magical creatures? I was offended about being left out, but perhaps it was for the best. Who knew what hateful things Jorg Ebola had to say in a dedicated section about witches? He probably had another entire volume about us dirty women and our wicked ways.

Eventually, my outrage subsided and sleepiness took over. The text kept blurring into upside-down economics lessons. I continued trying to read. My eyes continued moving while my brain fell asleep somewhere in the midst of a section on chimeras. I fell asleep.

With the book as my hard pillow, I had strange dreams, including one about Steve, the chimera lawyer at the DWM who had the body of a lion and the head of an iguana. In my dream, he was eating all the chairs in my house and then threatening to sue me for "wrongful indigestion."

CHAPTER 10

THURSDAY

I'LL SAY ONE thing about my new DWM Monster Manual: it's not much of a pillow.

Even a hot shower didn't iron out the book-shaped sleep wrinkles on my face.

I left the bathroom wearing a towel and stood at the top of the stairs, listening to Rhys and Zoey downstairs in the kitchen. How unusual to wake up to the sounds of two other people inside my home. And yet it also felt natural. How a family *should* be. A family with an active male role model, as opposed to the half-family I'd provided for my daughter. Had I already hopelessly screwed her up?

I used magic to tighten the top of my towel-wrap dress while I pushed away my guilt with positive thoughts. *Listen to how polite she is. Zoey is turning out great. That's the proof you're doing things right. There's more than one way to make a family.*

Laughter floated up the stairs. Pawpaw and his Zozo couldn't have been getting along better if I'd cast a bluffing spell on them both and declared them best friends. So why was I being such a sourpuss? Why couldn't I be positive about this reunion? Part of me wanted to play the role of a harried yet blissful mom on a sitcom, smiling through the morning gauntlet, pouring orange juice while nagging about the time. And my father's visit would go smoother if I could be pleasant toward him. Could I cast a bluffing spell on myself? Could I force myself to be happy?

Downstairs, Zoey kept laughing. "Make a bunny rabbit," she said breathlessly.

"We could start off with a simple rabbit," my father replied. "But for the next one, give me something tough, something more worthy of the astounding skills of a Master Pancake Maker."

"How about a fox jumping over the moon?"

More like a fox selling the moon to the highest bidder. Or a fox shirking any family responsibilities until it's suddenly interesting or convenient or he needs his side stitched up.

Rhys exclaimed, "Now you're talking!" There was the clanging of a spoon in a bowl, and then the sizzle of the batter hitting a hot frying pan. Vanilla scent wafted up the stairs. My mouth watered.

I returned to my small bedroom to get dressed. As was my daily routine, I cast a modified book-search spell to have my closet pick out the perfect outfit.

This time, however, my clothes only swayed. The perfect outfit didn't magically fly out. My spell fizzled out.

I tried the spell again, but again it only fizzled.

When my room had been squeezed, the closet had taken a big hit. My tightly packed clothes could no longer sort themselves at my command. The hangers on the rod could only squeak like frightened field mice.

Using my hands the old-fashioned way, I pried out a striped blouse that had once been part of a clown ensemble —theater costume sales were one of my guilty pleasures— and paired it with a conservative navy pencil skirt.

As I got dressed and combed my hair, I gazed longingly at the new book on my bedside table. I wished I'd been able to read more the night before.

I finished buttoning my striped clown shirt and looked around for a better, more hidden location for my book. Once Zoey left for school and I left for work, my father would be alone in the house, and I didn't want it to fall into his hands. My closet was packed tight, so I tucked the book into the bedside table's drawer, along with the nice note that Chet's coworker Charlize had slipped in for me.

The note read:

Dearest sister Zara,

Don't fall asleep with your face in this book! It's so boring. I'll show you some real action.

Let's hang out again soon.

Your friend,

Charlize

Her words had turned out to be a prescient warning. I smiled over that and how sweet she'd been to refer to me as her "dearest sister Zara." I hoped her *real* sisters, Chloe and Chessa, wouldn't be jealous.

I closed the drawer. I changed from my navy pencil skirt to the dark-green one. Finally, with nothing else to delay me, I went downstairs for pancakes.

As I entered the kitchen, Rhys yelled out, "Catch!" He lobbed a bottle of syrup at Zoey, who caught it easily.

He turned toward me, grinning like a, well, fox. "Good morning, sleepyhead. Did you fall asleep with your face in a book?"

I rubbed the deep vertical wrinkles on my cheek and grunted one word. "Coffee."

My daughter was already on the job, serving up a mug for me.

I surveyed the mess in the kitchen. There wasn't a square inch of counter that didn't have a dusting of flour or glop of batter. The floor wasn't any better.

Rhys held up the frying pan to show me a star-shaped pancake. "Zara, does this remind you of anything?"

It did. Years ago, during one of our annual daddy-daughter days, my father arranged for us to get a tour of the back of a fancy hotel's kitchen. He was buddies with the chef, who was a celebrity figure. This was back in the day before reality TV, when there were only a handful of celebrity chefs.

The chef had treated me like a princess. He promised to whip up anything I could imagine. Since I'd taken an interest in astronomy that month, I asked him to make me "edible stars." He happily served up star-shaped pancakes along with sliced star fruit, followed by star-shaped ice cream sandwiches made from fresh chocolate cookies and banana ice cream.

I relayed the story to Zoey then asked my father, "How did you know so many influential people?"

"You adored those ice cream sandwiches," he said, dodging my question. "It might have been the last time I saw you smile."

I immediately frowned. "Wasn't that celebrity chef caught up in a big scandal a year later? He wasn't exactly a good role model for a child."

"Admit you had fun," Rhys said. "You had a great time on daddy-daughter days."

I muttered something unrepeatable under my breath.

"Mom!" Zoey put my coffee mug into my hand. "Drink your coffee, and don't be mean to Pawpaw. He's sorry that he wasn't around much, but that's all in the past now."

I shook my head. "Zoey, when you get older and your timeline expands, you'll figure out the past wasn't so very long ago."

"Wise words," Rhys said in agreement.

I took a seat at the kitchen island and let the coffee get to work.

I noticed Rhys was moving awkwardly, favoring one side while he worked on the pancakes. I wondered how his injury site was healing but didn't ask. I'd given him the medication, and my house had given him a room. He had been provided with more than he deserved.

My mind floated back to the DWM Monster Manual.

When I got up for my second cup of coffee, I asked my father, "Do you think you were attracted to my mother because her red hair reminded you of happy family cuddles in a fox den?"

Without looking back at me, he said, "Someone's been reading a certain piece of literature written by that insufferable prat, Jorg Ebola."

I scowled at the rust-colored hair on the back of his head. Had he snuck into my room while I was sleeping and taken the book from under my face, read it, and then returned it to pillow position? That seemed unlikely, but then again, he was Rhys Quarry. The more time I spent in his presence, the more memories came back. I recalled him getting us backstage at events thanks to his "special handshakes," which contained wads of cash, and I also recalled us being escorted back out again by security.

One time, he'd coached me into faking a seizure, just to get us through a long line at the circus. But I couldn't tell Zoey about any of these things, because I knew how wonderful and fun they would sound to her young ears. Everyone loves a rogue, and Rhys Quarry was the original rogue.

I forged on with my line of questioning. "When you met my mother, was it love at first sight?"

Zoey chimed in. "Was it?"

"Yes." He flipped the final pancake onto a platter and brought the stack over to the kitchen island. "Zirconia Riddle loved me the instant she laid eyes upon me." He tossed a fox-shaped pancake onto my plate. "And that was before she'd seen my incredible pancakes."

The fox-shaped pancake was perfect. He added the second part, the moon the fox was jumping over. It was the most perfectly round pancake I'd ever seen.

"That's a lovely pancake," I admitted.

"Tasty, too," said Zoey.

"I should hope so. I stole the eggs from a farmer early this morning." He winked at me.

Zoey said, "No fair. You said I could watch you shift the next time you do it."

"I was only joking, Zozo." He reached over and ruffled her hair, messing it up spectacularly. If I had done the same thing to Zoey that early in the morning, I'd have gotten a finger bitten off. But Zoey just grinned.

My father sat on a stool across from me and began putting butter and syrup on his star-shaped pancake.

Zoey was already on her third pancake.

Rhys kept watching me with those twinkling green-gold fox eyes of his.

"Zara, if you do happen to have a copy of *Second Year Intermediate Economics*, I could broker a sale for you. The book is hardly worth reading, let alone keeping around collecting dust on your bookcase."

I raised my eyebrows. "If it's so worthless, who would buy it?"

He tilted his head to the side nonchalantly. "The information is pedestrian and outdated, but the volume has a certain sentimental value to collectors."

"I'll keep that in mind if I happen to come into possession of a copy."

He locked gazes with me. "Which hasn't happened yet?"

"Nope." I picked up my knife and cut the head off my pancake fox in one stroke. "Tell me about your accomplice," I said. "The one who paid the vet bill."

He blinked three times.

"Don't play me for stupid," I said. "You wouldn't have had your assistant pay the bill if you didn't want me to know about it. This conversation we're having right now is also part of your big plan, but I don't even care. I still want to know who he or she was."

He gave me a sidelong look. "What if I were to tell you I have no idea who or what you're talking about?"

"I wouldn't believe you for a minute."

He nodded slowly. "Tell me what you know."

I glanced over at Zoey, who was listening with interest. She hadn't heard this part of the story yet.

"Rhys, do you remember the talking blue jay in the forest?"

He winced. "Vaguely."

I explained to Zoey, "The blue jay knew my name. It also told me to be careful. Then it flew off."

She asked, "The blue jay was a shifter?"

"That would explain its human intelligence." I turned back to look at my father, who was frowning thoughtfully. Almost convincingly. Oh, he knew, all right.

"Interesting," he said. "Everything was a blur to me at that point. I don't remember any birds."

"Except the one who attacked you," I said.

"Right," he answered, a little too vehemently.

"How's your memory of your time inside the vet clinic?"

"Hazy," he said. "The doc gave me some good drugs."

"Did you happen to see someone come in and pay your bill?"

He blinked. "Huh?"

"When I went in to pick you up, the vet assistant told me the bill had already been paid by some benevolent stranger."

"That's nice," he said. "What a lovely town, full of nice people."

"Rhys." I tried to stare the truth out of him. "It wasn't some random nice person. It was someone who does magic. They must have cast a glamour disguise, because the assistant's description of the person, who I can only assume is some accomplice of yours, kept changing."

"How curious," he said neutrally.

Enough playing dumb. You don't get to crash into my life uninvited and lie to my face.

I cast my bluffing spell.

The air tightened up around us.

I smiled at my father and said, "You will remember. You *want to* tell me who it was."

His face relaxed, and he blinked at me. In a robotic voice, he said, "I want to tell you who it was."

"Yes," I said, artfully strengthening the bluffing spell that had worked so well the night before on the Thai restaurant's owner.

The air seemed to grow very tight around us. My spell was straining to break his will. It wasn't meant for brute force like this, just for mild suggestion. I felt something snap, and I couldn't tell if it was my father's will or the spell shorting out.

He tilted his head. Heavily, he said, "It might have been my associate, Reynard."

Zoey bounced on her barstool. "The French word for fox is *renard*. Pawpaw, is your friend a fox, too? Is he related to us?"

The heaviness lifted from Rhys's voice as he told Zoey, "Reynard is no friend. Just an associate. And the less you know about her or him, the better." He frowned at me. "I probably shouldn't have told you this much, but that bluffing spell of yours is very good."

"Spell?" I tried to feign ignorance, but it's hard to feign ignorance while gloating.

He groaned and adjusted his seat on the stool. A trickle of sweat ran down the side of his face.

"You could help your old man," he said, looking at my beheaded fox pancake and then up at me. "I could use you as backup for a meeting with my associate, Reynard. You wouldn't need to do anything out of the ordinary. Just stand there and look scary."

"No way."

His lips curled in a smirk. "Very good. I'll need you to look scary, just like you're doing right now. It's exactly the right sort of crazy eyes for this situation."

"I don't have crazy eyes."

My teen daughter snorted.

I blinked away my crazy eyes. "Whatever you've got going on, I want nothing to do with it. This town is where I live, and I've already had too much interaction with the local police this week. Remember that woman you bit yesterday? She's probably already filed a report on me."

Zoey's eyes grew as big as saucers. "Pawpaw bit someone?"

"I was in fox form," he said dismissively, as though that explained everything. "People should know better than to taunt a fox." To Zoey, he said, "It was nothing. How about you? Got big plans for the day? Big Thursday plans?"

"High school," I answered on her behalf. "And she's not playing hooky, so don't even think about roping my daughter into your schemes."

He made a pouty face.

"I'll unblock your number from my phone," I said. "If you go on your own and get arrested, I promise to bail you out." I held one hand up. "I promise."

He held one hand to his chest and pretended to blink back tears. "Unblocking my number *and* bailing me out of jail? You've made me the proudest father in the whole world."

"You're welcome."

He reached for another pancake off the stack. Casually, he said, "By the way, speaking of the police, you're currently under surveillance." He lifted his nose and sniffed. "Your man has circled around to the front sidewalk again."

CHAPTER 11

SOMEONE WAS WATCHING my house. As soon as I popped my head out the front door, he tried to hide behind a utility pole.

"Bentley, I can see your big butt," I called across the street. "If you want to be sneaky, you need to lay off the rainbow sprinkle donuts."

Detective Bentley stepped out from behind the pole and pulled his gray suit jacket closed in a self-conscious, protective motion. He looked about as happy to see me in front of my own house as he did when I beat him to Chloe's bakery and snagged the last sprinkle donut.

"My butt's not big," he said with a frown big enough for me to see across the street.

"Are you sure? Lift your suit jacket and show me the junk in your trunk."

He started to turn but then stopped.

"Don't be shy," I teased. "I bet you have a nice tush underneath that jacket. What a waste you're keeping it to yourself."

"You're a wicked woman, Zara Riddle."

I closed my door behind me and crossed the street so we could continue the conversation about Bentley's butt without the whole neighborhood hearing.

He gave me one of his steely, serious looks. "I still weigh exactly the same amount as when I finished my training at the police academy. Every morning, I do the same number of one-handed pushups."

I leaned back and looked him up and down. "I guess you're right. Everything is where it should be. In fact, you have the classic proportions of an Old Hollywood leading man. If I didn't know better, I'd say you were cloned from the cellular material of Cary Grant."

"You're saying I'm a clone of Cary Grant?"

"Do you have evidence to the contrary, Detective?"

His thick, dark eyebrows knitted together in a pensive, Cary Grant-esque expression.

"Let's go back to you insulting me," he said. "This complimentary side of you is much worse."

"Ouch." I glanced over at my house, which seemed to be a more vibrant shade of red that day.

The house had changed on the outside. It was taller by the height of one step. Crazy house.

I turned back toward Bentley's steely gray eyes.

"Detective, there must be a reason you're loitering around here on Beacon Street. Has there been a ghastly crime?"

"Maybe." He pursed his lips and looked up at the tree branches above us.

I followed his gaze to the leafy canopy. "Let me guess. You've come to rescue a kitten who's stuck up in a tree. You should have brought a ladder."

The leaves rustled, and a blue jay dove down from the branches. He landed on Bentley's shoulder and cocked his head at me. My fingers tingled with energy. The blue jay could very well be the same one I'd seen yesterday in the woods. Blue jays are known for their boldness, but landing on a person's shoulder was extremely bold.

Bentley's eyes widened. He didn't move, except for his eyes. The blue jay's perky crest rose up as though in greeting.

I asked, "Friend of yours?"

He slowly turned his head to face the bird. "Hello," he said.

"Hello," answered the bird.

Bentley slowly turned his head back to face me. "I could swear this bird just said *hello*."

"Blue jays are members of the corvid family. Like ravens, they're capable of speech, but it's just mimicry. They don't understand the words they're saying." I studied the blue jay, who seemed to be listening and understanding. In fact, the bird was listening more attentively than most humans. "Probably," I added.

Bentley jostled the bird by moving his shoulder gently. The bird dug in tighter, the tips of his claws disappearing into the wool of the police detective's dark-gray suit jacket.

"He must be someone's pet," Bentley said. He swiveled his head toward the bird again. The wrinkles on his forehead eased as curiosity replaced shock. "Hello, Mr. Blue Jay. Would you like a peanut?"

The bird bobbed his whole body up and down. "Peanut! Peanut!"

Bentley reached into his suit jacket pocket and pulled out a peanut, still in its shell. He held it out to the blue jay, who snapped the peanut up. Rather than flying off with the treasure, the blue jay stayed on Bentley's shoulder and began dismantling the peanut, expertly separating shell from nut.

The look on Bentley's face was one of wonder. I saw a glimpse of the child within him, the person he was before he became so serious, before he became Steely Bentley, the rules-enforcing striver.

As the blue jay consumed the peanut meat, Bentley murmured soft sounds of encouragement. The talk became mushier as it went on.

"Get a room," I muttered.

Bentley chuckled and handed me a peanut. "Here. You give him one."

I showed the peanut to the blue jay but didn't hand it over yet. "Do you two know each other?"

The bird squawked, "No!"

I said, "Methinks he doth protest too much."

"No," the blue jay squawked.

I lifted the peanut tentatively. The blue jay snatched it up and began ripping through the shell.

Bentley asked the bird, "Do you have a name?"

For the third time in a row, the bird squawked, "No!"

"My daughter went through that phase," I said to Bentley. "Every question got a *no*. It's called the Terrible Twos for a reason."

To the bird, I said, "I bet your name is Reynard."

The blue jay answered in a hesitant tone, "No."

"He paused," Bentley told me. "I think you're onto something."

I pointed my finger at the blue jay. "Reynard, I know all about you," I said.

The bird's blue-feathered head crest rose up aggressively. "Reynard," he squawked. "Reynard! Reynard!"

"That's right," I said. "I've got your number, Reynard."

The bird let out a squawky laugh. He shook his wings, darted his beak at a spot above Bentley's ear, and then took to the sky, still laughing.

Bentley's eyes couldn't have been wider if he'd had his eyelids propped up with sticks.

"Did he hurt you?"

Bentley rubbed his head. "He didn't draw blood. He just yanked out a strand of my hair."

"You've got more than enough to spare." Bentley's hair was thick and dark, with a widow's peak on his forehead and just a few flashes of silver at his temples.

When I first met Detective Bentley, I'd thought of him as a silver fox. Now that I knew more about the magical creatures around me in Wisteria, I wondered if my subconscious has been giving me a hint. Was Bentley supernatural? Did he do some of his best detective work in the form of a silver fox?

In fairy tales, Reynard is a fox who's also a trickster. I'd been looking at the bird when I'd tried the name, but had I been watching the wrong creature for a reaction? Was Bentley's first name Reynard?

"You're staring," Bentley said. "Is there something in my hair?"

"No. I was just thinking that your hair would make excellent nesting material."

He gave me a crooked frown as he kept rubbing his head. "Who's Reynard?"

"You tell me. You're the detective." I watched him closely. "Is it you?"

He tilted his head, glanced at my house and then at me. "Who's that man staying at your house?"

I turned to catch a glimpse of Rhys peering out the open door. He immediately stepped back and shut the door.

"Not that it's any of your business, but that's my father. He's visiting. His, um, traveling circus is getting some wagon wheels fixed so he decided to drop in on me."

"Ah." Bentley made a slow, exaggerated nod. "Your father is with the circus. You know, I always figured your family had a circus connection."

"You think?" I smiled and adjusted the collar of my clown-costume blouse.

Bentley flicked the peanut shells off his shoulder. "The circus connection explains why I saw you yesterday with that red fox wrapped around your shoulders. You scared the beans out of poor Margaret Mills. I had to talk her out of pressing charges."

Margaret Mills must have been the rhinoceros-like woman I'd saved from getting run over by a bus. She wanted to press charges against me? How ungrateful. Of course, she wouldn't have been in danger if she hadn't been fleeing my snapping, snarling, fox-shaped father.

"So, that's why you're watching my house," I said. "You're on a fox hunt. You should have brought some beagles and a horse. Plus bugles. Is that right? Beagles and bugles? That almost sounds like a tasty snack mix. *Hey, you start up the movie, and I'll open this box of Beagles and Bugles.*"

Bentley was anything but amused. "Ms. Riddle, it's against city bylaws to keep wild animals in a residence."

"I'm sure it is," I said. "Which is why it's a good thing I don't have a fox."

"There was a red, furry thing wrapped around your shoulders yesterday. Even from across the street, I know a fox when I see one." He stopped talking to take a breath. Amusement flitted across his face. He was enjoying this, enjoying grilling me. "I suppose you're going to tell me it was a red scarf, something from your always-surprising wardrobe?"

"Maybe it *was* a red scarf. Who are you going to believe, Detective? Sweet little ol' me, or your lying eyes?"

His eyes flicked over to my house and back again. "My eyes never lie."

"Go let yourself inside," I said airily. "You could search the place from top to bottom. I promise you won't find a red fox, but while you're at it, perhaps you could get to the bottom of something for me. Where do the unmatched socks disappear to? Does the dryer eat them?"

"I can't come in," he said tersely.

"Some sort of personal rules?"

He blinked twice. "I don't have a warrant."

"Detective Bentley, aren't we past the warrant stage by now? We just had a charming interaction with a talking blue jay. We're becoming friends."

He raised one dark eyebrow. "If we're friends, tell me my first name. I'll give you a hint. It's not *Detective*."

"Ben," I guessed. "Your name is Ben, as in Benjamin Bentley."

"Nice try," he said. "Not even close."

I looked up into his eyes, which were medium-set, hooded, fringed with thick, dark lashes, and perfectly symmetrical. Most people have one eye that's droopier or smaller, but Bentley's were perfect. And they were colorless. Perfectly gray.

As I stared into those colorless eyes, the edges of his face began to blur and fade away. Without boundaries, his face stretched out until it was everything, and there was no sky or trees or quaint neighborhood. Just gray.

The effect was pierced by my daughter calling out, "Mom? Oh, there you are! I thought you left for work without your purse."

Bentley's face snapped back into focus. He took a step back, bowing formally.

With a thick, gravelly voice, he said, "I should let you be on your way."

I reached out and put my hand on his forearm. The wool suit felt soft to the touch, but there was strength in the arm underneath. He wasn't joking about one-armed pushups.

"Let me introduce you to my daughter," I said.

Zoey skipped across the street toward us, the hard soles of her shoes scuffing on the pavement. She was wearing the ballerina flats that were a size too big and flopped around noisily whenever they weren't falling off and tripping her. The girl had plenty of shoes, but she chose to wear those silly loose flats for reasons that I, a grown adult woman, was not able to comprehend.

Zoey reached us and handed me my purse. "Here you go, Mom. Don't worry about walking me to school today. Pawpaw is going to give me a ride in his car."

Bentley turned to my daughter and said, "You must be a Riddle. You truly are the spitting image of your mother and aunt."

She stuck out her hand and introduced herself. "Zolanda Daizy Cazzaundra Riddle. Everyone calls me Zoey."

"You can call me Bentley."

My daughter sucked in air and let out a high, light laugh. "You're the detective? The way Mom talks about you, I expected someone way different."

He quirked an eyebrow. "Your mother talks about me?"

I elbowed Zoey. "You'd better make sure the kitchen's cleaned up before you leave for school."

Zoey took the hint and started back toward our house, stopping once to pick up her loose shoe.

Up the street, a car door slammed and then another. People were leaving for their jobs, just like any other Thursday morning. Except it wasn't that normal for me, because I wouldn't be walking my daughter to school. That made it two days in a row. She caught a ride with a schoolmate on Wednesday. We'd reached a fork in the road of our lives. My sweet, bubbly girl was headed off in another direction without me.

Bentley's deep voice startled me back to the present. "Do you always walk to work?"

"I don't have a car, and I can't fly." *Not yet, anyway.*

"I'll give you a lift. My car's just up the street."

"Thanks, but I prefer walking. Morning ambulation clears the head."

"Morning ambulation," he repeated. "Your vocabulary is as refreshing as your wardrobe." He raised his chin and looked down his nose at me. "That is quite the colorful outfit. I suppose later today we'll have a naked clown show up at the police station to report a mugging?"

"No way," I said. "The clown I got this shirt from surrendered it willingly. And he's not naked. I left him one of those wooden barrels with suspenders to wear around town."

"How thoughtful." Bentley started walking along my usual route. "Come on. I'm *ambulating* with you to the library," he called back.

"A police escort? For little ol' me?"

He gave me a steely look. "It's a new crime-reduction program."

"Can't hurt to try."

I hitched my purse strap up my shoulder and skipped to catch up with Detective Bentley.

CHAPTER 12

"THERE'S SOMETHING STRANGE going on in this town," Bentley said.

"Oh?"

"It's too perfect. Have you seen that movie, *The Truman Show*? Sometimes I think a big spotlight's going to fall from the sky and reveal that I've been part of an immersive, semi-scripted TV show this whole time."

We'd been walking for twenty minutes, making small talk about movies and the weather, and were now entering Wisteria's downtown core of shops and services. The street we'd turned onto was aesthetically pleasing to the point of being unreal, like the two-dimensional painted backdrops for an upbeat stage play set in a quaint small town.

Up ahead, a middle-aged man in a green apron emerged from a flower shop and began sweeping the sidewalk, whistling as he did. He swept rhythmically, stopping only to call out greetings to passersby—many of whom he knew by name.

"Good morning, Detective," the shopkeeper said to Bentley as we drew near. "And a good morning to you," he said to me. "Why, look at that lovely red hair! You're as luminous as these ranunculus blossoms. You must be Zinnia Riddle's niece."

"Guilty as charged," I said.

Bentley paused, looking at the display of cut ranunculus flowers and then at me, as though he was thinking of buying me a bouquet. His eyes twitched back and forth. Was I reading him like an open book, or imagining things? They say people see what they want to see. But I didn't want Bentley to buy me flowers. No. That would be weird.

After some small talk about the nice weather, he said goodbye to the shopkeeper and started walking again. I skipped to catch up, the hard soles of my boots making satisfying sounds on the cement.

"Every single one of those flowers back there was perfect," he said.

"I'm sure they throw out the imperfect ones. I bet if we go into the alley, we'll find a dumpster full of rumpled ranunculi. That's the plural of ranunculus."

He shot me a steely look. "I've seen their dumpster. It's clean and graffiti-free, just like everything in this town."

"I do understand what you mean," I said. "When Zoey and I first got here a few months ago, we joked about people being robots. Like in that show, *Westworld*."

He let out a sigh of relief. "So, it's not just my imagination."

We walked in silence. I should have dropped the subject, but I couldn't help myself.

"Detective, if there is something going on in this town, what makes you think I'm not in on it? Maybe I'll report your wild conspiracy theories to the head of the Department of Mind Erasing, and you'll be getting a visit tonight." I glanced over to give him a double eyebrow raise. "The sort of late-night visit nobody wants to get."

I was only partly joking. There very well could have been a Department of Mind Erasing in Wisteria, for all I knew—a subsidiary of the Department of Water and Magic. Vincent Wick probably ran it from his underground offices near the composting piles.

Bentley grimaced. "Funny you should mention mind erasure. That's a popular topic for the local eccentrics. They say that when the Pressman house burned down, it was actually a cover-up for some evil, mind-wiping mad scientist operation."

"Maybe it was," I said, flirting with the idea of a full confession. Why couldn't Bentley be told about the town's magical aspects? It would certainly make his job easier. In fact, it seemed cruel that he didn't already know. Wasn't the police department in on everything? One possible explanation was they were giving Bentley a trial run before letting him in on all the secrets.

Oh, but it would be so much fun for me to grab him by the arm right now and tell him everything. *Bentley, you're right about this town! It's full of magic!* What a fun job that would be. The expression on his face would be priceless when I levitated the peanuts out of his jacket. I could witness, up close and personal, a man's entire worldview shatter. His mind breaking. And then the crushing realization that everything he knew was a lie. He would be over on the other side of the revelation with me. Yet he wouldn't truly be part of it because he had no powers of his own. And then he'd be as depressed as my daughter.

On second thought, it would be a terrible job to have to tell people about magic.

Bentley slowed his pace. He reached into his pocket for a handful of peanuts, which he tossed into a planter box as we walked past.

"That's for the squirrel who lives around here," he explained. "His name is Petey. He's got a reputation for mugging people at the sidewalk seating for the cafes."

"Really? And the official Wisteria Police Department response to a known mugger, a buck-toothed buccaneer, is to pay protection money in the form of peanuts?"

"It's one of our many crime reduction programs." He dusted off his hands. "Plus the little guy's cute, like that blue jay by your house."

"Detective Bentley." I used both hands to mime framing a sign. "Friend of Woodland Creatures."

"At least Petey the Squirrel doesn't talk—not that I know of."

"And now I understand why you carry peanuts in your pocket. See, if you look hard enough, there's always a logical answer to everything. Wisteria is like that. It seems odd at first, on account of how happy people are, but maybe it's the rest of the world that's doing things wrong."

Bentley turned his head and watched me for several paces. "You're in on it," he said. "You're feeding me lines from a script."

"No," I answered, a little too quickly. Just like the blue jay.

"You're in on it," he repeated.

I rolled my eyes and answered with a sarcastic, "You got me, Detective." I pointed to a display of fresh mangoes and pears as we walked past a fresh produce store. "Don't eat those. They're all plastic, from the props department."

"All right," he said. "What are you authorized to tell me about Wakeful?"

"Wakeful?" *Wakeful.* The word resonated inside my head. It sounded like something I should know about but didn't yet. "Is that a coffee shop?"

He shook his head and looked straight ahead. He picked up his walking pace.

"Never mind," he said. "It's a shame you're not interested in getting to the bottom of things. You would have made a good partner. I always thought librarians were great at ferreting out information."

"We are," I said. "And don't give up on me that easily. What else do you know about Wakeful?"

He put his hands in his pockets. "Never mind," he repeated.

I fought the urge to shake him by the shoulders. How dare he tempt a librarian with the prospect of a juicy research project and then take it away!

Bentley cleared his throat. "You probably don't know this, but I only moved here a month before you did," he said. "I can't even remember why I applied for the position, or how, but I must have, because here I am."

A few questions came to mind, but I kept quiet and let him talk. Some men are stingy with their inner thoughts, and you have to draw the story out of them with questions. Then there are the ones who won't stop talking or explaining or bragging. I liked how Bentley fell right in the middle.

"It's almost comical how overqualified I am for this job," he said. "The majority of my calls could be handled by a rookie. I spent most of yesterday helping Old Man Wheelie negotiate with some neighborhood kids for the return of his prosthetic legs."

"Was he up drinking on his roof again?" Bentley had told me about a similar story a few weeks back.

"He was on a church roof this time. He rang the big church bell to get help." He glanced over at me. "Is it *rang* or *rung*?"

"I'm a librarian, not a grammarian." The answer bubbled up anyway. "It's *rang*. *Rung* is the past participle." I gave him a sheepish smile. "I try not to correct people's grammar, but I find language interesting, so I assume other people must feel the same way."

Out of the blue, he asked, "Why aren't you married?"

I felt the heat rise in me and the skin on my back prickle. No matter how many times people blurted the question at me, I always got a visceral, physical reaction.

I volleyed back, "Why aren't you?"

"Because I've been married," he answered evenly. "I didn't pack up and move to Wisteria just for the cupcake bakeries and sunny weather."

"Fair enough," I said. "In answer to your question, I guess the number one reason I'm not married is because nobody's asked."

He stopped walking. "Why not?"

I stopped and faced him. "I guess it's because I never gave anyone a chance to ask."

"Why not?"

"Because... I'm afraid of being let down."

"Why?"

"Because people always let you down. Always. Eventually." And by people, I meant *men*.

"Why does a smart woman like yourself believe something that's patently untrue?" He blinked in slow motion. "Look around you, Zara. Look at all the people hustling around with purpose. They're all trying so hard. Trying not to let anyone down."

I looked around. We had come to our standstill directly across the street from the library. People were walking toward the book-return drawer with bulging book bags. Kids with backpacks were hurrying toward school. All around us, everyone moved with purpose. Bentley, a striver himself, recognized the quality in others. They were all striving.

And was I one of the strivers? I worked hard at my job to serve the community and to support my family. I was letting my troublesome father stay at the house so my daughter could spend some time with a male role model. I even let ghosts hang out inside my head. Apart from a few pastries, most of my activities were in the service of others, so I didn't let anyone down.

Bentley said, "Look at me."

I did. I looked at the steely-eyed man in the gray suit who carried a pocketful of peanuts.

He asked, "Did I walk away from Wheelie before getting him his legs back? No. I didn't."

I continued looking at him. Really looking. Once again, I saw him for the striver I'd pegged him as when we'd met. Bentley was a driven man, and he valued it. He saw the quality in other people, the way I was able to spot a person's thirst for knowledge.

But he was also making a point about the lack of a wedding ring on my finger, which was none of his business.

"Good for you," I said, my tone ever-so-slightly patronizing. "I guess there's an exception to every rule."

He reached into his jacket's inside pocket and withdrew his phone. It was buzzing insistently. He didn't look at the screen.

"To be continued," he said, maintaining eye contact with me. "Let's pick up this interview again another time." His gray eyes shone silver in the bright sunshine, almost platinum.

"Interview? Am I a suspect for something?"

"You're always my number one." His phone stopped buzzing. He still didn't look at the screen. He looked over my shoulder at the library and then up the street. "I'm going to do my work on foot today, like the prototypical gumshoe detective. My gut tells me I'll see a lot more this way."

"You've got nice weather for it. Maybe you'll find some lady to rescue by making her the next Mrs. Bentley. Or should I say Mrs. White Knight."

He turned back to face me again. "And I plan to figure out this town's secrets," he said, ignoring my barb about him being a white knight.

"All of this town's secrets in just one day?"

He shrugged. "I already figured out yours, didn't I? You don't trust men, and it has everything to do with your father, who travels with the circus, trains wild birds to talk, and makes a mess in your kitchen."

I snorted. He wasn't entirely wrong.

Detective Bentley made an old-fashioned gesture like he was tipping an invisible bowler hat, turned, and walked away.

CHAPTER 13

FRIDAY

FRIDAY MORNING, I woke up in my small bedroom, in a bed that seemed smaller than the night before. My feet were hanging off the end. Either I'd grown, or my furniture had shrunk.

I sat up and listened to the sounds of my father cooking breakfast downstairs in the kitchen. The strange part was how this didn't feel strange at all. They say you can get used to anything if given enough time, but really? Two days?

The night before had felt practically routine. The three of us had shared a dinner of leftover Thai food and then gone for a walk to get ice cream from a local shop, to compare it to the takeout from the Northern Stargazer Cafe.

After the ice cream, which was deemed to be nearly equal in taste and texture, we'd strolled along the shoreline, where Rhys and Zoey had played at skipping stones for hours. When we got back to the house again, the two of them continued their poker game while I read my Monster Manual. I'd nodded off with my face in the book yet again. There was something about the way the book had to be read, in its upside-down, magically encrypted text, that made me sleepy.

Before my eyes had closed, I'd returned to the section about the Iguammit, a chimera with the head of an iguana and the body of a lion. The DWM employed one as their in-house lawyer, Steve, whom I'd only seen for a moment in the hallway—long enough to make an unforgettable impression. According to the book, Iguammits are shy and reserved until you gain their trust. When it comes to convoluted legal matters, they are ten times as sharp as human lawyers. However, they get hyperfocused on their work. They forget to eat regularly and get so peckish they consume anything at hand, including but not limited to office furniture. Their first choice is candy, preferably red, but they will consume anything from staplers to laptops. If I ever required the services of Steve—and I hoped I wouldn't—I'd be sure to have plenty of red licorice on hand.

I crawled out of my shrinking yet warm bed, sniffing for clues about breakfast. I smelled bacon, and something like onions but milder. *Shallots,* whispered the residual memory of Winona Vander Zalm. *Shallots are perfect for breakfast omelets, darling! Not too overpowering for sensitive guests.*

I hadn't heard from Winona recently, and I found her presence comforting. Her true spirit had moved on to another place, so what I held in my head was just a copy, a simulation, but I enjoyed it all the same.

In fact, I was fondly remembering Winona's lavish dinner parties when I walked right into a wall.

I rubbed my forehead. Walking into a wall was not my favorite way to wake up, but it sure did the trick. The wall now bore a faint oil mark from my face. Last night, I'd had a bedroom door where I was standing. Now I had a wall.

"Not funny," I said to my house. "Give me back my door." I poked the wall to make sure it wasn't an illusion. It was solid, and the bump on my forehead was certainly real.

I wondered aloud, "If I don't have a door, how am I able to smell bacon wafting up from downstairs?"

There was a creak, like a door opening. A breeze blew over my bare legs. The smell of breakfast got stronger, and I heard the voices downstairs more clearly.

I looked to my right and then down. The creak had been a door opening after all. The door was similar to the one I'd closed last night—same chipped paint job over square wood panels—but it was a miniature version. My new bedroom door was only four feet high.

"You've got to be kidding," I muttered, followed by some less ladylike expressions of my true feelings.

The house didn't respond, but I did get the sense she (or it) was snickering.

"I don't deserve this," I told my ceiling. "Am I being punished for something I've done wrong?" *Zara tries to be a good witch,* I thought. *She's always striving to not let everyone down!*

The door squeaked and became smaller by another inch.

"Not fair!" I cast my bluffing spell in the general vicinity of the door. "You're going to be a nice door," I said, weaving Witch Tongue words between my regular English speech. "Deep down, you're a good door, and you want to be big, and normal, and let me in and out of my bedroom with ease."

With a squeak, the door shrank another inch.

"Fine," I sighed. "You win."

I got down on my hands and knees and crawled through.

* * *

By the time I finished getting ready for work, which included no small amount of time spent cursing at my shrinking bedroom door, Zoey had already left for school. The house was quiet, so I assumed she'd gotten a ride with Rhys.

When I went downstairs, I was surprised to find my father sitting at the kitchen island with a cup of green tea that smelled like grass clippings.

I started making coffee, feeling self-conscious about being watched. I fumbled with the coffee filters. It annoyed me that I couldn't use my telekinetic powers to fluff out a single coffee filter the way I usually did. Sure, my father knew I was a witch, but there was no way I would be demonstrating any of my powers for him.

"No buffer," he said.

"What?" I whirled around, spilling coffee grounds on my socked feet.

"Zoey's gone to school," he said. "Our conversational buffer is gone. This is the first time you and I have had a moment to talk in private."

"I suppose it is." I forced a smile. "Big plans today?"

"Just admit that you liked me better as a fox."

Had I? His fur coat had been rather soft. Without knowing who it was, I'd enjoyed having a companion who curled around my shoulders and listened with big, pointed ears. Right now in my kitchen, however, I felt no desire to pat Rhys Quarry's rust-colored hair.

"You make a cute fox," I admitted.

His upper lip curled up to reveal a sharp-looking canine. "And we were having fun that day, you and I."

"Before you took a nip at Margaret Mills. She went straight to the cops and tried to press charges against me, thanks to you."

His upper lip curled all the way into a smirking grin. "Totally worth it. You saw the look on her face."

"She meant well," I said. "She was trying to raise awareness about *your kind* being trapped or farmed for the fur trade."

"My kind?" He raised a rust-colored eyebrow. "You've been hiding in your room reading that book every night, yet you still know so little about our kind." He gave me a pointed look. "That's right. I said *our* kind. You are my daughter, and that means you're one of us."

"A shifter? If I'm like you, why have I never turned into a fox?"

"Have you ever jumped out of an airplane?"

"What's that got to do with anything?"

"Maybe you'd sprout wings if you needed to. Your great-great grandfather was a crane."

I jiggled the coffee maker in a futile attempt to make it percolate faster.

"A crane," I mused. The idea of my great-great grandfather, whose name I didn't even know, elicited no sense of wonder. I'd have been much more interested in ancestors who were witches. Was I being prejudiced against shifters? Like Jorg Ebola? Probably. But in my defense, being just one thing seemed so much simpler than being a hodgepodge of magical bits and bobs.

"We could give your sleepy shifter powers a whirl," Rhys said. "Let's go up to the mountains and toss you over a cliff." He grinned. "Let's see what happens."

I snorted. "Over my dead broomstick."

"Over my dead broomstick? Mercy!" He wiped the corner of his eyes. "I haven't heard that expression in years. Where did you hear it?"

"It just came to me."

"The older generations used to say it. Not just witches, but also shifters and... others." He got a faraway look. "Wow. That brings back so many memories."

"I'm listening," I said. "You can tell me anything. Like, for example, how you and my mother met."

"That's easy. The Riddles hired me to find a suitable husband for your mother. I was working as a romantic matchmaker back in those days. She didn't like any of the candidates I brought her, which probably doesn't surprise you."

"It does not," I confirmed. My mother was perpetually unsatisfied. If being unsatisfied could generate electricity, she could have solved the world's energy problems.

"The potential mates were either too big and brash or too small and mild-mannered. Too hot or too cold. Too pompous or too common." His gold-green eyes twinkled. "Actually, most of them were deemed too common."

"Sounds like my mother, all right." I poured hot coffee into a takeout mug. "So, how did the pregnancy happen? The one that resulted in me?"

"In the usual manner," he said.

"You know that's not what I meant."

"Your mother tricked me," he said.

"Right." I scoffed.

"She had me meet her at a hotel to discuss a background check on a candidate. She opened a bottle of something. Not champagne, but something else. It was sweet, and red, and sparkling."

I gave him a sidelong look. The beverage sounded an awful lot like the Barberrian wine coolers that had led to my teen pregnancy. But those wine coolers hadn't existed before I was born. Or had they?

"Maybe it was sangria," he said. "Anyway, whatever it was, the drink was effective at removing your mother's icicles. Her chill melted right off, and I found myself in bed with a warm and vital woman. I forgot how much she despised me." He cleared his throat. "The next morning, when the sun came up, something dawned on me. I finally understood why finding a match for Zirconia Riddle would be an impossible task. The woman was unmatchable."

He looked to me for a response. I had nothing. I was still grappling with the visual he'd painted in my mind. Everyone knows what their parents must have done, but nobody wants to picture it. My father hadn't described the hotel room, but since I knew my mother's taste so well, I'd had no trouble conjuring up a detailed image. High ceilings. Gauzy curtains. A huge bed with a dozen pillows. Fresh flowers. Tall champagne flutes for the sparkling pink beverage of seduction.

"Zara, I loved your mother, but she didn't make it easy for us to love her."

"Don't lump me and you together into one group," I said. "You weren't around. It was just me."

He got up from his stool at the kitchen island and began to stretch. He winced with pain and stopped to brace his midriff.

"Zirconia Cristata Riddle could be a royal pain," he said

"Tell me something I don't know."

He got a mischievous grin. "I just did."

I rolled back the conversation and replayed it. *Zirconia Cristata Riddle could be a royal pain.* Royal.

"You said *royal.*"

His grin broadened. "That's right, Zara. You're descended from supernatural royalty." His eyebrows bobbed. "On both sides."

I blinked at him.

"Princess," he said mockingly.

I took a sip of my coffee. I didn't feel like a princess. Nobody had mentioned royal lineage to me before. It hadn't been part of the scroll I'd seen at the DWM. No, it was more likely this was another of my father's games.

"You don't believe me."

"Duh."

He tilted his head and took a long look at me. "Why do you think your powers are so strong, compared to other witches?"

"My sparkling personality." The truth was, in the few short months since I'd gotten my powers, I'd only been able to compare notes with one other witch, my aunt.

"Your sparkling personality is the trait you got from me," he said, puffing out his chest with fatherly pride. "Now put a lid on that coffee so you don't spill it in my sweet car. I'm giving you a ride to work." He grinned. "Princess."

"Don't say that."

"Princess?"

I shuddered. "That word is extra gross coming out of your mouth."

"Does that mean I shouldn't get you a pink T-shirt that reads *Daddy's Little Princess*?"

"Only if you want to be barfed on."

"Noted."

"What am I the princess of? Is there a magical kingdom that you access through the back of a closet?"

His expression sobered. "Oh, no. You wouldn't want to go there."

"Now I want to."

He handed me the lid for the coffee cup. "Forget I mentioned anything. It's been thousands of years since witches held any real power in the underworld."

I snapped the lid onto the cup. "You're such a liar."

He grinned. "Had you going for a minute, didn't I?"

CHAPTER 14

My father spent most of the drive to the library talking about his car, which was a 1986 Nissan 300ZX in a dazzling shade of deep orange.

"I call her Foxy Pumpkin," he said. "I won her in a poker game."

"And did you paint her this lovely orange hue to match your hair, or did she come this way?"

"She was an uninspired plain red when I got her, and very depressed about it."

"I didn't know cars could suffer from depression."

He patted the dash lovingly. "Not my Foxy Pumpkin. Not anymore."

We turned a corner, and my hair whipped around my face in the breeze coming through the open T-top roof. I was enjoying being in his car, but I wouldn't admit it. My father clearly *adored* the car, and it made me gag a little when he showed it affection. Was this an ugly streak of jealousy inside me, something akin to sibling rivalry? I'd grown up an only child, so I had no idea what such a thing actually felt like. I certainly hadn't expected to learn of my jealousy over an inanimate object when I'd accepted his offer of a ride to work.

"Foxy Pumpkin's a good girl," he said. "Very reliable, but also feisty. What do you think of the ol' gal?"

"I think... you take excellent care of your possessions."

"Maybe I'll stick around town a while longer. I'll get an extra set of keys made, and you can borrow Foxy Pumpkin for scenic drives along the coast. You've got some spectacular views around here." His head turned as we passed a trio of attractive young women walking together.

The girls noticed the flashy orange sports car and looked to see who was driving. One of them, who was barely older than my daughter, gave Rhys a flirty wave.

He waved right back.

I slouched down in the passenger seat so they wouldn't see me.

"Lots of spectacular views, indeed," he said.

We passed the girls, and he smiled as he tapped the controls for the stereo, which was a combination radio and CD player that had probably been state-of-the-art back in 1989.

"What do you think?" He grinned over at me. "Would you like your old man to stick around and let you borrow the car?"

"Don't delay your planned departure on account of that," I said. "I get by just fine without access to a car."

He said glumly, "Way to make a guy feel wanted."

Great. Now I've offended him. Should I apologize?

No.

He didn't deserve an apology. *He should be the one apologizing to me.*

He sighed. "I suppose I'm just an old fool for thinking I had a place in a real family for once."

As we rounded the corner and my hair whipped into my eyes, it all hit me.

Zoey and I were the real family. Plus Zinnia, of course. She complained a lot and was reluctant to get involved in my problems, but she always came through when push came to shove. The three of us were the real family. Rhys Quarry could be fun, but he wasn't one of us. He was just some random shape-shifting trickster who'd knocked up my mother.

He'd weaseled his way into my life by taking advantage of my compassion for an injured red fox. Then he'd repaid my generosity by nipping at that woman and getting Bentley on my case. Now my fair-weather father was taking over my house—taking over my family—when he didn't deserve any of those things.

"Such a shame," he sighed.

"What did you expect?" My tone was snappier than ever. "You haven't been a part of my life since, well, ever. And then you show up out of the blue without an invitation.

You hog up all my daughter's free time just so she can worship and adore you. You're having the time of your life, for now. But you'll get bored soon enough, because you always do. One day a year is all you can manage. You're going to bail on us the moment it suits you, leaving me to pick up the pieces."

"Ah. Where's this coming from? Do your powers extend to viewing the future?"

"Who needs the future when you've got the past and the present? Just look at what my own house is doing. We never had a spare room before you turned up. Now my house keeps reconfiguring itself, making my room and my bed smaller each day. It's shrinking me out, making me feel like a second-class citizen. I expect that sort of treatment from some people, but not from my own house."

"You mean *our* house," he said, flicking on the car's turn signal.

We'd already reached the library. He pulled into the staff parking lot with practiced ease. He'd been here before, which bothered me, but not as much as what he'd said.

He'd said *our house*. Not my house. *Ours*.

"Here it comes," I said through gritted teeth. "You promised me the loan for the house deposit came without any strings whatsoever, but here come the strings."

"I also cosigned, Zara. There's *no way* a bank would have given you a mortgage given your situation. Not in today's financial climate, not even in a town like Wisteria. You hadn't even gotten your first paycheck from your new job. It would have taken years to build up the credit, especially in light of all the debts you've racked up over the years."

"Those debts have been paid," I said stiffly. "All of them. Student loans. Everything. And I'll pay you back, too."

"I don't want your money," he said.

I pushed the door open. The 300ZX was a small sports car, and it had been well cared for, so the door swung open as though flung by magic. Or maybe I had boosted my power with magic. It was so hard to tell which physics were at play when I lost my temper. I stepped out of the vehicle and checked to make sure no one else was there to overhear us. My boss had arrived in her brown Honda Civic and was pretending to not be watching us.

He repeated, "I don't want your money." He leaned forward to look into my eyes under the T-shaped roof. "Keep the deposit as a gift."

"No way," I said. "You don't get to buy your way into the family you abandoned."

He gave me a hurt look.

"We're cheap, but we're not that cheap," I said.

I shut the door with a satisfying slam.

* * *

"You think I'm the world's most ungrateful daughter," I said. "You think I'm selfish and spoiled and generally wicked."

My boss, Kathy Carmichael, handed me a plate with a chocolate croissant. She hadn't heard much of my discussion with my father that morning in the parking lot, but she had heard the door slam at the end.

"Family dynamics are complicated," she said. "Every family is unique. Family brings out the best and worst in us."

I bit into the croissant. Flakes flew out of my mouth as I said, "He brings out the worst in me."

Kathy chuckled. "I'm afraid that part isn't very unique." She gave me a motherly smile and blinked rapidly, her golden-brown eyes owl-like behind her round glasses. Her curly brown hair was swept up in a messy bun that day. Three spiral curls had escaped the bun and framed her round face.

"I'm working on paying him back for the house deposit, with interest," I said. "That's all I owe him."

"You said he used to spend time with you for one day out of the year. Was it on your birthday?"

"Not my birthday. It was just some random day in the summer."

"Was it really random?"

I poked at the croissant with my fingertip. "I can't remember," I said. "He'd show up in the morning to pick me up, and then the whole day would be such a whirlwind. At the end of the day, when I crawled back into bed, it felt like I'd lived two or three full days."

"Sounds like you two had fun together."

"For the first few hours," I admitted. "It didn't hurt that he plied me with a week's worth of sugar almost immediately. He liked to fuel up before we got down to petty crimes and misdemeanors."

The head librarian nodded thoughtfully. "Mind if I make a personal observation?"

I stuffed the remainder of the croissant into my mouth and waved for her to go ahead. I didn't know many people who asked permission before giving their opinion. When it comes to advice, most people think giving is far better than receiving. This thoughtful quality of Kathy's was why she held the position of head librarian. Sure, she had her meltdowns, but they were in private, back here in the break room. And it was always pastries that took the brunt of her aggression, not people. Whenever she dealt with our patrons, even the challenging ones, Kathy was the epitome of manners and restraint.

"Your situation with your father is unwinnable," Kathy said sagely. "You're angry that he wasn't a part of your life in the past, and now you're angry that he wants to make amends by doing the opposite. It's unwinnable for him."

"You think?"

She answered my question with another. "Is there anything he can do right now that won't upset you?"

"He could go away," I said, pouting.

Kathy pursed her lips, emphasizing the pointed tip of her sharp nose. "Is that what you really want? For you and your daughter?"

My daughter. Zoey had been so happy over the last two days, skipping around the house instead of scuttling. She enjoyed spending time with her grandfather, and he easily drew out the bubbly little girl who'd all but disappeared into moodiness over not getting her powers. His presence had rolled back the clock, bringing us back to a more innocent time—a time of animal-shaped pancakes. What harm could be done by having him around? Zoey was barely sixteen, still a minor, so even if my father did get both of them arrested sneaking into somewhere they weren't supposed to be, Zoey wouldn't face adult charges.

"No," I admitted sullenly. "I don't *actually* want him to go away."

Kathy pointed at my chest. "What you want to go away is that *feeling* you have. The clinging bitterness that reaches up and consumes you from below, squeezing you in its jaws." She made a clawlike gesture with both hands.

"Squeezing me in its jaws?" Like how my house was squeezing me out?

Does she know?

I looked at Kathy in a new light. Her golden-brown eyes did seem to sparkle with secret knowledge. She might know about my shifting house. She'd never given me any signs of harboring supernatural powers, but then again, our other librarian, Frank Wonder, hadn't done anything but dye his hair pink before he suddenly turned into a flamingo shifter. Two out of us had magical powers. What were the chances all three of Wisteria's full-time librarians had supernatural abilities?

"Whooo knows," she hooted, waving one hand. "Listen to me carrying on about the heart's speech. This always happens when I read a bunch of self-help books back to back. I open my beak and out comes all this woowoo nonsense."

"It's not nonsense," I said. "A little woowoo, yes, but you make a good point. I don't want my father to leave. I want the anger to go, and for my house to go back to normal."

"Normal," she mused.

"I know, I know. Normal's just a setting on the dishwasher, between Lite Wash and Heavy Pot Scrub."

"Right," she said.

Kathy pulled one of her springlike curls and got a faraway look. She stretched out another curl and peered at it, as though looking for more of the stray twigs she'd had stuck in her hair two days ago. Something troubling must have happened Wednesday morning. She'd not spoken about it since, but she had been reading self-help books about family dynamics.

Kathy said in a dreamy tone, "We mothers and daughters, we *women*, say the word *normal* when we mean something else entirely."

"Maybe." What was she talking about? "But it's not like me to wish to be normal. That's my daughter, Zoey's, mantra, not mine. I'm all about embracing the chaos, loving the weird and wonderful."

Kathy's golden-brown eyes flitted over to mine and came into focus. "Yes, Zara. That's you, all right."

I asked, "What does normal mean to you?"

"Control," Kathy said without hesitation. "And knowing what everyone is at all times."

"Don't you mean *where*? Knowing *where* everyone is?"

She let out a forced laugh. "Yes, that's what I meant."

I looked down at Kathy's feet. Her shoes were mismatched. It wasn't uncommon for a librarian to show up at work with mismatched shoes, but Kathy's weren't simply two different shades of brown. One was black, and the other was blue.

"Kathy, is everything okay with you? Are the boys still on the road with your husband?"

She waved her hand. "Don't worry about me. I'm quite fine. Back to you and your father." She whipped off her glasses and started cleaning them with a white cloth from her pocket. Without looking up at me, she asked, "What if this is the new normal? Your father is here, and he wants to be in your life. Can you live with it?"

I could live *through* it, because I'd lived through worse, including electrocution, possession by ghosts, and dying briefly. But could I live *with* my father? What if it meant living with the tiny dollhouse-sized door on my bedroom?

Either I could get down on my knees to crawl through, or I could borrow a sledgehammer and start swinging.

Crawling or sledgehammer.

Going with the flow or throwing a tantrum.

I had a choice to make.

CHAPTER 15

THROUGHOUT THE DAY, I worked on finding my inner Zen. In between helping patrons with their materials, I took a few peeks at our self-help books, which collectively gave me a pep talk about boundaries.

According to the majority of books about relationships, an adult can deal with difficult people, so long as the situation isn't abusive or dangerous. The key is to draw up strong boundaries. What is a boundary? It can be as simple as a list of things you decide ahead of time that you will not tolerate. Or it can be more metaphysical. *When someone says something antagonizing, picture yourself surrounded in white light!* That made me smile. Self-help books aren't written with witches in mind. If I focused too well on being surrounded by white light, I ran the risk of actually turning into a glow stick.

Glow stick or not, I would handle the remainder of my father's visit with grace and tongue biting. My daughter loves him, and I didn't want to let her down. Whatever was bound to happen would happen, and the actions of other people were outside of my control. The future would unfold, and nothing was ever entirely good or entirely bad. Black-and-white thinking would only cause me pain. I had to be more gray. Gray like Detective Bentley, with his gray eyes and steely gray temples.

Speak of the devil.

Just as my shift was ending, Detective Bentley sauntered in.

The weather was warm that Friday—warm enough that I'd had to confiscate several drippy iced drinks from patrons in flip-flops, but Bentley wasn't in summer gear. He looked cool and unperturbed in his usual gray suit.

Yes, I would do well to be more like Bentley. Driven. Cool. Unflappable. Unless you got the last sprinkle donut.

The forty-something detective scanned the library, stopping when his gaze met mine. He sauntered toward the circulation desk, where I'd been working on something that suddenly felt unimportant.

"Bentley," I exclaimed. "I've been thinking about you all afternoon!"

He quirked an eyebrow. "Oh?"

All five of the patrons using the computer kiosks looked up in our direction. I'd spoken louder than my usual library volume, and my voice had cut through the same way TV commercials blast through the din of a family restaurant.

I grabbed the stack of books I'd pulled for him over the last two days and set them on the counter between us. He'd mentioned something called Wakeful, and I could never resist a juicy research project.

"Detective Bentley, this is everything we have on Wakeful." I spoke in my soft, business-like, nothing-to-see-here-folks librarian tone. The faces at the computers dropped back down, and the patrons returned to their homework and those other clandestine things they quickly hid whenever a staff member walked by.

Bentley perused the stack of books, which were mainly about local Wisteria history. I'd used one of my magic spells—the one for finding a specific page in a book—to locate mentions of Wakeful, and then I'd marked the pages with Post-It note tabs.

"The Wakefuls were one of the founding families of Wisteria," I said. "Not to be confused with the Winfields or the Winnfurs, who were also founding families."

"That's interesting. But you shouldn't have bothered." His hands fluttered over the stack, betraying his excitement. "I've already forgotten why I was interested."

Liar.

He opened one of the books to a full-page photograph of a general store. "Wakeful Home Goods," he said, reading the hand-painted sign above the tidy shop in the photo. "Established in 1910."

"The Wakeful name was on all sorts of businesses, from shops and services to train stations and coal mines."

Bentley glanced up at me, his steely gray eyes glinting silver. "And how many of these Wakeful businesses are still in operation today, Ms. Riddle?"

He already knew the answer and was trying to make a point.

"If you already know, just say so, Smart Pants."

"The answer is zero," he said. "There is not one business or historic site in this town that currently bears the Wakeful name." Bentley leaned back, pulled out his badge, and set it on top of the books.

"Are you arresting those books for obstruction of justice?"

"I was hoping to borrow them. Is that the right term?" He sounded it out to himself. "*Borrow.*" He looked up at the ceiling then at me. "That's the term a lot of thieves use when they're caught with something that's not theirs. 'Officer, I wasn't stealing this bike, I was only borrowing it.' It's a shame we don't have a public library for all things. It would really cut down on theft."

"A public library for all things," I mused. "Imagine all the librarians the city would have to hire."

"And all the detectives they'd have to let go."

"Ah, the yin and yang of life," I said. "Maybe you could become a librarian."

"Let's start with me becoming a card-carrying library customer."

"The term is patron," I said. "And it would be my pleasure to set up an account for you. I trust you have some means of identification other than your shiny badge?"

Bentley flipped over the badge to reveal his driver's license and address. I stepped over to the computer terminal and started setting up an account, starting with his full name, which was Theodore Dean Bentley.

"Theodore," I said excitedly. "Your first name is Theodore." My voice came out much louder than I'd meant. Loud for a library, anyway. Once again, all five faces at the computer stations looked up at me.

My pink-haired coworker, Frank Wonder, also heard. He actually shushed me as he came over at a fast-paced walk.

"Zara Riddle," Frank said with a haughty air. "If you can't keep it down, take it to the discotheque."

I stuck my tongue out at Frank. It had been our running joke that week that noisy people needed to "take it to the discotheque." What's funnier than a dated vocabulary word frequently used in French language textbooks from the 1980s? Not much!

I managed to finish setting up Detective Theodore Dean Bentley's patron card and check out his books without too much oversight by Frank, who I could tell was desperate to be a part of the interaction.

After hovering nearby for several minutes, Frank finally came over and put my purse on my shoulder. "Good work today," he said loudly. "Have a nice walk home." He looked at Bentley and then back at me. "Zara Riddle, I certainly do hope nothing happens while you're walking yourself home all by yourself right now, since you're done work for the day."

I gave Frank a strained smile. "Thank you *so much*, Frank Wonder. That's very thoughtful of you."

I moved toward the staff lounge. Frank shifted his body to block me.

"Bye!"

"Frank, I still need to..." I mimed punching out my timecard. The WPL had a strangely antiquated time-tracking system that included a machine that made an un-library-like KERCHUNK when it stamped a card.

"I already kerchunked your card," he said.

"That's strictly against WPL policies."

Frank flashed his ultra-white teeth at me. "I'll write myself up." He lifted his chin to point it toward the exit. "Get on out of here with your bad self. Take it to the discotheque!"

I shook my head.

"I'll walk you home," Bentley said gamely behind me. "I still need to pick up my car from your street, anyway. It's been there two days. I hope I didn't get a ticket."

"Thanks," I said.

Frank's eyes bulged as he inhaled with excitement. I shot him a quick eyebrow lift to let him know we could discuss the matter of Bentley's car being parked on my street *some other time*.

I walked out of the library with Bentley, who was carrying his borrowed books in a Wisteria Public Library canvas tote he'd purchased for ten dollars to help a national children's charity.

* * *

The walk home in the late-afternoon sunshine was everything I love about walking home on a Friday: dappled sunshine, families getting ready for weekend camping adventures, and the sounds and smells of barbecues. If a whole town can give off the sensation of putting its feet up while cracking open a tasty beverage, Wisteria was doing it.

While we walked, Bentley regaled me with his wild conspiracy theory. He suggested that the Wakeful family had committed crimes so unspeakable that they'd been erased from the town's memory. He felt he might find some evidence in the borrowed books. I wished him luck, but I knew from doing my own research on the library's materials that he wouldn't find any genuine talk of witchcraft or supernatural beings.

We slowed to admire a hedge that had been trimmed into the four-digit number for the home's street address.

At the corner, we both smiled over a resident's act of kindness. Someone had found a child's dropped teddy bear, given it a good wash and a mending, and affixed it to a fence with a note.

"Teddy has been found," I said. "Cancel the Missing Bear Report."

"I'll close the case when I get back to the station," he said with a chuckle.

"Teddy is a nickname for Theodore," I said.

He made a nonverbal sound of agreement.

"Did the girls in school call you Teddy Bear?"

"What do you think?"

"I don't know. Were you cuddly back then, or were you always how you are now?"

He glanced over at me. "And how am I now?"

"Never mind. You answered my question."

"You can call me Teddy if you'd like."

I shrugged. "I'll stick to calling you Bentley." I kicked at an old pinecone on the sidewalk. "Did you have much luck over the last two days as a gumshoe detective? Did you see anything you wouldn't have seen from your car?"

He didn't answer. I glanced over to catch him smiling.

"You did get lucky," I said. "You look like the cat who ate the canary."

"I might have met someone," he said cryptically.

I kept kicking the pinecone. "What? Who? A woman?"

He looked down at my feet. "That's odd. She was wearing the exact same boots as you."

"Now I know you're pulling my leg. Nobody around here wears these old-fashioned granny booties except me and my aunt, Zinnia Riddle. The shoe store only orders them in our size, because we Riddles are the only ones who buy them."

"I'm not pulling your leg, and I'm not one of those men who's fashion-blind. I know what I saw. She wears boots like yours."

"What did the rest of her look like? Is she a ravishing beauty, with red hair and hazel eyes?"

"She's... indescribable."

"Come on, Bentley. Is that the best you can do? Give me a height, a build, a general age range."

He stopped walking. We were in front of my house already.

"She's indescribable," he repeated, his tone flat, as though he'd been hypnotized.

"Nothing's indescribable," I said. "You could try."

"She's very tall and she wears green," he said flatly, staring straight at a neighbor's pine tree.

"Is she triangular?"

"Yes. Her hair goes like this." He made a pine tree shape with his hands.

This was all very familiar. Dr. Katz's assistant, Fatima, had sounded that way when she described the person who'd paid for the fox's medical bill—the person I'd assumed was my father's partner.

I wanted more information from Bentley. I wondered if Zinnia knew a spell that would help us break through a glamour.

Bentley, however, had other ideas. He crossed the street and climbed into his car. He started the engine and drove away.

I stood on the sidewalk, staring after his boxy gray car, long after he'd disappeared around the corner.

A feathery breeze caressed the back of my neck. Someone or something was watching me.

I looked up into the tree branches above me. Green leaves. No eyes.

But someone was walking toward me. My neighbor Arden and his brown Labradoodle.

"Hello, Zara," Arden said cheerfully. "What are we looking for?" He put his hand to his temple to shade his eyes and peered up at the tree.

"I was looking for a blue jay," I said. "He's really friendly. Have you seen him around?"

Arden gave me a confused look. "It's Friday today, so you won't see a blue jay."

"Why's that?"

"According to my grandmother, blue jays are never around on Fridays because they're busy fetching sticks down to hell."

"I didn't know there was a particular day of the week just for fetching sticks down to hell."

Arden shrugged. "It's just a thing she used to say. My grandmother was obsessed with devils and monsters. She used to tell me stories about the olden days. Our family comes from a long line of monster hunters."

"That explains why I've seen you boating with that pointy-looking trident of yours, looking for sea monsters."

Arden chuckled and rubbed his shiny bald head. "The truth is, it's just an excuse to get out on the boat."

"So's fishing."

"But I don't eat fish."

"Do you eat sea monsters?"

He chuckled again. "Zara, you do bring something fresh to this ol' neighborhood." He turned and started walking away.

"You shouldn't eat sea monsters," I called after him in a joking tone. "I hear they cause terrible indigestion." *And also because some of them might be people.*

He gave me a wave of acknowledgment without looking back.

I took one last look in the tree for the blue jay. He wasn't visible, but I sensed something hiding behind a clump of leaves. I used my telekinetic magic to gently swish some branches aside. This revealed the hiding spot of a red squirrel, who gave me a single chirp of surprise.

I demanded of the squirrel, "Who are you working for?"

The squirrel darted along the branch in a zigzag pattern and then scaled up the trunk toward better cover.

"Come back down here," I said. "Get your furry butt down here and face me like a... squirrel."

A woman walking by with a baby stroller gave me a wide berth.

The squirrel disappeared. Even using magic to swish the leaves from side to side, I couldn't spot it again.

I looked down the street for my father's car. The pumpkin-hued Nissan 300ZX was nowhere in sight. He'd had plans to get pizza for Zoey's school friends and take them all out to a movie. The adoration of teenagers was relatively inexpensive.

I wasn't too happy about him getting all the glory of being the fun grownup. I would have gladly taken Zoey and her new friends for pizza.

But at least Zoey was making friends. It had all happened suddenly, during the last week. And not a moment too soon. The school year was drawing to a close, and I'd feared she'd spend a long summer vacation without any friends.

I ran up the steps of the house and then raced up the stairs toward my bedroom door. No family inside my house meant I could jump right into my DWM Monster Manual undisturbed.

First, I stopped in the kitchen for provisions. With an assortment of leftover takeout food in hand, I raced upstairs to my room.

I noted bitterly that the door had shrunk even more. It was now smaller than a cupboard door.

If I went through, would my room take away the door entirely and trap me inside? My stomach growled, which gave me a funny idea. Could my house flood the room with juices and digest me? I laughed out loud and shook my head. *Don't be silly. Houses don't eat people.* It was just making some sort of point about my family relationships. Or maybe it needed the wood for something better, like an addition for the bathroom. I'd always liked the idea of having a cedar-lined sauna.

I stretched and rubbed my eyes. It had been a long week. Having my father show up on Wednesday had complicated my life and thrown off my routine. Thanks to my one outing with a fox on my shoulders, I'd attracted more attention from Bentley. I'd always considered him basically harmless, but perhaps I'd underestimated the man. When handling a gun, you should always treat it as though it's loaded. Bentley was a square, but he was still a detective.

I got down on the floor and opened the cupboard-sized door to my room.

More worries flitted through my thoughts. Was my sweet neighbor Arden really descended from monster hunters? Were witches considered monsters? What about shifters? And was a talking blue jay spying on me?

Maybe the DWM Monster Manual had some answers.

I pushed my plate of food through the door in front of me and then waited.

My bedroom appeared to be smaller than before, but it didn't do anything suspicious, such as eat my plate of food.

I got down on my elbows and wriggled through the doorway like a snake.

CHAPTER 16

MY HOT DATE for that Friday night, the DWM Monster Manual, was a bit of a tease. There was information on a number of subjects, but each answer led to more questions.

The section about blue jays read as follows:

Blue jays are occasionally used as remote eyes for creatures of the grave. When sent to watch a human subject, the individual blue jay may eventually become fascinated by the human subject and break its grave bond. The blue jay is more fortunate than humans, who are rarely able to break the grave bond. Little is known of the mechanism for enchanting a blue jay, as creatures of the grave are unhelpfully secretive, perhaps due to their unholy, abhorrent nature. Several creatures of the grave were asked to contribute to this index, yet as of the press deadline, none have acquiesced. Unhelpful as always!

"Speaking of unhelpful, Jorg Ebola, you are one unhelpful editor," I said to the book. "Grave bond? And what the heck is a creature of the grave? Is it a zombie? Ghost? Blood sucker? Mummy? Walking skeleton? Worms? All of the above?"

The book didn't respond, which was probably for the best. I didn't want a reply if it came in the judgmental tone of Jorg Ebola.

But I had my own ways of finding information. I twirled my finger and used the same page-finding spell I'd invoked multiple times over the last two days to find Wakeful family information for Detective Bentley.

"Find me a definition for *creatures of the grave*," I commanded, weaving in Witch Tongue.

The book grew hot in my hands, gave off an acrid smell, and abruptly slammed shut.

"Easy now," I said, as though calming a spooked horse. "I guess you don't like other spells, huh?" The book already had one spell running for the glamour on the pages. Mixing spells is like mixing two kinds of prescription medication—you could be fine, or you could turn purple.

The book let out a squeal like a balloon losing air and flew out of my hands. It flapped through the air, flying like a frightened bat. It didn't have far to go, since my tiny bedroom was barely large enough to contain my bed. With a panicked flapping sound, the book disappeared into the middle of my closet.

"Come back," I said soothingly. "I promise not to cast any more spells. Nobody warned me, okay?"

From the depths of the closet, the book made a sound not unlike that of a pouting toddler.

I went to the closet and tried parting my clothes, but my reduced-size closet was packed too tight for me to wedge more than my fingertips in.

I made the smooch-smooch sound people use to call animals. "Here bookie, bookie. Come out, come out, wherever you are."

Nothing.

I sat on the bed and made a phone call to Zinnia. For a change, she picked up on the first ring.

After I'd explained the situation to her, she said, "You should ask Chet for help. I've never had the good fortune to see that particular book." She sniffed. "Perhaps one day, I'll be invited to look at it myself. I might be of more help after getting first-hand experience."

"Aunt Zinnia, why can't you just say what you want? Does it always have to be a complicated song and dance with your hints and your guilt trips?" I sighed. "You're just like my mother."

"I am not," she retorted.

There was silence on the call for a full minute. Was I in the wrong? Probably. I'd been annoyed about the book and my shrinking room, but since I couldn't take it out on either of them, I'd snapped at my aunt.

"Sorry," I said. "That wasn't fair of me to say. You don't deserve that."

"No, no," she said thinly. "I probably do. I appreciate your honesty, Zara. I truly do. We ought to always speak the truth to each other, and help each other."

"Yes," I agreed.

"Well then," she started but didn't follow it up with anything else. The ball was in my court, so to speak with a sports metaphor. It was my serve, or volley, or whatever.

"Zinnia Riddle, I *officially* invite you to come over to my house and have a good, long look at my new book. You can hold it and read it as much as you like... provided you extract it from my closet first."

"Tonight? Right now?"

I glanced over at my tiny door. It was a good thing my aunt was the same size as me.

"Sure, come on over now," I said.

"I'm afraid I have other engagements. How about tomorrow morning? I could bring bagels for brunch. Plus cream cheese and lox. Oh, and I can prepare a nice fruit platter. I've got a spell for making perfectly round melon balls that I'd like to practice."

"You had me at bagels," I said.

* * *

SATURDAY

Saturday morning, I was sitting in the living room, quietly reading the obituaries segment of the local newspaper, when the doorbell rang.

I yelled over my shoulder, "Doorbell!"

My father, who was reading the business section of a national newspaper on the chair across from me, also relayed the signal. "Doorbell!"

Zoey came running down the stairs. "Doorbell!"

"Doorbell," Rhys replied, smiling at me.

"Doorbell," I said with a raised eyebrow.

Zoey paused in the living room. "Doorbell," she said, with the casual freshness of someone making an observation for the first time.

"Doorbell," I agreed.

She pointed at the front door and moved toward it. "Doorbell," she said by way of explanation.

Rhys chuckled in an amused, grandfatherly way.

I nodded and went back to my obituaries. If I sped up, I could finish my task by the time Zoey and her great-aunt finished greeting each other.

For the last couple of weekends, I'd made it my routine to read every obituary and death notice in the local newspaper. Being Spirit Charmed—or Spirit Cursed, depending on how you looked at it—meant that a stray ghost could invade my head at any moment. No notice, no takebacksies. Zinnia had been the one to suggest I keep tabs on the local dead people in order to help me identify new spirits more easily. And so I'd started the curious habit of reading the obituaries, several decades before a person naturally gets interested in such things.

To my surprise, the obituaries weren't depressing at all. If anything, reading about the wonderful lives of others, and how deeply one person could affect other people and communities, made my heart feel buoyant. What we do with our lives matters. No single act of kindness and grace is ever wasted. Seize the day and all that!

I folded up the newspaper with a happy flourish and jumped up to greet my aunt.

Rhys was already hugging her. Zinnia's arms flopped limply at her sides while he gave her what looked like an exuberant squeeze.

"Little Ziti Noodles, it's been too long!" he exclaimed. He stepped back and looked her over. "And you're not so little anymore. I'll have to call you Zirconia!"

Her hazel eyes flew open wide. "You mean Zinnia. I'm not Zirconia."

"Slip of the tongue," he said.

She huffed. "Rhys Quarry, I'm not like my sister. Not at all." She crossed her arms over her chest protectively. She wore one of her usual eclectic ensembles: flower-dotted leggings with a paisley-and-floral tunic. The tunic was cinched at the waist with a braided cord that might have once been a tieback for velvet drapes. Her red hair was tied back in a loose braid.

Rhys kept chuckling over my aunt's reaction to being called her older sister's name. He didn't know I'd already insulted her the night before by comparing her to my mother. I couldn't blame him for getting us mixed up. We Riddles all look so similar to each other, and the Z names don't help.

Rhys turned to Zoey. "Zozo, did you know that your aunt was about your age when we first met? She was such a shy little thing, compared to you. I wonder if it's a generational thing?"

"I wasn't shy," Zinnia said crisply. "I was younger than Zoey, and I was raised to have manners. I knew better than to—" She cut herself off and said simply, "It's lovely to see you again, Rhys."

"And under better circumstances," he agreed. "A brunch beats a funeral every time." He sniffed the air. "Bagels?"

"Yes!" She picked up the canvas tote bags she'd set on the floor a moment earlier. "I've brought a dozen fresh bagels, along with a selection of cream cheese flavors, as well as the world's most perfectly round melon balls. They're like marbles."

Zoey grabbed the bags with a happy whoop. "You had me at bagels," she called over her shoulder on the way to the kitchen.

Zinnia looked at me. "Like mother, like daughter."

Rhys chimed in, "I'll say. Isn't Zara the embodiment of all Zirconia's best features?"

They both stared at me. I felt like a bug under a glass.

"Zara does embody many fine Riddle traits," Zinnia said. "But she is her own person."

"She sure is," Rhys said.

They continued staring at me.

"She can be a mystery," Zinnia said.

More staring.

I took a few steps back cautiously. "You two look like you're planning an intervention. I should have known better than to host a family reunion. Now there are enough people here to gang up on me."

Rhys said, "That's what family's for. We play-fight to prepare for the real world. Like fox pups tumbling around."

"Speaking of which," Zinnia said. "I can't believe I never knew of your particular gift. Looking back now, it's all coming together, but I had no idea."

Rhys looked at me. "You told her?"

Zinnia gave him a playful whack on the shoulder. "Of course she did, Rhys. I'm her mentor. You don't keep secrets from your mentor."

He looked down at his shoulder where she'd whacked him and then directly at the redheaded witch. "Ziti Noodles, are you flirting with me?"

Zinnia opened her mouth and made a choking sound, halfway between a laugh and sucking in a bug. Her cheeks turned pink. Rhys waggled his eyebrows at her, which produced more of the bug-sucking sound.

"Gross," I said, and I turned around quickly to find something else to do. Surely there was a bagel that needed slicing. I'd rather grate carrots than watch my father flirt with my dead mother's younger sister.

CHAPTER 17

THE FOUR OF US eventually made our way out to the back of the house, where we'd be having brunch alfresco. I hadn't gotten around to buying patio furniture since the move, but Zoey had taken care of the seating earlier that morning. She'd set up a folding card table in the back yard, dressing it up with a colorful tablecloth and pairing it with chairs from the dining room.

"Great job," I said to Zoey as I took in the economical yet quaint setup. "All we need is the Mad Hatter, plus a mouse who lives in a teapot, and it'll be a storybook brunch."

"The shrubbery does have a Wonderland feel," she agreed.

Indeed, the jungle in the back yard had become even more overgrown in the last few weeks of summer weather. At least the bushes were blossoming now, blue and white and pink. All the flowers made the overgrowth look intentional.

"I made place cards with everyone's names," my daughter said, skipping around the table. "Pawpaw, you're over here, at the head of the table."

I murmured to Zinnia, "There's no *head of the table* if it's a square card table."

"We ought to humor the girl," Zinnia said. "These last playful vestiges of childhood will be gone before you know it."

"That's what I'm afraid of." I glared at my father pointedly.

They'd gotten home late the night before and had spoken to each other downstairs with hushed tones I could only call conspiratorial.

He was currently joking around with Zoey, rearranging the place cards on the table and juggling with the small granite creatures she'd set on a silver tray as the centerpiece.

My aunt was staring at my father the way she looked at cakes. I didn't like it one bit.

I elbowed her. "Shake your head. Your eyes are stuck."

She turned and blinked at me. "No, they're not."

"You were gawking at my father. I thought shifters were repugnant to witches?"

"Yes and no." She tilted her head nonchalantly. "He's good with your daughter. I can see what my sister saw in him."

"Gross. You're not going to hook up with my dad, are you?"

She gasped. "Over my dead broomstick!"

I pointed at her. "Where did you get that expression? I just said it the other day, and I can't remember hearing it."

"Your mother used to say it," Zinnia said. "Though it beats me how you picked it up. I certainly never heard it from her lips after she had you."

I gave her a hard look. "Was my mother a witch or not? You told me she wasn't, but Rhys says she was."

Zinnia's hazel eyes clouded over as she glanced around. She uttered the sound bubble spell to enclose the two of us. Rhys and Zoey were moving the table to a more level section of yard and weren't paying us any attention. We stayed in the shadow cast by the back of the house.

Zinnia spoke slowly and clearly. "Your mother chose to renounce witchcraft."

"She renounced witchcraft," I repeated. *Renounced*, as in *to formally declare one's abandonment of a claim, a right, or a possession.*

"She didn't want to be a witch."

"Can you do that?"

"Your mother did what she pleased."

"Yet she was never pleased," I said. "How ironic."

My aunt glanced up at the blue sky. "I hadn't even gotten my powers yet when she decided she was done with hers. Did you know I was a late bloomer?" Zinnia's voice pitched up girlishly. "I didn't find out I was a witch until I was nearly seventeen." She frowned at the sky as she bit at her lower lip. "Not until I nearly killed someone by accident."

"That must have been awful," I said.

She looked at me with a tight expression and spoke with bitterness. "My big sister might have seen fit to make the minimal effort to *warn me* about my own powers before she decided to no longer be a witch."

"How does one stop being a witch?"

Zinnia looked down at the concrete beneath our feet, at the blades of grass pushing up through the cracks. "It's not recommended," she said softly. "There were side effects." Her eyes flicked up and met mine. "Deadly side effects."

Her words were like a spell that shot ice water into my veins.

Deadly side effects.

I had to ask. "Is that what killed her?" The doctors had been confused about my mother's illness, right to the end. Right to her final raspy breaths.

Zinnia didn't have to answer. The glistening in her hazel eyes told me. My mother's decision to no longer be a witch had made her sick. It had made her... dead.

I felt a hand on mine. Zinnia held my hand, holding me steady. Everything was happening so fast.

A few moments earlier, we'd been joking around in the kitchen about playing badminton with her perfectly round melon balls, and then we'd stepped out into the yard, and now we were speaking of death. I could smell the disinfectant scent of the hospital, worming its way through my nostrils and into every cell of my body. My hands were funny. I could see Zinnia's hand on mine, but I couldn't feel it.

I was turning translucent, turning into a wisp of smoke, turning into a ghost again.

"Your mother did what she thought was best," Zinnia said, startling me back to the physical realm.

I wasn't a ghost. I was still there.

A buzzing housefly clumsily flew right into my cheek and bounced away. *Why do houseflies do that?* What is it about a human being, standing perfectly still, that invites midair collisions? My mind raced through insect trivia. Anything to not be there, the recipient of news I probably should have been sitting down for.

"Zirconia didn't want anyone to know," Zinnia said. "She didn't want anyone to know that it was her choice, her fault."

From a long way down inside me came my voice. "I thought we were done keeping secrets from each other."

"We are," Zinnia said. "You asked me the question, and I answered you honestly."

I looked down at the grass growing through the cement cracks. She had been honest. She just hadn't volunteered a bunch of secrets retroactively. Was it fair to hold that against her? Probably not.

"I still don't understand," I said with a thick voice. "Was it a spell? A ritual? Or did she just stop using magic one day, cold turkey?" I glanced over at my father, the fox shifter. "Is that why she had a baby with one of *his* kind?"

"All of that and more," Zinnia said. The seams of her lips kept sticking together as she talked. Her mouth had gone as dry as mine.

"What a waste," I said. "What a waste of this beautiful gift."

Zinnia's eyes widened. She was surprised by my reaction.

We stared at each other. Her face shifted, the edges losing cohesion as I stared into those eyes that were a perfect mirror of my own except older and wiser.

Zoey ran up and tugged on our hands, urging us to join the garden party before she fainted from hunger.

Zinnia and I both sat in the seats bearing our place cards.

My card bore my full name, written in calligraphy: Zarabella Diamante Riddle. I ran my fingertip over the swirling letters, remembering the sweeter things my mother used to say. One time, when she was tipsy from an afternoon of wine tasting at a fancy vineyard, she made me swear that I would never accept the imitation of anything.

Zirconia Cristata Riddle was named after zirconium dioxide, a white crystalline oxide used to make artificial gems, but I was the real thing; I was a *diamond*, and it said so right in my name.

Had she been talking about my witch powers, or about something else?

It was a shame she'd passed away before I could ask her about any of this.

Zoey chattered away about how much fun she'd had the night before with her grandfather, and how her new friends thought he was the coolest adult they'd ever met.

I passed the food around the table. Zinnia did the same, glancing over at me with a worry line on her forehead that let me know she was equally troubled by our discussion of my mother's choices.

Such a shame, I kept thinking.

Such a shame Zirconia Riddle couldn't be with us that Saturday morning in the garden, squeezed in between the overgrown bushes and a gussied-up card table, having brunch with all the people she'd once loved. It had been her choice to leave us, though. Her choice. I respected her decision, and yet I also hated her for it, among other things.

My mother had let us all down.

* * *

"Come with us to the zoo," Rhys said. "I know one of the zookeepers, and I can get us into the staff-only areas. Don't you want to cuddle a baby hippo?"

My father and I were currently alone together in the kitchen. We'd been cleaning up from brunch, and I had both hands in hot, soapy water. I was never the most domestic of people, but I found washing dishes by hand surprisingly soothing. For the past few months, I'd used telekinesis for such tasks, so I'd forgotten the mundane pleasures of rinsing bubbles off squeaky-clean glass bowls.

I did not, however, like the idea of sneaking around the non-public parts of a zoo.

"Baby hippos," he said teasingly.

"No, thanks," I said. "And you stay away from the staff-only areas with my daughter."

He made a rubbery innocent face. "But, but, but! These particular baby hippos are pygmy hippos. They get damp and covered in bits of straw. You know the ones. They're rubbery and wet and the exact opposite of cats."

"Rhys, I don't care if the baby pygmy hippos do a circus act with baby giraffes and purple unicorns. Don't you dare pull your sneaky tricks. Pay the admission, stick to the walkways, and stay out of trouble."

"Wow." His rust-colored eyebrows rose even higher. "You sound exactly like Zirconia, telling me to stay out of trouble with you."

I glowered. "Not that you respected her wishes." I yanked the plug from the sink, rinsed off my hands, and wiped them on a towel. "Since we're talking about my mother, can you answer a question for me?"

"Okay, it wasn't just the one night in the hotel. There were several nights."

I scrunched up my face. "Not that." I hung the dish towel on the stove handle to dry. Everything took so much more time without magic. "Why did she stop being a witch?"

He looked me straight in the eyes. "She never told me."

Too much eye contact. He was lying. "Not even a hint?"

He maintained the intense eye contact. "I would imagine it was the same reason anyone leaves a career or a relationship. The benefits don't outweigh the costs." He tilted his head to the side in a foxlike movement. "Haven't you noticed a few glitches along with your magic powers?"

I paused before answering, careful not to admit to being a witch. "You're the only glitch around here."

"A glitch and a witch. What a great duo." He smiled. "Come with us to the zoo today. We'll have fun like old times. Remember when you got to ride the racehorse?"

"That actually happened?" I stared at him in disbelief. "Whenever I told people about that, they said I must have confused a dream with reality. I can't believe you let a four-year old ride a galloping horse around a racetrack."

"It was your idea," he said defensively.

"I was four!"

"You were a natural rider." His gold-green eyes twinkled. "And the horse wasn't a regular horse, anyway. He was an old friend."

I shook my head. Even a shifter horse was still a horse. "On second thought, maybe you should stick around the house today, where I can keep an eye on you. Watch a nature documentary on the TV. No zoo today."

Zoey entered the kitchen, heard the tail end of what I'd said, and started whining. "Mom, you promised me we'd go to the zoo. We've lived here for months, and we haven't even gone once. I think it's important for my education that I experience a broad range of educational activities."

I snorted. "That's what I'm afraid of."

"Mom, I'd never do anything bad. Don't you trust me?" She widened her eyes and pouted, making the innocent face that scaled her age back to the single digits.

"Fine," I relented. "Enjoy the zoo with my blessing."

Zinnia appeared in the entryway to the kitchen. I'd banned her twenty minutes earlier for being bossy. She ducked her head and made a beeline for the microwave. She opened it up and grabbed the plastic dome that she'd bought for us to use when reheating leftovers. Even with all the witchcraft stuff, the state of our microwave interior was a big deal to her.

"Filthy, filthy, filthy," she exclaimed as she surveyed the crusty interior of the plastic dome. There was a maniacal gleam of excitement in her eyes.

Zoey and I exchanged a knowing look. Together, we'd done a fine job getting an artistic spray of spattered food all over the dome's interior. Zinnia's reaction had been worth the effort.

Zinnia made a tsk-tsk sound as she scurried over to the sink with the filthy plastic dome and got to work scrubbing it under the tap. "You do have to clean the plastic thingie on occasion," she lectured. "Some of this doesn't even resemble food." She turned and gave us a suspicious look. "Is this craft glitter?"

I caught Zoey's eye and held my finger to my lips. The craft glitter was our little secret.

My father smiled as though he'd been in on it all along.

We all watched my aunt scrub the lid. After you've eaten your body weight in brunch goodies and the tryptophan coma is setting in, it doesn't take much action to entertain you.

After a few minutes, Rhys clapped me on the shoulder. "I guess we'll be on our way. Can I pick up anything for the house while I'm at the zoo?"

"Please don't bring home any monkeys."

"I can't make any promises," he said, and he turned to go.

Zoey raced along behind him, zigzagging with youthful energy.

Once they were gone, and Zinnia had finished making a big production out of putting the clean plastic dome back inside the microwave, she and I headed upstairs to spend some quality time with my new book.

Unfortunately, my house had other plans.

My bedroom door, which had been cupboard-sized that morning, had become even smaller—way too small for a person, let alone an adult, to squeeze through.

"Oh, dear," Zinnia said. "Only a Barbie doll could walk through that door."

"Not without ducking. Barbie is eleven and a half inches tall." I crouched down and used my hand, which I knew had a span of exactly eight inches, to measure the height of the opening. "Ten inches," I said, and then, "Doctor, the cervix has dilated to ten inches." I stood up, grinning. "Get it? Cervix is another word for *neck*, as in *opening*."

Zinnia gave me a quick nod and rubbed her chin thoughtfully. "And the book you've been calling the Monster Manual is still inside your room, hiding in the closet?"

"It flew right in, like a bat, and started sulking," I said. "Let's witch up some spellcraft! Tell me you have a spell to make my house behave. Or a spell to bash a new doorway through the wall. Maybe right here." I rubbed my hands in eager anticipation. "A magical sledgehammer, if you will."

She dug around in her purse, pulled out what appeared to be a three-hundred-page paperback mystery novel, and knelt by the room's entrance. She opened the tiny door with a tiny creak and then pushed through the paperback. As the book disappeared from sight, I heard fluttering, the sound of pages flapping, and then silence. I took a step back and watched for a sign.

The door didn't get bigger. The wall didn't open up. The only thing that I noticed was my stomach shifting food around just enough that I considered the possibility I might be hungry again at some point in the future.

After a minute of nothing, I asked, "Is it one of those things that doesn't happen if you're watching?"

My aunt patted the wall. "Zara, we won't be doing anything to counteract the powerful magic of your house. A smart witch knows better than to take on a task at which she will certainly fail."

I groaned. "That's the weakest thing I've ever heard. You can't preemptively quit something just because you think you'll fail." I rapped on the wall with my fist. "Bust this wall down, Aunt Zinnia. I know you can do it!"

Shaking her head, she turned and headed to the stairs.

I followed her downstairs, asking, "Why'd you feed my bedroom another book?"

"I wasn't *feeding* the house. What I did was for the benefit of your new book."

"Oh! Like cloning a hard drive. You're making a copy?"

"Not at all. That wasn't even a magical book. It's just a mystery paperback, for company."

"Your master plan was to give my Monster Manual a little buddy?"

"Magical volumes get lonely if they're on their own too long. They have nothing to do but talk to themselves, and they become rather mad."

"Rather mad," I repeated.

She looked at me as though I was choosing to be dense just to annoy her.

"Yes, Zara," she said. "Lonely books can become quite mad."

"*We're all mad here,*" I said in a low, booming voice, quoting the Cheshire cat from Alice in Wonderland. "*I'm mad. You're mad.*"

Zinnia stopped at the foot of the stairwell and quoted Alice. "*How do you know I'm mad?*"

"*You must be,*" I said, using the cat's voice, "*or you wouldn't have come here.*"

Zinnia smiled. "Very clever," she said. "Since we can't examine the book today, grab your purse and accompany me on an errand."

"Is it a *mad* errand?"

"Let's find out."

"Purse!" I cast the spell to locate my purse and also have it come to me. After having to restrain myself and not use my powers all morning, my Witch Tongue was snappy, and my purse flung itself at me with enough force to send me reeling into my aunt's arms.

"Life with you is never dull," she said as she caught me, which I decided to take as a compliment.

And off we went on her errand, which would turn out to be quite a mad errand after all.

CHAPTER 18

"Zara, don't sulk. It's unbecoming."

I pointed to my face. "If you think this is sulking, you need to spend more time around a teenager."

Zinnia gave me an exasperated look before returning her attention to the road ahead. We were in her car, driving to her friend Tansy's house.

We'd been talking about the Riddle family and its many secrets. Zinnia had told me the truth about my mother earlier that day, but what if I'd never asked? Would she have ever brought it up?

"I've tried my best to balance my privacy with what's in your best interests," Zinnia said tiredly, her eyes on the road. "If you must know, I found it terribly difficult to divulge my secrets to you and your daughter."

"It didn't seem that difficult from my perspective. We bumped into each other at the shoe store, then you came over for dinner, where you dropped all sorts of hints about curses and such—which I should have paid far more attention to now that I think about it. Then the ghost of Winona Vander Zalm electrocuted me with the toaster, and when I woke up, I was at your house, and my daughter was fawning over your book collection. She breathlessly informed me that we are all witches. I had to hear it from my barely-sixteen-year-old daughter, not even straight from my mentor. You showed everything to Zoey while I was circling the drain. I could have died. You didn't even take me to a hospital."

"You were in no danger of dying."

"Not that time, anyway."

She stared straight ahead at the road. There was a chill in the air that didn't come from the car's air conditioning alone. Observing her stiff posture gave me a twinge of guilt. Zinnia was right about one thing. I did continually bring up that time she accidentally killed me.

"Secrets are bad," I said. "I'm part fox shifter, and I had no idea. What if I suddenly turn into a fox one day? Will I be stuck that way forever if I don't have any training in how to turn back? That's no way to live a life. No offense to foxes, but it's no way for me to live my life. People deserve to know what they are."

"I didn't know your father was a fox," she answered coolly. "Don't misdirect your anger at me."

"Fair enough," I said. "Do you think my mother slept with him as part of renouncing her powers? Or to get back at her family?"

"Probably the latter," Zinnia said with a chuckle. "It's a shame she took so many secrets to her grave."

To her grave. The words echoed in my head.

She slowed the car as we turned onto a gravel road. We had entered the nicest, richest quarter of Wisteria. This area connected onto Pacific Spirit Park and resembled the countryside with its large estates, ample lots covered in trees, and driveways so long you couldn't see the houses from the main road. Most of the driveways were blocked with gates and had multiple signs warning against trespassing.

"Your friend Tansy must be rich," I said. "Good for her. Assuming she pays her fair share of taxes."

"Oh, Zara. Please don't say anything like that when you meet her. I beg of you."

The estates were getting larger, judging by the distance between gated driveways.

"How rich is she? Is she swimming-pool rich? I should have brought my bathing suit. Wait." I reached in under my shirt. "Maybe I'm already wearing it. I haven't done laundry in a while."

My aunt made a disapproving sound.

"Nope," I reported after getting a good feel. "You'll be happy to know I'm wearing regular underwear. At least on the top."

"Tansy doesn't have a pool."

"What a waste of being rich!"

My aunt frowned. "I regret bringing you with me on this errand."

"What are we doing, anyway? Are you buying some weird magic herbs?"

"Probably not. Tansy had some greenhouse issues, and she lost some crops recently. It sounded like perhaps a magical creature broke in and ate everything."

"Like a giant glowing, radioactive bunny rabbit?"

My aunt shot me a frustrated look. "Must everything be a joke to you?"

I shrugged. "When you won't tell me stuff, I have to make up my own explanations. I wish there was a library just for magical resources, and I could go in and check out books whenever I wanted. Like Hogwarts, but for real."

"There used to be something like that, but the elders felt it wasn't safe to have so much power concentrated."

"Did those same elders volunteer to keep the books for safekeeping?"

She didn't answer.

"Figured as much," I said with a snort. I should have let the issue go, but my librarian side kicked in. "Knowledge belongs to the people. I'm all for the ownership rights of the individual but not when it holds back the academic and social advancement of the larger community."

"Your beliefs are admirable," my witch mentor said. "But you must understand that there are good reasons for those with powers to keep their secrets."

"It's always just two reasons. Money and power."

She winced. "You've heard of stealth wealth, right?"

"Sure. It's people with Old Money, who don't flash it around like the *nouveau riche* do, with their tacky McMansions and driveways full of brand-new Lamborghinis."

"Yes and no," she said. "With stealth wealth, the money doesn't have to be old, but the established families do have more practice. By keeping their wealth private, they don't have to worry about certain grim realities, such as having their school-age children kidnapped for ransom."

I sat up straighter in the passenger seat. In a flash, I'd recalled another of my one-day adventures with my father. He'd introduced me to one of his business associates. The young man was nondescript in every way, except for the contents of his beat-up green backpack.

I told Zinnia the whole story. "There must have been a million dollars' worth of gemstones in that ratty old bag," I said.

"A million dollars," she mused. "That's a lot of money. But let me ask you a question, and don't answer until you've given it some thought. Is a million dollars more or less than the value you would you place on your witch powers?"

I fell quiet. I hadn't considered assigning a monetary value to what I could do.

My mother hadn't valued witchcraft at all.

It had to depend on the individual, and what they planned to do with their powers. I liked using mine to chop vegetables without using my hands. That was worth about twenty bucks a week. Multiplied over the rest of my lifetime, that would be... significantly less than a million dollars.

I wandered down the rabbit hole of possibilities. If I wanted to monetize my powers, it could be done, but every dollar earned would open me to more risk, and not the kind you could get business insurance for.

"It's hard to put a dollar value on magic," I admitted.

"But if the wrong people found out about your abilities, you'd find out their value in a hurry." She let out a witchy cackle. "You'd have to protect your family. It would be private schools and armed bodyguards for Zoey, and I don't think she'd appreciate that."

I crossed my arms over my chest. "I don't like this mental exercise. I'm not sure how someone else would benefit from my powers."

"Use your imagination," Zinnia said. "Let's say you needed to fill your own backpack with gemstones. What would you do?"

"Is there a spell to make gemstones out of rocks?"

"Be more creative."

"I guess I could use my telekinetic powers to steal them. I could rob every museum and bank in town without lifting a finger. I could funnel jewelry through the air and out the building's mail slot." I smiled and quickly added, "But I never would."

"You *say* you wouldn't, but what if kidnappers had your daughter and demanded a sack of emeralds and rubies in exchange for her?"

"Then I'd phone you immediately and drag you into my mess, because you *love it* when I do that." I gave her a huge grin.

She chuckled. "I do believe that's exactly what you'd do. And then I'd have no choice but to help you pull off the greatest jewel heist of all time."

I turned to study her profile. "Aunt Zinnia, what do you do for a living, anyway?"

She laughed off my question, as she always did. Unlike me with my library job, my aunt didn't have anywhere she needed to be on weekdays, yet she was always very busy.

"Here we are," she said, stopping the car. She got out and walked toward a pair of wrought-iron gates blocking our way down Tansy's driveway. She began untangling the chain holding them closed, ignoring all the KEEP OUT signs.

Zinnia was focused on the chain, with her head down, so she didn't see the two dark shapes approaching.

Running toward her, on the other side of the gate, were two of the biggest dogs I'd ever seen. By the looks of their bared fangs, they weren't coming to beg for a dog biscuit.

Zinnia got the chain free of the gates. Without looking up at the approaching monster dogs, she began pushing the gate open. I yelled for her to look out, but my voice was muffled by the closed windows of the car. She didn't acknowledge hearing me.

The dogs were only twenty feet away now, and running at top speed.

As I pushed the car door open, I simultaneously used my magic to grab hold of the wrought-iron gates and keep them shut.

Zinnia muttered under her breath, "Rusty old things." I detected a spell being woven, counter to my own. My arms trembled, and the gates flew open.

"Zinnia!"

She turned toward me, her back to the dogs.

"Behind you!"

They were almost upon her.

I cast a motion disruption spell at the dogs. It was a new one for me, and I hadn't practiced it on anything bigger than a falling teacup. My telekinesis was only as strong as my body, and what I could move myself, but the motion disruption spell was more powerful. It could, in theory, be used to stop a moving vehicle or at least redirect it. Would it work on a pair of dogs? Purple sparks arced through the air from my fingertips to the enormous beasts. They passed through untouched, without a falter in their steps.

Since I couldn't move the dogs, I did the only thing I could. I focused all my telekinetic strength and wrapped it around Zinnia. It took everything in me to tug her straight up into the air.

Her feet left the ground, and she rose up two inches.

It was working!

And then she cast a counterspell, whipping my spell off.

The recoil sent me reeling backward.

She touched down on the ground and gave me a stunned, annoyed look.

And then the two enormous dogs tackled her.

CHAPTER 19

THE DOGS THAT had looked so vicious were surprisingly ineffective at ripping my aunt from limb to limb. She didn't even cry out. The duo split up, and one came for me.

The shadow that fell upon me blotted out the sky. I shot blue lightning from my palms, but the streams of blue light arced through the shadow, touching nothing. Fangs were flashing, but they didn't connect. Was my motion disruption spell working after all? Was this the effect it had on living creatures?

The shadow dog continued its ineffective attack. You could say the dark beast was "all bark, no bite," except it didn't even bark. The attack was silent. Eerily silent.

The only sound was my wheezing, my effort to catch my breath. The recoil from my aunt's counterspell had tossed me on the ground next to the car. Either the spell or the fall had knocked the wind out of my lungs.

Zinnia didn't react to the shadow dogs. She did look around to see what I'd been shooting blue fireballs at. With her feet spread apart in a warrior's stance, she seemed to be guarding the open iron gates. Her tight leggings showed off her musculature. Even pushing fifty, she was formidable, like a red-haired superhero. One of the gates squeaked in the breeze. Other than my own labored breathing, there was no sound.

The shadow dog who'd jumped on me now stood on my rib cage. It weighed nothing.

Zinnia stayed where she was, still in her superhero pose. The fringed end of her corded belt swung slowly, like a pendulum.

She asked in a low tone, "Zara, what is the threat?"

"Ghost dogs," I said, my voice raspy from having the wind knocked out of me. "If you can't see them, I guess they're ghosts, not holograms."

Zinnia whispered a spell and swept one hand in an intriguing gesture. In a low tone, she replied, "No living threats here. Not now, anyway."

A threat detection spell? I needed to learn that soon. I pushed myself up onto my elbows. The shadow dog on my chest jumped off lazily. The other dog stayed by Zinnia's side. It was either licking or biting her left arm.

"Zinnia, the dog is touching your left arm. Do you feel anything?"

She looked from one arm to the other. "Are you sure? I don't sense anything." She rubbed her left arm. "Maybe a slight coolness."

The dogs blurred when they moved. They were a similar size, and either a mixed breed or a type I wasn't familiar with. Both wore red leather collars with no identifying tags.

Zinnia walked over to help me to my feet. Her hand was dry and hot. Touching it sent a jolt through me—like that time my friend got me to stir two pots at once on her grandmother's ungrounded stove, and I got an electrical shock. Or that time Winona Vander Zalm nearly killed me with a toaster. I yanked my hand back, grazing my elbow on the dirt road.

My aunt apologized, whispered something to her palms, spat on both of them, and extended her hand again.

I didn't take her hand. "No offense, but I'm not interested in becoming Spit Sisters with you." I pushed myself upright on my own, groaning. "You really gave me a good wallop with your counter spell."

"You'll be fine," she said with a sigh. "If you need a bandage, ask Tansy for one when we get to the house. I certainly don't need your blood on my car upholstery. Even a couple of drops of witch blood can cause an infestation of bloodweevils."

I checked my elbow. Thanks to my self-healing powers, my fresh scrape was already covered in a pink layer of skin cells.

"Your concern for me is touching," I said sarcastically. "Dial it back, or you're going to make me cry."

"Your injury is your own fault," she snapped. "Ghost dogs or not, you shouldn't have performed spellwork on me without my consent."

"Oh, no you don't." I bobbed my head from side to side. "This is not my fault. The first spell I did was to hold the gates closed. I tried to keep the gates closed so I could warn you. If someone's falling in front of a bus, you yank them out of harm's way. You don't lecture them about the importance of looking both ways before crossing the street."

She pursed her lips. "Is that so?"

"Listen. If you actually trusted me, you would have turned around for an explanation about the gates. But oh, no. You had to prove a point. You're *so much stronger* than me. Fine. I get it. But you didn't need to bash through the gates like a battering ram and then knock me on my butt."

"My counterspell may have been an overreaction," she replied coolly. "Even so, your spell was the wrong tactical decision."

I wiped the road dirt off my legs and shorts. "No way. I did the best I could with my limited knowledge of novice spells. The *real* problem is you don't trust my judgment." I pointed at her emphatically. "I did something unexpected, and your first assumption was that I was wrong. You had to cancel me out because you assumed I was... What? Just messing around?"

"Yes," she said with a certainty that made me think she'd been waiting for me to ask that very question. "Because you are *almost always* messing around, Zara. You choose to play the fool when you should be paying attention. Is it any wonder trouble keeps finding you? And can you really blame me for not taking you seriously?"

I looked down at the two ghost dogs. Both were calm now, silently watching us. Two dark shadow dog heads tilted sideways in confusion. Human beings were so strange! But the dogs were also strange, especially the way they sat, with their non-corporeal bodies partly merged.

One or the other wasn't aware of its own ghost physics, and so they were overlapping in space, their bodies conjoining.

"Get her," I told the dogs. "Bite that lady. Bite her right on the a—"

"Zara!"

"Absolutely fabulous buttocks," I finished.

She tugged her flowered tunic down over her hips. "That's what I get for trying to dress in a more youthful manner."

One of the dogs stood and began pacing, crossing through the other ghost dog, which set off mute barks of alarm.

"The dogs are pacing around," I said. "Does your associate Tansy always send a couple of ghost dogs to greet visitors?"

"Not ghost dogs." She followed my gaze and turned to where the ghost dogs were pacing. "Jasper and Coco, is that you? Jasper? Coco?"

Four dark ears perked up.

"They heard you," I reported. "And by the wagging of their tails, you got their names right."

"Oh, dear," she said. "That's not a good sign. Are they still here?"

"Yes. They're milling through each other's non-corporeal bodies. Now they're jumping through each other, trying to get petted, I think."

Zinnia put out her hand and petted the air. The dogs arranged themselves to share the space under her hand. This petting seemed to satisfy them. I gave her a running commentary of what they were doing.

"I've never seen animal ghosts before," I said. "Which was probably for the best, since I'm not vegetarian." I shuddered at the thought of every chicken I'd eaten following me around, seeking closure before moving on to the Next Great Barnyard.

After a minute of petting the ghost dogs she couldn't see, Zinnia turned away from me. She pulled a tissue from her purse and wiped at her eyes. When she turned back, her eyes were gleaming, but her expression was composed.

"The ghost dogs are more than a dark omen," I said.

She nodded. "Jasper and Coco were both alive and well the last time I came out to meet with Tansy. It was that day several weeks back, when you saw me bottling herbs in my kitchen. Speaking of which, I don't know what you said to my Black Startwists, but they've been misbehaving ever since."

I'd used the plant for free talk therapy one night, but she didn't need to know that.

"I plead the fifth," I said.

"Zara, you must not touch, poke, or otherwise agitate magical ingredients. Magic has a mind of its own, and magical items are not to be taunted."

"What should we do about these ghost dogs? They're still pacing." The ghost dogs appeared to be agitated, perhaps by a nearby threat. I couldn't see or hear anything in the trees and foliage.

"Whatever it was, it's already happened," Zinnia said. "Tansy's beloved dogs never left her side." She paused dramatically. "Something dreadful has happened to poor Tansy."

We both looked at the winding driveway ahead of us.

"Time to call the police," I said, pulling out my phone. "Or not." I stopped short of pressing the numbers. What was I going to report? A sighting of two big ghost dogs that only I could see? Detective Bentley would love that.

Zinnia must have been having the same train of thought. "We need to check the grounds ourselves," she said solemnly.

CHAPTER 20

UNDER BETTER CIRCUMSTANCES, I would have enjoyed touring the lush country estate's grounds.

Tansy had a sprawling collection of potting sheds, gardens, and greenhouses. There were many interesting oddities, including one circular garden dedicated to left-handed snails. The condition of being a left-handed snail is extremely rare. On slow news days, newspapers run articles about the plight of some lonely left-handed snail who is unable to find a mate without boarding an international flight with a wingman human.

My aunt and I discussed this, and she said, "Who knew snails were so picky about mating?"

"It's not a case of being too picky," I said. "And it's not prejudice, like shifters and witches."

"I wouldn't expect so. They're just snails. But why can't the left-handed ones mate with the ones whose shells swirl the regular way?"

"I'm glad you asked! It's because the organs necessary for mating are over on the wrong side, and nothing matches up." I used my hands to make some crude mating gestures.

My aunt cast her gaze up to the blue sky. "Oh, Zara. Thank you *so much* for that particular visual."

"You asked," I said. "If snail love makes you nervous, don't look too closely at that gurgling fountain up ahead. By the look of the snails gathered around the rim, the fountain puts them in an amorous mood."

Shaking her head, she walked past me out of the garden.

I chased after her. "Actually, calling these snails *left-handed* is a bit of a misnomer. A human being with the equivalent of the same genetic mutation would have their organs completely reversed, with the heart on the right-hand side."

She picked up her pace.

I called out, "Fun fact: the human heart actually sits in the *center* of your chest, in between your lungs. It's only tilted slightly to the left. Your pancreas, however, is on the left."

The ghost dogs bounded after her as she approached a small wooden shed with an adjoining pen enclosed in chicken wire.

I caught up with her and asked, "Does Tansy raise chickens?"

Zinnia opened the door to the wooden shed. "Not anymore," she said.

The shed held only empty nest boxes and a few loose feathers. Out in the open-air pen, there was a scattering of chicken feed on the ground that hadn't been taken away by smaller birds or wild rodents.

"The chickens disappeared recently," I noted. "But I don't see any chicken ghosts roaming around, if that's of any comfort." And then, with optimism, "Maybe they busted out and flew away?"

"Perhaps." Zinnia closed the door to the chicken shed even though doing so was pointless, now that the chickens were gone. We moved on to the next building.

It was another greenhouse, not unlike the first few we'd toured, and this one was also empty of plants, except for the ground, which was covered in a smooth carpet of green leaves.

Zinnia knelt and examined the leaves. "This is a ground-cover plant I don't recognize."

"Let's call it shag," I said, because it was soft underfoot, like shag carpet.

Zinnia dug through the shaggy leaves and picked up something gray and stick-like. "What does this look like to you?"

I walked over to get a closer look. "That's a chicken bone," I said. "Specifically, the drumstick."

"Tansy's chickens didn't fly away." Zinnia frowned at the drumstick. "She had a dozen hens."

"I guess we're up to a death toll of fourteen. Two dogs and a coop full of chickens."

"And Tansy makes fifteen," she said softly.

"Don't say that yet. We don't know for sure."

"What was the description Rhys gave you? For the creature that attacked him on Wednesday? We're not far from Pacific Spirit Park."

"He said it was a flying creature. A giant winged beast, black, with razor-sharp talons. He also said it was snarling. Not cawing or hissing but snarling."

"That could be any number of things."

"Or it could have been purely imaginary," I said. "He probably had an accomplice give him a non-fatal wound."

"That's a possibility," she said softly.

I kicked at the green leaves. I didn't like the way the ground-cover plant was undulating around my sandals, tickling my toes.

Still holding the chicken drumstick, Zinnia stood up. "Where are the dogs now?"

I'd gotten used to the silent black pooches and hadn't been tracking them closely, so I had to look around.

"They're back at the entrance to this greenhouse," I said. "They're sitting obediently on the outside. They must have been trained to stay out of this building."

As I turned my head back toward my aunt, a glinting flash overhead caught my eye. A metallic object hung from the apex of the greenhouse, glittering like a disco ball in the sunshine. Except it wasn't a disco ball. It was a hand-held gardening tool. A small, pointed shovel. A trowel. Why had Tansy hung a trowel all the way up there? It must have been a personal joke or some gardening superstition.

"Coco, Jasper, come here," Zinnia called.

I turned to watch the shadow ghost dogs. "Their ears perked up at their names," I reported. "But they're not coming in."

"They must be afraid of whatever got to the chickens." She put the bone into her purse. "The creature must have been an omnivore, because it also consumed whatever plants Tansy was growing in here." She looked up and squinted at the brightness coming through the clear, corrugated plastic roof. "This is Tansy's best greenhouse, for her most valuable crops."

"Something ate tasty chickens on a bed of greens," I said. "Sounds like a Chicken Caesar. Now we just need to find the crouton crumbs and the empty vat of Caesar salad dressing, and the mystery will be solved."

Zinnia nearly smiled. "Chicken Caesar? That sounds exactly like something Tansy would say. The longer she lived on her own out here, the stranger her sense of humor became. Is she here now? Inside you?"

"Oh, please. That was a good joke, and I came up with it all on my own."

"If you say so." She led the way out of the greenhouse and toward the one building we hadn't searched yet—Tansy's house. We'd knocked on the door earlier but hadn't gone inside yet. We'd been hoping to find Tansy in her garden. Alive.

My aunt tried the door. "Unlocked," she said. "Do you hear anything?"

We stood on the front step, listening. You'd think the countryside would be quiet, but it's not. I heard the bumbling buzz of honeybees, distant croaking frogs, gurgling water from the snail fountain, water rushing in a nearby creek, as well as the songs of several birds. The air was fragrant with roses, both wild and cultivated.

My aunt pushed the door to the house open with a creak.

"Tansy, it's Zinnia Riddle," she called out. "I'm coming inside with my niece, Zara. I've told you about her."

"All good things, I hope."

She didn't comment. The dark shadow dogs, Jasper and Coco, came running at top speed as though someone had called them for dinner. They had no physical form to knock me down, which was a good thing, or I'd have been sent sprawling for the second time that day.

My aunt stepped into the house, and I followed, keeping my senses on high alert for a monster that had recently eaten a dozen chickens plus two dogs, a monster who might be feeling peckish for a pair of redheaded witches.

CHAPTER 21

TANSY'S HOUSE WAS decrepit by today's standards, but sixty years ago, it might have been featured in glossy architectural magazines. The furnishings were well worn but loved. A classic leather-and-wood Eames lounger sat in front of a picture window. Judging by the condition of the tattered leather, the reclining chair had been Tansy's favorite place to sit.

Zinnia led the way, calling out for Tansy as we methodically checked every room. My aunt didn't say it, but we both knew we were looking for a body.

Our search took a solid twenty minutes and concluded in the kitchen. We'd checked every room and closet. We'd even looked inside the woman's laundry hamper. There'd been no blood or sign of foul play. The only thing suspicious was Tansy's absence and the two ghost dogs.

I wandered over to the dining room table. Some opened letters caught my eye, and I felt a shudder of dread. *Bills!* I should have averted my eyes immediately, the way I did at my own house.

Zinnia also saw the mail and went right to the stack. "Tansy would want me to understand what's happening here," she said, and she began reading.

I joined her at the table and took a seat. My feet had gotten hot from all the walking in the summer sunshine. I pushed down the straps at the backs of my heels and loosened my sandals.

Zinnia pushed half the mail over to me, and we began our investigation.

Tansy's bills were up to date, but there were several other letters that painted a clear picture. A property development firm wanted to purchase Tansy's land, and they weren't taking no for an answer. They'd started months earlier by making offers at assessed value. More recently, they'd doubled the offer. The most recent letter had a more sinister tone and alluded to calling in authorities to investigate everything from zoning infractions to unauthorized growth of controlled substances on the property.

When we were done, my aunt stacked the papers into a neat pile. She looked me in the eyes and tented her fingers thoughtfully. The air inside the house was stagnant. Sitting down with loosened sandals hadn't cooled me down at all. My mouth was gummy, my face felt sticky, and my antiperspirant had given up on its life's purpose.

My body had recovered from the tumble outside, but I felt light-headed, and there was a tickling at the back of my neck, as though I was being watched. The tickling on my neck turned into something else, something like a Popsicle being pressed against the back of my hot neck.

The chill became more pronounced. Something was at my back.

"Zinnia," I whispered, careful not to make any sudden movements. "I believe there's a ghost behind me."

"Probably you-know-who," she said, careful to omit Tansy's name.

"What should I do? Should I invite her inside my head or try to communicate with her the way I did with the dogs?"

Zinnia slowly reached for her purse. She pulled out two cotton balls plus an unmarked plastic bottle. "No, no, not that one," she muttered to herself. She exchanged the bottle for a tube, not unlike a toothpaste tube but with no label. She deftly squeezed lavender-hued goop onto the cotton balls.

"Put these up your nostrils," she said.

I took the lavender-soaked cotton and did as I was told. She didn't fully trust me, but I trusted her.

The cotton balls had smelled pleasant enough, but once I got them fitted into my nostrils, it was a different story. Had the cotton turned into a furry creature that was experiencing violent stomach flu inside my nostrils?

I gagged noisily.

"Try not to inhale through your nostrils," she said.

I opened my mouth to breathe more easily, but that seemed to oxidize the scent and make it even worse.

"What is this?" I couldn't stop gagging. "Concentrated *eau de halitosis*?"

"More or less," she said.

"From what creature?"

"You don't want to know." She motioned for me to turn around. "Is it her? Do you see Tansy?"

I turned around to find a woman standing behind me. I had already known, on some level, that she was there, but I was still shocked. I startled in my chair and made a non-verbal sound like HRBBBBRRR. That's the sort of thing you say when you see a ghost lady behind you, even if she looks pleasant enough.

Zinnia asked, "What do you see? Tell me everything, but you must keep your mouth as closed as possible while you talk."

"Why?"

She sent a wave of light and energy at my chin. The energy locked onto my jaw and held it up, effectively wiring my mouth shut.

"You can talk," she said. "But don't let your mouth open any larger than a nostril, or she'll slip in."

Through a narrow crack in my lips, I said, "I'm not a ventriloquist." And then, "Hey, not bad," because my enunciation hadn't been bad at all.

Tansy's spirit stood motionless, her eyes unfocused. She had the what-did-I-come-to-this-room-for look on her face.

Careful to keep my lips close together, I asked my aunt, "What about my ears?"

"Spirits travel on breath," she said.

I nodded. That answered my next question about areas that might need protecting.

Doing my ventriloquist impression, I described the ghost before me. Tansy was about eighty percent opaque, like the dogs, but she had light skin and wore light clothes, so her transparency was more obvious. I'd seen photographs of Tansy upstairs, so I had no doubt the ghost was her.

Tansy's face was deeply lined, and her hair was as gray as mine was red. Her clothes were shades of green, but the details were hard to distinguish. When I tried to focus on her clothing, her blouse shifted to a T-shirt and then a blouse of a different style. A clear view of her attire was always out of reach, like the end of a rainbow as you approach. Her face, however, stayed crisp and clear. Tansy was Caucasian, with a weather-beaten oval face, light-blue watery eyes, thin gray eyebrows, and an equally thin yet crooked nose. Her gray hair hung down past her waist, as though it hadn't ever been cut. She wore two pairs of glasses—one on the high bridge of her nose and another on top of her head.

When I was done describing her, my aunt spoke with a sad sniff. "That's Tansy, all right. People in Wisteria mistook her for a homeless person at times. She was a walking contradiction, as brilliant and sharp as she was absentminded. One time, I saw her put on a pair of glasses in front of the pair she was already wearing." Another sniff. "What's she doing now? Is she trying to communicate with us?"

"She's looking at the stack of mail on the table. Now she's moving." I turned on my chair to watch as the ghost of Tansy walked around the table to the mail. She put her translucent hand through the letters and paused, frowning. Then she glanced around.

I described this to Zinnia, who replied, "She can't see us. We must be on different planes. They slip around, which is why the dogs could see us. Time moves differently between the realm of the living and the in-between."

"Are you saying there's a plane of existence with a dozen chicken ghosts wandering around?"

"It's possible."

Tansy continued swiping at the mail, apparently unaware of us.

I reached for the putrid cotton balls that were still jammed in my nostrils. "If she can't see us, I'm pulling out these plugs before my brain turns into Blue Stilton cheese."

"Don't," she barked.

I dropped my hands reluctantly.

She explained, "Just so you know, that barrier compound is not bacterial in nature. I'd be very surprised if you could make cheese with it." She paused. "However, it could come in handy for certain kinds of sauerkraut."

"Here we go," I said. "Tansy's on the move again." I described how she was puttering around her kitchen as though preparing a meal. None of the objects she reached for moved, but she didn't seem to notice.

We observed her for several minutes. My eyes began watering from the scent of the gooey cotton balls in my nostrils. I wiped away the tears as they came down my cheeks.

Was I crying? I'd thought my eyes were watering from the tincture, but there was also a heaviness in my chest. The ghost before me had recently been a living, breathing person, with gardens to water and dogs to feed. She'd lived a long life, but she'd been taken too soon. She wouldn't have lingered around as a ghost if she'd gone peacefully.

I'd never met the woman, and watching her toss back her long gray hair while she puttered around her kitchen felt like a violation of her privacy. I felt guilty, as though I'd stolen something from her. *Survivor's guilt.* I was still alive, and she was not.

Tansy's translucent hand passed over the microwave's control panel. Suddenly, the appliance came to life. The buzzing fan and gleaming yellow light filled the kitchen. The ghost had apparently turned it on. I turned to my aunt, whose cheeks were paler than usual. She was delicately blowing her nose.

"She turned on the microwave," I said through tight lips. Zinnia's jaw-wiring spell had faded, so I had to remember to keep my chin up on my own.

"Spirits can manipulate electricity," Zinnia said. "As for the how and the why, I'm afraid you'll have to find a physicist who believes in magic to explain it to you."

"Do you think she's trying to communicate with us?"

"Through the microwave? We ought to consider the possibility." She squinted at the microwave's control panel without getting up from her chair. "Forty-five seconds. Now forty-four. Forty-three."

We waited in silence for the next forty-two seconds, until the microwave finished with a beep.

The noise seemed to startle Tansy. She whipped her head around, gray hair swinging, then left her kitchen on soundless feet and peered out of the picture window by the recliner nervously. She was fading. Down to fifty percent opacity and then forty percent. I reported this to my aunt, noting that my lips were getting tired from staying in ventriloquist mode.

She faded to ten percent, looked up to the vaulted ceiling, and disappeared entirely.

"Now she's gone," I said. I rubbed my jaw and yawned. My whole body was stiff, as though I'd been on a road trip for the past five hours. We couldn't have been sitting at Tansy's table for more than thirty minutes, but I'd been tense ever since she'd appeared. Time can move strangely on our own plane of existence as well.

Zinnia asked, "Are the dogs gone as well?"

"I don't see them." The two oversized dog beds were forlorn in their emptiness. A half-eaten piece of rawhide punctuated the nearer of the two. The rawhide would never be finished. Not unless whatever ate the dogs came back for a midnight snack.

Zinnia spread Tansy's mail back out in an approximation of how we'd found them.

Together, we left the house.

She was quiet on the walk back to the car. We'd left her vehicle at the gates, which were a quarter mile from the house. I had a million questions about Tansy, but I held back out of respect for my aunt's grief.

We passed the threshold of the open gates. There'd been no sign of ghosts, neither human nor dog, so she told me I could remove the cotton plugs from my nostrils.

I moaned with relief.

"You can toss the cotton balls in the bushes over there," she said. "No point in keeping them. The effectiveness wears off as the compound oxidizes."

I expected to find relief upon removal of the stinky plugs, but it was the opposite. Fresh air inside my nostrils activated the residual scent. I leaned over and spat on the ground, waiting for the nausea to pass.

After my aunt closed the gates, we got back into her car. The passenger door creaked noisily when I slid in. It felt like years had passed since I'd last been in that contoured seat.

Something moved at the corner of my vision. We weren't alone in the car. Someone was in the back seat.

I opened my mouth to tell my aunt the ghost was in the car, but I didn't get far.

The ghost's watery blue eyes locked on mine. There was a blast of light like a camera flash going off in my face. The ghost's form compressed into a glowing bead the size of a garbanzo bean and then shot into my mouth.

"Ack," I said as the ghostly garbanzo bean hit the back of my throat. "Ackakak."

"Stop with your nonsense," Zinnia said.

I coughed. "This isn't my usual nonsense," I said. "Your buddy Tansy was in the back seat, waiting for us, and now she's... You know. In me. Possessing me." I snapped my fingers. "But she hasn't taken full control over me. Not yet." I snapped my fingers some more. "And I haven't blacked out!"

My aunt gave me a hopeful, earnest look. "Tansy?"

"Still me," I said.

She nodded slowly. "We need to contact the authorities. But first I need to inform her next of kin."

"Isn't that something the police do?"

"Yes, but I need to get ahead of them. She didn't have much of a crop growing, but there are a few things that need to be cleared away before the police start stomping around. Like any wise person who deals with magical items, Tansy had a posthumous destruction plan, sort of a Living Will for people in her line of work."

"Who's her next of kin? She's not related to us, is she?"

My aunt pointed through the car's windshield at an overgrown sign. I hadn't noticed the sign on the way in, due to the fading on the letters. The sign bore a family name.

Wick.

Is her next of kin Vincent Wick? As soon as I'd wondered the question, I knew the answer, thanks to Tansy's spiritual residence inside my mind.

Her full name was Tansy Aphrodite Wick. She was the sister of my least favorite municipal employee, Vincent Wick.

CHAPTER 22

ZINNIA AND I sat in an interview room at the Wisteria Police Department, waiting for someone to come and take our missing persons report for Tansy Wick.

My aunt had already called Vincent Wick before driving away from Tansy's property. Vincent confirmed that he didn't know of his sister's whereabouts due to having not spoken to her recently. And by *recently*, he meant about five years, give or take a few months. But he didn't hesitate to help. He promised to carry out his older sister's posthumous plans, and promised he would remove all the magical herbs in the greenhouses and stored in the cellar before the police descended.

The interview room was chilly with air conditioning. The patch of skin between my knees and the seam of my shorts was all gooseflesh. I rubbed my legs and eyed the camera, which was placed prominently in the corner of the ceiling. The red recording light was off, but that didn't mean we weren't being observed. There was a one-way mirror on the wall behind the desk.

Zinnia leaned over and whispered, "Let me handle this. Not one word from you about the g-h-o-s-t."

I snorted. "If someone's listening, they're probably trained in basic spelling."

She elbowed me. I would have elbowed her back, but the woman had just lost a dear friend, whom I'd unwittingly inhaled.

The two redheads reflected in the mirror across from us shifted from left to right with matching body language of impatience. What a pair of limp flowers we were, with our faces shiny from sweating while searching Tansy's property and our shoulders drooping from the revelation of Tansy's demise. We both had a wilted appearance, like rhododendron blossoms three days past their prime.

Now I was thinking about flowers.

I leaned forward and grabbed a sketchpad and pen from the room's desk. The pad was probably intended for something other than doodling, but I had some ideas in my head that needed to be let out. I began sketching.

After a few minutes, Zinnia peered over and asked what I was drawing.

"I don't know," I said quite honestly. I held the pad away from me, like someone in need of reading glasses might do with a menu in a dimly lit restaurant. "Abstract art of some kind," I answered.

"Try again." Zinnia gently pried the notepad from my hands. "This is a top-down view of a landscape design. These circles represent trees. The big square is a house." She tilted the notepad to the right. "Your house, I believe. There are sidewalks on two sides."

I gently smacked my forehead. Once she'd pointed it out, it was so obvious. Patio design and landscaping books are some of our most popular nonfiction titles at the library, especially in the spring, when I've seen patrons barter trades with each other at the circulation desk.

"This can't be *my* house," I said. "The overgrown bushes at the back would be better represented by scribbles, or a spill of black ink." I'd been thinking about the back yard that morning while we'd been having brunch next to the bramble bushes. But I had never studied landscaping books closely. The lines of my drawings were strong and confident.

I looked into Zinnia's hazel eyes, which were glistening.

"These are Tansy's plans," I said. "Remember what Beatrizz Riddle wrote in that old Geocities posting? They want to feel useful. She said so right under point number two, what do they want?" My witch relative, whom I had never met, had written: *Spyryts wish to share their wisdom, spend more time with family and friends, or to see and do the things they enjoyed when they were alive.*

Zinnia looked at me a long time before speaking. "I suppose you're right, Zara."

I cupped my hand around my ear. "Sorry, I didn't catch that. Could you repeat it a little louder?"

"I suppose you're right, Zara." She shook her head.

A man had entered the room while she was complimenting me.

He asked, "What's Zara right about?"

I smiled up at Detective Theodore Dean Bentley.

"Wouldn't you like to know," I teased.

Zinnia elbowed me again. She must have used magic to make her elbows more sharp, because they really dug into my ribs.

* * *

Bentley took down the details for our missing persons report. He tried to downplay his interest, but he seemed excited about the case, talking more quickly by the minute.

He fixed his steely gray eyes on my aunt. "This would go a lot smoother if you told me what your friend was growing in her greenhouses."

"Not marijuana," she said.

He raised one dark eyebrow.

"I swear," she said.

He looked down at his computer screen. "Tansy Wick has been charged multiple times with possession for the purposes of trafficking. The laws are changing these days in regard to this particular cash crop, but the record remains."

"That was so many years ago," Zinnia said. "She made some mistakes in her younger days."

"As did you, from the look of these reports." Bentley tapped away at the keyboard. "Look at all these hits on your name!" He glanced over at me. I shrugged. His steely gray eyes flicked back to my aunt. "Explain yourself."

"Wrong place, wrong time," she said. "You'll note that my name is only mentioned in your reports as a witness, an innocent bystander."

"Lucky you," he said dryly.

He tapped away at the keyboard and asked a few more questions about Tansy's business associates. My aunt couldn't tell him about Tansy's secret business operation of growing magic herbs, but she did have some contacts for Tansy's legitimate cover business. For the last decade, she'd been growing specialty houseplants ranging from African violets to low-maintenance spider plants.

He was more interested in the threatening letters from the property developers.

"If it turns out something criminal has happened to your friend, we will look into all angles," he promised. "I'm familiar with that real estate development corporation. Akorn Development." He paused. "Oh, I just heard it. Akorn is like acorn, but with a K. Interesting."

Zinnia asked, "Are they dangerous?"

"Akorn Development has a few questionable practices, but I doubt they have anything to do with your friend's disappearance. They're always sending letters, but they never follow through. They're all bark, no bite."

Zinnia frowned. "But what else do you have to go on? The real estate company is the only suspect."

"Suspect," he mused. "Your friend might simply be on a trip out of town for a few days. You said yourself, you two weren't that close."

"A bad thing has happened to Tansy Wick."

"Ms. Riddle, there's something you're not telling me." His keen eyes stayed trained on her. "You know more than you're saying."

"Nothing relevant," she replied icily.

He looked at her for a long minute before speaking again. "I would imagine your niece has already informed you that I'm looking into some of this town's stranger occurrences."

Her face went as stony as the granite animals decorating a certain gorgon's yard.

He continued, "Particularly, I'm reopening some old cases involving the occult."

"I don't see what that has to do with the disappearance of Tansy Wick," she replied with a chilly tone. She was so icy that both of my forearms scrunched up with goose bumps.

"You would see if you were in my position," Bentley replied with combative, fiery warmth. "Tansy Aphrodite Wick is a name I've been coming across frequently during my review of old cases."

She shifted forward on her seat, preparing to get up. "Good. Then I expect you should be able to locate her in no time. Thank you for your help."

"Sit," he barked, then, "Stay."

Zinnia made a sound that was both high and low frequency at once. The side of my body next to my aunt buzzed with electricity. She did not appreciate being ordered around. And Bentley was being so rude to her. No wonder my attempts to set the two of them up on a date had failed. He was kind of a jerk.

With a low, growling grumble of a voice, he asked, "Zinnia Riddle, have you ever been, or are you currently, a member of a secret religious sect?"

I'd been keeping quiet for too long. My compulsion to interrupt and deflate the tension with a quippy comment was as powerful as any magic. I clenched my jaw.

My aunt lifted her chin defiantly. "That's preposterous."

"There are many reports of secret cult activities in this town."

She said nothing.

"Just as I suspected," he said.

I finally chimed in, "Oh, come on, Bentley. If she told you all about it, then it wouldn't be much of a *secret cult*, would it? You can't put the genie back in the bottle. And if word of some new secret religious sect got out, everybody would be trying to join in, like they do with fad diets whenever the reporters on TV run a story about the dangers of the latest crash diet featuring a tea made from fermented rutabaga and cinnamon sticks. If you keep asking around about monsters and the occult, you're going to find yourself in a heap of weird trouble. It's not magic, Detective. Most of what has passed for witchcraft over the centuries is simple human nature, wishful thinking, and pattern recognition. It's just the Law of Attraction. Haven't you ever read *The Secret*? We've got plenty of copies at the lib—"

Zinnia elbowed me to shut up. I leaned away from her pointy elbow and shut my mouth.

Bentley sniffed the air. "Speaking of crash diet teas, what is that putrid smell?" He looked up at an air vent on the ceiling. "Something must have crawled into the air ducts and expired."

I rubbed the tip of my nose guiltily. I'd used a tissue in the car to wipe out my nostrils, but the stinky ghost-barrier compound wasn't going away without a fight.

Zinnia got to her feet, tugging my arm so I did the same.

Bentley also stood and walked around the desk to the door with surprising speed.

In a professional, authoritative voice, he said, "Ladies, I will contact you if I have any more questions."

"Don't bother calling unless you have an update," Zinnia said. She shot me a quick look and then, weaving spellwork between her words, she added, "Detective Bentley, you *will* keep us informed about your search for Tansy Wick. You will call us daily with regular updates. This case will be your *top priority*."

His gray irises shone like liquid silver briefly before returning to normal. Her spell had taken hold.

"The Tansy Wick case is my top priority," he said evenly.

She gave him a curt nod and continued toward the door.

"Wait," he said. "Your boots."

All three of us looked down at Zinnia's boots. I'd been wearing sandals all day, but Zinnia wore old-fashioned boots that matched a few pairs I had at home. They had an all-leather upper with old-fashioned laces, combined with a sensible yet snappy heel. When I'd been a teenager, we'd called the style Granny Boots. My daughter called them our *Anne of Green Gables* boots.

Zinnia tapped her pointed toe impatiently. "What *about* my boots?"

"Never mind," he said. "Your boots reminded me of someone, I think, but I already forgot what I was going to say. I forget…"

I grabbed my aunt's forearm and gave her a meaningful look. "Detective Bentley is dating a woman who wears boots like yours." I flashed my eyes at her. "And also like the person who paid the vet bill for the fox on Wednesday."

Bentley asked, "What vet bill? You said you didn't have a fox."

"Inside joke," I said, weaving in my own bluffing spell. Mine wasn't as powerful as my aunt's, but I could count on it to boost my lie. "There's no fox, silly. You know me. I'm always joking around."

He kept giving me a suspicious look.

"Tell us more about this new lady friend of yours," I said, pushing more of the spell his way. "What does she look like, other than the boots?"

His eyes got a faraway look. "She's indescribable," he answered.

"Don't be silly," Zinnia snapped. "You're not a victim in a Lovecraft tale. Tell us what she looks like."

Her command was so powerful, I felt compelled to describe the woman myself. "Leather boots," I whispered before I caught control of myself.

Neither of them reacted to what I'd said.

Bentley's face grew red. A croak came out of his mouth. "She's indescribable," he wheezed. "I can't."

Zinnia nodded. "Very well, then. Thank you for trying." She grabbed my hand and tugged me to follow her.

We sped out of his office and all the way out of the police station.

Once we were outside, I asked, "What was that all about? With the indescribable woman?"

"I would tell you if I knew," she said, breathing heavily and glancing back over her shoulder. "Someone else has been enchanting that man."

"He could be *more* enchanting," I quipped. "He can be so rude. And arrogant."

"Someone is intruding upon our affairs."

"Someone who wears our boots." I leaned back and gave her a sidelong look. "Are you sure you haven't been dating ol' Teddy Bear Bentley in secret?"

She blinked rapidly. "So secret that I don't even know?" Her brow wrinkled.

"I do things I don't remember when a ghost takes over. Maybe you've got a secret personality who's been dating Bentley."

The wrinkles on her brow smoothed out. "You're being ridiculous," she said. "It's far more likely that whoever got to Tansy has also gotten to the local police."

"Do you suppose my father's involved? It can't be a coincidence that he showed up right as Tansy disappeared."

"Rhys Quarry may be a lot of things, but he'd never harm a woman."

"How can you be sure? You didn't even know he was a shifter."

She looked down at the sidewalk. "But..." Her mouth twitched, but no more words came.

I rubbed the goose bumps on my forearms. The sunshine was warm on my skin, but the air conditioning inside the police department had sunk into my bones.

Was it Tansy's spirit that was causing the chill? I felt for her and sensed only stillness. She'd been quiet since moving into my head, providing little beyond her full name and relation to Vincent Wick.

With my previous ghosts, they'd responded to the familiar. Winona Vander Zalm showed up when I had a cocktail in my hand and a house full of guests. Perry Pressman was a penny pincher who'd gotten excited about my online bill payments. Chessa had manifested when I was in or near water. Or Chet.

Tansy Wick loved her quiet country life, her dogs, and her plants.

There weren't any dogs nearby, but there were some planter boxes stationed around the entryway to the police department. I walked over to one and perched on the concrete rim.

Zinnia said, "Good idea. Let's sit and think."

"I'm going to try summoning Tansy," I said, and I explained my line of thinking.

"That's a bad idea," she said. "We're in public, Zara. What if she takes over your body and does something unexpected?"

"You're here," I said. "I know you could work my body like a marionette if you wanted to. And if that doesn't work, you can force-feed me some of those pills you mashed into Frank's mouth that day."

She shook her head, but she didn't try to talk me out of it.

I turned toward the leafy green plants in the box and touched them gently.

"These planter boxes could use some love," I said. "Geraniums are fine, but..."

My spine tingled.

Multiple Latin names for plants flashed through my head, courtesy of my new resident with the green thumb. I listened to plant names for a while, and then gently pushed them aside. Enough with the plant names. What we needed was for Tansy to tell us what happened to her.

Could she tell me? Or show me?

I carefully spoke inside my head, *Tansy Wick, I know we never met in person, but I'm your friend Zinnia's niece. You can trust me. Can you tell me or show me how you died?*

The stream of Latin names for plants abruptly cut off.

My mind had been feeling green and lush, but now the landscape turned to red, like molten lava.

Everything burned and turned to smoke.

A dam broke, and a boiling hot wave of anguish gushed through me. My mind screamed.

In the physical world, my body doubled over. My hands flailed, clutching at my aunt for support.

Another woman's voice roared inside me. *I died? No! I don't want to be dead! You're a liar!*

My physical self was trembling, seizing in pain. I was standing, on shaking legs. My aunt was casting spells. My body convulsed.

In my head, the boiling lava of anguish rose like flood waters, covering everything.

The few remaining green leaves and flowers baked in the heat, turning black.

There wouldn't be another spring. Not another summer. Tansy was me, and I was Tansy. We were one, and we were done.

My death was final. Everything I'd ever meant to do would remain undone. Bitter was the regret on my tongue.

I'd never allowed myself to feel how precious everything was, because I'd always feared losing more than I could bear at the end, but now it was here, and what a waste. What a waste that I hid away by myself, that I never took it all—the pain, the sweet agony of loss, the triumphant beauty of surrender. Life. Ever fleeting, mysterious, unknowable.

The world was dark now. Dark and smoking, charred wreckage.

Dimly, I was aware of people walking by on the sidewalk, and the cold, stone police department building looming overhead. But that was not in my world. That was all some distant plane I viewed through borrowed eyes.

Zinnia was pulling me off the sidewalk, guiding me over to a patch of grass. The blades were like shards of green glass under my skin.

I was dimly aware of the woman in shorts and sandals writhing on the grass, shaking with gut-wrenching sobs.

The other woman patted her—me—on the shoulder.

"Hush now," she sang soothingly. "Hush now, Zara. Everything's going to be okay."

Tansy and I didn't believe her. Not for a second. We knew better. Everything was infected with a blackness, a dark mold that clouded the light and ate the sun. Nothing would ever be okay.

CHAPTER 23

Darkness lingered.

It had been an hour, maybe two, maybe more, since I'd tried breaking the news of Tansy's death to her ghost.

My aunt had driven me back to my house and offered to come in with me. I'd assured her I would be fine on my own and simply needed rest. But now here I was, stuck in my hallway.

I couldn't get to my bed because my bedroom had no door at all. The wall was as smooth and featureless as a sheet of blank paper.

I pressed my back against the wall and slid down to a sitting position. After the day I'd had, all I wanted was a nap before dinner, a little peace and quiet before Zoey and my father returned from the zoo. I needed the sweet oblivion of the dream world. Anything to block out the waves of sorrow that kept radiating from Tansy's spirit. She was doing the ghost equivalent of sobbing in a corner, and it was all I could do to not join in.

But I'd learned a valuable lesson.

Never again would I try to break the bad news to a spirit that he or she was deceased.

Beatrizz Riddle should amend her list to include a very specific warning about that.

I curled onto my side on the floor, crooked my elbow to use my arm as a pillow, and closed my eyes.

* * *

I dreamed of the grave.

Dirt below me, dirt above me.

Bugs crawling over my hands, my face.

The creaking sound of distant crickets singing down the sun.

The squeaking of tree branches rubbing against each other in the night breeze.

I was cold. So cold.

* * *

"She's still breathing," someone reported.

I knew the voice. Zoey?

A man said, "She must have tuckered herself out doing all of this yard work."

Warm hands wrapped around my upper arms and tugged me upright.

I opened my eyes to the glare of a flashlight. I couldn't see the face of the person hoisting me up, but I recognized the hands as my daughter's.

I croaked out, "Is there a problem, Officer?" I used one hand to shield the bright light from my eyes. "Please tell me you're the police and not aliens. I'm not in the mood to be probed."

"Mom, stop joking around. What are you doing?"

The other person, my father, angled the flashlight down so I could see something besides the red veins inside my eyelids. I blinked away floating discs of burned-in light.

Rhys chimed in, "Yes, Zara. What *are* you doing back here?"

I answered defensively, "What does it look like I'm doing?"

What was I doing? I recognized the red siding of my house as the flashlight glinted over. We were in the back yard. My hands felt grimy. They were covered in dirt. So were my clothes, my hair, and—by the taste of it—the inside of my mouth. I leaned to the side and spat dirt onto the ground.

"Classy," my daughter commented.

Rhys Quarry, who was crouched next to my daughter, gave me a look of genuine concern. Fatherly concern. It was the first time I'd seen the expression on his face. I only knew about fatherly concern from TV and movies.

He grabbed my filthy, dirt-encrusted hand and helped me to my feet.

"It looks like you were taking a dirt nap," he said.

"I was," I replied brightly. "There's nothing quite like a dirt nap, under the stars." I waved up at the sky.

"It's overcast," Zoey said. "There aren't any stars visible. And I think there's a summer storm coming."

As if magically summoned—and maybe it was—a bolt of lightning lit the back yard and briefly illuminated our faces.

Zoey looked skyward and counted off. "One one-thousand, two one-thousand, three one-thousand—"

A sky-ripping crackle of thunder cut her off.

I heard the rain going pat-a-pat-tat on the leaves around me before I felt the drops on my face.

"Get your mother inside," Rhys said to Zoey. "Her lips are gray. She's freezing cold, and all that dirt's turning to mud." He made a parental tsk-tsk noise.

They each grabbed an arm and walked me toward the golden light of the back porch lamp.

"Look at those muddy footprints," Zoey said, playing the grownup. "I think we should get the garden hose and hose you down out here so you don't make a mess in the house."

I stomped my muddy feet defiantly.

"The house can suck it," I said. "She's not my favorite dwelling at the moment."

Zoey asked, "Did your room get smaller again?"

"I noticed my room's been getting bigger," said my father.

"Congratulations," I said flatly. "My door's completely gone. I've been squeezed out." I stomped dirt through the back entryway. "Stupid jerk house."

Rhys muttered about putting on the teakettle.

Zoey muttered about getting my sandals off and then tossing me in the shower, clothes and all.

With her help, I managed to get my sandals unbuckled and off. She led me through the house and past the kitchen, which smelled like food. Good food. My stomach growled.

"You two ate dinner without me?" My voice was tinged with the hurt of betrayal.

"When we got home, you weren't around, so we thought you were still with Auntie Z. It wasn't until a few minutes ago, when she phoned me to check on you, that we started looking for you."

I sniffed. Nobody had missed me. Tansy's icy-cold fingers tickled my spine from the inside. *We loners will never be missed,* she whispered. *Nobody comes to our funerals, no matter how virtuous a life we lead. The town drunk would draw a bigger crowd. Our dogs will grieve. Our cats will eat our flesh.*

I shivered so violently my teeth chattered.

That's enough for tonight, I told Tansy.

She went quiet.

My daughter and I reached the bathroom. I stood there stupidly while she got the water temperature set on the shower. I used the rubber plug to close off the drain, switched off the showerhead, and let the tub fill with hot water. I climbed into the tub, muddy clothes and all.

My daughter watched with concern, saying nothing.

"Look," I said, waving at the muddy brown water pooling around me. "Witch soup."

"Something's different," Zoey said. "You've been acting weird ever since Pawpaw got here, but this is beyond your usual weird. Have you been Spirit Charmed?"

"Right in the mouth," I said with a weary sigh.

"For real? Was it someone from the obituaries?"

"Fresher than that. It was a woman named Tansy."

"The one Auntie Z gets her plants from? Well, that does explain your new passion for late-night gardening."

I sniffed the air. The insides of my nostrils no longer reeked like a harpy's used dental floss. Suddenly I was very interested in what the two of them had eaten for dinner while I'd been gardening or dirt napping.

Zoey read my mind the way only a daughter can. "I'll bring you up some dinner leftovers on the tub plate, and you can tell me everything."

I licked my lips. "Super."

She left, and I settled into the hot bath, letting the heat chase the chill deeper into my bones. My shirt and shorts billowed loosely in the water around me.

Tansy had gone quiet, her spirit somewhat soothed by or tuckered out from digging in the dirt. All she gave me now was a line that kept rolling around in my head like stuck song lyrics: *I feel good, from my head to-ma-toes*.

I tried to think of something else, anything else, but Tansy's gardening pun was on a loop.

I feel good, from my head tomatoes. Ha-ha.

From ma-head to ma-toes.

My daughter returned with a heaping pile of food on the tub plate—a blue plastic serving platter that had a curved rim, so it could be floated on water like a boat. In the Riddle household, ever since Zoey was four years old, the blue platter had been called the tub plate. Most "normal" households would refer to such an item by its commercial name, Frisbee.

I relaxed in the tub and ate dinner from the floating Frisbee. Tonight's meal was a mélange of spaghetti and meatballs plus chow mein with sweet-and-sour chicken balls. It was a special dish we Riddle girls referred to as Balls to the Walls.

While I ate, Zoey asked questions about Tansy, and I filled her in on the events of my day.

When I was finished, Zoey stared at me with huge eyes that were nearly as round as the final chicken ball on the tub plate.

She asked, "Do you think Tansy was murdered?"

"Possibly," I said, trying to be honest but not alarming. "But she could still be alive somewhere, in a coma."

"Along with her two dogs and a dozen chickens?"

"Probably not." I used my toes to work the faucet at the end of the claw-foot tub to blast in a warm-up.

"Let's hope that Bentley guy can find her body and figure it out. Maybe Pawpaw can help?"

"Maybe." I hadn't told her about my suspicion that he could be involved, perhaps working for the real estate developer.

"But let's not get ahead of ourselves," Zoey said. "Not all hauntings are caused by violence. A surprise death, or a sudden illness, or even unfinished business can make spirits stick around."

I used my hands to make a whirlpool in the tub to distribute the fresh hot water. "Tansy might need one more summer of gardening to get closure."

"But now she knows she's dead, right?" Zoey walked over to the counter and started brushing her wavy red hair with smooth strokes. "What does a ghost think when she looks in a mirror and sees your face staring back?"

"We all see what we want to see."

Zoey kept brushing her hair as she came back over to the tub and sat daintily on the rolled metal edge. "How does she know it's okay to dig up a back yard she's never seen before?"

"Maybe she'd been to our house before. She probably knew Winona Vander Zalm, since it's a small town and they were both involved in magic."

Zoey's hair-brushing hand slowed. "Do you think Tansy's spirit believes she's helping Ms. Vander Zalm with some landscaping? I wonder, what *is* she thinking?"

"If you happen to catch me burrowing into the earth like a fox digging a new den, you should ask."

"You need to be careful," Zoey said.

I chuckled. "Honey, I try, but I think we're past that point."

"With the dirt," she said. "Have you had a tetanus booster shot lately? There are plenty of microbes in the local soil that could cause a serious infection if you get a cut on your hands. You should be wearing gloves." She reached into the muddy water and picked up my hand. She eyed my dirty fingernails before giving me a serious look. "Mom, promise that from now on you'll practice safe gardening."

"No glove, no garden love," I promised.

"And put the gloves on right at the start," she said, pointing her hairbrush at me accusingly. "Not halfway because you got 'carried away' with the excitement and kinda-sorta forgot."

"Right from the start," I promised. "The thickest gauge available."

She nodded. "That's what I like to hear." She let go of my hand, dried her fingers on her pants, and went back to brushing her hair.

"I do appreciate these little talks we have," I said. "Most teens wouldn't be comfortable talking to their mother about safe gardening."

"Ours is a special relationship," she said sweetly.

CHAPTER 24

SUNDAY

SUNSHINE WARMED MY face, gently waking me. And was that a soft pillow under my cheek? Oh yeah, it sure was. Without even looking, I could tell I was in the lap of luxury, or at least not taking a cold dirt nap in the back yard.

I opened my eyes and stretched. The house had provided for me, in its own weird way. My bedroom was closed off, yet Zoey's bed had given birth to a second bed, which was now stacked above the original one in a bunk bed formation.

We'd been uneasy about the surprise furniture procreation the night before. We were both reluctant to take the bottom spot. It was, after all, a magical bed that might suddenly decide to become a single bed again. What would happen to a warm body between the mattresses? A smothered redhead sandwich, that was what.

But then we'd concluded that if our house had wanted to kill us, it would have done so by now. To be heroic, I took the lower bunk. "Just one of the many sacrifices a parent makes," I'd said before zonking out.

Zoey's bedroom was silent now, the only breathing my own. My teenager was downstairs already, having breakfast. The fridge held plenty of food left over from Saturday's brunch, yet I smelled Pop Tarts toasting. Raspberry Pop Tarts. And something else. Eggo waffles.

I climbed out of the lower bunk, careful not to bang my head on the upper bed's support.

As I crossed the hallway to the bathroom, I heard Zoey telling her grandfather about a TV series with a character who loves Eggo waffles.

He replied, "Hey, maybe that can be my signature food! I like Eggos as much as the next guy, maybe more. Watch me eat this whole stack in five bites. No. Three bites."

I brushed my teeth, freshened up, and then automatically turned down the hall toward my bedroom. I bumped my hand against the wall where my doorknob used to be. Old habits die hard. I stood there a minute. No door meant no closet and no clothes.

I returned to my daughter's room and surveyed her closet. She had given me permission the night before to borrow anything I needed. We had giggled in our respective bunk beds like two teens at a sleepover. My father had actually knocked on the wall and barked at us to get some sleep, which only made us gigglier, of course.

What to wear today? I had no idea, so I cast my spell. Zoey's closet shimmered. The clothes slid left and right on the hanging rod. After a minute of fluffing things around, the closet offered forth a pair of green jeans, a minty blouse with a deep-green ivy pattern, and a green corduroy headband. I looked like someone you might find working a gardening-themed booth at a trade show.

I got dressed and found that everything fit well enough. Why the garden theme? Was the spell responding to Tansy's green thumb? If I would be doing more gardening that day, a better color would have been dark brown, for dirt. I considered overriding the spell's choice with plain jeans and a white T-shirt. But my closet spell hadn't let me down yet, so I decided to trust that my outfit was the perfect choice for the day's activities.

And what activities were those? My memory was foggy, but I did recall agreeing to something between giggling and falling asleep. Something tacky and regrettable, though I couldn't put my finger on what.

Decked out in my green jeans and ivy blouse, I went downstairs. In the kitchen, I found my father and my daughter laughing about some woman with a big hat.

"She probably wanted a date with you," Zoey said, laughing.

"No way," Rhys said. "The only sort of dating I would be performing on her would be *carbon dating*."

"Pawpaw, she was your age!"

He made a horrified gasp. "How old do you *think* I am?"

She laughed uproariously.

I walked between them, toward the coffee maker. "Sounds like you two had fun at the zoo," I said, pouring a cup of wake-me-up.

"We got in for free," Zoey said proudly. "Pawpaw turned into a fox and rode on my shoulders. The lady at the admissions believed me when I said we were hired to be weekend entertainers."

I shot my father the dirtiest of dirty looks. "That's stealing," I said.

"I prefer the term *creative payment*," he said loftily. "We still paid our way, trust me. I allowed myself to be mauled and poked at by dozens of children, and I didn't bite any of them. Not even when they dribbled ice cream on my fur."

"He nipped at one," Zoey said.

"She pulled my tail," he said.

"That's what toddlers do," she said.

I opened the drawer where I kept an old checkbook. "I'll write the Wisteria Zoo a donation check equivalent to two admissions," I said.

"Mom, save your money," Zoey said. "It was fine. Nobody's going to know."

"Save your money," Rhys said. "That zoo appears to have better funding than most private schools, anyway."

"We don't steal," I told him.

"We can pay double next time," Zoey said. "Don't send a check. You're so embarrassing with the things you write on the memo lines." She turned to my father and told him, "At my previous high school, the secretaries used to give me pity eyes. One of them invited me to a self-help group for the children of alcoholics."

My father looked at me. "Is this true?"

I dropped the checkbook back into the drawer. "They shouldn't serve margaritas at their stupid school fundraisers that start at five o'clock without any food around for parents who've come straight from work."

"Always blaming others for your choices," my father said with a nod. "You are so much like your dear mother."

Zoey chortled.

I swiveled my head and said, "Run upstairs and get me a pair of socks, would you? I didn't want to go snooping through your drawers."

She glanced at Rhys and said, "What's different about today?"

I narrowed my eyes at her. That wasn't fair of her to say. I'd always respected her privacy. Most of the time.

"Socks," I said with my I-mean-business tone.

She slowly finished flattening the empty Eggo waffles box, sighed dramatically, and left me alone in the kitchen with the bad influence.

"Don't you dare undermine me," I said to him. "I've always done my best to set an example for my child. Whenever we were in the grocery store, I wouldn't even eat a grape to taste-test the batch without putting a quarter in the little box. And if it was the kind of store that didn't have a box, I wouldn't sample. I'd buy a pound or two and play grape roulette. Do you know how many times I paid a small fortune for grapes that were full of giant seeds or too sour?"

"Sounds like someone has a case of... sour grapes." He grinned at his joke.

"Why bother," I muttered under my breath. "You can't explain parenting to someone who's never been one."

The rubbery grin on his face fell off so fast I almost heard it thud.

"That's not fair," he said. "I never had a chance to be a parent."

"And you never will."

I dumped my coffee in the sink, untouched, and turned to leave.

"We've got mini golf today," he called after me. "We have a reservation for a tee time, and you promised you'd come with us."

Right. Mini golf was the horrible thing I'd agreed to. Whacking a plastic ball through a tacky theme park was the kind of thing I normally enjoyed, but I didn't want to taint it with my father's company.

"Yeah, yeah," I called back over my shoulder. "I'll go, but you're paying."

I headed toward the front door, planning to take a walk to clear my mind.

While I pulled on some tennis shoes by the door, I called up the stairs, "Zoey, I'm stepping out for my coffee. I'll be back in an hour."

"What about your socks?" She stood at the top of the staircase with a handful of socks.

"I changed my mind about the socks."

She glared down the stairs. "It was never about the socks, was it?"

"We'll discuss socks later," I yelled back, reaching for the front door.

I yanked open the door. A man was standing in the doorway. It was Detective Bentley, one fist raised at knocking height.

"Oh," he said, blinking. "Were you just headed out?"

"No," I said sarcastically. "This house has very old hinges on the doors. You need to whip the door open regularly so it doesn't seize up." I whipped the door back and forth in a fanning motion. "Like this. Listen. No squeaks."

"No squeaks," he agreed.

CHAPTER 25

After three more swings of the door, I closed it behind me and stomped down the porch steps. Detective Bentley ran after, jogging to catch up. He was wearing another gray suit, or possibly the same one he'd been wearing the day before.

He called after me, "Wait up, Red."

I stopped and whirled around. "You did *not* call me Red."

"Riddle," he said. "I was calling you Riddle, but you didn't let me finish."

A likely story. I resumed walking at top speed. "What are you doing here?"

He fell into step beside me. "I'm here as requested, to provide an update on the Tansy Wick case."

"It was my aunt who cast..." I coughed into my fist and started again. "It was my aunt who *asked* you to stay in touch. You should be lurking around outside her door, not mine. How long were you out there, anyway?"

"Long enough to hear you yelling at your daughter about sex."

"Sex?"

I was temporarily speechless. Had I been yelling about sex? I reviewed what had happened and what Bentley must have heard. I'd been talking to Zoey about the zoo, and about socks. *He heard me yelling about socks, not sex.*

The mix-up was so absurd that my outrage drained out like water from a busted irrigation hose. So what if my father snuck Zoey into the zoo for free. She was a good kid. She knew the difference between right and wrong. A single incident of bending the rules wasn't going to spoil her permanently.

"I was yelling about socks," I said to Bentley. "As in s-o-c-k-s. I asked her to get me some *socks*, and then I changed my mind."

"I swear I heard you say *sex*."

I gave him a playful smile. "Detective Bentley, they say people hear what they want to hear."

He didn't smile back. "You're not wrong," he said stiffly. "The ears are not perfect digital recorders. The brain is only too happy to fill in the blanks. That's why witness testimony is notoriously unreliable, and I'm afraid it only gets more corrupted as time passes."

We reached the corner of the street and looked both ways in unison. A car drove by, and I caught a glimpse of our contrasting appearances. He was the dark-haired square man in a gray suit. I was the bright, fun one, with my red hair and green clothes.

He asked me, "Where are we going, anyway?"

"I'm not sure, but I have a feeling there's a place a few blocks from here that makes the most incredible mint mochas, blended with ice. I've got a wicked craving for something minty fresh."

"You are dressed for something minty fresh." He looked pointedly at my ivy-patterned blouse and green jeans. "I'll go with you."

"Good, because you're buying. I stormed out of my house without my purse. It really kills the impact of a dramatic exit if you go back for your handbag."

"I'll buy." He rubbed the light stubble on his chin. The dark circles under his eyes and the new stubble reminded me of how Chet had looked the previous week. Bentley wore his stubble almost as well. In fact, it made him seem more human and less like a robot.

"Bentley, have you been up all night?"

"Time is of the essence with a missing person," he said.

My pace faltered, and I stubbed the toe of my tennis shoe on a raised sidewalk slab. I did that thing where you skip for a few paces to pretend the tripping was on purpose.

Bentley regarded my dance moves with suspicion, as was his way.

"I'm sorry you lost sleep over the case," I told him, and I meant it. I truly was sorry I hadn't told him the full truth. He would never find Tansy alive, because she was already dead.

"Well, I'm sorry your friend's gone missing," he said.

I would have said Tansy wasn't my friend, and that I didn't know her, but that was no longer true. I'd met her dogs and seen her left-handed snail garden. We'd shared an existential death tantrum. And we'd gardened.

After a block of walking in the morning sunshine, I asked, "Do you have any news?"

He seemed to have been awaiting an invitation to speak. "We found bones on the property."

"Oh?" Bentley wasn't too sharp if he was reporting to me about the chicken bones.

"Canine bones," he said. "They match the description of Tansy's two dogs, but our crime scene techs noticed something strange."

"How strange?"

"The bones are stripped clean. Whatever happened to Jasper and Coco, it might have happened years ago."

"That is strange," I agreed. It occurred to me that the chicken bone my aunt had found had been as clean as a boiled bone pulled from soup stock.

"There's more," he said, and he listed off juicy details he'd uncovered about the woman.

I nodded and reacted appropriately with soft cries of surprise, even though the stories he'd uncovered about Tansy would have been easily explained if he knew the true nature of her business. The woman grew magical herbs for witches. The rumors about her supplying love potions and such were, in all likelihood, true.

We reached the entrance for the nearest location of Dreamland Coffee, a locally-owned small chain. Dreamland had the most amazing iced mint mochas. I had been there before, but it had fallen off my radar, despite having the best coffee in town. It must have been Tansy's spirit who'd led me there. Bentley leaned toward the door but didn't open it yet.

He stared at me carefully and asked, "What do you know about Tansy's involvement with your aunt?"

"Just that they've been friends for a few years. Why?"

"I heard a strange story."

"I'm sure you did. Plant it on me. I'll tell you if it sprouts."

He frowned at my metaphor but continued. "The two of them produced a zero-calorie sandwich spread that tastes exactly like mayonnaise but has zero calories."

"Actually, I have heard about that." I hadn't. Tansy pushed the information through my head. "They called it Zeronnaise. Unfortunately, Zeronnaise was not a viable consumer condiment, due to unanticipated side effects."

"Did you know Zeronnaise was officially classified as a bio-weapon?"

Now I did. "Oh?"

"And it's currently in use by the military."

I gave him a sidelong look. "You're pulling my leg."

"Maybe I am." He gave me a slow wink. "If I did have information such as that, it would be highly classified, and I'd be in big trouble for sharing it with you." He looked down and shuffled his shiny black shoes. "In fact, I don't know why I told you at all. I don't even know why I'm here."

I knew. He was there because of my aunt's spell. She was one powerful witch.

A trio of young women filed out of the cafe. The last one smiled at me as she held open the door for us. Bentley and I had been standing outside the door long enough to attract some curious stares.

I smiled at the young women, made a comment about the heat being "great weather for pollination," and waved for my detective friend to go inside.

"Come on, Bentley," I said. "You can tell me more of your highly classified secrets over some icy-cold caffeinated beverages."

* * *

The mochas were cool and extravagantly minty, as promised by the cafe's signage.

Bentley filled me in on more details of his investigation. He'd gotten a lot accomplished in less than eighteen hours. Much of his work had been computer-based, as rich people don't appreciate being phoned in the middle of the night to chat about the last time they've seen a reclusive neighbor.

Tansy Wick had last used her bank card on Thursday at 3:10 p.m. at a coffee shop near the outskirts of Wisteria, not far from her country estate. The coffee shop was part of a local chain called Dreamland Coffee. They had several locations in the area, including two in Wisteria, one of which Bentley and I were currently sipping mint mochas inside.

At the other location, the owner, a woman named Maisy Nix, recalled seeing Tansy on Thursday afternoon. Tansy was a regular customer who came in about twice a week. That afternoon, she'd tied up her two dogs at the front, ordered her favorite drink plus a Montreal-style smoked meat sandwich, then sat on the sidewalk patio. She'd been alone as usual, but she wasn't lonely, thanks to her loyal dogs Jasper and Coco, who were well trained and didn't beg for table scraps. The owner came outside to chat for a bit and gave the dogs their biscuit treats, as was their routine.

That was the last time anyone had seen Tansy. She'd missed a Friday-morning appointment with her massage therapist. Her vehicle was parked in her garage, and her house was unlocked. There was no sign of any theft or violence on the property.

"Except for the dog bones," I said.

"I have a theory about those," he said. "They might have been from her previous pair of dogs, Jojo and Casper."

That would explain the condition of the bones, but it was strange. "Tansy had dogs named Jojo and Casper before she had Coco and Jasper? That's diabolical."

"People keep telling me she's an eccentric woman."

"Have you met her brother, Vincent Wick? He's my least favorite municipal employee."

Bentley fidgeted with the straw in his iced coffee. "Where do I rank on your listing of municipal employees?"

Higher than Chet Moore. "You're doing all right."

Bentley leaned forward and looked around furtively, even though we were the only two customers currently inside the coffee shop and the whirring fans of the refrigeration units covered our voices from the staff. I hadn't deemed it necessary to cast a sound bubble spell.

He said quietly, "I found geological surveys that show underground caves beneath the Wick property, but we haven't been able to locate an entrance." He raised an eyebrow meaningfully. "And there are other surveys that are more recent, except they don't show any caves. Just solid bedrock."

"The caves are secret caves," I said, nodding. "If I had caves on my property, I wouldn't want people to know, either."

"Who'd want caves?"

"Caves are wonderful. You can use them to grow mushrooms or to age certain kinds of cheese, like Gruyère."

"Gruyère? You know what? I've never been interested in any kind of cheese that doesn't come on a pizza." Bentley frowned and added, "Why am I telling you that?"

"Why not? We're friends."

I leaned forward to sip my frozen drink. I hit a pocket of air, making a noisy slurping sound with the wide red straw. He watched me.

"Don't stop," I said, gesturing with my hand for him to continue. "What else are you thinking about?"

"Tansy Wick dressed in shades of green," he said. "From her official government ID to social media photos, she wore green in every picture. And the drink she ordered from Dreamland Coffee that day was an iced mint mocha."

I finished slurping my drink and pushed it away.

His steely gray eyes narrowed. "What kind of game are you playing, Ms. Riddle?"

"I don't know," I answered quite honestly.

"You're dressed like Tansy, drinking her favorite drink. There has to be an explanation."

There was, but telling him wasn't my job. Not until I cleared it with at least one other adult.

"Detective, have you heard of people who are highly sensitive? Empathic?"

He only watched me.

"Sometimes I pick up on things," I said. "Certain energies." It wasn't far from the truth. "I don't mean to, but I start doing the things they like to do. I must be highly suggestible. I'd probably be a stage hypnotist's dream."

"You take on the qualities of missing people?"

"Or the deceased."

"Is Tansy deceased?"

I bit my lower lip. "The energy does feel quite strong," I said.

"That must be very difficult for you." He reached across the table and put his hand on mine. "Maybe with the right dose of medication, you can shake these paranoid delusions of yours."

I pulled my hand away. "Forget what I just said." I wove my bluffing spell through my words. "Forget that. Forget this whole interaction, from the minute you showed up at my door."

The air around us tightened. His eyes flashed as my magic took hold. "Okay," he said.

Okay? Was it really that easy?

He turned his hand over on the table to be palm up and stared at it. "My life line is changing," he said.

"You're not going to trick me into doing a palm reading."

He curled his fingers into a fist. "Why was your aunt following me last night?"

"It's a small town. What makes you think she was following you?"

"Never mind," he said. He lifted his hand from the table as though it was very heavy and began rubbing the bridge of his nose. "This is the sleep deprivation talking. I didn't see your aunt last night, just an old man with a cane. But the man reminded me of her."

"Oh, that's her disguise," I said in a joking tone. "Zinnia does her best spying dressed up as an old man with a cane."

He kept rubbing the bridge of his nose. "You really do have the most robust appreciation of the absurd, Zara Riddle."

"Thanks," I said for the second time, with even more pride. "You're very perceptive."

And he was.

He'd apparently seen through my aunt's magical disguise. But why had she been spying on Bentley?

CHAPTER 26

ATLANTIS MINI PUTT and Water Adventure Park looked about as busy as you'd expect a mini golf place to be on a Sunday afternoon with great weather. My father steered Foxy Pumpkin into one of the farthest parking spaces. We'd arrived there in time for our tee-time reservation, but just barely. I found it preposterous that a mini golf place took reservations and suspected it had been a lie my father told to get us out the door at a reasonable time.

Tansy, who'd been fairly quiet that day, from my coffee date with Bentley to the drive to Atlantis Mini Putt and Water Adventure Park, began stirring when I got out of the orange car.

The minute I stepped onto the plastic artificial turf that mimicked grass, the gardener ghost inside me bristled with annoyance. Why not real grass, like a real golf course? Didn't small children who'd been dragged away from their computer screens for one measly afternoon deserve a more natural outdoor experience? I found myself agreeing with the cantankerous lady. Real turf, such as the manicured Crenshaw bent grass used on upscale courses, would cost a fortune to maintain, but it would be more aesthetically pleasing and thus more nourishing to the nature-craving soul.

We hadn't even paid our admission tickets yet—in full, no cheating—when Tansy suddenly took over. I watched from within myself as the spirit used my body to treat my golfing foursome to a rant about the horrors of artificial greenery and its impact on today's youth.

Zoey, Rhys, and young Corvin Moore stared at me with wide eyes.

Honestly, I could have wrestled back control of my mouth, but I was as amused as anyone. The rant went on for several minutes.

Spit flew out of my mouth as she, or *I*, or *we* concluded, "Why not go all the way? Let's get to the endgame now, with a perfect low-maintenance world. Let's replace all the pesky humans with cyborgs and robots. Or better yet, artificial intelligence."

I'd barely caught my breath before more of Tansy's words erupted from my mouth. "Keep on poisoning the environment, humanity! Soon you'll get the squeaky-clean plastic world devoid of all insects and living creatures that you deserve! I hope you dummies like sand, because it's going to be sand for breakfast, lunch, and dinner in your desert world. Nothing but red, wind-ravaged deserts and dead seas of poison!"

My daughter grabbed my arm and pinched the back of my bicep. "Mom, you're getting carried away over just a bit of Astroturf." She bounced her eyebrows in a get-it-together suggestion.

Meanwhile, the poor teenaged employee who'd been standing inside the admissions booth looked like she might burst into tears. The girl in the blue sun visor didn't make the landscaping decisions. She probably earned minimum wage and had only the lofty career goals of being promoted to Mermaid. The Mermaid got to sit atop the castle, wearing a shimmering fish tail and waving regally, and because she was mute, she didn't have to talk to anyone.

My father was casually browsing the rotating wire stand of postcards, doing his best impression of someone who didn't know me.

The only person who appeared to be on my side was Corvin Moore, Chet's little boy, whom Zoey had invited along so we had an even foursome for mini golf.

"A dead sea of poison," Corvin echoed, his big eyes wide under his fringe of blue-black hair. "You tell 'em, Zoey's mom."

Zoey's mom. Right. That was who I was. Not a kooky hermit gardener with magical herbs and an army of left-handed snails.

I relaxed my face into an approximation of sanity. Tansy retreated to the back corners of my mind.

The teenager in the sun visor stared at me with a trembling lower lip. "Do you still want tickets?"

"Yes. That'll be two adults and two children," I said sweetly. "Is it still the children's rate for kids over twelve? My lovely daughter turned sixteen in the spring, and I don't consider her a child."

Zoey groaned.

Louder, to prove a point, I told the young employee, "I insist on paying the *full and fair* admission price because, in our family, we have values." Tansy's spirit kicked in, and she added, "If you stand for nothing, you'll fall for anything."

Corvin touched my hand and held up a crumpled wad of bills for his own ticket.

"Save that for a snack," I told him with a motherly pat on the top of his head. "Today's round of golf is on me."

Corvin crammed the bills back into his pocket.

The meek employee took my money and fumbled with the cash register for several minutes while her face reddened, and then finally we were on our way.

Rhys rejoined us as we picked up our golf clubs and balls.

"How are we doing this?" He crossed his arms and sized us up one at a time. "Boys versus girls? Young versus old?"

Corvin went to my father's side and grabbed his elbow. "It's always us against them," Corvin said with a serious tone. "Always."

I caught my daughter's eye for some wordless communication. Did Corvin mean shifters versus witches? His father was a wolf shifter, but we still didn't know what Corvin was, assuming he was a shifter. The boy could see ghosts. That much I knew.

Rhys chuckled and ruffled his hand through Corvin's raven-black hair. "You're not wrong," he said.

Did my father mean guys versus gals, or guys versus witches? I hadn't told him the neighbors were supernatural.

Zoey must have been wondering the same as well. She put her hand on her hip and asked her grandfather, "What's that supposed to mean? I could be one of *you*, if I wanted to."

Corvin tilted his head to the side. "Really?"

Someone behind us cleared her throat. "Excuse me," she said. "I don't mean to interrupt—"

"And yet that's exactly what you're doing," Rhys interrupted right back.

The stranger made an indignant rhinoceros sound.

I turned around to find the same woman whom my father had snapped at in fox form. The same woman who'd repaid me for saving her from a bus by tattling on me to Detective Bentley. Margaret Mills. She had five other people with her—family members, by the look of the frizzy hair and rectangular heads on all of them, for a grand total of a half dozen Mills, or *Millses*. Too many Millses.

"There are rules," Margaret Mills said, gesturing toward a fence-mounted sign about mini golf etiquette. "If you're going to stand around making jibber-jabber, you have to let the next party play through."

Rhys made a rubbery, mocking face of concern. "Ma'am, that sign says *nothing* about jibber-jabber."

Margaret Mills's hand was still waving toward the sign, but it was getting closer to my father's mouth. He suddenly lunged forward, snapping his teeth at her fingers, just like he'd done the previous week when he'd been draped around my shoulders in fox form.

Margaret Mills shrieked and stumbled backward into her family. All five of them knocked over like bowling pins.

The teen employee in the sun visor jumped over the counter and came running over. She was joined by two other uniformed employees who started picking up the fallen Mills family. The most senior employee, who might have been all of seventeen, tried to calm down Margaret, who was bellowing about being bitten.

Rhys simply smiled, as though this had been planned. He nodded for us to get started at the first hole, which was a simple putt on blue artificial turf with a seahorse theme.

I kept my head down and went along, eager to get some space between us and the Millses.

Behind us, I heard Margaret declaring there to be "too much riff-raff on the green" today. The senior employee offered the whole group free vouchers to come back for three more sessions at a later date.

Rhys said to the kids, "Watch and learn, Zoey and Corvin. Just by putting up a fuss, that woman's getting a total of eighteen free passes. Six people times three visits!"

Corvin said, "Only twelve, because she paid for today but she didn't get to play because you bit her."

Rhys ruffled Corvin's hair again. "Aren't you a clever little pup?"

Corvin grinned proudly. The kid didn't smile much, so the sight of his teeth was unsettling. Perhaps it was that he had all his adult teeth already, with no gaps, and they were perfectly straight.

Corvin stepped back so Rhys could start off the round. Rhys took careful aim. The hole for that challenge was covered periodically by a six-foot-tall sparkling seahorse's undulating tail. Rhys sunk the shot on the first stroke. Of course.

I pointed two fingers at my eyes and then at my father.

I'm watching you, I mouthed.

He mouthed back, *Why would I cheat at mini golf?*

Because you cheat at everything, I mouthed.

I made the I'm-watching-you gesture two more times.

* * *

Fun was had at the Atlantis Mini Putt and Water Adventure Park.

Fun was had by Rhys, Zoey, Corvin, me, and even by Tansy Wick. She grumbled internally about the tacky artificial turf, but like all the other adults on the course that day, she gave in to the pure joy of playing a silly game.

Unfortunately, both she and I had terrible aim. Zoey wasn't much better, so we lost.

"Winner has to buy the ice cream," I said to my father. "You two boys can gloat all you want, but you're buying us losers a consolation prize."

My father was only too happy to comply.

At my suggestion, we drove up the coast to the Northern Stargazer Cafe—the same place I'd visited with Chet on Wednesday night. The two kids engaged in childish eating contests and taking turns hanging their spoons from the tips of their noses.

Other customers complimented Rhys on his "adorable grandchildren."

"The dark-haired one's just a loaner," he joked with a woman his age. "Poor lad didn't luck out and get the red hair gene like the rest of us." This made everyone laugh, even Corvin.

And then, just when I was enjoying our family outing, Rhys decided to educate the younger ones on how to get free ice cream.

The tactic involved waiting until someone with a small child ordered a children's cone. You followed the kid out of sight of the staff, only to return a few minutes later to ask for "a fresh cone of whatever the little tyke was having." You explained to the employee that the kid dropped it on the dirt, and the mean or cheap parents refused to buy a replacement. Nine times out of ten, the employee working the counter would hand you a replacement ice cream for no charge, gushing over your kindness and wishing you a pleasant day.

"Golly, gee whiz, Mister," Rhys said, imitating the employee in this scenario with a dumb-sounding voice. "You tell those folks to come right back for a third one if this goes in the dirt next."

"That's enough," I said. "That was a great story, but it was just a story. We don't do those things."

"I think it's good to know about these tricks," Zoey said. "In case I get a summer job serving ice cream."

"More," Corvin said, staring at my father in awe.

"More," Zoey agreed.

"No more," I said sternly. "Especially not in front of young, impressionable Corvin."

"Boo," Zoey said.

"Boo," my father agreed.

"Tough turnips," I said, borrowing one of Tansy's expressions. "If Corvin passes along any of these tricks to Chet, I'll be getting a big lecture about my parenting abilities, and we don't want that, because, as you all know, I'm an excellent mother. Unless anyone disagrees?"

They all knew well enough to be quiet.

* * *

We returned to the house around three o'clock Sunday afternoon. Together, we started prying the kids out of the small back seat of the 300ZX. Both of them had fallen asleep on the long drive back from the neighboring town of Westwyrd.

Zoey woke up as soon as I touched her shoulder, but Corvin remained unconscious.

"He looks so innocent when he's sleeping," I said, admiring the way his long dark lashes extended over his pale, round cheeks. "Not creepy at all."

Zoey shook her head at me. She'd butted heads with Corvin when they'd first met, but then the two of them had become friends within a few days. She found him unusual, but he didn't give her the creeps at all. She climbed over him and then helped me with him. With the kid in my arms, I walked him over to his house. Grampa Don came to the door and took over.

"You wore him out," Grampa Don said, patting Corvin on the back. "Who won the golf game?"

"His team."

Grampa Don grinned. "That's our boy." He stepped back from the doorway. "Care to come in? She's not here today."

"I'd better not," I said. Chessa was liable to smell me on the furniture or something.

"Can't say I blame you." He glanced around and whispered, "She scares the willies out of me, and I've seen plenty of scary things. Have you ever seen a nest of brainweevils?"

"Are those any relation to bloodweevils?"

"Much worse." He tilted his head and frowned. "Oh. Hello, Zara. Are you here to take Corvin to mini golf?" He stepped forward, offering me the sleeping boy.

"We've already been," I said gently. Chet's father had a memory condition that caused these time jumps for him.

"You're a witch," he said. "Nothing but trouble, you meddlesome witches."

I backed away from the door. "Nice to see you again, Don. Catch you later."

He gave me a wild-eyed look. "They'll never catch me," he said, and he closed the door between us.

* * *

Finally, I could breathe again.

I was in my back yard at last, my fingers deep in the dirt. I'd heeded my daughter's warnings about safe gardening and donned a pair of gardening gloves to help protect me from harmful microbes.

I let Tansy Wick take over the wheel. Or should I say the reins. Or the remote control? There is no perfect metaphor to describe the surrendering act of letting the deceased use your body for their favorite hobbies.

I remained somewhat present, though, so I was aware when Zoey came out to let me know a deliveryman was bringing a shipment of soil, seedlings, and mulch in through the gate on the alley side. My daughter was concerned about the cost, but I waved her away. I recalled that Tansy had put in the order by phone the day before, and she'd negotiated an excellent discount.

The back gate was tricky to get open, but we managed, and the landscapers brought in all the supplies I'd need to make the back yard into a paradise.

Hours later, the sun had set, and the yard was dim enough that even with Tansy's expertise, she and I couldn't distinguish between the weeds that needed pulling and the herbs we'd just planted.

She gave me back control rather than hunkering down for a dirt nap.

Inside the house again, I rubbed my back muscles while I showered off the muck. Once again, I was thankful for my regeneration powers. I tossed the clothes into the washing machine and then put on a pair of Zoey's stretchy yoga pants along with a hip-length fuzzy purple sweater. For a summer night, the evening had gotten chilly.

Zoey was downstairs, watching a movie. Her grandfather wasn't with her. The guest bedroom door had been closed, so I'd assumed he'd gone to sleep early—all the better to stay ahead of our slumber party giggles in the bunk beds.

I started braiding my damp hair and said, "I guess we wore out Pawpaw just as much as we wore out Corvin today."

She barely looked up from the movie on the screen. "He had to go do something. Meet with someone, I think."

"Did he say when he'd be back?"

She hit Pause on the movie and checked the time. "Actually, he was supposed to be back by now." She sounded worried.

"Who was he meeting with? Was it a woman? Someone named Reynard?"

She paused thoughtfully. "I got the sense it was a woman. He was on his phone, and I heard him saying 'she' a few times, like someone was mad at him and he was trying to blame it on someone else."

"Like me?"

Zoey rolled her eyes. "Mom, he *adores* you. Why do you have to act like he's trying to ruin our lives? Ever since he got here, you've been stomping around like a grump. And all he's done is make breakfast, help out around the house, and try to have fun with us. This reunion is going great, as far as I'm concerned."

"Great? Zoey, my bedroom has no door. There might not even be a room on the other side of the wall. It could be the black vacuum of space for all we know. What would you say if you were walking down the hallway and the membrane between dimensions got pierced by accident, and you got sucked through a hole in the wall into the cold emptiness of space?"

"I'd grab onto something before I got sucked through," she said. "Duh."

"That's when the tentacles from the space monster shoot through and latch onto your legs. Then what?"

"I dunno." She shrugged. "I'd scream for help, and then you'd do some witch stuff and save me."

"Zoey, what if the tentacled space monster already had me and I was incapacitated? Then what?"

She shrugged again. "Die screaming, I suppose."

With grave seriousness, I said, "In space, no one can hear you scream."

She pressed Play on the remote control and started watching the movie again.

I used telekinesis to press the pause button.

She looked at me with annoyance and said, "I thought you were having fun bunking with me as my roommate."

"That part is fun," I admitted.

"It's like when we lived in that funky art studio with the tub in the kitchen. That place was so funky."

"*Funky* is an adjective you use when you're too broke to afford other apartment adjectives such as *adequate* or *rat-free* or *not a firetrap*."

"Funky is fun. Didn't you have fun today? You did your victory stomp dance after you sunk the trick shot at the flaming mermaids."

"That was a very difficult shot, and I didn't use any magic at all." *Zara doesn't use her magic at the mini golf course! Zara is a good witch!*

"Pawpaw's not so bad, if you give him a chance."

I crossed my arms and looked at the front door. "You'll be eating your words when he comes running through that door with a pack of cops and security guards after him."

We both stared at the door in silence.

There was a knock.

"Very funny," I said to Zoey. "How'd you do that? Are you kicking the bottom of the coffee table?"

"Don't look at me. You're the one who did it."

"Did not."

"Did too."

There was another knock, and then the doorbell rang.

"Doorbell!" Zoey jumped up and ran toward the front door.

I grabbed the back of her sweatshirt and yanked her back. "Let me get this one," I said. "Find something good and heavy for bludgeoning in case I need backup."

She went for the heavy candlestick holders just like I'd trained her to.

I opened the door.

Standing on my porch was Tansy's brother and my least favorite municipal employee, Vincent Wick.

"I've got something of yours," Vincent said.

I lifted my hand to eye level. "This thing of mine, is it about this tall, with rust-colored hair, and found somewhere it shouldn't be?"

Vincent leaned over to look past me at Zoey, who was clutching two candlestick holders in a boxer's stance. Zoey and Vincent Wick had never met, but each knew about the other. He was so creepy that I hoped to delay their first interaction as long as possible.

"Close but not quite," Vincent said. "We should talk in private."

I gave Zoey the hand gesture to back down. "At ease, soldier. I'm going outside for a minute to talk to Mr. Wick." I winked at her. "Mr. Vincent Wick."

She nodded to let me know she understood who he was, and I went outside.

"I'm sorry," Vincent said, his voice deep and serrated in the darkness. His apology was as unexpected as it was unsettling.

"No. I'm the one who's sorry," I gushed, only it wasn't me talking. Tansy said in her gravelly voice, "Oh, Vinnie, this rift between us has gone on for too long."

I glanced down to find myself gripping Vincent Wick's hairy forearm.

I continued gushing, "I've missed you so much, Vinnie. It's lonely on the estate without you dropping by like the good ol' days."

Vincent yanked his arm away. "Enough of your parlor tricks, witch. I've got your friend in a burlap sack in my van, and he's not breathing so good."

My skin prickled all over. Vincent Wick gave me the creeps at the best of times, but I'd never heard something so chilling.

I've got your friend in a burlap sack in my van, and he's not breathing so good.

CHAPTER 27

Vincent Wick resembled a movie gangster in the darkness of the quiet street, with his angled features lit dramatically by street lamps.

His van gave me an equally bad vibe as I approached. And for good reason. The last time I'd gotten too close to his rear bumper, a booby-trap device had sent enough electricity through my body to run a hydroponics greenhouse for three days.

Vincent opened the back doors of the van. "Ladies first." He waved me in.

I held back and waved him in first. "Age before beauty." The words had come from the ghost within me.

"Tansy used to say that all the time when we were growing up." He poked me on the shoulder. "Is my sister really in there?"

"What do you think?"

He looked down his hawk-like nose at me, his dark eyes beady under the streetlamp. "That's what you do, isn't it? You collect dead people. Like trinkets."

Tansy took control of my arm. I lifted my hand, braced my middle finger against my thumb, and then thwacked Vincent right between the eyes.

He inhaled sharply.

"Dung beetle," I said. That was Tansy's childhood nickname for him.

"Hey, now," he growled, rubbing the red spot above the bridge of his nose. "This ain't how I wanted to spend my Sunday evening."

"But here we are, so let's see what you've got." I climbed into the back of the van.

The interior of the vehicle was a miniature version of Vincent Wick's control center underneath his office at the waste management station. He didn't know I'd seen his secret lair, because I'd been there in spectral form. On the floor, illuminated by the eerie blue light of a dozen screens and monitors, was something inside a burlap sack.

I knew what the lump was even before I pulled open the sack.

A red fox. Curled on its side limply, its breathing ragged. Injured. Like he'd been that day in the forest, except worse.

I didn't even ask what had happened. It didn't matter. Now was the time for me to use my gift.

I put my hands on the animal's fur and willed my healing energy to flow through to him.

Focus the way you would when threading a needle, I heard my aunt's voice in my mind. *Steady both of your sides, pull them in sync, and let go of everything else. Let go of every emotion and memory that doesn't help.*

My fingers didn't crackle. They barely fizzed. Had I tried to heal before I was charged and ready? I pulled my fingers from the red fur, pressed my palms together, and closed my eyes. I heard the metallic clunk-clunk of Vincent Wick closing the van's doors, and then the sounds of his breathing. His nose had a slight whistle. The left nostril. I knew without opening my eyes because Tansy knew. Vinnie had a deviated septum.

I let the whistle of his nose fill my head without fighting it. I amplified the sound, so that it was a rushing wind, white noise to aid my concentration.

Something brittle cracked within me, like ice breaking on a winter pond. Finally, the blue fire manifested between my palms, cool yet hot, like cinnamon candies swirled in mint ice cream. *Sweet and liquid, like nectar from the petals of flameweed,* Tansy noted.

Holding focus carefully, I cracked open my eyelids and carried the healing energy, cupped in my hands, over to the fox.

"This makes us even," I whispered. "I don't know what trouble you've gotten yourself into now, but I don't care. Don't bother trying to talk your way out of this one. You'll be packing your bags first thing in the morning."

The blue fire flowed downward between my fingers like melting ice cream and then guttered like a drowning candle flame. I shook and cupped my hands. No more healing energy.

Why wasn't it working? I'd practiced dozens of times with Zinnia. I was holding my focus, threading the needle, balancing both sides, even holding the tip of my tongue in a sharp point the way she'd coached me.

I heard a voice in my head. *A cut flower cannot grow.*

I growled at Tansy's spirit. *Hey, thanks for being my personal gardening Yoda, but does it look like I'm arranging a bouquet?*

Vincent's hand landed on my shoulder like a chunk of sod. "We don't have time for second thoughts about your witcher-i-doo techniques. Do what needs to be done before the creature expires inside my van."

I ran my useless fingers through the fox's red fur. "What happened to him, anyway? I can't locate the injury site." I gently rolled him over and checked his flank in the area where he'd needed the stitches four days earlier. Half the stitches were gone, chewed or plucked out. The wound wasn't bleeding, but the skin didn't look so healthy, either. The partly healed flesh was puffy and asymmetrically swollen.

Tansy's spirit had me lean forward, sniffing the wound. *Sickly sweet,* she noted. *Pseudomonas aeruginosa.* It was a common yet serious infection.

"He's got an infection," I told Vincent. "And a burning fever."

Either my father hadn't followed the veterinarian's aftercare instructions, or the pills and creams hadn't worked on his human form. Or my magic was to blame. I'd forced him to shift while injured. Now he was very ill, and my powers weren't doing anything to help.

Panic rose up in my throat like a wash of acid.

If he dies, it's my fault. If he dies, I'm letting down Zoey.

Then Tansy gave me the ghostly equivalent of a slap across the face. She calmly showed me exactly which plants we needed to combat his infection. Unfortunately, even if I'd had the herbs, I didn't have the time to prepare the ointment. And the veterinary clinic was likely closed for the day.

I asked Vincent, "Did you find him like this?"

"Not exactly," Vincent said.

"What did you do?"

"He may have been shocked."

I whipped my head around to glare at the sharp-featured older man. "He *may* have been shocked?" I trembled at the memory of my own blast that had come courtesy of Vincent Wick. "Why would you electrocute a harmless little fox?"

"Calm yourself down," Vincent said. His command had the exact opposite effect.

"Tell me everything," I growled.

"I was out at Tansy's place, finishing up some plant disposal, and I found this critter inside the house, using Tansy's computer."

"So you electrocuted him? With what? Was her computer booby-trapped like your stupid van?"

Vincent lowered his head as though shamed. He slowly pulled a gun-like device from his jacket pocket.

"With this," he said. "It was only supposed to stun him, but he was sick. You said so yourself. He's got a fever and an infection. He was already sick from something else before I shocked him."

"Then you brought him to me," I said. "How'd you know he was mine?"

Vincent lifted his chin with unmistakable pride. "I've got access to every database in this town, and then some. The most recent hit for a fox was your visit to a veterinarian."

With that mystery solved, I turned my attention to the fox. He was sprawled limply on the rubber-matted floor of the van. His fever was so strong, the heat radiated through his fur. His paw pads were burning up. I scooped him up, using the bottom of my sweater as a sling. He hardly weighed anything.

Vincent's nose whistled.

I tried charging my hands and applying my healing energy to the fox, but it still wasn't working.

"Maybe it's because of the electricity from your Taser," I said, thinking out loud. "This power I have in my hands is specialized for battle injuries. Cuts, and bone breaks, and arrowhead wounds, and the occasional limb detachment."

"You can reattach limbs?"

"Let's find out, dung beetle." Tansy's spirit twisted my mouth into a wicked grin. "You go first. Chop your arm off."

He gave me a sidelong look. "Worm? Is that you?"

"She's around," I said. "You two must have had an interesting relationship."

Almost as interesting as my relationship with my father. I looked down at the fox cradled in my sweater. He was still breathing, but his eyes hadn't opened.

"We need to get him to a medical center," I said. "Now."

"Who is he to you?"

There seemed to be no point in lying. If Vincent didn't already know, surely he would soon enough.

"My father," I said.

Vincent swore an oath and got to his feet. "Why didn't you say so?" He shot past me to the front seats of the van and started the engine.

"Zara, find something to hang onto," he called back over his shoulder. "We'll be breaking some traffic bylaws." A few jostling movements later, he added, "And possibly the laws of physics."

CHAPTER 28

WHERE DO YOU bring a supernatural creature in need of medical treatment?

The Department of Water and Magic, of course.

We approached the DWM via a different underground entrance than I'd used previously, but I recognized the security equipment at the entrance, as well as the female voice coming out of the speakers.

Vincent Wick was doing a lousy job of convincing the female voice that we had legitimate business at the DWM. And the more agitated and demanding he got, the worse he communicated.

I asked him, "Don't you have an access card?"

"I don't work for the DWM," he said. "I'm an independent contractor."

"Can't you just hack into their system and get us in? I thought you were some sort of top-level hacker, with access to everything." It had certainly seemed that way when I'd spied on him in his underground lair.

"Patience," he barked at me.

The limp fox on my lap twitched at the loudness of Vincent's voice. We were both up front, in the passenger seat. I had moved up when Vincent's driving had threatened a new wave of injuries.

"I'll be patient if you'll be competent," I muttered under my breath. Why had he brought us there if he couldn't get us in? I should have called Chet. I should have run next door rather than staying in Wick's van.

Vincent shot me an evil look before turning back to the security panel.

"Connect me with your supervisor," he barked into the speaker. "I demand to speak to someone on the A unit."

A familiar female voice poured out of the speaker like cool, rolling fog. "It's past ten o'clock at night on a

Sunday, sir. As far as you're concerned, I *am* the A unit. Me and my curvy buttocks, which you're welcome to—"

"Charlize!" I leaned over to the driver's side of the van and called out to her in front of Vincent's chest. "Charlize, it's me, Zara."

The speakers crackled with static. "Zara!" The cheerful pronunciation of my name was followed by a sibilant hiss —probably her gorgon hair snakes getting excited.

Charlize had taken an immediate liking to me when we'd met. I had gone the other way, despising everything about her, especially how other people found her dumb jokes funny. But ever since our boozy slumber party at Chessa's cottage, my feelings toward her had mellowed. There were times, like now, when I actually *liked* her, and appreciated that she and Chloe considered me an honorary sister. Their other triplet sister, Chessa, had been neutral toward me, which was fine. I would take neutral over having my skull used as a candy dish.

Charlize asked over the speakers, "Are you the one who's hurt?" She sounded genuinely worried.

"Not me," I answered quickly. Vincent Wick had been vague when demanding access, so I couldn't blame her for the misunderstanding. "The sick patient is my father," I said. My throat clenched up, making it hard to get the next words out. "He might be dying."

The red lights on the gate in front of us turned green.

"You should have said so in the first place," she replied with kindness and professionalism. "Take the vehicle up to Bay Five. I'll have the medics waiting. You're in luck, actually. Some of the A unit are here."

"Good," Vincent Wick said gruffly.

I settled back into the passenger seat just as Vincent's sister took over my speech. "The phrase you're looking for, dung beetle, is *thank you.* Why not spread a little sunshine to help your relationships grow? It would be a fine complement to the fertilizer you're always spewing."

"Stop doing that," he growled.

"I would stop her if I could," I said, which wasn't true at all.

* * *

Once we reached Bay Five, the medics carefully loaded the sick patient onto a gurney. The limp red fox was so tiny on the large gurney; he looked like a mere throw pillow on a king-sized bed. We could have fit two dozen foxes on the gurney.

"He's so small," I said, to nobody in particular. My eyes were burning.

Vincent Wick answered, "Those gurneys are larger than average, and reinforced. Each unit costs a small fortune. Look at that smooth movement. They roll with an electrical power assist."

"Very smooth," I agreed weakly. When you have a sick family member, they look tiny and helpless no matter the size of gurney.

A glass door slid open, and the gurney wheeled away with an electric hum, unguided by human hand.

The attending doctor was a woman whose lavender eyes were even more striking thanks to the rest of her face being concealed behind a green mask.

She introduced herself. "I'm Dr. Ankh, and I'll be looking after your friend."

"Don't let me keep you," I said, my eyes on the receding gurney. "Go. Save him."

"I will," she answered confidently.

"Why are you still standing here wasting time?" I glared at her.

The strange purple eyes blinked. "Since he's incapacitated, I'll need to ask you some admission questions. Are you his designated next of kin?"

"Yes." *Short answers only, Zara. Let's get through this quickly.*

"And what is the patient's legal name?"

"Rhys Quarry. He's my father."

Her light-purple eyes opened wider. "Can you prove this?"

I stared at her, transfixed by those strange lavender eyes as much as I was stumped by the question. How could I prove the helpless, rust-furred creature was my father? He was currently a fuzzy forest creature. He wasn't wearing clothes, let alone pants with pockets in which to carry his driver's license.

"I guess I can't prove it," I answered. "Does it matter?"

The corners of Dr. Ankh's lavender eyes crinkled up like a smile. Had she really said her last name was *Ankh*, as in the Egyptian symbol for long life?

"It's not important," she said with a lilting, singsong melody. "He appears to have an infection. Who is his primary care physician?"

"Dr. Katz."

"I'm not familiar with that doctor. Does she work for the division?"

"Dr. Katz is a male, and he's a veterinarian in Wisteria." I quickly explained how I had brought the fox into the vet clinic on Wednesday for treatment of a wound.

"How did your father receive this wound?"

"He says it was from a flying monster. A bird who was growling and had sharp talons."

She blinked rapidly. "There's been another bird attack?"

"Honestly, I think that was just something he made up. We have a complicated history. He probably inflicted the wound himself. It was one of his scams. He played the victim, so of course I had to rescue him and then take him in. All so he could turn my whole house against me, literally and metaphorically."

"What an intriguing relationship." Dr. Ankh's lavender eyes deepened in color, becoming burgundy. "This is what happens when two kinds mingle indiscriminately. It's the children who suffer. The offspring. They always suffer in the ensuing complications." She watched me with unblinking intensity. "I have so many questions."

"Save it for your medical journals," I snapped. "Would you please go save him now?"

The burgundy of her irises turned to a deep, dark scarlet. Barely perceptible, I heard the word "mutt." Or maybe I just imagined it.

With a more civil tone, I said, "Please, Dr. Ankh, get my father patched up, and I promise you can ask me all the questions you want."

Her irises immediately lightened, all the way back to sunny lavender.

She gave me a mechanical nod and turned to go. "I shall return with an update shortly."

"I'm not going anywhere," I replied.

"You may stay," she said to me and then looked pointedly at Vincent Wick. "Not him."

"I can take a hint," Vincent said, turning to leave.

The sliding glass door opened again, and purple-eyed Dr. Ankh left, her soft shoes silent on the concrete floor. The only sound was her stiff cotton scrubs rustling.

Vincent headed for the exit without even looking back. I ran to catch up and caught him by the elbow. As soon as my fingers dug into the thick leather of his jacket, I clicked into him, like a piece of a quality jigsaw puzzle snapping into place. His sister's feelings toward her brother mingled with my own toward a man I barely knew.

And then... I *did* know him.

I knew, without all of the specifics of their shared history, that Vincent Wick had always made mistakes. He'd always hurt people, but he'd also made amends. Eventually. His code of honor was not the same as others, but he did have a code, and he stuck to it. He strove for balance. For relationships to be equal. One gives, the other gives the same amount. One makes a mistake then makes amends and finds balance again.

Vincent Wick had electrocuted my father without giving him a chance to explain his presence in Tansy's home, but then he had made amends by coming to me. You could always count on Vincent Wick to make a mess, but you could also count on him to clean it up. *Always,* Tansy's spirit whispered.

I was on the verge of saying something, but I immediately forgot what.

Vincent glared at my fingers on his jacket arm. "What?" His beady eyes flicked up to my face.

"Nothing," I said, and then, "Thank you for trying to set things right by me and my father."

"Stop it," he said gruffly, yanking his arm away. "I won't be charmed by you, witch. Save your glistening eyes for another sucker."

I stared at him, refusing to back down. I'd been trying to thank him, and he'd insulted me.

He stared right back. He leaned forward, getting his face into my personal space.

The words came from Tansy and onto my lips.

"Vincent Wick, you really are a big, stupid dung beetle." I reached up and flicked him on the forehead again.

His face contorted into pure outrage.

"Tansy made me do it," I said.

He looked down his hawkish nose and sneered at me. "Worm," he said.

"Dung beetle."

He turned and left.

I was alone in the waiting room, which was more of a concrete-walled hallway than a room. A proper waiting room would have some magazines or signs touting the benefits of frequent hand sanitizing.

I sat on a plastic chair and waited for news from Dr. Ankh.

I rubbed the sweat from my palms onto my long purple sweater. *This sweater matches Dr. Ankh's eyes.* Had Zoey's closet been able to foresee the details of tonight's events when it had offered the clothing hours earlier? I'd thought its prognostication abilities were limited to the weather forecast.

I pondered this, since I had nothing else to do while waiting. I had left my house with nothing but the borrowed clothes on my body. No purse. No phone. Nothing to distract myself with.

Purple, I mused. I'd been wearing a purple blouse the first time I'd encountered my father as an injured fox. *Probably a coincidence,* I decided. If my house's closets could tell the future, it would be a waste to use them only for wardrobe storage and selection.

My mind raced with the possibilities. I could use my all-seeing, all-knowing closets to become the Queen of the World. And then what? Besides increasing the funding for libraries, and ending all war and famine and disease and human greed and whatnot. Then what?

Tansy threw in a few suggestions about outlawing mini golf courses and artificial turf. She also had some decent ideas about true representational government.

This is good, I told her. *Let's start drafting up a manifesto.*

She started onto a rant similar to the one she'd given earlier that day at the Atlantis Mini Putt and Water Adventure Park. This one, judging by the snippets I could catch, was about socialism versus pure communism. In a matter of minutes, she was out of control. Unrestrained by a physical body, she spoke at a speed I couldn't comprehend. My whole head ached.

Thankfully, I was saved by the distraction of someone else joining me in the hallway. Tansy's spirit retreated to the dark edges, and the headache receded as well.

The newcomer was a huge man with a familiar face I was happy to see.

"Knox!"

The big, muscular, dark-skinned man walked up to where I sat.

In his deep gentle-giant voice, he said, "Zara, you look like you could use a hug, and people say my hugs are the best." He stretched out his trunk-like arms. I got to my feet and took him up on the offer.

Hugging Knox was like hugging a giant oak tree, if an oak tree could hug back. It was because of agents like Knox that the DWM had to get reinforced gurneys.

We sat down, and Knox listened as I relayed what had happened over the past five days, from my father's dramatic arrival, to my current role as host to Tansy Wick's spirit. If my father hadn't been connected to Tansy's disappearance before, getting caught inside her house had certainly done the trick now.

"He might not be involved," Knox said, frowning thoughtfully. "You said it yourself, your father's an opportunistic man. He might have broken into the estate for other reasons."

"To steal anything that's not nailed down?"

"Zara, have you considered that he might have been there to help you with your problem?"

I snorted. "Some help he's been."

"He's staying with you, in your house. Didn't he think it was weird when you suddenly started digging up the back yard? He might have heard about Tansy and put two and two together."

"You think he's investigating the case on my behalf?"

Knox smiled shyly. "What do I know? I'm just a big lunkhead. They didn't hire me for my lateral thinking skills." He flexed his big bicep to illustrate his point.

"Come on," I said. "Don't sell yourself short."

His brow wrinkled. "Tell me about the bird attack. The one in Pacific Spirit Park."

I rolled my eyes. "My father claimed the bird was roaring," I said. "Sounds pretty made-up to me."

Knox rubbed his big hand over his mouth and chin. "I just wish we could make it a whole week without hearing about yet another bird attack."

I raised an eyebrow. "Was my father's attack part of some spree? Is there another monster on the loose? Maybe a former associate of Dr. Bob's? He could have been working with others."

"There's no monster on the loose," Knox said, his voice rumbling with annoyance. "Bird shifters are always the scapegoat. Throughout history, my kind has always been mistrusted and reviled." He wrinkled his broad, flat nose as his nostrils flared. "It's not fair for us to be treated with so much persecution."

I waved one hand as though asking a question in a classroom. "Hello? There's a witch sitting in this chair. Do you know how many women have been executed for practicing witchcraft? It's always been a convenient way for the people in power to get rid of women who stir up trouble."

His expression softened. "But you *are* always getting yourself into trouble." He leaned back casually in his chair, looking me over. "Have you thought about teaming up with the good guys?"

"Me? Working for the DWM? I guess I'd consider it... if the Wisteria Public Library suddenly dropped into a giant sinkhole."

He frowned. "Don't say such things." He glanced around furtively.

I patted his knee. "Thanks for the offer, but I love my career. I get to help people every day, and it's the least I can do. Humanity's collective knowledge is the result of countless hours of sacrifice and dedication. You know, you can tell a lot about a culture by how much they value knowledge, and by how committed they are to sharing it with everyone."

"Good to know," he said. "Never mind about working with us. You would fail the psychological tests with that pro-sharing attitude."

"Are you saying I'm a security risk? Because I believe in libraries?"

He didn't have to answer, because I knew the answer was yes.

Chet had provided me with a single book, which was a drop in the bucket compared to the information the DWM had.

But as strongly as I felt about sharing knowledge, I did have some sense. The library doesn't carry books about how to make illegal drugs. Or explosive devices. It's not censorship, but we do adhere to community standards. And we use our heads.

I would, for example, never hold a press conference and announce to the world that witches were real. Did I want to be responsible for the mass genocide of magical beings? I'd sooner set off World War Three.

Not that I was against the idea of sharing more of the secret world of magic with others. Not entirely. I'd love to get a neurolinguist's take on how Witch Tongue worked its magic. I'd been tempted to let Detective Bentley in on the truth. And even my boss, Kathy. The poor woman was probably developing a complex from all the times Frank and I suddenly stopped talking whenever she walked by.

And *that* was exactly why I would fail the DWM's psychological tests. They would detect my slight wavering and reject me. With a complimentary mind wipe. Or if I put up a fuss, a dirt nap of the permanent kind. Knox and Chet referred to their organization as "the good guys," but you know what people say about secret supernatural underground operations that wield untold powers. They don't say much of anything! (Because of the aforementioned mind wipes and the dirt naps.)

I sighed.

"Don't you worry," Knox said. "Dr. Ankh will have your father's tail wagging in no time."

"About Dr. Ankh," I said casually. "What is she?"

He grinned, his Knox-sized teeth gleaming between full lips. "Zara, you know I'm not supposed to tell you stuff like that."

"But she's good, right? By which I mean her moral alignment. She's *lawful good*, not *chaotic evil*?"

He tilted his head. "You play Dungeons and Dragons?"

"Knox, we're currently underground, sitting on cheap plastic chairs inside the hallway of what's basically a high-tech dungeon. I've met your in-house lawyer, Steve, who's about as close to a dragon as anything I've seen. Plus I've been reading the department's own Monster Manual to educate myself on various magical creatures and what they eat." I paused for drama. "Knox, I don't need to play Dungeons and Dragons, because my regular life *is* Dungeons and Dragons."

His grin got even bigger.

I punched him on his big bicep. "Plus your name is Knox. It doesn't get more D and D than that."

"If you say so, Zara Riddle, level four witch with a plus two base attack bonus."

"Excuse me? Only plus two?" I shook my head. "I'm deeply offended. I should cast an animation spell and entangle you with that plastic ficus." I pointed to the world's least convincing artificial greenery.

"Do it," he said with excitement.

Before I could admit I'd been bluffing and knew of no such spell, we were interrupted by the sound of approaching footfalls. A woman emerged from a nearby hallway and came toward us.

It was Charlize, dressed in a silver jumpsuit that would look right at home on the deck of the USS Enterprise. Her golden curls fell loosely to her shoulders.

"Sister Zara," she squealed. "Wait. That makes it sound like you're a nun."

I replied, "Zara tries to be good, but Zara is not a very good nun."

Charlize laughed. "I don't get it." She laughed again anyway and gave me a hug. She smelled like cupcakes. She squeezed me with snake strength. "Your dad's going to pull through, I promise. Dr. Ankh will have his tail wagging in no time."

"So everyone keeps telling me," I said once she'd released me from her boa constrictor grip. "What I'd really like is for him to shift back to human form so he can answer a few questions."

"Such as?" Charlize raised a blonde eyebrow.

I glanced over at Knox. "Stuff," I said. "Knox thinks he might have been trying to help me with something."

"On Tansy Wick's computer," she said. "I got the details from our pal Vincent on his way out."

Knox said, "Let's not jump to any conclusions. Shifters are always getting blamed for stuff. There are a lot of bad stereotypes our kind has to deal with."

"I wish I knew what he was doing on Tansy's computer," I said.

"I can answer that," Charlize replied.

"Really? That would be amazing," I said. "I shouldn't be surprised. Chloe's always saying you're a genius on computers."

"We can't all be pastry chefs," Charlize said with a wink. Then in a spooky, drawn-out tone, she said, "Come with meeeeeeee, Zara. To my seeeeeeeecret underground labooooooratory."

Knox gave her a confused look. "All the labs are both underground and secret. The whole building is."

She patted him on the shoulder. "Knox, never stop being so literal. Even if they find a way to regrow your sense of irony, just say no."

Knox shrugged and looked at me. "If it's okay with you, I'll hand you off to Charlize so I can get in a quick third workout."

I gave him a sidelong look. "Third one today, or third one for some other period of time that would be more reasonable?"

"Today, I think. It's hard to tell the days apart when you're underground."

"Well, have a good third workout," I said. "Do a chin-up for me. I've never done one, and it's on my bucket list. I mean, it's not, but I can write chin-up on there and cross it off right away for the buzz of accomplishment."

"Will do," he said without a trace of irony.

Charlize gave me a sympathetic look and then led the way toward her office.

CHAPTER 29

I USED THE phone in Charlize's office to call Zoey and give her a quick update. I downplayed her grandfather's injuries as best I could and told her to go to bed, since she had school in the morning.

Charlize glanced over from her computer screen. "It's crazy that you have a sixteen-year-old daughter. That's, like, a whole entire other person you're responsible for. And you're basically my age. I can't even imagine."

"Do you want kids?"

She grimaced. "I can barely look after my nephew for ten minutes without a major incident."

"That's all parenting is. Stretching out those minutes between major incidents."

She chuckled and went back to her typing. "This will take a while. The server's updating."

"Can I ask you a few questions?"

Her golden-blonde eyebrows bounced. "You can ask."

"How does the DWM coordinate investigations with the Wisteria Police? I've been getting to know Detective Bentley—"

"I bet you have," she interjected.

I snorted. "As I was saying, he doesn't seem to know about the town's special qualities. Won't that prevent him from doing his job?"

"Yes and no," she said. "As for our system, I can tell you that all information from the police flows freely into the DWM, as I'm sure you've guessed."

"Does it flow through Vincent Wick?"

"More like in spite of Vincent Wick." She rolled her eyes. "Cases that involve supernaturals are worked on in tandem by both departments. We do have trained agents in place at various other agencies, including quite a few in parks and rec. But here's the thing. The regular human cops who don't know anything about magical creatures, it turns out they're excellent investigators. They're always chasing that thing that's just out of reach. Mystery is the single greatest motivator, better than money."

"Better than power? Or sex?"

She frowned. "Equal, maybe." Her computer beeped. She began typing again. Without looking at me, she said, "The best detectives throughout history are the ones who are driven to madness by puzzles, by their own desperate quest for the truth.

"Like Fox Mulder from the X-Files," I said. "*The truth is out there.*"

With her eyes still on her screen, she pointed her finger at me. "Exactly."

"You're trying to turn Detective Bentley into a UFO-chasing Agent Mulder."

"He's got the rugged good looks." She tittered girlishly.

"What happens when he does uncover something? Assuming he doesn't get mind-wiped or dirt-napped. Does he get promoted to the DWM? An all-access pass to Strangeville, Population Unknown?"

"That's not up to me or you," she said. "Now, let's see what your bushy-tailed father was up to on Tansy Wick's computer."

For the next few minutes, my gorgon friend dove into the data stream, becoming one with the computer. She explained in a robotic tone that Tansy's computer would be physically taken to the police headquarters on Monday, when the tech unit was given authorization. It had only been left at her house due to normal procedural delays, which had made it vulnerable to incursion by a sneaky fox. However, the DWM had previously attained a full data download from all of Tansy's devices. That had happened within minutes of my missing persons report going into the system.

"This data is a perfect copy," Charlize intoned, still eerily cyborg-like. "It includes a log of your father's keystrokes." She paused, transfixed by her screen. "He accessed some of Tansy's file folders." More typing. "What's Project Buttercup?"

I leaned over to peek at her screen. It was a code view that looked like something from a sci-fi movie to me.

"Project Buttercup," I mused. It didn't sound evil or nefarious at all. *Tansy, does that ring a bell?*

My ghost was silent. Very silent. It was the kind of suspicious silence that a mother recognizes.

I shook my head. "My ghost isn't telling me anything. Tansy's hiding it from me. Guilty conscience, I bet."

Charlize jerked her gaze away from her screen and stared at me. "She's dead? I guess I shouldn't be surprised, but I still am. Is she inside you now? What's that like?"

I shrugged. "What's anything like? There are good parts and bad parts. She hasn't shared with me what happened to her. From what I know of ghosts, they're confused most of the time, and they either don't know what happened to them, or refuse to remember. Denial ain't just a river in Egypt."

"You'll get better at this," she said, lifting her chin. "Hard work and methodical practice. Like a lion tamer. The job's dangerous, but remember, there are lion tamers in the world."

Lion tamers. Picturing that triggered a nagging suspicion I'd forgotten all about something. But what? The harder I tried to remember it, the further away it got. Was Tansy shuffling around my memories? *Calm down in there,* I thought loudly. *Behave yourself.* Or what? I didn't have a good punishment, other than singing annoying pop music over and over in my head, but that would punish me as well.

The air in the small office smelled sweet, like candy. I leaned my head back and rested it against the wall.

Inside my mind, I tried to chase down that lion. It was pale and silky. But Tansy, dressed in green, kept opening doors and ushering the white lion away. She didn't like them. Only dogs. She liked dogs first, then a whole pyramid of things. Toward the bottom were humans. Lower down were creatures like lions. She didn't like how they hid in the darkness before pouncing.

The small office filled with the waterfall sound of Charlize typing quickly. "This encryption is going to take some time to break," she said. "Tansy must have had her brother set up her security. I hate it when I have to admire the skill of his tech. Vincent Wick is a..."

"Dung beetle?"

"Exactly. He's a dung beetle of a person, but he's great with security. I don't know where he finds the time. Did you know he also trains falcons to keep other birds away from the airport? The man has skills."

"How big are these falcons he trains?"

"They're not supernatural, if that's what you're asking. One of them's a kestrel falcon, barely bigger than your hand, but he is ferocious."

"Are the birds always accounted for at the airport? I'm just wondering if my dad's story about being attacked by a bird might be true."

"The safest place for the truth is to disguise it as a lie," Charlize said.

She asked a few more questions about the events from earlier in the week, and I answered as best as I could.

"This woman with the boots might be the solution to the puzzle," Charlize said. "You think she was using a glamour?" At the mention of a glamour, her own glamour either activated or deactivated—I didn't know which version of Charlize was the truth. A dozen coppery snakes slithered from her golden curls, writhing as though stretching their muscles before snapping at each other. If anyone knew about glamour spells, it was Charlize.

"It's just a guess," I said. "The veterinarian's assistant described her two different ways."

"Intriguing." The snakes in her hair rose up together like the leaves of a red-flowering *Bromeliad guzmania* caught in a breezy updraft. I had Tansy to thank for the Latin name. She was trying to help, in her own way.

"That's our next lead," my gorgon friend said. "These encryption-cracking algorithms will keep running whether

I'm here or not." She turned her swivel chair. "Shall we go pay that veterinarian a little visit?"

I glanced around for a clock. "Isn't it the middle of the night? This place is like a shopping mall. I don't know what time it is, but I'm guessing it's around midnight."

"Zara, you nodded off for a while when I was talking to you about encryption."

Had I? The word *encryption* did make me yawn. And my neck was stiffer than I remembered.

Charlize gave me an amused look. "Let's have a look outside." She pressed a button on her desk, and the ceiling of her office became sky. Just like that. It had been basic acoustic panel, the type commonly found in offices, and now it was sky. Blue. With fluffy clouds and flying birds.

She saw me admiring the view and said, "Go ahead and touch it."

I got to my feet and reached up. I saw only open blue sky, yet my fingers bumped the nubby plastic covering of an overhead light. If I focused, squinting, I could see the sky and also see the true physical ceiling at the same time, but holding both images simultaneously was difficult, like trying to believe that two plus two equals five. Like *doublethink*. That was the term used by author George Orwell in his classic novel, *1984*.

"This is beautiful," I said. "And I bet it really helps with Seasonal Affective Disorder in the winter."

"Since we're underground, it's practically a necessity." She clicked the button again, and the skyscape shifted to a star-speckled sunset sky, then gray storm clouds, then another azure wash of pure blue with no clouds. "These are all real-time images from our other departments around the world."

A shadowy figure appeared at the ceiling's edge and drew closer. It was a flying creature, dark green, with the head of a dragon, bat-like wings, two scaly legs with sharp talons, and a long, snakelike tail. Instinctively, I ducked toward the doorway to take cover.

Charlize giggled. The beast loomed larger and larger, its gleaming eyes scanning the room. Or at least it *appeared to be* scanning the small underground office. But how could it be seeing in, if the ceiling projection was a glamour?

I whispered hoarsely, "Can that thing see us? Are we in danger?"

She snorted and waved one hand. "That's just Ribbons. He likes to perch on the roof of the castle where this camera is located. It must be part of his wyvern magic that he can sense when someone's accessing this channel, because I swear he's always flying in for a landing whenever I flip over to this view. Cheeky wyvern."

From the false safety of the doorway, I watched in awe as the dragon-like creature leaned in over the camera, its head expanding to take up a third of the office's ceiling. A long purple tongue slipped out between green, scaly lips. The creature delicately licked the surface of one gleaming black eyeball and then turned its head for an unobstructed view as it licked the other. Up close, its head looked more like that of a seahorse than a mythical storybook dragon.

Charlize asked, "Cute, isn't he?"

"*Darling,*" I said with a snort. "Is he named Ribbons because he rips people and horses to ribbons?"

She smirked. "Zara, he's only about seven inches tall. Haven't you ever noticed that when things get closer to your face, they appear larger? Camera lenses work the same way." She stood and circled around her desk. She snapped up a red apple from the top of a stack of file folders and brought it close to my eyes. "See? Big." She stepped back and held the apple away from me. "Now it's small again. It's called *perspective.*"

"Ha ha."

She leaned in, giddy about teasing me. We'd had a few moments like this at the slumber party in Chessa's cottage, only there'd been wine involved as our excuse.

"Big," she said, bringing the apple to block my view. "Small." She yanked it away.

I used my magic to snap the apple from her hand and slice it into quarters with a blade spell that had become a new bread-and-butter addition to my spell library. I hadn't mastered the round melon balls my aunt was so proud of, but I did manage to magically scoop out the apple's seeds with minimal waste.

Charlize clapped her hands girlishly. "Neat trick! Halfsies?"

"Halfsies," I agreed. It had been her apple, after all. We each munched on two quarters.

Ribbons the Wyvern watched the apple being eaten with keen interest. He licked his scaly lips left and right and then over his eyes once more before giving the camera a slow, deliberate wink. He could see me, all right. I gave him a timid wave. He responded by whipping out one bat-like wing and wiggling tendril-like green fingers at the tip of the wing.

"Well, aren't you the sweetest little baby," I said. "I could put you in a big tin of peanut brittle and scare the sassafras out of my coworker, Frank."

Ribbons turned his head to peer at me with the other eye, puffed out his green-scaled cheeks, and blew a tendril of smoke from both nostrils.

"Goodbye, Ribbons," Charlize said. She licked the apple juice off her fingertips before leaning over her desk to click the button again. "Say hello to the rest of the gang for me."

Ribbons made a gesture that looked a lot like the rude one made iconic by New York City taxi drivers.

"Cheeky wyvern," she said. "I think he's been up to something, but I don't know what."

"Is he dangerous?"

"Anything can be dangerous if it wants, but I wouldn't worry about Ribbons," she said and clicked the ceiling back to plain acoustic tiles again. The sudden transition from sky to mundane materials was surprising. "The projection is a drain on the power supply," she explained. "We're trying to go green here."

Just like a regular, non-magical corporation, I noted.

Corporations will never go green, Tansy noted right back. *The only green they care about is money.*

I was starting to see why Tansy lived by herself out in the country.

Charlize stepped out of her office and led the way down the hallway. "We can check in with the medical bay then hit up your veterinary clinic."

"I can't believe it's morning already."

"Believe it. The first sky shot was real-time, above the building. Our sister Chloe's already been up baking for hours."

"This place is like a casino," I grumbled.

"If by *like a casino*, you mean a drain on financial resources and an exploiter of human gullibility, then you can say that again."

"I meant the no-windows and no-clocks part."

"That, too," she agreed.

* * *

We got our medical update from Dr. Ankh's intern, a willowy blonde woman with elfin ears.

Rhys Quarry was a tough fox. He was still alive and getting stronger by the minute. He would not, however, be wagging his foxtail for a few more hours, as he was heavily sedated. And he needed to wait days, if not a full week, before shifting back to human form.

The willowy blonde intern with the elfin ears, identified on her security pin only as Ubaid, reported that my father's original wound had been deep and nasty. The veterinarian had done an adequate job treating the wound, but the stitches had been no match for my father's premature transformation into human form. Ubaid asked me several more questions about the circumstances surrounding Rhys's harm-causing shift. She kept drilling me, until finally Charlize snapped at the woman to let up on me.

"Can't you see she feels terrible enough as it is?" Charlize snaked one arm around my shoulders and hugged me to her side in a sisterly gesture. "We take care of our own here, and Zara is one of us."

"But she's a witch," said the willowy intern.

"She is one of usssssssssss," Charlize hissed, her hair snakes joining in the chorus.

The intern trembled visibly before retreating.

Charlize gave my shoulder another reassuring squeeze. "Let's go pop in on that vet. What's his name again? Dr. Puppies? Dr. Octopus? Dr. Cheese and Lettuce Sandwich?"

"Dr. Katz." My stomach growled. "But I've never wanted a cheese and lettuce sandwich more in my life."

"We'll stop by Gingerbread on the way to the vet."

CHAPTER 30

MONDAY... APPARENTLY.

SINCE THE LAST time I'd been in Charlize's car, a current-model Beetle, she'd acquired more debris in the back seat.

"Did you go camping recently?" I asked, eyeballing the top layer of the junk, which included a tent, a sleeping bag, and a plastic baggie of what I hoped was charcoal briquettes.

"I go camping all the time. I love to get out in the woods, where I can think and breathe and enjoy the quiet contemplation of nature."

A stone squirrel in the back seat caught my eye. The expression on its pointy rodent face was one of surprise. Or so I guessed. Squirrels always look a bit surprised.

I asked cagily, "And how *do* you enjoy the quiet contemplation of nature, Charlize? By turning small creatures into garden tchotchkes?"

Ignoring my question, she gushed, "You should come with me some time! We can roast marshmallows and tell spooky ghost stories."

"Spooky ghost stories?" I gave her a you-must-be-joking look. "You must mean tales from my regular, everyday life."

"Sure, why not? We'd have so much fun."

"Sure," I said, because *why not*? Even in nothing more than a flimsy tent, we'd be safe. I had my powers. Plus any bear or cougar that messed with us would quickly find itself embarking upon a new career as a concrete lawn jockey.

We stopped by the Gingerbread Bakery for a quick breakfast with Charlize's sister, Chloe, and baby Jordan Junior. The pastries and coffee were excellent, as always.

I still didn't have my purse or phone, so I used the bakery's phone to check in again with my daughter. She was even more concerned than she'd been the night before, but I convinced her to go to school like it was a normal Monday morning.

We thanked the Taubs for the breakfast, I gave Chloe a sisterly hug goodbye, and then we were off to the veterinary clinic.

Just the three of us.

Me, Charlize, and the surprised squirrel. I wondered if he was Petey the Squirrel, the one Bentley carried peanuts for.

We arrived at the clinic and parked the Beetle in front. The vet's lights were on already. All along the street, the other shopkeepers were shaking out their welcome mats and getting ready for another busy week.

Charlize switched off the ignition and yanked out her key ring, which was accessorized with a plush orange octopus. She looped the ring over her index finger and swirled the mass of keys and octopus three times noisily.

Her blue eyes twinkled as she asked, "Ready to roll, partner?"

"Ready as I'll ever be. How are you planning to jog the assistant's memory? Do you have one of those neat clicky pens or something else to break the glamour spell?"

She blinked innocently and drawled, "Why, just my Southern charm."

"You're Southern?" I hadn't detected any sort of accent before—not in Charlize or either of her sisters.

"Zara Riddle, you don't have to be Southern to have Southern charm."

"No, I think you do. That's sort of the whole schtick."

She tossed her head back in laughter before drawling, "Well, shut the front door! You can just watch me work my charms in there and decide for yourself, Little Miss Doubter."

She popped open the Beetle's door and stepped out into the bright morning sunshine. Wincing under the harsh rays, I followed.

As soon as I walked into the clinic, the short assistant greeted me cheerfully. "Welcome back, Ms. Riddle! How is your little fox man?"

"Perfectly healthy," I lied. "And so well behaved. I really lucked out with that one."

Charlize leaned on the counter and looked down at the assistant, who looked shorter than ever in proximity to Charlize.

Fatima said, "H-H-How can I help you, ma'am?"

Charlize looked at the young woman's name tag. "Are you working alone right now, Fatima?"

"I-I-I think so," Fatima.

"That'sssss nice," Charlize said with a hiss.

Fatima's round face relaxed. Her wide-set brown eyes relaxed to a semi-lidded state behind oversized white glasses.

Charlize moved her head rhythmically. The hidden snakes within her golden curls began to undulate.

"I have a question to assssssk you," Charlize hissed.

"Yessss," Fatima replied in a monotone voice. "Asssssssk me anything."

"Who paid for Zara's bill last week?"

"A woman," Fatima said without hesitation. "A woman like both of you. She had great power."

"She looked like us?"

Fatima swayed from left to right, like a snake being charmed by a flute player.

"I don't know," Fatima answered. "Like her." The short assistant pointed a stubby finger at me. "Like her, but different. Older."

I groaned. "Aunt Zinnia. I should have known."

Charlize asked if the clinic had security cameras.

"No cameras," Fatima said.

"Did she pay by credit card?"

I nudged the gorgon on the arm. "I already covered this the first time around."

Charlize poked my shoulder, turning my flesh to stone. It wouldn't last, but it still hurt, like walking on your numb foot when you have pins and needles in your leg. I decided to keep quiet and let her ask the questions.

She repeated the question, getting the same response I had. The stranger had paid in cash. Charlize asked again about a physical description, a scent, a type of clothing style, anything at all.

"Black hair," Fatima said. "She had long black hair."

"Are you sure?"

"Like yours, but black," Fatima said.

Charlize hissed with frustration. "I need something physical," she said.

"Like a tooth," Fatima said.

Charlize and I spoke in unison. "A tooth?"

Fatima opened a drawer and passed us a plastic bag containing a large tooth. A fang.

Charlize picked up the bag. "The black-haired woman left this?"

"Yes," Fatima answered, then, "No." She shook her head. "I'm so confused. It was... left behind that day."

I whispered to Charlize, "Ask her if it was found inside the fox's wound."

My snake-haired partner asked.

Fatima's brown eyes sparkled. "Yes," she exclaimed. "That's where it was. Whatever tried to eat the fox must have left it behind."

A few questions later, Charlize was satisfied we'd gotten all we could.

"A tooth is better than I expected," she said to me.

We were about to leave when a cat meowed pitifully from somewhere inside the clinic.

The white cat! That was what I'd been trying to remember, the thing Tansy had been smuggling away due to her prejudice against cats.

I asked Fatima, "Is that fluffy white cat you had here last week still in need of adoption?"

"Cat?"

"The one who looks like something you'd pull out of the lint filter after a load of white towels."

Fatima pushed her white glasses up her nose. "Yes! If you're interested, I can get you the adoption request forms. If everything clears, you could take her home in a few weeks."

"A few weeks?"

Charlize elbowed me out of the way. "Cat," she said, in a language that was not English yet I understood as English all the same. "Now." She pointed to a spot on the counter. "Cat. Now. Pleasssssssse."

Three minutes later, we were walking out the front door with a fluffy white cat in a cardboard pet carrier. I'd been thinking about adopting the cat, but with everything that had happened last week, I'd forgotten. Tansy would surely have reminded me if it had been a dog needing adoption.

"Her name is Boa," I said to Charlize as we climbed back into the car. I set the box on my lap. "Kind of an interesting coincidence, don't you think?"

"Boa? As in Boa Constrictor? I can't believe you'd make such a tasteless pun." She stared at me. And kept staring. For a full minute. Was I turning to stone? I wasn't sure. I did feel strangely tingly. My eyes began to water, but I stared right back, because I sensed she was testing me somehow.

Someone who wanted our parking spot pulled up behind the Beetle and gave a polite toot of the horn.

The shock of the sound made me break eye contact.

Charlize laughed and slapped her knee. "Boa, as in the feathered kind," she said. "I get it. I'm only teasing you, Zara. That was my impression of Knox."

"Good one," I said. "I thought I was going to suffer the same fate as that poor squirrel in your back seat. Is that Petey?"

"You tell me." She reached back and grabbed the stone statuette.

The car behind us beeped again, this time less politely.

Charlize suddenly thrust a squirming, living and breathing red-furred creature into my face. "Does this guy look like a Petey to you?"

The squirrel chattered angrily as it twisted free of her hand and jumped onto the top of my head. I instinctively pushed open the passenger side door. The squirrel scolded us as it jumped out of the car and zigzagged up the sidewalk. Petey the Squirrel lived!

Charlize didn't just turn living creatures to stone. She could also turn them right back again. Suddenly my witch skills felt like a useless degree from a bankrupt school.

Charlize winked and blew over her fingertip, just like a gunslinger in an old Western.

"Neat," I said, making the understatement of the day.

She twirled her mass of keys. She squealed the car out of the parking spot.

Boa reached a paw through a circular hole in the box and groped the air.

I have a cat. A fur-kid, as they say.

Charlize asked, "Are you coming back to the department with me to run a bunch of lab tests on that fang?"

"As fun as that sounds, my shift at the library starts pretty soon. Can you drop me there?"

"Want me to take the cat?"

"No," I answered a little too vehemently, thinking of Petey the Petrified Squirrel.

* * *

My coworker, Frank Wonder, didn't miss a beat.

"Zara Riddle, that's a box of cat," he said. We were in the staff lounge, making the first pot of coffee before we officially opened for the day.

"Yes, Frank. That is, indeed, a box of cat," I agreed.

"Wine," he said. "If you're going to smuggle in a box of something, it should be wine." He made a tsk-tsk sound and shook his pink-haired head.

"Don't worry. I'll call a taxi and take her home on my lunch break."

Frank opened the cardboard pet-adoption carrier and scooped up an armload of white fluff.

"No way," he said. "I'm going to make up a timecard for this fluff ball. She can work the full shift. What's your name, pretty lady?"

In a squeaky voice, I answered for the cat. "Hi, Frank. My name is Boa, and I am a pretty lady."

He held her at arm's length. She went limp and mewed softly.

"Boa?" Frank kept his eyes on the fluffy newcomer. "What manner of creature are you?"

"She's a regular cat, as far as I know. Charlize gave her a good sniff in the car and said she checks out as a standard feline."

Frank brought the cat in for a hug. Boa wrapped her front paws around his neck adorably.

"This is no standard feline," Frank said. "She's a diva. Isn't that right, Boa? You're just a feathery ballerina in a little white tutu, aren't you?"

"She can't stay here all day without cat stuff. She needs food and somewhere to go to the bathroom."

Frank grinned as he cradled Boa like a baby. "Zara, you're hardly the first librarian to smuggle a cat in here. Check the supply closet."

I did, and he was right. All those clichés about cat-smuggling librarians are true.

* * *

Boa took to the library like a natural. We tried to restrict her to the staff lounge, but she insisted on exploring the whole place, jumping from shelf to shelf like a feathery circus acrobat. She climbed higher and higher, up to the skylights. I worried I'd need magic to locate and extract her at the end of the day.

The patrons were delighted to make her acquaintance. When they learned I'd just adopted the cat that day, they told me their own heartwarming pet-adoption stories.

My lack of sleep became more pronounced throughout the day. I wasn't sleepy, exactly, but my mind was playing tricks on me.

Wherever I was in the building, I had the sense someone was watching me. Following me. Creeping up on me. I thought it was the cat, jumping from shelf to shelf, but I caught glimpses of something dark, not white like Boa.

I was tidying up the floor pillows in the children's storybook corner when a shadowy figure crossed by at the edge of my vision. I don't know how I knew this, but I sensed it was better to not look directly at the figure.

I kept tidying up the storybook corner. I nonchalantly approached a trio of brothers, all with the same light-brown hair, who were sharing a graphic novel.

"Enjoying the book?"

The middle-sized boy looked up at me. "Can we really take this home?"

"You can borrow it," I said. "All you need is a library card."

"Wow," he said and went back to reading.

I leaned forward to pick up a pillow and then abruptly glanced past my shoulder.

The shadowy figure moved like a blur, disappearing around the corner of a shelf.

Oh, no you don't. I ran after the dark blur.

Nothing but books and two teens who might have been about to kiss.

I kept going, weaving up and down the aisles. Was Frank playing one of his practical jokes on me, or was there a mysterious entity following me?

I gave my resident spirit a poke in the ribs.

Tansy, did you see who that was? Did you see someone with dark hair, a woman?

The spirit gave no response. I would have thought she'd be more active due to my tiredness. Honestly, I'd hoped she might take over for a bit so I could slip into the backstage of consciousness for a nap. But for my entire Monday shift, she was absent.

* * *

I had just tricked Boa back into the temporary pet carrier when Charlize showed up, looking serious.

"Oh, no," I said. My father hadn't made it. I grabbed onto the circulation counter to steady myself.

"Relax," Charlize said. "I'm just here to give you and the cat a ride home."

"How's my father?"

She glanced around. "His tail's wagging."

I breathed a sigh of relief. He wasn't my favorite person, but he was the only father I had. The only living parent I had.

Charlize eyed the pet carrier. "Need some help with that?"

"Sure, but no funny business." I slid the carrier across the counter to her. "Play nice."

Charlize rolled her eyes and took the carrier. Boa poked a paw through a circular hole and batted at one of Charlize's blonde curls.

"Aren't you a cutie," Charlize said. "Yes, you are. Yes, you are!"

I smiled as I watched my gorgon friend make embarrassing baby talk with my new fur-kid. I hadn't experienced this emotion since Zoey had been a baby, and it filled me up with emotion. *They grow up so fast.*

I was so glad to see Charlize, though. I hadn't felt so excited about a friendship with another woman since before I'd become a parent.

My feelings must have also excited my resident spirit in a way that regular librarian duties did not.

Grow only true friends in your garden, Tansy's spirit whispered in my head. *You'll know when you have the right ones because they'll sprout up and bush out like weeds, even if you neglect them from time to time.*

Wise words.

CHAPTER 31

I MUST HAVE nodded off in Charlize's car.

I remembered leaning my head back on the headrest.

The next thing I knew, my shoulder was both burning and freezing at once. Charlize was jostling me awake by shooting her stone powers into my shoulder.

"A gentle shaking would have sufficed," I grumbled, swatting her hand away. My defensive magic flared up, and I shocked her hard enough to make her shriek.

"Zara! I nearly wet myself!"

The cat inside the box on my lap meowed in alarm.

I made the horns sign with one hand and waved it at my blonde chauffeur. "You mess with the bull, you get the horns."

She eyed my finger-horns warily. "You would know, *devil's spawn*."

"Snake monster."

She grinned. "Soul sucker. Daughter of flame-haired demons."

"Ouch." I reached for the door handle. "I'd say something horrific about *your* lineage, but I might accidentally guess right."

"Probably."

We got out of the car and walked up to the front door. The cat in the box seemed heavier with each step.

"Boa, this is your new home," I said.

The fluffy white cat in the box meowed pitifully.

"She's excited," Charlize said. "I don't speak cat, but I do know excitement."

I wasn't so sure.

We walked into the house, and I called for Zoey.

My sixteen-year-old came down the stairs slowly, warily glancing between me, the meowing box, and

Charlize, whom she'd heard all about but had never met before.

I made introductions, we gave her an update on her grandfather, and then I quickly moved on to releasing Boa from her corrugated cage.

The fluffy white cat hopped out like a bunny being summoned from a magician's hat.

Zoey gasped and clapped her hands together in a childlike expression of pure delight.

I couldn't be happier. *Zara is a great mother!*

With her white feather-duster tail held high, Boa sniffed the air delicately, her tiny pink nostrils flaring. She began to explore the main floor of the house, ignoring the three of us. We trailed behind her like groupies, watching in fascination, and whispering about what she might be thinking.

"This is mine now, and so is this, and this," Zoey said, speaking on behalf of the cat. Indeed, Boa was rubbing her whiskered cheeks on furniture legs and corners as though staking her claim. "Oh, and this window is mine." The cat struck a pose on the den's windowsill. "Yes. Very nice. I shall return later to sunbathe."

The cat jumped off the windowsill and strutted past us, toward the downstairs powder room.

Boa's keen attention to every item in every room made me think of the white glove a butler might use to inspect a mansion for dust. She completed her "white paw inspection" of the main floor and stopped at the foot of the stairs, turning to look at us as though asking for permission to proceed upstairs.

"Go ahead," I told her. "This house is yours now."

Zoey raced up the stairs and stopped halfway. "Come on, Boa! Come see my bedroom. You can sleep on my bed after Auntie Z fixes you for allergies."

"We might not need that spell after all," I said. "She's been with me all day, and I haven't sneezed once."

Zoey frowned. "Sure, but that's *you*, Mom." The fluffy white cat passed her soundlessly on the stairs and began her inspection of the upper floor. "You got stronger in every way after..." She gave Charlize a cautious look.

"Charlize knows everything," I said. "Technically, she knew about us being witches even before we knew."

Charlize spoke through an embarrassed grin. "Not something I'm proud of, but it's true."

"You're the computer hacker," Zoey said. "You committed reckless conduct that created a risk of serious physical injury to another person." She pointed to her chest. "Me. Because you brought me and my mother here, straight into danger with all the weird stuff in this town. That's a class D felony, punishable by up to five years in prison, a fine of up to five thousand dollars, or both."

"You were at risk of living a boring life," Charlize said, meeting my daughter's accusatory tone with equal fire. "It would have been a far greater crime to let you continue the mundane life you were leading. Before Chet and I intervened, the most exciting thing you had going was planning a coup in your school's newspaper committee with Francie and Jade."

Zoey's eyes widened. We both knew that Chet and Charlize had hacked into our internet accounts to orchestrate our move to Wisteria, but hadn't considered the entirety of what that meant. If Charlize had read all our private correspondence, all our personal notes, she might know us better than we knew each other.

"Your plans worked, by the way," Charlize said snarkily. "Francie and Jade got support from the two Tanyas, and they overthrew Brianna. If you'd kept in touch with your so-called friends, you would know that."

The two stared at each other in stony silence.

I got the protective urge to defend my daughter. "Francie and Jade were no great loss," I said. "Those two were obsessed with rumors about celebrity pop stars being replaced by look-alikes, or clones, or reincarnated Illuminati priestesses, which, come to think of it, in light of everything I know now, might not be so crazy after all."

My daughter said nothing. She continued staring at Charlize, who also said nothing.

I sighed. "I miss Francie and Jade," I admitted.

That snapped my daughter out of the staring contest.

"It was nice to meet you," Zoey said to Charlize with a syrupy tone. "And congratulations on your own plans working out." And then, in the most syrupy, cruel tone only a teen can conjure, added a poisonous "I hope you're happy now." She went the rest of the way up the stairs, following after the white cat.

Charlize turned to me, looking sheepish. "I'm not great with children."

"She was planning a coup with Francie and Jade? I had no idea."

"Oh, she's got some Machiavellian traits, all right."

"Takes one to know one," I said.

Charlize put her hands in her pockets and looked down at the floor between us. "I shouldn't have said anything. Now your daughter hates me."

"Never mind what you said—it was what you did. You reading her private emails and messages." I tapped my fingers on the newel post. "And mine, too."

"It was more of a light skim than an in-depth read," she said. "Except for the part about the school newspaper coup, which was strangely fascinating."

"Mm-hmm." More finger tapping.

"And I only did it because my poor, innocent sister was trapped in a coma."

I rolled my eyes. How often was she going to play the coma card to get out of trouble?

The snakes in the blonde gorgon's hair remained invisible, but I did hear them hissing.

"Zara, I'm not one of those gushy girls who makes the big heartfelt speeches, but I want you to know I really like you. When I read your emails, I could tell you were funny and smart and kind. I hoped that one day we would be friends."

I took it all in. I didn't know what I felt. Everything? Nothing? The tiredness from staying up most of the night was hitting me with a fresh wave of exhaustion. I was too tired to feel.

Charlize added, "Honestly, I'm a bit jealous of how cool you are."

"It's hard for me to hold a grudge when you say nice—and entirely true—stuff like that." I tapped the wood again. What would Winona Vander Zalm do right about now? It came to me immediately.

In my delicate Winona voice, I asked, "*Cuppatea, dear?*"

The pretty gorgon looked up from the floor, her blue eyes bright and shining. "*Cuppatea?* Like a pair of girly girls?"

"Or a pair of adult women."

"Yes, please. I need to talk to you about the lab results from the fang, anyway."

I waved for her to follow me. "The kitchen's this way. Or at least it was when I left the house last night. With this place, you never know."

* * *

"So you can see my dilemma," Charlize said after it had all been explained.

"Not exactly." I took another sip of tea.

We were sitting on the new wrought-iron chairs we'd discovered in the back yard. The sturdy yet elegant dining set had arrived during the day, courtesy of arrangements Tansy's spirit must have made when she'd ordered all the plants and landscaping materials.

"This looks lovely, by the way." Charlize waved at the new lush greenery. "Let me know if you'd like any stone decorations. In case you're worried about the mistreatment of animals, don't be. I can turn the recently deceased and make them appear lifelike. Like the ones in front of Chessa's cottage."

The mention of Chessa's name made the hairs stand up on my arms. Or maybe it was learning that her lawn ornaments were roadkill.

I thanked her for the oh-so-generous offer. After checking that our privacy sound bubble was still in place, I got back to the main point of our discussion.

"Let me see if my overtired brain is getting all of this," I said. "The fang belongs to one of Tansy's dogs. Specifically, Jasper. You know this only because you happened to have the DNA of Jasper's littermate on file due to a dispute between two of the department's agents over whose pet was leaving droppings in a common area."

Charlize nodded. "Even the results of unauthorized use of the department's resources become property of the department."

"And because the fang of Tansy's dog was found inside my father's wound, that means he lied to my face about the bird attack. I suppose Knox will be relieved. But that does make him a suspect in Tansy Wick's disappearance."

"A suspect in her *death*," she corrected.

I winced. "My father has many flaws, but he's no killer. I'm sure that once the agents question him, he'll turn on this accomplice of his. The one who wears boots like mine. He or she is the one you've got to arrest."

"And that's my dilemma," Charlize said. "How do I put this delicately?" She looked into her teacup and casually turned it from porcelain to granite then back again. When she looked back up at me, her blue eyes were bright and ringed in red. "The department doesn't exactly follow the same rules as a municipal police department."

I stopped breathing. "They'll torture my father," I said. "But they don't need to do that. He'll cooperate with the investigation, I promise. Let me talk to him. As soon as he's well enough to shift into human form, I'll convince him."

"You won't get the chance," she said. "You saw what happened to Dr. Bob, as soon as the truth came out. He didn't get a fair trial. He didn't get a trial at all." The red around her eyes grew brighter. "Except trial by bloodshed."

I started breathing again, and it came in a ragged sob. I had thought I was too tired to feel anything, but I was wrong. The ache started in my chest and went all the way up to my ears. I hated Rhys Quarry, but I also loved him. I didn't want him to die.

Charlize took my hand in hers. She stroked my palm with icy-cool fingertips.

"Shush," she hissed. "It's going to be okay, Zara."

I bit back my emotions, pushing them into the dark basement. I had to be strong for my daughter. I had to keep my head above the water. I had to get help from someone more powerful than me.

"The department doesn't know about the fang yet," she said. "And they also don't know where Rhys Quarry was when he got shocked by Vincent Wick."

"They don't know?"

"I changed the details in the report the medics opened last night," she said with a soft hiss. "And I filed the fang request under the code for a different case."

I forced myself to stare into her eyes, even though the red rims looked like seeping blood. "Thank you," I said. "I owe you."

"All I did was buy you a bit of time. It's up to you and your father to save his furry hide. You need to find out who's responsible for Tansy's death so I can unleash the full fury of the DWM on *them*."

"Are you sure they won't just question him and let him go?"

"It's complicated. Once upon a time, Tansy was one of us. She was an agent. The department treats the death of one of their own very seriously."

"I'll talk to my father. Let's get him out of there so I can take care of this myself."

She blinked. The redness around her eyes only got more vivid, yet I could also see that her eyes were a healthy white and her eyelids were a soft, fleshy pink. The blood-hued redness was similar to the snakes in her hair. The redness was either a glamour, or the truth beneath the glamour. It was both things. Charlize was both things. Monster and friend.

Charlize let go of my hand and reached again for her tea. "It sounds like you two don't have the most honest relationship with each other, but it's time for honesty now. Don't make the mistake my sister Chloe made by not telling anyone about Chessa's gift. The only way to save your father is for all your family secrets to be revealed."

Familiar words echoed in my head. *Secrets revealed are trouble unsealed.*

"I'll do my best," I promised.

CHAPTER 32

TUESDAY

I woke before the alarm clock went off, and lay still, staring up at the bottom of Zoey's bunk.

Since my father hadn't been there the night before, and the cat hardly needed her own room, I could have slept in the guest room. But I hadn't wanted my persnickety house to get annoyed and brick me in like some victim in an Edgar Allan Poe story. That particular method of murder was, incidentally, a fate so popular at one time that it earned its own name. *Immurement.*

When I'd climbed into bed the night before, I'd tried not to think about immurement. Or my father being tortured for information by DWM agents. Torturing him for information was my job. Charlize had promised she would get my father out, smuggling him under her sweater if she had to.

Zoey and I didn't have our slumber party giggles on Monday night. With nobody to be annoyed, what was the point?

Boa jumped on the lower bunk, gave me a whiskery kiss goodnight, and then used her spectacular leaping skills to get up to Zoey's level. That was where she remained. Boa was Zoey's cat, that was clear.

I slept, though my dreams were so vivid, I might as well have stayed awake watching David Lynch films.

I was watching dirt, waiting for something to grow, when a tiny pointed leaf of pale green emerged. The loamy soil shifted. Another point came up from the dirt. This one was a bird's beak. The blue jay dug itself out of its grave and shook the dirt from its wings.

Be careful, the blue jay spoke without opening its beak. *Watch yourself, Zara. Watch yourself.*

The blue jay stretched out its wings and took to the air. But the bird couldn't fly away. No matter how hard he beat his wings, something held him down. A swirl of wire was wrapped around his legs, connecting him to the ground. More shoots of wire—barbed wire—pushed up through the dirt and lunged at the struggling bird.

The bird flapped harder and cried out in horror.

More wires shot up, looping around the bird's head and wings, dragging it down.

The ground rumbled, and then something a hundred times larger than the blue jay shot up from the ground and swallowed the bird whole.

When I awoke on Tuesday morning, the image of my nightmare lingered so vividly that I got out of bed early rather than risk returning to the same dream.

Zoey stirred in the upper bunk and made a contented noise.

Boa slept beside her head, with her fluffy tail draped across Zoey's upper lip like a comically large white mustache.

* * *

Frank handed me a book about the interpretation of dreams, plus a book about Freud, and a third one about medieval legends.

"Maybe these will help," he said.

We were upstairs, in the library's storybook corner. Frank was working on a display, and I was jokingly "supervising."

I'd planned to keep my latest worries to myself, but the storybook area reminded me of the previous day's sneaky visitor. I told Frank about that incident, plus the strange dreams that had plagued my sleep.

I checked that no patrons were watching then used my page-finding spell to query the books about blue jays and monsters from the grave springing up to eat them midair. The pages riffled with magic. Frank whistled his admiration of my nifty spellwork.

Alas, there was nothing under that search. I checked the word *immurement* next. And then I wished I hadn't.

"People used to enclose a lot of weird things inside their walls for good luck," I said to Frank. "The sort of things people nowadays would pay good money to have *removed* from their walls, like nasty old bottles with waste and bent nails." I chuckled. "Good luck keeping witches out with *that*."

I read a little more while Frank worked on his display.

After a while, he asked, "Anything good?"

"More like the opposite of good. All these old stories about superstitious builders sacrificing children to entomb inside foundation walls..." I shook my head and glanced over at a display of the latest teen novels. "All those young adult dystopian books, with all their kid-on-kid battles, don't seem so far-fetched in light of history." I sighed and closed the book. "Nothing in here about blue jays or their connection to *creatures of the grave*, whatever those are."

Frank clapped me on the shoulder. "We all have weird dreams. They don't always mean something."

"But you used to dream about flying every night before you finally found out what you are."

"Good point." He rubbed his chin. "How big would you say was this bird-snatching monster from your nightmares? Big enough to eat, say, a flamingo?"

"Of course not," I lied. The blue jay had been a speck inside the thing's large jaws. The hungry beast had been all mouth.

Changing the topic, I asked, "How's the flying club?" He'd been meeting with Rob and Knox for flights in the mountains, away from curious eyes.

Frank waggled his eyebrows. "The first rule about Flight Club is you don't talk about Flight Club."

I groaned. "How long have you been waiting to use that line?"

"Too long," he said with a smile.

Frank returned to putting up summer decorations. We'd chosen a bird theme for the children's summer reading program, much to Frank's delight. There were pink flamingos everywhere.

I picked up a pair of plastic martini glasses. "I'm not sure these are appropriate for children." They had flamingos on the bases, but they were still martini glasses.

He put a hand on his hip and gave me a sassy look. "Zara Riddle, I never took you for a prude." He plucked the glasses from my hands and returned them to the display. The centerpiece was a lamp with a shade covered in white feathers. It was an art piece by a local artist, titled Scenes From a Pillow Fight.

Frank flicked at the white feathers. "And how is the new member of the Riddle family?"

"My father? He's in big trouble as soon as I get him alone in human form."

"I meant the cat," Frank said. "Is the Divine Miss Boa settling into her new fashionable digs?"

"She's already better adjusted than the humans who live there. She walks across everything like she owns it. Furniture, counters, even people. I wonder if she might be possessed."

Frank frowned at me. "Zara, you do realize that's normal cat behavior, don't you?"

"I've never had a pet before."

"It shows," he said. "Cat-mom newbie."

I chucked a pillow at him.

He caught it and prepared to lob it back at me but stopped when he noticed a man approaching the story-time area.

"Busted," Frank said in a singsong voice.

To the man, he said, "Detective, it was self-defense, I swear." He pointed at me. "She started it." He chucked the pillow at my head.

Detective Bentley gave me a steely look. "I believe you," he said to Frank without taking his eyes off me. "Mind if I borrow your coworker?"

Frank picked up his toolbox of crafting supplies. "Sure. I need a refill on glitter anyway."

Bentley walked over to the display of birds and picked up a blue jay holding a sprig of holly. It was a Christmas ornament, and half the size of the blue jay who'd visited us. He put the bird back without comment.

He turned to me. "I'm here with your update on the Tansy Wick case." My aunt's spell was still working.

"Have a seat." I waved to the story-time pillows on the floor.

"Those aren't chairs," he said.

"You are really good at detecting things."

He frowned and took an awkward cross-legged seat on a gray velvet pillow.

According to his research, the property development company who'd been pressuring Tansy Wick to sell her land had also been involved in other recent cases. Their crimes were mostly trespassing and aggressive phone calls, but it showed a pattern of bullying. The company had at least a dozen employees involved in closed or current investigations.

I asked, "Do you have a list of names I can look over?"

He didn't even find this odd. That was some powerful spell my aunt had cast. He pulled his phone out and showed me a column of names listed alphabetically.

One of the named jumped out at me immediately.

"This one," I said excitedly. "Reyna Drinkwater." Her first name was so similar to Reynard that it had to mean something. "What does this MM next to her name mean?"

"Malicious mischief," he said.

"Did she toilet paper someone's tree?"

He gave me a wait-for-it look. "Reyna Drinkwater, with the help of an accomplice, released several wild animals inside a property while the owners were on holidays. The Pendersons, a law-abiding retired couple, returned home from vacation to find their residence infested with wildlife. There was a scurry of squirrels, a surfeit of skunks, and a passel of possums."

"That's it?" It was a far cry from murder. The infestation sounded both mischievous and adorable—but then, it hadn't happened inside my house.

"And a donkey," he said.

"You're making this up."

"I assure you I am not." He went on to show me photographs of the damage to the residence.

He explained that whoever had released the animals inside the house must have known that damage done by those specific animals was excluded from the couple's insurance coverage. The elderly couple decided to take the predatory offer from Akorn Development and use the funds to retire elsewhere.

"Reyna Drinkwater," I said, letting the name roll around in my head. Tansy's spirit had been quiet all day, and even now she didn't react. *Tansy Wick, were you being harassed by someone named Reynard? Or Reyna Drinkwater?* No response. *And what's Project Buttercup all about, anyway?*

Silence from the ghost in the peanut gallery.

I asked Bentley, "Do you know of something called Project Buttercup?"

He looked around at the bright-colored children's books surrounding us. "Should I?"

"Never mind."

He regarded me with suspicion. "You know something," he said. "You're keeping secrets."

"Tansy Wick was working on a Project Buttercup," I said. "I can't explain it, but I have a hunch that this Reyna Drinkwater might be involved."

"Does this come from that thing you do? Where you use empathy or psychic powers or whatever you call it?"

He remembered that after all. "That sounds silly," I said. "Bentley, I was just teasing you that day."

He rubbed his forehead. "This isn't right. Something's wrong. I shouldn't be here. I shouldn't be talking to you." He got up from his pillow and looked down his nose at me. "This is inappropriate."

"Probably," I said. "Before you go, do you have any photos of Reyna?"

He clutched his phone protectively. "No."

"Does she have pale skin and long black hair?" If I could connect her to the woman who'd paid the veterinary bill, we would almost certainly have our suspect.

"No," he said.

I made a disappointed noise.

"Her hair is dark auburn," he said.

I made a hopeful noise.

It wasn't much, but we had another lead.

Reyna Drinkwater, what have you been up to?

CHAPTER 33

CHARLIZE BREEZED INTO the library five minutes before the end of my shift. She looked ready for the gym in a baggy sweatshirt, tight leggings, and athletic shoes.

She caught my eye and puffed out the bottom of her sweatshirt, where she had presumably stuffed a fox earlier that day to smuggle him out of the DWM.

I asked in a whisper, "Is he in there now?"

She flattened the sweatshirt again to show her trim figure. "He's waiting in Bugsy, wagging his tail because he's so happy to be up above ground," she said.

I didn't want to see his tail wagging. I wanted to hear him answer my questions. "He hasn't shifted?"

"Not yet. He can understand us, but he can't talk."

"How convenient," I grumbled.

But even if he couldn't talk, I would mention the name Reyna Drinkwater and try to bluff a reaction out of him.

I said goodbye to my coworkers and punched out my timecard with a noisy KERCHUNK. Charlize teased me about making noise in the library, and we joked around for a minute. On the way out, I caught the head librarian staring after us wistfully. I pulled away from my new blonde friend guiltily.

From the expression on Kathy Carmichael's face, I could read her emotions like the synopsis of a book. I, too, had looked longingly after girlfriends joking around without me. For the past sixteen years, I'd gone without. I'd been too young to fit in with Zoey's schoolmates' parents, who were all easily a decade older, but too tied down to socialize with people my own age.

When Kathy had offered me the job, she'd offered to introduce me to her favorite crafts. She had expected that we'd be friends outside of work. I had expected the same, yet months later, it hadn't worked out.

I smiled at my boss and gave her a cheerful wave, holding eye contact longer than necessary. *I haven't forgotten about you,* I beamed in her direction. She turned away quickly.

* * *

My father's ears pointed up when he saw me. He stood on the passenger seat with his white-tipped tail whipping from side to side. The windows were down, so I heard his high-pitched yipping noises. It was the first time I'd been around the fox since learning he was my father. He was so cute. I wanted to hug him. But I wouldn't hug him. No way. Not after all the trouble he'd caused.

I opened the door. "I know about your friend," I said.

He tilted his head to the side.

"Your friend Reynard. I know it's a woman named Reyna Drinkwater."

He yipped once.

I asked, "Is that twice for yes and once for no?"

Two yips. Yes. Which meant no to Reynard being Reyna Drinkwater.

"Whatever," I said. "I'm not in the mood for playing games. We know you were attacked by Tansy's dogs."

He blinked his big gold-green eyes innocently.

"Play cute and innocent all you want, but we know about the dogs. I've got a few friends who have a bone to pick with you for trying to blame it on a bird attack, too. Keep playing mute if you want, but it's only a question of time before we figure out everything."

He lowered his head to the seat and put one paw across his eyes.

I wanted to be angry, but I couldn't. Why did he have to be so adorable?

Charlize patted my shoulder. "Let's get you home before you draw a crowd."

A few people walking their dogs were watching from a distance with interest.

The back of Charlize's car was too full of junk for my father to sit anywhere else, so he had to sit on my lap for the ride to my house.

I gave him a pat on the head and scratched his chin anyway. He was still in trouble, but some instincts you can't control.

Charlize squealed out of the parking spot. "How was your day?"

I told her how I'd been troubled by nightmares the previous night, but at least I hadn't imagined anyone was stalking me in the library today.

She said, "Stress has many adverse side effects on the unconscious mind. When my sister was trapped in her coma, I kept seeing her everywhere. Whenever I went out on the ocean, she seemed to be there, just far enough below the surface that I couldn't make eye contact. But she was always watching me. Of that I'm sure."

"Maybe she was. How powerful is she?"

The fox on my lap whimpered.

"You don't want to know," Charlize said grimly.

We pulled up in front of my house.

"I really owe you," I said. "You're already the best friend I've ever had, even better than Hannah Gerber, who loaned me her gym shorts in the first grade when I went down the big kids' slide and landed in a big mud puddle. If she hadn't done that, the other kids would have called me pee-pants the whole year."

Charlize shifted uncomfortably in the driver's seat and flicked at the plush octopus on her key ring.

"Zara," she said in a we-need-to-talk tone.

Here it comes. "What?"

"Nothing. Just that I care about you, too," she said. "Whatever happens, you need to know I'm on your side."

"You're scaring me. Are you in trouble?"

She turned her plush octopus toy to granite and then back to orange fabric again. She didn't make eye contact with me.

"I'll be fine," she said with a grit that didn't inspire confidence. "Take care of yourself."

"Would you like to come in? *Cuppatea?* You can see how well the white fluff ball is settling in."

She shook her head stiffly. "I've got work to do."

I opened the door, and the fox sprung out ahead of me. He walked easily toward the house, glanced back to see me watching, and began to limp. *You rotten little faker.*

"Wait," Charlize said.

She pressed a plastic baggie into my hand. It was the yellowing fang we'd gotten from the veterinarian.

"Maybe you can use this for some witch stuff," she said, spitting out the words as though talking against her will. "I don't know much about witchcraft, but maybe there's a way for you to use this to find Tansy's body. That would help the investigation a lot. You can call the police department once you find her. Don't touch anything."

"You sound pretty confident that I'll be able to help."

She looked me right in the eyes. Her pupils were so red and raw, I wished she hadn't.

"Zara, I can't do much until we find Tansy's body," she said plainly. "That part's up to you."

"Okay," I said. "I'll do some witch stuff. Or, as Vincent Wick calls it, witcher-i-doo."

"You do that." She leaned over and called out the window, "And you, be a good boy," she said.

Too late for that.

* * *

A pair of green-gold eyes with oval pupils stared mournfully at the glass of red wine I was drinking.

"This sure is a fine bottle of *Valpolicello* that I've been saving for a special occasion," I said from my lounging spot on the sofa. "Oh, isn't that your favorite type of wine, Dad?"

The fox whimpered and licked his lips. The green-gold eyes flicked from the wine to the assortment of fancy cheese, stuffed olives, spicy dips, and crackers spread out on the coffee table. More lip licking.

"Sorry, fox. This is *people* food. For people." I sipped the wine. "Mmm, this people wine is delicious. It's a shame we can't give this delicious *Valpolicello* wine to foxes." I took another sip and smacked my lips. "And it's a *crying* shame that you're still injured and it's not safe for you to shift back to human form."

He let out a heart-breaking whimper. He could have easily swiped whatever food he wanted. I wasn't about to shock him or harm him, but something about him being in fox format must have made him believe me that he wasn't allowed to partake of people food.

Boa, however, didn't see the distinction. Or simply didn't care. She jumped on the coffee table, grabbed a three-quarters-full wheel of Brie with her feline fangs, and was gone in a heartbeat.

The fox barked like a dog and skittered away on the wood floor, chasing after the cat.

I called out, "Bad fox! We don't chase kitties!"

Animal nails skittered over the kitchen floor. More hissing, yowling, and yipping. Boa let out a bone-chilling howl that was ten times the cat she was.

Zoey, who'd been watching the whole scene with interest from her seat in the comfy chair, raised her eyebrows at me. "I thought getting a pet would make us more normal," she said.

I waved one hand. "You and your obsession with being normal. Have you had any allergic reactions, by the way? When you were little, cats and dogs made you sneeze."

"I haven't sneezed once."

"That's what I figured. You must be cured, which is good, because you had a cat-tail mustache this morning."

"Boa must be one of those less allergenic cats. I was reading that certain colors of cats produce fewer allergens."

"Or your lack of sneezing could be a sign of your powers kicking in," I said. "A very positive sign."

She wrinkled her nose adorably. "Mom, give it up. I'm just a regular kid. If I really was a witch, something would have happened by now."

"All you need is the right motivation, or stronger stimulus. I didn't know I could shoot lightning bolts until

Dr. Bob swooped down from the sky and tried to rip me to ribbons."

A white blur swished onto the coffee table, nearly knocking over the bottle of red wine before I balanced it with magic. Boa nabbed a chunk of aged cheddar cheese and dashed off with it once more.

"She must be building a cheese nest," I said to Zoey. "That's something cats do, right?"

"Oh, yes. The *Felis catus* is valued for its companionship as well as its ability to build elaborate nests out of cheese."

Boa dashed through the room with the cheese. The fox wasn't far behind, yipping his head off. Both of them scrambled up the stairs, their sharp nails putting even more dents and scratches on the old wood.

Once they were above us, my daughter looked up at the ceiling, which emanated scuffling sounds.

"Mom, are you sure that fox is really Pawpaw and not some random red fox?"

"Uh..." I hadn't considered that. Charlize had been acting strange. Had she made a swap?

Zoey locked her hazel eyes on mine. "It could be a DWM agent sent undercover to spy on us."

"You never know around here," I said. "How do we know Boa's not a spy? She could be deep undercover, like the you-know-what in *Harry Potter*."

Zoey smirked. "The you-know-what? Mom, I've read that series multiple times."

I shrugged. "My librarian's instinct to avoid spoilers runs deep."

The doorbell rang, and Zoey ran to let in my aunt, who we were expecting. The two of them chatted in the entryway for a few minutes before joining me in the living room.

"What a lovely spread you've set out for us," Zinnia said. "Only a half glass of wine for me. I need to stay sharp for spellwork."

"What about me? We can't let the bottle go bad."

"Zara, you're a natural. You'll be surpassing your mentor in no time." Her lips puckered. The compliment was bitter on her taste buds. She was a witch, but she was still human.

"I don't get it," Zoey said. "If Mom is such a genius witch, why did her house lock her out of her own room?" She pointed at my leopard-print dress, which I'd borrowed from her closet. "Don't stretch out my Audrey dress with your adult hips." We'd picked up the brown-and-black-spotted form-fitting dress at a theater's costume department sale. She had never worn the figure-hugging dress but was still weirdly possessive about it. "And don't stretch the top out with your adult boobs, either."

Zinnia and I exchanged a knowing look. My daughter was sensitive about her late-blooming powers and sometimes took it out on me. But... adult hips? Adult boobs? Ouch. Low blow.

"Don't do that," Zoey said.

We answered together, "Do what?"

"Don't talk about me with your eyes. I can see you."

The cat tore through the room like lightning, followed by the fox. They tipped over a wooden chair and skittered their way back up the stairs.

Zoey gave me a dirty look, as though everything in the entire world was my fault suddenly, and followed the animals upstairs.

"Zara, your house is getting more crowded each time I come over. Was that a cat or an animated feather duster?"

"It's a cat who resembles an animated feather duster. Her name is Boa, and... Let me get you that wine."

She was already pouring her own, levitating both bottle and glass gracefully.

"*Valpolicello*," she commented. "Your mother's favorite. I believe Rhys was the one who introduced her to it."

"Not a coincidence," I said. "I'm using it as incentive to get my father to turn back into a person, or as much of a person as Rhys Quarry can be."

"He does strike me as the type who is motivated by rewards, and not deterred by punishment," she said.

I made her promise not to give any wine to my father until he turned back in his smug-faced Rhys Quarry human form. I caught her up on the rest of the story while we sipped wine and nibbled the cheese that had not yet been stolen for Boa's cheese nest.

I also told her about Bentley's suspicion that she'd been spying on him. The past two days had been so hectic that I hadn't had the chance to talk to her about my Sunday-afternoon coffee date with the detective.

"Nothing came of that," Zinnia reported. "I had hoped to learn the identity of Bentley's indescribable new friend, but he was alone all night."

"You should have taken me with you. It's been ages since you disguised me as a bush."

"Zara, you were in no condition to do spellwork. I'm still not sure what happened to you outside the police station. One minute you were fine, and the next you were writhing around on the grass, moaning about being absorbed by the darkness, being consumed."

"I broke the news to Tansy that she was dead, and she didn't take it well."

Zinnia pursed her lips. "To be expected."

"Is communicating with spirits always like that? She didn't just make me feel sad. She fire-hosed me with anguish. If I'd been standing next to a cliff, or on a subway platform, I don't know what I might have done."

"Direct communication is extremely dangerous," she said. "That's why we're doing this spell in tandem, to split the flowback energy. Even so, it could be tricky."

"Great," I said with an enthusiastic swing of the arm. "Let's get to it."

She reached for her purse and started pulling out potions.

We planned to summon the spirit of whichever one of Tansy's dogs had lost the fang. We would use the fang as an anchor to communicate with the dog. If our spell worked as planned, we'd have the dog lead us to Tansy's body. Then the police and the DWM could take over the investigation, and I would putter around in the garden with Tansy until she'd been avenged and buried properly so her spirit could move on to a greener greenhouse. Easy peasy.

And so, while my fox-shifter father chased a white cat around the house, and my daughter sulked about not being a witch yet, my aunt and I drank wine and set up the ingredients to perform a tandem-witch spell to summon a pair of dog ghosts. Just a typical Tuesday night for the Riddles.

CHAPTER 34

EITHER THE RITUAL was working, or I'd accidentally sat on an electric eel.

My body hummed with power, and tooth-colored sparks circled over the dog fang on the silver platter. Zinnia let out an unselfconscious witchy cackle. She felt it, too. We were successfully summoning the spirit of a ghost dog using its fang. What witcher-i-doo!

A dog spirit appeared. The darkness entered through a wall with a lumbering gait.

Boa sounded the alarm, hissing at the spectral presence. The white cat, who'd been curled up on the back of a sofa, watching us with one sleepy eye, was fully alert now. She arched her back, making herself taller. Her feathery tail twitched like a whip. She yowled at the translucent dog, who eyed the cat warily and gave me a guilty look.

Zinnia still couldn't see the ghost dog, but apparently the cat could. Based on what I knew of cats, this didn't surprise me much.

"Is it Coco or Jasper?" Zinnia asked me. "Jasper had a white diamond on his forehead."

"Coco," I said. "And now that I'm looking for it, I can see she's missing an upper fang."

Coco lumbered her way over to my feet. She warily kept her big brown eyes on hissing Boa, who was doing a fine impersonation of a snake.

"She's enormous," I said to Zinnia. "Is she part hellhound?"

"Neapolitan Mastiff," Zinnia said with a chuckle. "Coco's most evil traits are drooling and snoring."

"That's not very evil."

"You haven't been kissed by her."

"I take it you have?"

Zinnia made a funny face and mimed using her hand to squeegee drool off her face.

"Good girl," I said to Coco. "Thank you for coming to help us."

The Neapolitan Mastiff had a beastly appearance, with her heavy-boned frame draped in an oversized skin. Her abundant hide hung in wrinkles around her head and under her chin in a dewlap. She was beautiful in her own magnificent way. She glanced up at me and sat obediently. Her relatively small ears twitched between me and the hissing cat.

"She's not interested in chasing the cat," I said.

"Coco's got better manners than your father."

I reached out to pet the dog. "Coco tries to be a good girl." My hand passed right through, but she perked up visibly at the praise, so I continued. "Coco doesn't chase kitties, does she? No. Coco is better trained than some foxes."

The fox in question was upstairs in the guest room. We'd put him there to keep him from chasing Boa through our spell ingredients. I'd taunted him to turn back into human form so he could work the doorknob. So far, he hadn't. But his ploy to avoid questioning wouldn't last forever. With any luck, we'd have a breakthrough tonight that would force a full confession from him by morning.

The huge, wrinkly dog remained before me, her face the same height as mine and her comically small ears twitching with alertness. *Yes? You summoned me?*

Zinnia handed me our pointing tool, which was a modified hand-held compass. I pressed Coco's fang into a chunk of poster adhesive, affixing it to the bottom of the compass. Following Zinnia's instructions, I leaned forward and held the compass inside the ghost dog's head. It seemed a very rude thing to do to a ghost, but Coco didn't seem to mind me scooping my hand through her ghostly brains.

"Find Tansy," I said. "Take us to your owner."

The dog cocked her head and pawed my knee with one ghost paw.

"She's pawing my knee," I reported to Zinnia.

"She's not wrong. Tansy's spirit is inside you."

"Perhaps. She's been awfully quiet today. As dormant as tulip bulbs in the dead of winter."

"Tulips? Sounds like she hasn't crossed over yet." She leaned over to look at the compass. She couldn't see the ghost, so she had a clear view of it. "The needle's still spinning. Ask Coco to take us to Tansy's body."

"Coco, can you do that? Take us to where your master lies, um, physically."

The dog blinked. She remained silent, as before.

"Her bones," I said, and I conjured in my mind an image of a woman with long gray hair, dressed in green, lying down. I let her clothing and flesh fall away so that all that remained was her skeleton. I beamed this image at the dog. "Find her bones," I said.

The dog backed up, rolled onto her side, and tipped back her head, possum style.

"You're playing dead," I said. "You are such a smart dog, Coco. You do understand me."

Her tail wagged.

"Now take us to where Tansy played dead." I got down on my knees. Instead of holding the compass in the dog's skull, I held it where the dog could see the face. "See this pointy thing? You can talk to us if you try really hard. Make the arrow on the compass point to where your owner played dead."

This can't possibly work, I thought.

But then the arrow on the compass slowed its spin.

Someone squealed and clapped. It was Zoey, who'd come downstairs soundlessly to watch.

"It's really working," Zoey said. "You've poked a hole through to the other side, and now a ghost is talking to you. Just like when Ms. Vander Zalm wrote on the bathroom mirror!"

"This is nothing like that," Zinnia said defensively.

I gave my aunt an *oh really* look. This was exactly like that, except she'd been terrified because she'd attempted the tandem-witch spell on her own.

"How long will it last?" Zoey asked.

The arrow stopped spinning. I rotated the disc in my hand to be certain the arrow was pointing in a specific direction and not simply stuck. It was definitely pointing in a set direction.

"The connection won't last forever," Zinnia said. "We need to get to my car. Zoey, you can drive. I'll sit in the back seat with your mother so we can focus on keeping the channel open."

"She only has her learner's permit," I said. "She's barely touched a steering wheel."

"Pawpaw let me drive Foxy Pumpkin," Zoey said.

This was news to me. I didn't comment. A stream of energy was arcing through me, making my whole body buzz. I couldn't spare the mental resources to get annoyed about my father teaching my daughter bad driving habits.

We had a job to do.

Find Tansy's body.

* * *

The compass took us toward Tansy Wick's property, which was surprising. I'd thought for sure Coco and the compass would take us to the rural property that belonged to Reyna Drinkwater. I even had a speech prepared to give Reyna as soon as I came face to face with her.

But that seemed unlikely to happen if Tansy's body wasn't on Reyna's land.

I wondered, why had the location of Tansy's body evaded the Wisteria Police Department? They'd brought a cadaver-sniffing beagle, which had turned up the canine bones, but nothing human. I wondered, was it because Tansy wasn't human after all? Something snickered in the dark closets of my mind.

Tansy Wick, are you something other than human? No response. *Tansy, what were you doing before you were inside my mind? What is Project Buttercup?* Still no response.

I turned to my aunt in the back seat. The enormous Neo Mastiff seated between us was blocking my view, so I had to lean forward to ask her my question.

"I know we've been over this, but are you entirely sure Tansy was a hundred percent human with no witch powers?"

Zinnia replied calmly, "The only magic she had was in her plants, and I don't even know who supplied her seeds."

"Did you know she used to work for the DWM?"

"I didn't even know the DWM existed until recently. I mean, I knew there were people who had power and used it, but I had no idea it was all so organized. I thought everyone else was operating in the dark the way I have been." Her lower lip trembled ever so slightly. "I'm a clueless old fool, Zara. You should find yourself another mentor. One who actually knows things."

I felt her power contribution to our shared spell waver with her flagging confidence. The effort of keeping the channel open was exhausting her. And like most people when they get tired, she was falling prey to negative thoughts.

I reached around the ghost dog and grabbed her hand.

"You've got me," I said.

She startled. "I do?"

"Whether you want me or not. You've got me."

The ghost dog licked my face. Thankfully its saliva was spectral.

"Oh," Zinnia said softly.

From the driver's seat, Zoey said, "And me, Auntie Z. You've got both of us. Whether you want us or not. Because that's how our family is. We Riddles stick together, through thick and thin."

My aunt swallowed. "I should have eaten more at your house. I'm just a bit tired from the spell."

I squeezed her hand. "Let's just run this body-locating errand quickly, and then we'll get sundaes bigger than our heads. My treat."

"Yes. We'll do this... errand, and then have ice cream." She settled in her seat and gazed out at the passing terrain, which was becoming wilder. The sun was low in the sky, causing a strobe effect as we passed slender trees that blocked the golden rays.

* * *

We reached the gate at the front driveway. There was no yellow-striped police tape, but the gates were closed. Zoey stopped the car with a lurching halt that was not unexpected, given her level of driving experience. I reached forward and gave her a pat on the shoulder. Her shoulder was noticeably moist to the touch through her T-shirt. She'd been sweating from the concentration of driving.

"Nice driving," I said.

"You're just saying that because you're my mother, and all the parenting handbooks say you have to encourage your children with praise, even when they have no physical coordination skills."

"Yeah, well, the handbooks also said to feed you five to nine servings of fruits and vegetables per day."

She snorted.

My aunt opened her door, and we followed. The ghost dog jumped out my side and lumbered along next to me.

Zoey said, "Gate's locked."

After a brief discussion about battering through the gate with my aunt's car—a discussion my aunt didn't find funny at all—we decided to leave the lock in place and proceed on foot.

Zinnia and I had left the car by the open gate during our previous visit as well, because we'd discovered the ghost dogs and thought it wise to follow them. They hadn't brought us to Tansy that time, but now we had our magical compass. The arrow wavered, but it seemed to still be working.

As soon as we squeezed through the narrow opening between the iron bars, we were greeted by Coco's cohort, Jasper. Coco and I were the only ones who could see Jasper, so I described the scene to the other Riddles.

"They look like two old college buddies in big wrinkly sweaters," I said. "Now they're sniffing each other from nose to tail. Do you think they can actually smell each other?"

I leaned over and sniffed them myself. There was a faint aroma of dogginess.

Zinnia, who had started walking down the long driveway, paused to look back at me. "What on earth are you doing?"

"The ghost dogs have an odor," I said. "Come here and see if you can smell them."

Zinnia didn't, but Zoey came right over. I guided her to where the dogs were, and she took a few deep sniffs.

"I don't smell anything," she reported grumpily. "You're the special one, and I don't have any skills at all."

"You're highly skilled at feeling sorry for yourself."

She crossed her arms and fixed me with the most evil of teenaged glares. Attempting something she wasn't immediately brilliant at brought out the worst in my sweet Zolanda Daizy Cazzaundra Riddle. Such is the curse of the gifted, for they give up too easily.

Tansy's spirit surfaced and made me say, "Your mind is like soil, and your thoughts are all seeds."

"You're acting crazy."

I smiled. "You can sow flowers, or you can grow weeds."

She rolled her eyes. "Rhyming only makes you sound more crazy."

Zinnia cleared her throat to get our attention. "The sun will be setting soon." She shook the pair of flashlights she'd taken from the trunk of the car. "And these don't shed much light."

* * *

An hour later, the sun had set, and the novelty of stomping around bushy forest terrain by flashlight had worn off.

I regretted wearing the leopard-print dress for this expedition. A pair of jeans would have been much smarter.

The skin on my shins healed almost instantly after being scraped by brambles and undergrowth, but I still felt every scratch.

The compass was only working intermittently. We'd move in the direction it pointed for several minutes and then find the direction had changed. Either the spell was busted, or Coco kept changing her mind about where her owner had played dead. Both of the dog spirits followed us around the property, from one greenhouse to another.

"At least I'm getting my exercise for the day," I said.

"I have to use the washroom," my daughter grumbled.

"There's one behind every tree," I said.

She smacked her lips. "We should have brought something to drink."

Zinnia said, "Let's go into the house, Zoey. You can use the washroom, and I'll have a look around in there." She reached out for the compass.

I held it possessively. "It's not even pointing at the house." I pointed to the greenhouse's far exit. "The arrow wants us to check that way."

"We already looked over there. It's almost as though Tansy's body is moving around."

"Maybe it is. Bentley said there might be caves underneath the property."

All three of us looked at the compass. The pointer was wavering again.

Zoey said, "She's pretty active for a dead lady."

Zinnia shook her head. "It was worth a shot, anyway."

Zoey asked, "Can we still get ice cream? Can I drive?"

"Yes and yes," I said.

I handed over the compass to my aunt. "Take this in case you get a reading in the house," I said. "I'm the only one who can see the ghost dogs, so I'll just keep following them around."

Zinnia looked down at the flashlight in my hand. "You're a bit dim."

"Ouch," I said. "When you get tired, you get mean."

She shook her head and traded me for her flashlight, which was still bright. Then she clapped her hands together, uttered a phrase I'd never heard before, and pulled her hands apart slowly. A skein of light stretched dazzlingly between her palms. It looked sticky, like warm sap.

Zoey whistled in appreciation. "Does it hurt, Auntie Z? It looks like your skin is melting."

Through gritted teeth, my aunt said, "It's not comfortable, or my first choice for light. But my energy is low from the channeling spell, so this will have to do for now." She started walking toward the house.

Zoey paused, looking at me. I held my flashlight at my hips like a gunslinger.

"You look ready for action," she said.

"Pew pew," I said, pretending to fire the light at her feet.

"I think you should come to the house with us," she said. "People in horror movies always get into danger right after the group splits up."

"They'd be a lot safer if they didn't get themselves into horror movies in the first place."

"True." She turned to leave, skipping to catch up with my aunt.

I was alone with one flashlight and two ghost dogs.

They circled nearby, sniffing the ground and the perimeter of a greenhouse. The white diamond on Jasper's forehead glinted in the moonlight. He looked at me as he parked his big, wrinkled body in front of the entrance to the greenhouse. Coco joined him, scratching on the door.

"We already looked in there," I told them. "Twice."

They didn't budge.

"Third time's the charm," I said as I pulled open the door and stepped inside.

The greenhouse had trapped the day's heat. The warmth made me notice how much the temperature outside had dropped in the last hour. I should have brought the fifties-style cardigan that went with my Audrey dress.

The moon was bright overhead, shining through the clear plastic roof of the greenhouse. I clicked off the flashlight to conserve power for the darker, forested areas of the property. My stomach growled. I hadn't noticed how hungry I was. I could eat something enormous. A whole horse. The spell must have already burned off all the calories from the red wine and fancy cheese. I would hike up my leopard-print dress and do a flirty dance for a granola bar. Unfortunately, this offer wasn't on the table. It was just me, an empty greenhouse, and two ghost dogs.

Both Jasper and Coco had come into the greenhouse with me, unlike my previous search. They huddled together in one spot, near the center of the greenhouse. They began barking, or so I assumed, by the snapping of their muzzles. If a ghost dog barks and nobody hears it, does it make a sound?

My stomach growled again. My price was dropping. I would do a striptease for half a granola bar.

The dogs huddled so close to each other, they became a single wrinkled beast with two heads. It felt significant.

"Jasper, Coco, what is it? Is this the place where Tansy played dead?"

Coco rolled over on her side and splayed her paws in the air. Jasper circled and circled, walking through his sister. Both of them kept looking up at something. The moon?

I followed her ghostly gaze all the way up.

There was something twinkling in the moonlight on the ceiling. It was metallic and roughly triangular in shape. The hand trowel. I'd seen it up there when we'd been there during the day. It was up too high for me to reach with my hands—at least twenty feet—but I was able to use my magic. The trowel came free easily. I floated it down and caught it in my free hand.

It was just a basic gardening trowel. There was a hole in the handle, the right size and shape for a hook. It must have been caught on a hook that held up the irrigation hoses. But how? Tansy wasn't a witch, so she couldn't have floated it up there. Had she flung it during a confrontation?

Jasper continued to circle his sister, at a dizzying, supernatural speed.

"Slow down, boy," I said. "You're making me dizzy."

Except he wasn't. It was the ground itself that was losing cohesion. The ground beneath me was disintegrating.

Images from my nightmare flashed through my mind. The monster rising from the ground and snapping the blue jay from midair.

I turned to run, but there was nothing under my feet. I'd never felt like a cartoon roadrunner before, but here I was, legs moving through nothing.

I was falling, but not for long.

My feet hit something soft, about five feet below the ground of the greenhouse. I was now eye level with Coco, who was still on her side, playing dead.

Sinkhole. Bentley was right about the caves after all.

I reached out to grab onto something so I could hoist myself out of the sinkhole.

No sooner had I grabbed one handful of loose dirt than I felt something snaking around my waist.

I still had the trowel in my hand, so I stabbed it downward, into the thing encircling my torso.

The thing, which was neither plant nor beast yet both at once, rumbled and gripped me tighter, squeezing the breath out of me.

But it couldn't squeeze the fight out of me. I dropped the flashlight and used both hands to grip the handle of the trowel. I bought the blade down again and again. A chunk of something flew off. *Take that!*

And then, like a five-scream ride at an amusement park, the fun started.

CHAPTER 35

WHATEVER HAD GRABBED me suddenly shot upward, sending me toward the peak of the greenhouse. My head struck the ceiling's hard plastic panel.

"Ouch," I complained, which was pretty stupid. The monster hadn't hit my head on the ceiling by accident. It was trying to knock me out. This became painfully clear when it thumped my head on the ceiling a second time.

I yelled like a warrior and stabbed at the rubbery flesh wrapped around my torso. Except it wasn't flesh at all. And it wasn't a snake-like loop around my waist. My entire lower body was encased. My waist was encircled by the rim of something powerful. The lips of an enormous mouth? In the dim light of the moon, I examined one of the chunks I'd gouged out with Tansy's garden trowel. The chunk was shades of green.

I'm being eaten by...

I could hardly finish the thought without hysteria.

A carnivorous plant.

Screeching choruses from *Little Shop of Horrors* danced merrily around my brain. I was about to suffer the same fate as the Broadway play's character named Audrey. And I'd unwittingly dressed up for the part, too.

I screamed for help. My aunt and daughter were a quarter mile away from the greenhouse. Or was it farther? It didn't matter. They were witches. Or at least Zinnia was. If she couldn't hear me or sense me screaming for help, she wasn't much of a witch.

But was I screaming? I couldn't hear anything. I opened my mouth wider, clenched something in my throat, and tried to scream.

Nothing came out.

I drove the garden trowel down into the green flesh and scooped out a divot. But the plant was thick. At this rate, it would take me hours to dig myself free.

I clenched the trowel's handle between my teeth, braced my hands on the green rim, and tried to wriggle myself free. No luck. Curse my adult hips!

But I wasn't down for the count. Not yet. I hadn't used a single spell. And I'd been learning so many new spells lately. The task of choosing one made me giggle hysterically. This carnivorous plant messed with the wrong witch.

To start things off, I cast the blade spell I'd used recently to core and slice an apple midair. The plant quivered as the magical blades of energy swept up the outside perimeter of the bulb that held the lower half of my body. The spell worked on most fruits and vegetables. Was my captor a fruit or a vegetable? I felt its grip loosen. I kicked, and my foot emerged through a slit. I kicked again, lengthening the slit as I searched my inventory of spells for some way to cushion my two-story fall.

But then the slit pulled back together and healed itself. The surface of the bulb crackled and turned a darker shade of green.

I cast the apple-slicing spell again. This time, it did no more than scratch the surface.

Think, I heard Zinnia say in my mind. *Peaceful solutions before violence.*

Had I jumped to violence too quickly?

I took the garden trowel out from between my teeth, cast a bluffing spell, and asked nicely to be put down. But my voice still wasn't working. Whether the plant had ears or not, I couldn't convince it of anything without my voice. It must have numbed my vocal cords somehow. Maybe a neurotoxin. *All the better to quietly eat prey without calling attention to itself.*

If my voice was numb, how much longer did I have until full paralysis?

Something soft squished against my bare legs. A tongue? I really should have worn jeans. *It's rolling me around on its tongue. Tasting me.*

I hoped I tasted terrible.

Spit me out. My diet is lousy. I eat far too much junk food. I'll give you indigestion.

The slurping continued. I couldn't see what was happening below my waist, but the creature seemed to be salivating. The bulb around me was filling with liquid. I was reminded of sitting in a hot tub. I used to *like* hot tubs.

Time for more violence. I cast the blade spell a third time. Nothing happened. The surface didn't even scratch like before.

My head was woozy. The plant was undulating on its long stalk, swaying me from side to side. *Stop the world, I want off.*

I cast my new motion disruption spell. It wouldn't get me free, but at least it might buy me time.

My magic popped and fizzled, like a struck match that smokes but doesn't light.

I was new at the spell, so I blamed myself and tried again.

More fizzling.

The plant's acidic saliva gurgled around my waist. Was it laughing at me?

I was running out of tricks. I cast the spell for detecting ripeness in a cantaloupe, partly because it was a no-fail spell and partly because I wondered what new information I might glean.

But the ripeness spell wouldn't run.

I tried telekinesis on the dirt far below me on the ground. Not a single speck flew up. The ghost dogs watched helplessly. They'd suffered the same fate, I realized. The only thing left had been their eerily clean bones.

Can't think about that now. Gotta keep thinking.

My magic definitely wasn't working. The plant gurgled. Had I been shorted out by the liquid? Apparently so. Next, I would be digested, from the bottom up.

On the plus side, at least I would die knowing exactly what horrific fate had befallen poor Tansy Wick. I mentally kicked her spirit. *Hey, thanks a lot for the warning about the carnivorous plant under your main greenhouse. When I meet you on the other side, let me thank you in person.*

I stabbed at the plant angrily with my trowel. Green fluid oozed from the wounds I'd inflicted, but they were no more threatening than ladybug nibbles on a watermelon.

To my amazement, my rage called forth some blue lightning. It was weak and sputtering, but I might have one good shock left in me.

I tucked the trowel into the mouth of the thing, at the center of my chest, and rubbed my hands together.

You mess with a witch, you get the blue fireballs.

Once the charge was focused, I slapped my hands down and blasted. A web glowed over the surface, bright green, and quickly faded. It gave off a scent like baby spinach wilting in a hot frying pan.

Fry up real good. Yum yum.

But the plant didn't stop undulating or even break its rhythm. And was the grip around my torso tighter now? The bright moon overhead became dimmer. I was losing oxygen, losing my senses. Losing time.

The stem beneath me suddenly whipped. My head connected with the overhead panel hard enough to break something. As I slipped into darkness, I hoped the cracking had been the translucent panel and not my skull.

The death will be painless, a voice told me. It was Tansy Wick, finally speaking up.

Over my dead broomstick! Painless or not, I wasn't going to feed this beast.

The Droserakops needs to be nourished.

Droserakops? *Tansy, is that what this rancid salad monster is called?*

Yes, she replied, as calm as a tour guide at a museum. *This fine specimen is a hybrid of the sundew, a member of the* Droseraceae *family. It lures and digests insects with its mucilaginous glands.*

But I'm no insect, I said.

Tansy's spirit continued in a detached voice. *You're probably wondering what the sundew was spliced with to create such a lively little sprout!*

A lively little sprout? Tansy was clearly not in the here and now. Her spirit was giving a relaxed demonstration, which meant I was accessing one of her memories. I could do nothing but let the recorded clip play out. And why not? I had nowhere else to go.

She continued. *Why, it was the critter you provided me with, Reynard! Look how beautiful our baby is growing up. Careful. Don't touch.*

She laughed, her voice like an old gate squeaking in the wind.

I waited for more, but the memory replay had finished.

The only sound was the plant, which rustled and squeaked, like a fallen tree in the woods, caught upon a green branch not yet ready to give way.

Tansy? Get back here with your green thumbs! Who is Reynard?

She didn't respond. Fickle ghosts.

If only there were some way for me to get better access to what was left of her mind.

My witch powers weren't working, and I couldn't scream. I had to use my wits and stay alive until my family happened upon me.

The plant might have some weakness I could exploit, some weakness Tansy knew about.

Something rubbed against my leg in the whirlpool. Not a tongue, at least.

Earlier that evening, we'd used a dog fang to connect with a dog spirit. I remembered most of the spell for the ritual. I could wing it. Now, if only I had something of Tansy's, I might be able to run the same spell now.

Bones. What had my aunt said a few days ago at the Thai restaurant? Something about bones and spitting them out. The memory fit against something else in my mind, courtesy of Tansy. I caught a glimpse of her instructing the plant to spit out the bones when it was done digesting the chickens.

Tansy had fed her chickens to the plant.

I used my knees to grab the hard object floating in the soup. It was a bone, all right. Probably a tibia.

I squeezed Tansy's tibia bone between my knees and prepared to do the spirit-communication spell. This spell was different from the others I'd tried because it interacted with energy on another plane. It might work. As I began casting, the mental spellwork and hand movements came back to me. I didn't have the magical ingredients, so I would have to improvise by stripping the spell down to its basics. I threw caution to the wind and left out the safety protocols. If something nasty slipped through from another plane, I'd deal with it next.

Unfortunately, the carnivorous plant wasn't giving me much time. My leg movements must have tickled it into action. I found myself being whipped violently, jerked up and down, and smacked against the roof.

Smartening up quick, I went limp. *You got me, Droserakops. I'm knocked out. I'll just be here, limp as a boiled dandelion, while your digestive enzymes go to work on me.*

Playing dead worked. My captor stopped rattling me like a Rumba shaker. I carefully located the bone in the whirlpool again, with minimal movements, and quickly cast a pared-down version of the spell. It was messy and chaotic, but it was a thing of beauty, because it worked and it was all I had.

My pulse quickened as the connection snapped together. I saw her face clearly, and in my mind's eye, she was looking at me. Her hair was long and gray, her face was unremarkable, but her eyes were brilliant green.

Tansy, please help me, I said. *Does the Droserakops have a weakness?*

Mucilaginous glands, she said. Her voice was so quiet.

I repeated the spell to boost the volume.

Tansy, how is that a weakness?

It comes from the roots, she said. *Sever the stem, and the glands will empty. Remove the heart, and you take its powers.*

Sever the stem? Remove the heart? Would if I could, sweetheart!

In my vision, Tansy shrugged. She'd cared more about the state of the plants in my back yard than whether I lived or died. Maybe she lived in seclusion because she was a jerk and nobody liked her.

It's true, she said, even though I hadn't verbalized my thoughts. *Nobody likes me. There won't be a memorial service for Tansy Wick when I die. Who would come? Just my dogs.*

But her dogs were already dead, and so was she. I did the psychic equivalent of putting on a mask with a smile. She was denying her death, or confused. Either way, I didn't want to break the news to her and suffer another existential tantrum. I'd probably get so depressed I'd beg the Droserakops to finish me off quickly.

I pulled away from the vision in my mind. She'd given me what I needed.

The creature's weak point was the base of its stem.

I slowly leaned over to get a visual. The base was thick and coarse. How could I effect any damage from fifteen feet up, with no corporeal powers?

I turned over the trowel in my hands and looked around. Above me was a network of water irrigation pipes. Why hadn't I thought of this sooner? I could use the trowel to pry free some pipes and use them to jab into the base of the stem. I reached up, but even with my arms fully extended, the pipes were still two feet from the tip of my trowel.

How could I get lifted higher? If only I could press a button to operate the plant's hydraulics, like an orchard's cherry picker.

All I could do was make the creature angry enough to bash my head into the ceiling, then not get a concussion or lose consciousness while I pried loose a makeshift javelin. Easy peasy.

I kicked at the plant's innards, digging my heels into what felt like a squishy tongue.

The reaction was immediate and painful. My head missed the corrugated plastic and struck the metal supports.

The whole greenhouse rang like a church bell. Or maybe it was just my head.

Darkness crawled up my spine. I heard the clunk of the trowel landing on the dirt far below me. My whole body was numb. I lost consciousness and went to a place within myself.

In the darkness, a vision appeared. It was the image that went with the audio I'd heard already.

"You're probably wondering what the sundew was spliced with to create such a lively little sprout!" Tansy Wick held a terra cotta pot with both hands. *Growing from the pot was a much smaller version of the creature that now held me. "Why, it was the critter you provided me with, Reynard! Look how beautiful our baby is growing up. Careful. Don't touch."*

And then Reynard, who wasn't great at listening to warnings, reached forward and touched the bulb of the plant. With a flick of its stem, the juvenile plant opened wide and latched onto his finger. He cried out in surprise and yanked his hand free.

"Tansy, you've outdone yourself," he said, rubbing his *finger.*

She tossed her gray hair over her shoulder coquettishly. "Why, thank you, Reynard."

"Give me this one," he said. *"My buyer is impatient and putting pressure on me."*

"No!" She yanked it toward herself protectively.

The plant whipped again and latched onto the nearest thing, which was Tansy's bare arm. She shrieked and dropped the plant pot. The terra cotta container shattered.

"Look what you made me do," she said angrily. *"Filthy trickster fox."*

My father held up both hands and smiled his rubbery salesman grin. "Easy now. A deal's a deal, Tansy. I brought you the cuttings, and now I need the heart so I can get paid."

Tansy tipped her head back and laughed.

My father knelt down and felt around on the greenhouse floor. "Where'd it go?"

"*Where do you think? It burrowed down. It's probably in the caves by now.*"

"*I'll get it out.*" *He changed into fox form and started digging.*

She kicked him out of the way. "Don't you dare," she said. "I'll send my dogs after you."

He whimpered and returned to human form. "We can't leave it growing free down there," he said. "Think of the consequences."

"*That plant is my baby,*" *she said.* "*I raised it and nourished it myself. You're not going to cut out my baby's heart. I'd rather die.*"

He backed away, toward the door. "It's so early in the day," he said in a placating tone. "Let's go get some of those iced mint mochas you love. We can talk about this."

"*No, we can't,*" *she said.* "*No more talk. I'm sick of people like you trying to manipulate me.*" *She rubbed her arm where the plant had bit her.*

The two big dogs, who'd been sleeping on the ground, watching lazily, got to their feet.

"*I'll go,*" *he said.* "*I'd rather not be slobbered on, so don't bother with your threats.*"

Tansy pulled two satchels the size of oranges from her pockets and broke them over the heads of her dogs. A powdery mist floated down over the animals. Their posture changed immediately.

"*Jasper, Coco, kill that man,*" *she said.* "*Kill.*"

My father's eyes widened.

The dogs advanced, looking less like dudes in wrinkly sweaters and more like hellhounds.

One of them growled menacingly.

My father shifted into fox form in the blink of an eye, and then he was off and running.

The blackness turned to gray. I was conscious again. The vision had been illuminating, but it hadn't done a lick of good to get me out of my predicament.

I'd dropped the trowel, so now I had only my hands to work with. My numb hands. I was closer to the ceiling than before, though. I stretched up and managed to reach one of the pipes. I've never been happier to grab onto something. My muscles strained as I tried to pry the pipe free.

I didn't have enough leverage. When I pushed against the plant, the plant simply bobbed lower. I had to use the plant's strength against it.

I grasped the irrigation pipe tightly and started kicking the plant again. Either the pipe would come free, or maybe it would stay fixed and the human clinging to it for dear life would come free of her watery prison. My first kick didn't register. I'd gotten tripped up on more of Tansy's bones. A skull, by the feel of it. I twisted my body and prepared for a harder kick. My fingers were locked on the pipe tightly.

And then I caught a new movement out of the corner of my eye.

The door of the greenhouse was opening.

In walked a white cat with a puffy tail. Boa glanced around, sat prettily, and slowly looked from the plant's base all the way up to me.

"Meow," she said.

CHAPTER 36

Boa!

My fingers slipped off the pipe. My hands were so numb I didn't feel it.

I pointed accusingly at the white cat. Or at least I tried to point. The paralysis from the plant's juices had extended to my upper body. I could barely control which direction my eyes were pointing.

I knew it, I thought, even though I hadn't actually suspected the cat of anything until just now.

Helpless as a kitten myself, I watched as the white cat padded over to the base of the plant and sniffed it. Boa must not have liked what she smelled. She hissed and backed away, her tail straight up and puffy.

A noise came from my throat. I could hoarsely whisper now. Had the loss of muscle tension somehow reversed whatever had paralyzed my vocal chords? I was grateful to have my voice back but disturbed by how little control I had over my mouth.

"Boa," I croaked, spit flying out freely. "Who are you? *What* are you?"

A man's voice answered, "She's just a cat. I brought her along as a decoy, to feed the Droserakops, but it looks like you're taking care of that."

"Rhys," I croaked. "Or should I call you Reynard, like your friend Tansy did." As much spit as sound came out of my numb lips.

My father, in human form and wearing the same cheap salesman suit he'd worn during his first surprise appearance, circled around the base of the plant, inspecting it. He'd brought a glowing lantern with him, and as he circled the plant, it cast comically large shadows on the greenhouse walls.

"Try to relax," he called up. His words were light and casual. "The more you jiggle around, the more you activate its trigger hairs."

"Get an ax and chop me down!"

He set down the glowing lantern, reached into his jacket, and pulled out a pocketknife. "This should do the trick," he said cheerfully.

I spat, "An ax, Dad. Get an ax."

"No need," he said. "Any good tradesman knows the right tool is the best way to save time. And the right tool is the one you have in your pocket." The blade of the knife flickered in the lantern's light as he approached the base of the stem. "Measure twice, cut once, and all that."

I snapped back, "Don't measure. Just cut." I tried to say more, but my voice was gone again. Only wheezing, spitty breaths came out.

He used his knife to cut into the stem, between the two largest leaves at the base. He had the focus of a surgeon removing an organ, though, not the gritty determination of a lumberjack. I smacked my limp, numb hands together to get his attention, then made a chopping gesture.

"Zara, relax," he called up. "I'm removing the central gland of the Droserakops. As soon as I get it out, the enzymes will stop flowing. After thirty minutes or so, the stem will relax, and you'll be able to wriggle out of the mouth."

Thirty minutes? I gave him a panicked look and mimed chopping movements frantically.

"You're going to hate me for this," he said, and then he chuckled. "So what else is new, right? At least now you'll have a reason to hate me."

I pointed my finger and made a wheezing accusation. "You... killed... Tansy." My words came out like a buzzard's throaty hisses.

"I didn't kill Tansy," he said. "She and I met here on Wednesday to have a look at our project. I wanted to harvest the heart before the Droserakops got too big for its britches. But she and I didn't see eye to eye. I told her it wasn't safe. She had already fed it most of the chickens from her coop, and she wanted to wait another week before the harvest."

"You're lying," I said. "She sent her dogs to kill you."

"She told you about that? I would have thought her guilt would keep her silent."

"I know everything."

"Yeah? Did she tell you about her crazy idea to produce three flowers from one root? She was greedy." He paused in his surgical cutting and looked up at me. "Her greed was what killed Tansy."

"No," I said. "She loved this plant."

"Exactly. She was greedy for love. The love of an extremely dangerous plant. That's what killed her."

My eyes started rolling around out of control.

"Help... me," I gasped.

"I'm trying," he said, focused on the work before him. "I have to be careful, because removing the heart is a bit like defusing a bomb. There's an order to cutting the supply lines, and if I get it wrong, the whole thing could blow up in my face."

I held still and waited, because I was now paralyzed and could do nothing else. I caught a glimpse of Boa, who was still there, wandering around the greenhouse. The poor thing had no idea she'd been brought there to be sacrificed to a carnivorous plant. Mind you, neither did I.

"Done!" Rhys stood up and proudly held the thing in one hand, like a prize fish—if a prize fish looked like a dark-green beating heart. "Isn't it a thing of beauty?"

It was a thing, all right. But not one of beauty.

Boa came running to his side. She swatted playfully at the pulsing heart's trailing green tendrils.

"This is goodbye for now," Rhys said. He gazed up at me, catching the moonlight on his face. The lantern on the ground next to him flickered like a guttering candle flame.

I croaked out gibberish and flopped my head from side to side. It was all I could do. Nothing worked. Not my telekinesis. Not my defensive fireballs. Not even my mouth. A wacky refrain kept circling inside my head. This one wasn't a tune from *Little Shop of Horrors* but a line from the Shel Silverstein nursery rhyme about being eaten by a boa constrictor. The narrator sings *oh fiddle* and *oh heck* as the boa constrictor swallows up to her middle and then up to her neck. The popular children's rhyme played in its entirety in my head, where such things were not prevented by modern song copyright laws.

My upper body felt different. Warmer. Wetter.

Oh heck. My captor had swallowed me up to my neck.

I flopped my head once more and tried to make eye contact with my father. Why couldn't he chop the stem like I asked and release me? Was this all a big joke to him? I gurgled what I hoped would be a convincing plea.

He tucked the pulsating heart into a grocery store tote bag that I recognized as having come from my kitchen. *My bag!* The nice blue one from the organic place! Then he picked up the lantern in his other hand and headed for the door.

"Zara, don't hate me," he said.

I spluttered out an approximation of, "Too late."

"You'll be fine. Maybe better than ever. They say whatever doesn't kill you makes you stronger."

I tried to tell him off but only made an undignified raspberry noise.

"Trust me, Zara. This outcome is for the best." He paused, as though about to explain more, but then he opened the door and left.

I was alone.

Alone in the moonlit greenhouse, trapped in the maw of a carnivorous plant. Up to my neck.

Boa meowed.

Scratch that. I wasn't alone. At least I had my cat.

Boa meowed again as she scratched at the stem of the plant.

My face felt funny. Was I smiling? No. It was the mouth of the plant, slurping its way up my jaw and over my mouth. I breathed rapidly through my nostrils only.

This wasn't supposed to happen. My father had promised the plant would fade without its heart. It was supposed to be drooping down and releasing me. Instead, it was continuing to digest me. I could barely keep my nose from being covered by its sickly green flesh. At the current rate, I'd be cut off from my oxygen in just a few minutes. Then six minutes until brain damage and death. Ah, if only I'd thought to bring my rented scuba diving gear and oxygen tanks with me. Cue the hysterical laughter.

Boa, my fluffy little white knight, was still scratching away at the stem like a champion. *You go, kitty! Chop this nasty ol' tree down like a lumberjack cat!*

She kept scratching and meowing in earnest, louder and louder.

Just as I thought she might be doing real damage to the plant, a second pointed tip emerged from the ground next to the stem. I hadn't seen the Droserakops blossom open when it had snatched me up, but now I could do nothing but watch.

It was a thing of beauty, even in the dim light of the moon. The giant petals were green and tough on the exterior, but shades of red, orange, and pink on the inside. The flower rose up to where I was being held and then dove down. In one smooth motion, it scooped up Boa in its maw. The cat didn't even see it coming. I swear I heard the plant go GULP.

The door to the greenhouse opened once more.

Dad! He came back!

But it wasn't my father.

"Auntie Z, I swear I heard meowing in here. It sounded like Boa."

"How can that be? She's at the house with Rhys. It's probably just a stray."

"I'm going to check in this greenhouse again anyway."

Dimly, through drowsy eyelids, I saw two redheaded women enter the greenhouse.

One let out a blast of blue lighting bolts.

Yay! My hero!

And then she was immediately swallowed head first by the same blossom that had gobbled Boa as an appetizer.

Zoey flung her flashlight at the flower and screamed.

A third flower emerged from the ground next to her feet. In the blink of an eye, she was gone as well. Snapped up by the third blossom of the three-headed Droserakops.

No wonder it hadn't succumbed to injuries after my father removed its heart. It had two more pulsing at its base.

In a fit of motherly fury, I summoned great forces and burst the plant surrounding me to smithereens. *Yes, yes, that's it,* I thought dreamily. And then I cast the blade spell flawlessly and chopped the other stems to pieces. It was all going so easily. So perfectly. As though in a dream. And then, after, we hosed ourselves off and went for ice cream, laughing over our sundaes over that time we were nearly eaten by a carnivorous plant. *This is heaven,* I said as I dug into my enormous ice cream sundae. *I've died, and this is heaven.*

Those are the sorts of happy hallucinations a person might have when paralyzed by a neurotoxin and deprived of oxygen.

CHAPTER 37

WITH THE BRAVERY and heroism of the highest-paid action movie star, I saved all three of us plus the cat from the Droserakops. I saved us a *whole bunch of times*, which didn't even strike me as odd at the time. First, I eviscerated the leafy thing like a green smoothie in a blender. The scene started over, and I burned it down like a blowtorch on gnarly weeds between pavers. Then I used a new kale-to-dessert spell to magically transform the plant into soft, fluffy, harmless pink cotton candy.

Except I didn't do any of these things. Each heroic rescue was a hallucination, a dream within a dream, a byproduct of the panicked synaptic flashings of my oxygen-deprived brain.

One vision, however, seemed more real than the others.

This was what *really* happened that night in the greenhouse, as witnessed through one of my eyes.

The third and smallest blossom shuddered and shook, and then something emerged near the bottom of the bulb. Teeth flashes. Sharp teeth. A creature was biting its way through the green membrane. More teeth flashing, and an elongated muzzle emerged. Then the whole head, with triangular ears. As it emerged, the face dripped in primordial goo. The plant's thick stem bent as though bowing. Front paws came out next. The flower split at the base like an embryonic sac, and it birthed a four-pawed creature.

A red fox.

The fox whipped its fluffy tail and shook the green goo from its fur.

Snarling, the fox attacked the second-largest flower stalk with its teeth.

Sparks of blue flashed from its teeth, for this was no ordinary fox.

The fox bit out a smaller version of the green, pulsating heart my father had left with.

The second stem bowed graciously. The fox bit into the blossom base, sharp teeth flashing with blue sparks, and helped birth a pair of creatures. A redheaded female in a flowered vest and a white cat.

Zinnia got to her feet. She and the fox came for me.

But I was no princess in a castle who needed rescuing! Not me! I burst out with magic and tore free of my prison, tossing bits of plant like boiled spinach. Except I didn't do that, because I couldn't control anything except one eye, and only barely.

The plant shifted, and I lost the visual of my rescuers.

Was my daughter really a fox? Were she and Zinnia about to rescue me? Or was it just another hallucination?

The darkness in my spine overtook me. I slipped down inside the plant and went limp inside the whirlpool of digestive juices.

* * *

Zinnia and Zoey had approached the greenhouse to investigate the meowing sound.

My aunt expected to find nothing but a malfunctioning sprinkler hose as the source of the sound.

What they actually found was a huge plant with two stalks and two flower buds. There was a cat-sized bulge in the smaller flower bud, and a Zara-sized bulge in the larger one. The Droserakops held perfectly still, doing its best impression of an innocent corn stalk, only instead of corn silk sticking out of the top, there was a hank of my red hair and half of my face.

My aunt, being a skilled witch, wasted no time in jolting the plant with her defensive magic. But the Droserakops had much more mass than a typical foe. Its root system ran for miles underground. It felt no more than a tickle from her strongest blast.

The plant was no slouch in the intelligence department —at least when it came to self-preservation. Its counter-move came without warning. The smaller bulb with the cat-sized bulge elongated itself and lunged, snapping up Zinnia in one bite. Rather than attacking her from underneath, like I had been ambushed, the plant had gained the wisdom to swallow troublesome witches headfirst.

Zinnia was plunged face-first into a pool of digestive, sticky plant goo. She will, however, tell anyone who asks that she was ready to bust out some high-level magic on the creature, and she would have, if Zoey hadn't rescued her first.

Ah, Zoey.

My sweet-and-sour moody teenager with the heart of gold and the fox-shifter DNA.

It turned out the only thing standing between her and magic was the right kind of stress.

The blossom hadn't fully closed around her when she shifted into fox form. There were two major benefits to doing so. First, the thick red fur was perfect for keeping snow and rain from reaching fox's skin, and equally effective at keeping the plant's numbing juices from touching Zoey's skin. Second, Zoey's fox form had much sharper teeth than her human form. It wasn't easy for her to bite her way out of the blossom, but her survival instincts had kicked in, and she'd managed to do what I had not.

Once she got Zinnia free, it was simple enough for them to use a combination of Zoey's teeth and Zinnia's magic to get me free.

However, there was the small issue of me being nearly dead. Not all the way dead, or I might have witnessed these events clearly from above, but very nearly dead.

They cleared my airway and treated me for drowning, rolling me onto my side and administering mouth-to-mouth resuscitation.

I began breathing, albeit raggedly, but the larger issue was my heart. I was in tachycardia. The poison in my body was battling my own healing abilities, and the poison was winning. My heart was racing wildly fast.

"Foxglove," my aunt said. "We need foxglove." But there was panic in my aunt's voice. Even with her skills, she didn't have the time to synthesize the medication I needed to get my heart under control. She barked at my daughter to call for an ambulance.

My daughter barked back. Literally. She made yip-yip fox noises. She had no phone, no pockets to hold a phone, and on top of that, no fingers with which to make a call.

And that was when the cavalry arrived.

An armor-wearing team of DWM agents crashed in through the side of the greenhouse. They busted in like a team of superheroes who took special glee in destroying private property.

At the front of the team was Charlize. While armored members circled the limp green wreckage that was the Droserakops, Charlize and the medics knelt over me. They called over the leader of the medical team, Dr. Ankh. The lavender-eyed woman was assisted by her intern, Ubaid. They made the assessment to transfer me to the DWM for treatment there.

Charlize, however, had a different idea. She pushed my aunt and daughter away from my body and straddled me. I was barely conscious, but I saw her face above me. She looked calm and serene. I knew in that instant that everything was going to be okay.

Then she put both of her hands on my chest and turned my heart to stone.

That got my attention. My lungs had also turned to stone, so I couldn't even gasp.

My eyes flew open, and suddenly I was dragged away from my happy hallucinations. The weight I felt was the weight of the world, a mountain atop me. I was granite on the inside, fused with flesh, and if you think that sounds painful, you're not wrong.

Charlize tilted her head. A single tear dropped from her eye onto my cheek.

Don't be sad, I thought. And then there was only pain. Everything went white.

After I lost consciousness, she turned my heart back to flesh.

Dr. Ankh threw a fit, grabbing Charlize by the arm and throwing her through the only intact greenhouse wall.

But the gambit had worked. Being turned to granite and then back to flesh was an *unusual* treatment for tachycardia, but it had worked.

What happened next was a frenzy of activity.

The DWM took my daughter into custody, mistaking the red fox for her grandfather. If someone had used their good sense to ask questions or peek under the fox's tail, they might have saved my aunt from having to pull out her fightin' words.

"Turn back into yourself, Zoey," my aunt said. "Shift back."

But Zoey didn't have any practice at turning back into human form, plus she was frightened.

The armored men tossed her in a cage and took her away, despite threats from my aunt. The medical crew jabbed her with something to keep her from following through on her promises.

When Zoey did finally shift back, she was in a cage in the back of a van, halfway to the DWM headquarters. On the plus side, at least she was greeted by a familiar face. Chet was driving the van. He let her out of the cage, and she rode the rest of the way in the passenger seat. Days later, she reported back to me that she and Chet had bonded over their shifting experiences, and he'd really stepped up. "Just like a father," she'd said, which hurt my heart in a way the granite hadn't.

* * *

Dr. Ankh, Ubaid, and the rest of the medical staff took good care of me during my overnight stay. Or so I've been told. I drifted in and out of consciousness while recovering from the plant's poison.

I kept hearing people talking about some other patient they were concerned about. Who was the other patient? Zoey and Zinnia had been shaken but able to walk and talk or bark.

In the morning, I found out from a nurse that the other patient everyone had been fussing over was the gosh-darned plant, the murderous Droserakops.

As soon as the nurse left my room, I jumped out of the hospital bed and bolted for the door. As grateful as I was to be alive, I didn't want to be underground with any part of that thing.

My daughter and my aunt, who'd been waiting in the hallway, ran after me.

Zoey cried out, "Mom, your butt's hanging out of your gown!"

Zinnia said, "Zara, slow down. We ought to make sure you're properly discharged."

I ran for the exit. There would be no more slowing down for me.

"Mom! At least try to cover yourself! Ugh. Are you wearing underwear covered in happy faces? You're so embarrassing."

CHAPTER 38

WEDNESDAY MORNING, TWO hours after making my escape from the DWM, I walked to the Wisteria Public Library as though nothing had happened the night before.

I'd considered calling in sick, but I wasn't sick. There was a lot on my mind, including stuff I had to emotionally process, but physically, I was just fine. Thanks to my witch powers, I'd survived yet another near-death experience.

As for Tansy Wick's spirit, she didn't come with me to work.

Earlier that morning, when I was in my bathroom, brushing the plant-goo off my teeth, she'd made an appearance. You know how in horror movies, ghosts love to appear behind people while they're looking in bathroom mirrors? She did that to me. Cheeky ghost.

I whipped around, spraying toothpaste foam from my mouth like a rabid dog. She looked serene, dressed in green, with her long gray hair in two braids, as she stood next to my antique claw-foot tub. It struck me later that the bathroom was the logical place for a ghost to appear. People die in bathrooms all the time. When you're not feeling well, where do you go? The bathroom. To splash cold water on your face, take a bath, or get something from the medicine cabinet. The previous owner of my house had passed away in my tub.

"Hello," I said.

Tansy nodded. Her loyal pets, Jasper and Coco, flanked her.

"You tried to kill my father," I said. "I know about everything."

She pointed at me.

"Good point. He left me to die, which means he's not the World's Greatest Father, but in his defense, he thought I'd be fine."

She said nothing.

"What you did was intentional," I said. "And you put that murder potion on your dogs, making them accomplices. As a new pet owner myself, I condemn that."

She made a grim expression and bowed her head.

"But then your monster plant ate the dogs and you, too, so I guess it all balances out."

She looked more faded than she'd been at her house, maybe fifty percent visibility.

"Tansy, do you know you're dead?"

She gave me a sad look, blew me a kiss, and then turned and walked straight out through an exterior wall with the dogs right behind her.

Case closed.

For me, anyway.

The DWM had her bones, as well as the shredded remainder of her final botany experiment. My father remained a "person of interest" they wanted to interview. Good luck with that.

But based on what Charlize had uncovered on Tansy's computer, it appeared the woman's death had been an accident.

Speaking of Charlize, you may be wondering, how did she know to bring a DWM tactical team to the greenhouse at precisely the moment I needed rescuing?

The short answer is she didn't.

She had been following the transmission of the tracker that had been placed in my father during his medical treatment at the department. Her big plan of "sneaking" my father out of the department had been a ruse. A misdirect. All part of her plan to follow him straight to the Droserakops. Her meeting with me in her office, when she'd claimed she couldn't access all of Tansy's notes due to encryption, had been an act.

She'd played me for the fool.

And I'd been so blinded by my growing fondness for her that I'd believed every bit of it.

I don't mean to be overly dramatic, but it must be stated: Charlize betrayed my trust.

And for that, she would pay.

All in the fullness of time.

For now, I had a job to do.

I had to punch my timecard and start the day anew.

My name is Zara Riddle, and I'm proud to be a librarian.

Zara tries to be a good librarian!

Zara does not roll her eyes when a patron states that a two-dollar overdue-materials fine is akin to being picked up by one's feet and shaken for loose change. Zara must remember that not everyone has been gifted with the life-altering, perspective-gaining experience of having literally been picked up and whipped around like a Rumba shaker then smothered by a plant's digestive enzymes before having their heart turned to granite by a snake-haired demon and then back again.

* * *

All of Wednesday, I tried to act "normal." But as my daughter frequently complained, I'd never been good at playing normal. The head librarian cornered me in the staff lounge during my midmorning break. She closed and locked the door behind her, which she'd never done before.

I'm being fired.

"You've got to tell me your secret," Kathy said, pushing her round glasses up her owlish nose.

"No," I said, quite seriously. "I don't have to."

"Zara, your skin is positively glowing today. Your hair is brighter, and even your posture is incredible. Are you on a juice cleanse? Is it makeup?" She closed the distance between us and sniffed the air audibly. "You smell good. Like raw vegetable juice."

I self-consciously stroked my jaw. Kathy did have a point about my appearance. Thanks to the exfoliation I'd received in the plant's acidic bath, my skin was softer than new rose petals. Was that all Kathy wanted from me? Beauty tips? It seemed a bit gratuitous for her to lock the door to the staff lounge for girl talk, but Kathy could be strange.

She asked, "What is that scent? Is it a skin lotion?"

"Sort of. Are you familiar with the *Droseraceae* family of tropical plants?"

Kathy blinked twice. "Venus flytrap plants?"

"Yes, that's the idea. Last night, I took a bath in an experimental all-over exfoliation lotion extracted from one of the larger plants. I was... a volunteer. Sort of. I'm afraid the product's not ready for the market yet."

"Whooo knew," she hooted. "An extract from carnivorous plants." She gave her head a shake and smiled. "Let me know if they want more volunteers for testing. I'm willing and able."

"I'm not sure you would be so eager if you were aware of the side effects."

She frowned. "Fine. If you don't want to share your beauty secrets with me, just say so." With a half shrug of dismissal, she walked past me to get something from the refrigerator. She opened a rectangular plastic container with a blue lid and began spooning up brown goo. The gelatinous treat was *dotori-muk*, an acorn jelly made for her by her Korean neighbor. On my first day of work, I'd made the mistake of throwing an earlier batch out of the fridge. I could see from Kathy's expression that she was also accessing the memory of that interaction. And regretting her decision to hire me.

I had to make things right.

"Kathy, I'll get you a jar of something better," I promised. "My aunt makes a zero-calorie salad dressing that's terrible for the digestive system but works miracles dissolving dry calluses on the feet."

Her expression brightened, and she hooted softly. "Ooh, ooh, that would be something." She went back to eating her acorn jelly with a smile.

What now? I looked over at the locked door and back at Kathy. She wanted something else, but what?

I asked in a friendly tone, "How are you doing? I haven't seen any leaves or sticks in your hair recently."

"Oh, that." She rolled her eyes. "Have I ever told you about my father? He can be challenging."

"Sounds about right for fathers." I leaned back against the lounge's kitchenette counter and looked into my mug of microwaved coffee. Last night, my own father had left me to be eaten by a carnivorous plant. I didn't know what Kathy's father had done to upset her, but I had a feeling it wasn't quite as bad.

"He's got some issues with hoarding," she said. "He's always complaining to me about how he would be happy to clean up his back yard if only he had some help. So, I went over there last week before work to give him a hand, and we pushed our way through the back bushes to where he's got an old car graveyard. I was taking photos of the cars with collectible value, so we could list them for sale, and suddenly he had one of his mood swings. Everything had been just fine, until a fox came running through the yard, chased by the neighbor's dogs."

"A red fox?"

"Yes. A red fox. It ripped between us and then disappeared into a hole in the ground. I told my father that the fox was probably headed toward the underground cave system that runs under the edge of the city on that end. You know about the caves, right? They pop out under Pacific Spirit Park."

"They do?"

"It's a secret," she said, flashing her eyes mischievously. "Well, my father went into one of his rants, about how the whole town's going to hell these days, thanks to the ungodly supernatural beings that keep flocking to Wisteria. Then he got onto a huge diatribe about the DWM, and how they're not doing anything right under the current leadership, and they haven't done anything right since Don Moore was forced to take early retirement. I told him, 'Dad, we're all doing the best we can to battle the forces of ignorance and evil,' and I even told him there were some new witches in town who've been fighting the good fight, but he's just one of those guys, you know? He thinks his generation is the only one that can keep the peace. And by *his generation*, I mean specifically just the men. You know what I mean, don't you, Zara?"

She raised a jiggly cube of acorn gelatin toward her mouth and paused.

"Sure," I said. "I know the type."

And that was the day I learned that all three of the full-time librarians at the Wisteria Public Library knew about magic, and spells, and things that go bump in the night.

CHAPTER 39

Zoey's summer moping was worse now that she could turn into a fox at will. She could do a melodramatic full-body drape over furniture even better in fox form.

My education-loving daughter had always been touchy during the first week of summer holidays. In the past, this had been expressed through loud sighing and limp body posture. After a few days, she would get into the summer routine and be fine. She usually babysat for other families in the building where we used to live, or did odd jobs, including her plant-watering service. The days would pass easily enough. And then most of August was about preparing for the September return to school, which made her giddy.

Sometimes I worried about her love of school. Was she the picture of health, or had I failed somehow in raising her? My "free range" method of parenting might have caused her to crave the comfort and security of a set routine, with bells ringing regularly to signal movement from one task to another. The summer she was thirteen, I'd experimented with our own schedule of activities, right down to an electronic timer that buzzed every hour. She gamely went along with the schedule the first few days, but then as soon as I left for work, she removed the batteries from the timer because a neighbor "needed them" for her remote control.

This year, now that everything was different, I'd hoped to skip the summer slump.

For one thing, she had her learner's license for driving, as well as access to a fun car.

Rhys Quarry left town with the heart of the Droserakops, as well as my last bit of goodwill for him, but he didn't take Foxy Pumpkin. When we returned home after the incident at Tansy Wick's property, we found ownership transfer papers on the kitchen counter, along with the keys. No note.

Zoey showed little interest in the car. She avoided talking about Foxy Pumpkin or riding in it. She was dealing with the confusing aftermath of what my father had done to us. It didn't help that whenever I brought up the subject, my face would make the I-told-you-so expression.

I swore to her that it gave me no pleasure to have been proven right about the man she called Pawpaw, but we both knew I was lying. Of course I was happy to be proven right. Even if it meant breaking Zoey's heart, it was better now than later. Better to rip off the bandage quickly than to pick at it once a year.

My father had shown himself to be the kind of man who would leave when I needed him the most. He'd let me down just as much as my so-called friend, Charlize, who lied to me to further her career. Most days it was a tie for which one of them made me angrier. The bitterness in vegetables is caused by alkaloids and sulfamides. The bitterness in adults is caused by life, and all the ways other people disappoint you. At last, I understood why Tansy Wick preferred her solitary life in the country with only her dogs and her plants.

But I put a smile on my face, and I kept the bitterness from my daughter as best I could. She was sixteen, and it was summer, and unlike I'd been at that age, she wasn't swelling with pregnancy.

On Saturday morning, I yanked the box of Eggo waffles from her hand before she could put another one in the toaster.

"The sun is shining, and it's a beautiful day," I said. "Let's take Foxy Pumpkin out for a spin. You can drive there and back. I promise not to grab the wheel."

She glowered at me. "It's not the steering wheel that's the problem," she said. "You always use your magic to push the brake pedal, and the turn signal, too. How am I supposed to learn if you're magically side-seat driving?"

"Drive better, and I won't have to jump in," I said. "You've got potential, but you've got to work at it. Driving isn't a book you can memorize and get a hundred percent on the test."

"But I did get a hundred percent on the written driving test." She grabbed the box of Eggos from midair, where they'd been floating, and jammed one into the toaster.

I floated the waffle out of the toaster. "No more sadness eating," I said. "We're going out. Young lady, you're going to get some fresh air and have fun, whether you like it or not."

A mischievous grin twisted her lips. "Fine. But I'm going on my terms."

She crouched down, jumped into the air, and twisted into her fox form instantaneously. She landed on the kitchen floor on four soft paws.

"You cheeky little vixen." I shook my head. "You know you can't reach the pedals in fox form, but I'd sure like to see you try." I pictured the scene. An adorable red fox driving a bright-orange Nissan 300ZX, ears buffeting in the breeze from the open T-roof.

Fox-Zoey yipped.

"No, you're not driving in fox form. But I'd sure love to see the look on Detective Bentley's face when he pulls me over for letting a fox drive our car. If he hasn't discovered magic by now, it won't be long."

Fox-Zoey cocked her head to the side. In her animal form, she had hazel eyes that were the same color as her human eyes, but with a vertical cat-like iris. She spoke to me in a chatty fox vocalization that sounded like mocking laughter.

Boa came in on silent white paws to see what the commotion was about. She was still missing half her whiskers. They had burned off during her brief swim in the plant's digestive juices. Thanks to the quick thinking of DWM agents Knox and Rob, the cat hadn't suffered any damage to her eyes or other organs. They'd given her a chilly bath at the scene, using a garden hose to get the acidic, numbing goo cleaned off all four of us. It was a clever gesture that was not appreciated by the feline.

Boa showed no signs of lingering damage, though sometimes when I looked into her green eyes, I sensed a special connection. We'd both survived something together. I wondered, what crazy adventures were awaiting us in the future? There are spells that witches can do with cats. They can serve as our spies, getting into places we can't go and then sharing their memories with us.

I picked up Boa, who melted into my arms and started purring immediately. She rubbed her cheek on my chin while keeping one eye on Fox-Zoey. Boa had been wary of Zoey in fox form, thanks to all the barking and chasing done by my crazy father, but she'd been warming up to her. They chased each other around the house, but Zoey traded off, letting Boa do the chasing half the time. The cat seemed to enjoy the playtime, but she preferred her mistress in human form. Humans had hands to hold the blue brush that was Boa's favorite. What was the appeal of the blue brush? I tried it out on Zoey in fox form once, and she reported later that she didn't see what all the fuss was about. Perhaps it was just a cat thing.

Boa stretched down from my arms and swatted at the wriggly white fur at the tip of Zoey's foxtail.

The tail twitched again, irresistibly.

Boa jumped down from my arms and chased the fox through the main floor of the house and then upstairs.

Five minutes later, when Boa came sauntering back into the kitchen as innocent as could be, I put out a fresh bowl of food for her.

Boa dug right in. A bit of "fox hunting" helped stimulate Boa's appetite. She'd been a tad skinny when we adopted her, but she'd been gaining mass nicely.

Zoey-fox slunk into the kitchen, sniffing the air with interest.

"You want cat food?"

She shook her muzzle, no, but her eyes stayed locked on the stinky bowl of cat food.

"Let's go for that drive up the coast," I said. "Are you sure you want to wear your thick fur coat? It's a hot one today."

Zoey-fox swished one dark ear at me. Yes, she would be fine in the fur coat.

* * *

Foxy Pumpkin wouldn't have sold for the price of a modern sports car, but it was just flashy enough to attract attention.

With the T-top roof open and pop tunes playing on the Pioneer stereo, we were a sight: A woman with red hair whipping in the breeze, driving an orange sports car, her companion a grinning red fox in the passenger seat. The fox had her glistening black snout hanging out of the side window like a dog.

When we reached the seaside ice cream shop at the edge of the next town, Westwyrd, my fox companion hunkered down on the floor in front of her seat. Out of sight of onlookers, she shifted back into her teenage girl form.

"How convenient," I said. "You've suddenly got hands with opposable thumbs now that we're at a place that sells cones."

"Foxes don't like ice cream," she said, wrinkling her nose. "It's still tasty, but not in the same way. I had to think logically about how much I wanted ice cream right now and then manually override my impulses to go hunting for rats under the wharf."

"You're teasing, right? Like you were with the cat food? You didn't *really* want to hunt and eat a rat, did you?"

She looked straight into my eyes. "Mom, don't freak out or anything. I'm still myself when I shift. I'm still Zoey Riddle, but everything's different."

"How different?"

"Let's just say that adopting a hamster or a gerbil for the house would be a bad idea."

"You wouldn't."

She shrugged. "I might."

I shuddered at the idea of my daughter eating a live rodent.

"There." She pointed at me. "That look on your face. Judgment. That's why I can't talk to you about this stuff."

"But Zoey..." I'd been about to deliver a motherly lecture about keeping up the lines of communication, no matter how gross or uncomfortable, or else we would be no better than people like Jorg Ebola, the editor whose prejudice made reading the DWM's Monster Manual difficult. We Riddles were a *mixed family*, a blend of witch and shifter, and we couldn't allow our differences to tear us apart.

I lost my train of thought. I was distracted by the fluttering of blue wings directly overhead.

A blue jay.

Maybe it was *the blue jay*, the one who'd given me the warning in the woods.

We had solved the mystery of what happened to Tansy and why, including the revelation that Project Buttercup was a flesh-munching triple-headed monster plant, and that Reynard was one of my father's pseudonyms. But we hadn't uncovered the identity of the person who'd paid the vet bill and been talking to Bentley.

I reached for my purse and the bottle of sight-enhancement gel my aunt had prepared. The gloop smelled bad, but not as bad as the spirit-blocking stuff I'd put in my nostrils.

Zoey followed my eyes up to the bird and groaned. "Here we go again on another one of your wild goose chases."

"More of a wild blue jay chase," I corrected. "Would you say that blue jay is staring at us with beady eyes that are controlled remotely by a creature of the grave?"

Zoey turned her head and gazed longingly at the ocean-side ice cream shop. Happy families were laughing together on the patio. "All I can see is ice cream," she said.

"One last try." I gave the bottle of viscous fluid a shake. I had been chasing blue jays for days and was down to the dregs. I pulled out the special polarized sunglasses and squirted the last of the fluid onto the lenses. The bottle made a humorous sound, like a ketchup bottle giving up its final squirt. "Keep an eye on the bird while I get this set up."

Zoey's posture went dramatically limp. She rested her head on her hand and stared up through the open T-top roof. The blue jay didn't budge from his branch.

"He's up there, all right," she said. "Just minding his own business."

"What sort of business? Eating seeds and insects?"

My daughter suddenly jerked her head up. "I think he's listening to us. His head turned toward you when you talked, and now it's turned back to me." She rubbed her forearms. "I just got chills. Maybe this one really is a *seer for the dead*."

"Zoey, we ought to keep our voices down when we say things such as *seer for the dead*. We're already attracting a lot of heat just being in this car."

She giggled. "You sounded just like Auntie Z."

I made a gagging face as I finished spreading the viscous gel over the sunglasses. When applied to a specific brand of polarized sunglasses, the magical compound allowed the wearer to see certain kinds of magic, such as the tracer lines connecting a *seer for the dead* with, well, *the dead*. Just like the tracer that the DWM had placed in the back of my father's neck, this blue jay could lead me to the other person involved in the Project Buttercup puzzle.

If this accomplice had been smart, he or she would have fled without a trace, like my father. Rhys Quarry had apparently removed the tracer from the back of his neck and put it in a postage-paid envelope. The tracer had traveled halfway around the world by the time a DWM agent intercepted it from a confused mail carrier in Madagascar.

My father was long gone, and Tansy's bones had been laid to rest, yet I kept seeing blue jays around. Peering in the window at the library. Hopping around on the roof of my house. Flapping overhead as I walked through the park. I couldn't chalk up all the sightings to simple coincidence. The bird was watching me.

My aunt had helped me prepare the vision spell. She didn't like me going after someone so powerful without her, but the blue jay could be long gone by the time she drove up to Westwyrd to meet up with us. She would want me to learn the identity of the accomplice. She feared it was someone she knew, and that was why they'd been tipped off by her old-man disguise and evaded her the night she'd followed Bentley. Both of us were keenly interested in finding out what person—or thing—was watching us.

I donned the sunglasses.

Two thin blue lines traced north from the blue jay in the tree above us.

Ziggity!

The spell was working perfectly. I must have gotten better at casting the verbal spell. Either that, or the bird's master was closer.

I hurriedly explained everything to Zoey, and we switched seats so she could drive while I followed the lines. She didn't grumble once. In a pinch, I could always count on my daughter.

CHAPTER 40

We followed the tracer lines five miles up the highway, to a luxury resort inside a tall stone building that looked like an old castle from Europe. A European castle? How could that be?

No sooner had I asked the question in my mind than my daughter was answering.

"This is Castle Wyvern," she said. "We learned about it at school."

"It looks like a real castle," I said.

"It is. I mean, it's a luxury spa now, but the main building was once a castle. The story is, an eccentric countess had her family's castle taken apart, stone by stone, and shipped over here. She didn't get to enjoy it for long, though, because she died tragically before the decoration was complete." With a campfire-ghost-story tone, she said, "People say her spirit still haunts the building."

I rubbed my neck, where I'd gotten a crick from craning up at the thin blue lines we'd been following.

"Castle Wyvern," I said. "I thought Wisteria was wacky, but the town of Westwyrd is certainly full of surprises."

We parked the car in a lot marked as visitor parking and turned off the engine.

"Mom, we drove here in a straight line, with the lines visible the whole way. That can't be a coincidence. What if this is a trap? We can't walk right in, unarmed."

"What do you mean, unarmed? I've seen those teeth of yours in action. And let's not discount the fact I've learned dozens of spells. Sure, half of them are related to food preparation, but I've got some skills."

"You sure showed the Droserakops who was boss," she said snarkily.

"Hey! I softened it up to make it easier for you."

"Sure, you did."

I knew she was rolling her eyes, but I didn't dare take my focus off the glowing lines that cut through the sky. The signal terminated in one of the luxury spa's third-floor windows.

"Third floor," I said. "Time to storm the castle."

Zoey said, "I've got a bad feeling about this."

"Because of the ghost of the countess?"

"The whole thing."

"But maybe the countess could be my next spirit guest," I said. "At last, I'll finally learn me some of them highfalutin manners I've been hearin' about."

"I think we should call Auntie Z for backup. Or at least Mr. Moore. He's been really helpful with my questions about being a shifter. He wants to be more than just a neighbor to us, Mom."

I snorted. I didn't need Chet and his wolf breath. I was a strong, confident, powerful witch, and I could get into trouble just fine on my own, thank you very much.

I opened the car door and headed for the castle.

My daughter tried to talk me into waiting while she made some phone calls, but the farther away I got, the less convincing she sounded. Soon she was chasing after me as I jumped over fences and elbowed my way through perfectly manicured shrubs.

The spell on the glasses was finally fizzling out. There was only the blue summer sky, but it didn't matter. I had seen which room the *seer for the dead* spell was emanating from, and as soon as I could find an entrance, I would be confronting the person who'd conspired with my father.

I found a side exit door. Locked. I almost laughed. A locked door was no match for a witch. I visualized the door handle from the other side and gave it a twist. The door popped open.

My daughter trailed along behind me, muttering about all the laws and bylaws we might be breaking.

"Put it in your report for Bentley," I teased as I raced up the old stone stairs to the third floor.

We pushed open the interior fire door, which had to be a modern addition and not part of the old stone castle. I counted my paces until I reached the door connected to the room that held the person with whom I had a bone to pick.

I lifted my fist to knock and then paused.

I was panting and sweaty. So was my daughter.

I wore a pair of slime-covered sunglasses.

I whipped off the sunglasses and handed them to Zoey.

She stared back at me, her hazel eyes wide. She whispered, "You're going to bang on the door? Just like that?"

I looked down at our feet. A shadow between my feet was moving, yet I was perfectly still. The person on the other side of the door knew we were there. The person was standing there, waiting for us. Waiting for me.

A curling, twisting, tickling sensation of fear snuck into my body. I hadn't felt this hesitant since the morning I'd stood outside of Chet's house, desperately wanting the book I'd been promised. I'd worried about what Chessa might do to me, but then she hadn't done anything at all. I had been hurt by a new friend I trusted, plus my own father, and a hungry plant.

What good was being afraid if you were afraid of the wrong things?

Whoever was on the other side of this door, they might be my salvation or my downfall, but I wouldn't know until I knocked.

In the pit of my stomach, I felt the pull of something stronger than my own curiosity. A powerful entity waited on the other side of the door. A being who wanted me to make the first step. *Knock on the door, Zara.*

No!

Please? For me?

I took a step back.

That last plea had sounded eerily familiar. *It can't be.*

Zoey's whole body was tilted, leaning toward the door. Her red hair fell loosely to one side only. She felt the attraction, too. I grabbed her hand and yanked her back, back toward the stairwell.

"We're leaving," I whispered in her ear.

The voice called to me again. *Just knock on the gosh-darned door, Zara. Don't keep me waiting.*

Knock on the gosh-darned door?

I knew that voice.

No! It can't be!

Rivulets of sweat trickled down my back. I turned and shoved my daughter toward the fire door.

"Move your butt," I whispered. "We're leaving."

The door to the room swung open.

My eyes seemed to move in slow motion, turning away from my daughter and toward the person standing in the doorway.

Scratch that.

Not *the person*.

The woman.

She was in her early fifties, but I didn't need to assess the fine lines around her eyes and mouth to know her age.

She had long, flowing hair, as black as a raven's wing. She wore a terry-cloth luxury robe, probably the resort's, judging by the insignia on the pocket. The woman's feet were bare, as though she'd just stepped out of the shower. Inside the doorway was a pair of familiar-looking boots, like the kind my aunt and I wore.

On her face, the dark-haired woman wore a smile as beautiful as it was horrific.

Zoey spoke first. "Gigi?"

Gigi was my daughter's name for her grandmother.

For my mother.

Standing before me was Zirconia Cristata Riddle. Even with the strange black hair, I knew her. But it wasn't just a hair dye job that was new. She looked taller and thinner. Her freckles were gone, replaced with creamy-white unfreckled skin. Yet I would know her anywhere.

She smiled that beautiful yet horrific smile that could not be and prompted me with a raised eyebrow. "Well?"

"It's been a while," I spat out.

"Too long," she said. "When was that, exactly? The last time we saw each other?"

"At your funeral," I said. "The last time I saw you, you were lying in a coffin. Dead. Quite dead."

Silence passed for several seconds. Were any of us breathing?

"Your eyes were closed, so I don't know if you saw me that day at your funeral," I said. "Also, as I mentioned already, you were dead."

More silence passed. More horrific smiling.

And then, improbably, I used a name I never thought I'd use again, except when referring to myself in third person. "Mom? Is that really you?"

She kept smiling.

For a full list of books in this
series and other titles by
Angela Pepper, visit

www.angelapepper.com